THE DYEING ROOM

by Robert T. McMaster

UNQUOMONK PRESS

Williamsburg, Massachusetts

U.S.A.

The Dyeing Room

Printed in the United States of America.

www.TrolleyDays.net

ISBN 978-0-9856944-3-2

Published by Unquomonk Press, P.O. Box 126, Williamsburg, Massachusetts 01096 USA

This is a work of fiction. Names, characters, places, and incidents either are the product of the author's imagination or are used fictitiously. Any resemblance to actual persons, living or dead, events, or locales is entirely coincidental.

Cover design by Sean P. McCarthy

F MCM
McMaster, Robert T
The Dyeing Room (Trolley Days Series, bk
2)

~ 1 ~

Jack Bernard knelt in the garden straddling a shallow furrow in the soft dark earth. From a rickety wooden wheelbarrow he drew a handful of onion sets, small bulbs with green shoots swaddled in papery brown scales. With one hand he planted each set firmly, with the other he scooped moist soil around it, then moved a few inches along the row before planting the next.

It was a Saturday morning in late April and a long, cold winter was finally yielding to spring in Westfield. The rich, black soil smelled of new life, breathed as surely as does a living thing, taking in the moist, warm air. Jack had been looking forward to spring and to planting ever since the harvest of the previous autumn was finished. He tolerated winter, but the farmer in him lived to work the land and smell the sweet earth.

At seventeen years Jack was slender and tall. His hair, cut short and a bit ragged by his sister over the kitchen sink, was dark brown, although soon the summer sun would lighten it several shades and put a broad wave in it. His facial features were sharp, his eyes soft and pale blue, like his mother's. He wore faded overalls over a brown flannel shirt and loose-fitting trousers that partly covered a pair of tattered leather work boots caked with mud.

As Jack completed planting a third row of hundreds of tiny onion plants, the morning sun was rising just high enough to warm him. He stood mopping his forehead and the back of his neck with a handkerchief, then stuffed it in the breast pocket of his overalls. Looking upward and to the east, he followed the flight of a line of crows over the distant fields, black dihedrals silhouetted against the yellow morning sky. Beyond stood a strand of hardwood trees in their early spring colors, ash a coppery red, beech a pastel green, and maple, its tiny flowers forming a fringe of scarlet starbursts at the tips of the branches.

From behind him came a shrill whistle. Turning, he rested one hand on his hip and looked off in the direction of the sound. It was his neighbor, Émile Bousquet, driving a huge workhorse with chestnut coat and steaming flanks, harrowing the lower field along the river, a field that would soon be planted to corn. He stood and watched the boy and his horse for several minutes. When they turned at the end of the field and started back in his direction, Jack caught Émile's eye, waved, then walked slowly toward them. As he approached, Émile pulled gently on the lines and spoke softly to his horse. Jack stroked the massive animal's muzzle.

"How's old Thor?" he asked slowly, clearly, his eyes fixed on Émile's.

"Tho's gra, Jay-Jay, jus gra…" replied Émile with a broad smile. Then he turned to the horse. "'Tcha boy?" and rubbed the animal's glistening neck. Thor's ears pricked forward, then his gray eyelids quivered and closed with equine pleasure. "Tho's alus gra, eh boy?"

Jack grinned at Émile and nodded, then spoke slowly. "And the harrowin', how's it coming, 'Mile?" Jack and Émile had been friends as long as either could recall. Émile was a year younger than Jack, but stood nearly as tall. His black hair, glistening with sweat, was matted against his head, his round face burnished by the wind as well as the work.

2

The Bousquets had acquired Thor when he was a year-old colt, and the bond between horse and boy was forged at once. A Percheron like Thor was a powerhouse, and handling him was demanding work. Émile would grasp the lines gently but firmly in both hands, keeping one eye on the row ahead and one on the horse, yet still minding his footing on the uneven ground. The pair would work for hours together, tilling, harrowing, plowing, dressing, with only occasional breaks for horse and driver to rest.

Like Thor, Émile loved his work. His large, clear eyes shone, as if hard work was his greatest pleasure. But he was always ready to talk to his neighbor whom, it was clear, he greatly admired. He called Jack by the nickname Jay-Jay because he had difficulty pronouncing final consonants. Émile was deaf, having lost his hearing when he contracted German measles at the age of two. Only in the last few years had his speech and lip reading improved, thanks to the aid of his tireless tutor, Jack's sister Marie.

"It's comin' 'long, Jay-Jay, comin' 'long. So, when you leavin' for collesh?" Émile asked that question of Jack nearly every time they talked.

"September, still a while yet. Lots to do first, 'Mile."

Jack felt sorry for Émile. He was a smart boy, capable of more than plowing a field, but unfortunately his teachers were not trained to teach a deaf student. Jack knew too well the hurt his friend felt when, at the end of grade six, Sister Superior curtly informed Pierre and Madeleine Bousquet that the nuns of St. Agnes School had done all they could for their son.

"You puttin' in ung-yins, Jay-Jay?"

"Yep, Gibraltar and Prizetaker, 'bout two acres, best cash crop we got," said Jack, knowing he was not telling Émile anything he didn't know. Jack gestured to the freshly harrowed field. "Corn again?"

"Yeh - yeh," replied Émile, smiling and nodding. "How's yer job goin', Jay-Jay - the mill?" Émile knew all about Wellington Textiles where Jack worked. "Biz-niz gud?"

"Uh-huh, yep," replied Jack, nodding his head several times, "pretty busy, pretty busy." Even at his young age Jack already had several years' experience working at the largest woolen mill in Holyoke. He had left school in grade nine to work in the mill when his father lost his job with the same company. Fortunately, Jack was able to return to his studies the following September, but he worked the same job the following three summers. He planned to go to college and had been offered a generous scholarship to attend Worcester Polytechnic Institute, but was taking a year to work and save money, more for his family than for himself.

"The sortin' house?" asked Émile. Jack nodded. Émile's father had worked in the sorting house at Wellington Textiles when he was younger. "Tha's haad wor', eh?"

"No harder than what you and Thor do every day, I wager," replied Jack, again stroking the animal's head. Thor stood at least six feet at the withers and his head loomed above the young men standing beside him. His coat was reddish brown, his mane white. Long, graceful feathering of white and gray hairs covering each platter-sized hoof lent a festive look to the massive animal, even as he labored through muddy fields.

Smiling, Émile grasped Thor's flanks with the palms of his hands. Jack often wondered, when Émile held Thor in that way, if there were vibrations only he could detect, a kind of secret language between horse and boy.

"You still swee' on tha' girl Anne, aincha?" asked Émile with a grin and a twinkle in his eye. Jack blushed and tried to change the subject but he wasn't quick enough for Émile. "Perdy girl, Jay-Jay, yera luggy guy." Again Jack smiled and nodded.

"I heard you're goin' back to school, 'Mile?"

4

Émile hesitated, still grinning, then looked away. "I guezzo." But when he turned back toward Jack, he was no longer grinning.

Jack struggled for words. "You'll like it, I bet - you'll see. Any news from Stephen?"

Émile shook his head and smiled. Only two weeks earlier his older brother had left for Montréal to enlist in the Canadian army. He'd been working in one of the whip factories in Westfield since he was fifteen and had surprised his family when he announced he was joining up. The last Jack had heard Stephen was training near Québec City. Any day now his unit would ship out for England. In weeks they could be in the trenches, fighting back the German war machine as it swept across Europe. At least a dozen other young men from Westfield had already returned to their native Canada to enlist. Now that the United States had cast its lot with England and France, many more would no doubt be enlisting in the American services. The war in Europe was starting to hit close to home.

"Tomorrow, 'Mile, at church…it's a special Mass in honor of Father Lévesque. You goin'?"

Émile looked uncertain. Jack wasn't sure whether his friend wasn't planning to attend or simply hadn't understood him. To the Bernard family Father Lévesque had been more than pastor of St. Agnes Church, he was also a family friend, having come from Sherbrooke, Québec, as had Jack's parents. Father Lévesque was retiring and that Sunday would be a day of both celebration and sadness for Jack, his father, and his sisters.

"Well, I gotta finish puttin' in the onions, 'Mile. Maybe I'll see you at Mass."

~ 2 ~

The Bernards rose early the next morning. After breakfast every family member had chores to do. Jack cleaned out the family's rusty old Model T and tended to the cow and pigs. Charles sat in the kitchen waxing and polishing four pairs of Sunday best shoes. Fifteen-year-old Marie ironed shirts and trousers for Jack and her father, dresses for herself and her sister. Twelve-year-old Claire fed the chickens.

At 8:30 sharp a long, black motorcar pulled into the gravel driveway. Bromley, the Wellington family chauffeur, stepped out first, walked around the car, then helped seventeen-year-old Anne Wellington from the car. Anne's facial features were delicate, her eyes bright, her lips always poised to smile. Her complexion was the color of pale roses, her lustrous auburn hair done up in a chignon and topped with a small hat of cream and pink lace. Her dress was simple, white muslin with the neckline trimmed in filmy gauze and adorned with a cameo brooch.

Jack emerged from the front door and strode across the grass smiling. "Hello, Anne. Hello, Mr. Bromley, sir."

The old man smiled, tipped his hat to Jack, then turned and spoke to Anne. "I'll be back at four, then, Miss?" Anne nodded and thanked him. He climbed into the gleaming car, then slowly backed it out of the driveway. Jack and Anne walked up the flagstone front walk side by side.

Ten minutes later Anne and the four Bernards clambered into the family's Model T. It sputtered and chugged down Southampton Road to St. Agnes Church, a mile away.

Reverend Timothy O'Rourke, Bishop of the Springfield Diocese that included Westfield, gave a rambling homily on the topic of faithfulness. Being true to Our Lord, he reminded the congregation, required more than simply attending Mass each Sunday. It meant obeying the edicts of the Church, the Holy Father, and the Ten Commandments. It meant observing the Rites of the Church. And it meant supporting the Diocese in its time of need.

The Bishop went on longer than anyone wanted about the Bishop's Fund that would begin canvassing in a few weeks. Nothing made the parishioners of St. Agnes more uncomfortable than being reminded of their financial obligation to the church. Most had barely enough money left at the end of each week to put food on the table, much less to make a special contribution to the church. Some resented what they considered meager support shown by the Bishop and the Diocese for their parish and particularly for their school.

Finally the Bishop spoke of Father Lévesque. He called him a man of humility and devotion, of decency and kindness, a faithful servant of Christ. Not a dry eye could be found among the congregation when at last Father Lévesque rose from his seat beside the altar, stepped forward with the assistance of an acolyte, and grasped the lectern with both hands. While his body was obviously in decline at seventy, the old priest's mind was still sharp, and he spoke to the congregation like the friends they truly were.

At that point Anne placed her hand discreetly on Jack's. He had been surprised when, just a week earlier, she had asked to accompany him and his family to this Mass. She knew how much Father Lévesque meant to all of them. He had said the Funeral Mass for Jack's little sister, four-year-old Thérèse, when the child was taken from them by diphtheria a decade earlier. He had presided over First Communions and Confirmations for the other three Bernard children. And when Jack's mother, Evelyne Bernard, succumbed to influenza just a year and a half ago, it was Father Lévesque who ministered to the stunned and heart-broken family. This day marked more than just the retirement of a priest and rector. It was the end of an era for the Bernard family, and Anne wanted to be a part of it.

After Mass the Bernards and Anne stood in the chill April air in front of the church talking to friends and greeting the Bishop and Father Lévesque. The retiring priest would be returning to Québec in time, but for the next month or so he would be staying on at the rectory. That knowledge made it easier for parishioners to take their leave, trusting they would see him again before his departure.

"Hello, Father. My name is Anne - Anne Wellington. From Holyoke. I'm a friend of Jack's."

"How do you do, Anne Wellington?" replied the priest with a warm smile. "Thank you so much for attending Mass today. What brings you to St. Agnes?"

"I just wanted to say thank you - for all you have done for Jack and his family."

"Well, that's very nice of you, young lady, very nice indeed - God bless you. And what church do you attend in Holyoke? St. Mary's? Mater Dolorosa?"

"St. John's," replied Anne.

"The Wellingtons are Episcopalian, Father," interjected Jack nervously.

"Oh, St. John's, yes, yes. I know Father Curran well. Fine man - very fine man," replied the priest. Then he added with a twinkle in his eye, "Even if he is Protestant."

"Good luck in your retirement, Father," said Anne, her eyes sparkling.

As the couple strode down the slate sidewalk toward the street, Jack felt a tug on his sleeve and turned. It was Émile Bousquet smiling shyly. "'Lo, Jay-Jay." Then he turned to Anne. " 'Lo Anne, nice day, eh?"

"A very nice day, Émile, very nice indeed. It is so good to see you," replied Anne warmly.

"How's the harrowin' comin', 'Mile?" asked Jack.

"Almos' done, Jay-Jay, almos' done." Émile beamed with pride. "Thor - he mays id easy."

"'Mile's goin' back to school, Anne," said Jack enthusiastically. "Isn't that good?"

"That is splendid, Émile, splendid," replied Anne. But as she spoke she could see a wave of doubt sweep across the boy's normally sunny countenance like a dark cloud against a blue sky. Just then the rest of the Bousquet family joined the trio, exchanging greetings with Anne and Jack. A sudden blast of cold wind drove everyone toward their motorcars with hasty good-byes offered all around.

Back at the Bernard home, Anne and Jack stood in the barn dressed in their church clothes. Jack proudly showed off his current woodworking project, a set of pine shelves that would hold condiments and other preserves in a disused corner of the kitchen pantry. Claire led Anne through a narrow door into the chicken coop and pointed out two newly acquired roosters with white feathers on their legs.

"Don't they look like they're wearing spats," asked Claire, "like they're going courting?" She laughed, then turned and looked at Anne, her round face turning pink. "I suppose they *are* going courting in a way, aren't they?"

Anne laughed and tousled Claire's hair. "Yes, I suppose they are, Claire."

"Me and Anne are going out to look at the onions, Claire. Why don't you go inside and change your clothes before you get that pretty dress dirty?"

Claire looked boldly into her brother's face. "I'm not a child, Jackie, I can take a hint." Then she turned to Anne. "You'd better not get your dress dirty either, Anne." And she turned and walked toward the house. Jack shook his head and smiled at his sister's impertinence, then led Anne through the back door of the barn.

Just then a motorcar pulled into the neighbors' yard. Anne and Jack waved as Émile and his parents, Madeleine and Pierre, and his sister Elaine climbed out of the vehicle and walked across the lawn to their front door.

"I haven't seen Émile since last summer, Jackie. He's gotten so tall. He's quite a fine looking young man. But did you notice how he acted when I asked him about that school? He seemed so - so *phlegmatic*. What do you suppose is bothering him?"

"It's that school," replied Jack dismissively. "It's a training course for cripples and simpletons. They teach 'em to do the most menial tasks - busy work, Émile calls it. It's just not right, Anne. He can drive a team as well as any grown man. He can fix a thrown shoe on a two thousand pound draft horse like a farrier. I swear he's read every book in the library a couple times over. And now he's learning sign language. If people would give that boy a chance, he could do so much more."

Now that they were out of sight of the house, Jack took Anne's hand and the couple walked gingerly across the damp grass. "Thanks for coming to Mass. I was surprised when you - well, I didn't think you'd..."

"I know how much Father Lévesque means to your family, Jackie - I just wanted to be part of the occasion, that's all. But I thought the Bishop would never stop talking about the canvass. I almost expected him to come down from the pulpit and start passing the hat."

"Yeh, he's always asking people to give up their hard earned cash. I guess that's his job. But Father Lévesque hated that business. He just wanted to tend to his flock. That's what made him different. He was a pastor, not a businessman. You know?" Jack paused, looking off across the onion patch. "We'll miss him."

Anne pulled Jack close to her and kissed him on the cheek. Jack's eyes briefly met hers, then looked away.

"What's the matter, Jackie? What is it?" Anne could tell when something was troubling Jack. They had known each other since Jack entered grade eight at the Forestdale Grammar School in Holyoke. He and her brother, Tom, had quickly become best chums and Anne had taken an immediate liking to *the quiet French boy* as her classmates referred to him.

It was the death of Jack's mother, Evelyne, that drew Anne firmly into the Bernard family. She stayed with them for several days after the funeral. She walked Marie and Claire to school on a blustery March morning, their first day back to school after the death of their mother. Since that day she had been more like an older sister to the two Bernard girls than their brother's girlfriend. Even Jack's father was warmed by Anne's presence.

Jack looked nervously at Anne, then at the ground, then off toward the maroon Berkshire Hills that lay like a sleeping giant to the west. Finally he spoke. "I - I'm thinkin' of lookin' for a new job, Annie, at the mill."

Anne looked surprised. "Why is that, Jackie? I thought you liked working in the sorting house."

"Well, I do, but I gotta make more money. If I'm goin' to college, I gotta save up a lot this summer for Dad and the girls. Otherwise it's gonna be awful tight around here next year." He looked back toward the house, shaking his head.

"So what do you have in mind?"

"I don't know. I'll ask around, see what's what."

"Couldn't you stay in the sorting house and ask for an increase? I could talk to Uncle Richard." Anne's uncle and her father were co-owners of Wellington Textiles.

"No," said Jack sharply. Then he looked into Anne's eyes and spoke in a more measured tone. "I don't want any special favors, Annie, I want to do this on my own. I'll be all right. Just - just don't mention it to Dad or my sisters, okay? I haven't told them yet."

Sunday dinner featured one of the Bernard family's favorite meals, *tourtière*: spiced ground pork and beef baked in a thin, flaky crust, then served piping hot with parsnips, beets, and potatoes. It was a specialty of Evelyne Bernard and Marie was proving she was as skilled as her mother at preparing it. All heads were bowed as Charles said grace. Then the meal began.

"You must be excited to be graduating, Anne," Charles offered. "When's the big day?"

"The thirteenth of June, a Wednesday evening. You are all invited - if you would like to attend."

"Well, thank you, we'd love to," responded Charles.

"I'll be passing out programs at the front door, Anne," chimed in Marie, "for the Purple and White Club."

With a mischievous grin Claire addressed her question to Anne: "What about the Senior Formal? Any plans, Anne?"

"Well, no, Claire," replied Anne with a wry smile. "Actually I have received several offers from young men interested in escorting me, but I haven't made up my mind as yet. I'm holding out for a certain someone, but unfortunately he has not spoken up." Jack's face turned red as the beets on his plate. "Marie, what about you? Sophomores can attend the Senior Formal, you know." Marie shook her head and looked down at her plate. "It's early yet. I'll bet there will be some entreaties," added Anne.

Marie looked up and smiled briefly. "Did everyone get enough meat pie?"

Then Charles spoke. "How are your parents, Anne? Is your father well?"

"He's all right," replied Anne guardedly. "His doctor says he mustn't exert himself, not with the condition of his heart. He has a full-time nurse, Miss Beldon, who watches over him all the time. He still insists on seeing the company's financial reports. He stews and fusses over them for hours each week. It worries us when he gets himself worked up like that."

"And your Mother?"

"Mother is fine. As usual she's all wrapped up in the Women's Home. They're trying to raise funds for a new project in Chicopee Falls."

"What about young Tom, what's the news from him?" asked Charles.

"Well, he's still in Williamstown. We expect he'll be there until the end of June. We don't hear much from him. He sent me a short note last week, but it didn't say much. I just hope..." Anne's voice trailed off and she bit her lip nervously. Several months earlier Tom had agreed to admit himself to a sanitarium in the Berkshires that promised to cure drinking problems. That sounded like an odd thing to promise, but some former patients vowed their condition had improved thanks to the clinic. With all that Tom and his family had been through in the previous year, many hopes were pinned on a successful outcome for the troubled young man.

"I can't wait to see him," said Jack. "It's been ages."

After dinner Marie and Anne stood side by side at the kitchen sink washing dishes.

"I want to go, Anne, I really do. But the only boy who has asked me is Herbert Miller. I put him off - told him I wasn't certain I could attend."

"But why, Marie? He can't be *that* bad." Marie rolled her eyes and shook her head slowly. "Marie, may I say just one thing? And please, please do not take umbrage, I only want to help."

Marie froze, clasping a dinner plate. She nodded slightly. Anne turned toward her and spoke softly and sweetly. "Marie, you're sixteen, and you have such a comely smile. You should use it more often. Show it off, especially to the boys."

"Oh, Anne, I..." Marie was shaking her head slowly, her eyes fixed on the dinner plate in her hands.

"I know you have many responsibilities, more than most girls your age - more than I ever had. And I am sure it must be difficult at times, but you need to cultivate friends - of both sexes. A little smile now and then wouldn't hurt, would it?"

Marie had great affection and admiration for Anne, so she was willing to listen. She nodded, then smiled weakly.

"A while back when I visited," recalled Anne, "you were seated at this very table with a rather handsome young man."

"Émile?" said Marie in a whisper.

Anne nodded. "Remember how you were taking turns reading *Huckleberry Finn*?" Marie nodded again. "I couldn't help but notice that, as you read, Emile's eyes were on *you*, not on the book."

"That's because he was reading my lips, Anne." replied Marie in a scolding tone. "He's trying to learn to lip read."

"I don't know," replied Anne with a sly smile. "I had the feeling he was doing more than *reading* those pretty lips."

Marie's face turned scarlet and she spoke in a whisper. "Anne, Émile Bousquet is seventeen years old and all he cares about is that horse. Besides, he's a neighbor. We've known each other since we were babies. I'm sure he's never thought of me in *that* way..."

14

"Trust me, Marie, if he's a boy and he's seventeen, he *has*. I can guarantee it."

Marie blushed again but was smiling. "Stop it, now, Anne. Enough."

Just then Jack appeared in the kitchen. "Looks like the dishes are almost done. May I steal our guest away for a while?" asked Jack.

Marie nodded. "Yes, Jack, please do." And she threw a look of mock anger toward Anne. The two girls giggled as Jack escorted Anne into the parlor.

"What was that all about?" inquired Jack when they were seated on the upholstered couch together.

"Just girl talk, Jackie, just girl talk."

Jack cleared his throat. "About the Senior Formal, I thought I should - well, it's your school and your dance so I wasn't sure that I should be inviting myself - you know?"

Anne smiled. "Yes, Jackie, I understand. But it is not really proper for a girl to invite a boy, now, is it?" They both smiled and laughed and there was another pause.

"Okay. Miss Wellington - can I - I mean, may I - have the honor of escorting you - to the Senior Formal?"

"Weeeell," replied Anne, "I've had several other *very* interesting offers." She paused for dramatic effect. "But, since you ask - yes, I suppose I could permit you to escort me."

Jack's face glowed. But then his smile disappeared momentarily. "Just out of curiosity, who were those others?"

"Wouldn't you like to know?" replied Anne with a beguiling smile.

Soon it was time for Anne to leave. She spoke to Marie and Claire, then to Jack's father, thanking them again and again and repeating the invitation to her graduation. Finally she and Jack stepped out of the front door and walked slowly across the yard to the waiting motorcar.

"Now that spring is here, Jackie, maybe we can have a picnic lunch one day a week by the canal," proposed Anne brightly. "How about Tuesday at noon? I'll bring everything."

"How can you do that? Are you planning on playing hooky or something?" asked Jack.

"No, no, nothing like that. I'll tell you all about it on Tuesday."

Jack nodded in agreement. "Okay. Tuesday, twelve o'clock, by the canal."

"See you then," replied Anne with a wink. Jack nodded again, helped her into the car, and watched as it backed out of the driveway and headed toward Holyoke.

~ 3 ~

MONDAY, APRIL 30 – TUESDAY, MAY 1

Jack rose at five the next morning. Barely awake, he pulled on a broadcloth shirt and trousers, loosely fastening his black suspenders, then stood by the kitchen stove drinking strong black coffee from a gray porcelain mug. Soon Marie had a steaming bowl of farina ready for him.

Fifteen minutes later he strode briskly along Southampton Road in the dull light before dawn, the sky over East Mountain just beginning to brighten. The crowing of a rooster greeted him as he approached the trolley stand; a horse-drawn wagon filled with timbers creaked as it passed, steam rising from the backs of the team of gray Belgians. A distant whistle told him the Boston and Albany train was approaching Westfield on its route to Boston.

Just then a Holyoke-bound trolley arrived and Jack clambered aboard. Several other riders were slumped against the windows, half asleep. As the car clattered down the tracks, Jack gazed out across the fields, then over the glassy waters of Hampton Ponds, then up toward the jagged ledges of Rock Valley, lost in thought.

In twenty minutes the car was bumping down Sargeant Street as the sun shone through the steam and smoke that rose from the mills on Holyoke's riverfront. Wellington Textiles was the largest woolen mill in Holyoke and one of the busiest, most successful textile businesses in all of New England. Its five four-story brick buildings stretched nearly a half mile along Race Street next to the Second Level Canal. Founded over a half-century earlier, the business had grown rapidly, supplying wool fabric to a growing nation. Its first big contracts were to provide uniforms for Union soldiers during the Civil War. Fifty years later the factory was thriving still, now driven by demand for blankets for the Allied forces fighting in Europe.

The entire wool-processing business occurred in the Wellington Mill. Freight cars loaded with fleeces rolled up to the receiving platform several times daily and were quickly unloaded. Flatbed trucks carried the bales of wool through wide wooden doors into the cavernous sorting house where Jack had worked since he was fourteen.

Work in the sorting house was hard. Thick dust hung in the air and quickly congested a worker's lungs. Men who labored inside were prone to all manner of respiratory complaints from colds to bronchitis to shortness of breath. Cases of brown lung were not uncommon; even anthrax occasionally took the life of a sorting house worker. Fortunately, Jack's job involved moving from inside the sorting house out onto the loading platform or into the elevators that carried wool to the dyehouse, carding rooms, or weaving rooms, so he found the conditions tolerable. Furthermore, he enjoyed the constant activity and the conviviality of young men much like himself.

Jack worked alongside Jim Trottière, an old friend and classmate from St. Agnes School in Westfield, and Leo Lacroix, whose family had arrived from Québec only a few years earlier. Outside the sorting house they dragged and shoved bales of wool from the railcars onto platform trucks. Inside the trio winched each bale onto one of many piles depending on the type and quality of wool. Mr. Leduc, the sorting house supervisor, selected bales to be moved to the other end of the room and broken open. Sorters then pulled and separated the wool, each fleece sometimes containing six or more types and qualities of fiber. When orders arrived, Jack and his co-workers loaded heavy drays with wool selected by the sorters, then muscled the wagons up a sloping ramp that led to the dyehouse where the wool would be scoured, dried, and dyed.

Jim was far and away the strongest man in the sorting house, and Jack and Leo relied upon him for the extra force needed to move the biggest, heaviest loads. Everything about Jim was oversized: massive hands, bulging muscular arms, and enormous feet. His co-workers often exchanged amused glances when Jim made child's play of a task the two of them had struggled at.

Time went by quickly that morning as it did most days in the sorting house. During the lunch hour, Jack walked the short distance to the dyehouse, a building he passed every day as he arrived for work. Mr. Tuttle was the dyehouse boss and a gruffer, more distasteful figure Jack could not have imagined. He was like a character out of a Charles Dickens novel - a jailer, a con-man, or a professional thief. His grotesque, red-veined face was dominated by a huge, bulbous nose. His thick purple lips always held the stump of a cigar, though smoking was strictly prohibited in the dyehouse for everyone else. He growled and cursed at his employees and barked orders constantly.

Jack knocked on the office door. "I'm busy," came the sharp reply from within.

"It's Jack Bernard, sir, from the sorting house. Could I speak to you for just a moment?"

"I told you, I'm busy. Go away."

Jack had been forewarned about the man's manner. He spoke loudly through the shut door: "I - I just wanted to know if there are - well, if you might have some work for me."

Tuttle's reply was immediate and unequivocal. "Nope. Nothing. Now get lost."

"Mr. Sullivan told me to speak to you, sir."

19

Jack turned and began to walk away, but Tuttle's voice followed him: "Maybe in a couple weeks, Bernard. Maybe."

Jack thanked the man without ever seeing him face to face, but somehow he felt he'd made a small bit of progress. The name Bernard was well known at the Wellington mill; his father had been a dependable, skilled worker for nearly fifteen years. And Jack had always conducted himself well in his work in the sorting house. Frank Sullivan was the head dyer at Wellington Textiles. He'd learned his craft in Ireland and brought those skills with him to Holyoke nearly thirty years earlier. His neighbor, Mr. Donahue, had been Jack's high school chemistry teacher and had spoken highly of Jack. He knew that dyeing was both art and science, and Jack had shown very good promise in high school chemistry. So Jack hoped that his efforts might be successful with Mr. Tuttle, surly old viper though he was.

Throughout the morning on Tuesday Jack was thinking about lunch and his assignation with Anne. As soon as the noon bell sounded he ran out of the sorting house onto Race Street and hurried along the canal toward Dwight Street.

"Jackie - Jackie," called out a familiar voice. It was Anne, waving from the bridge over the canal. He darted between a motorcar and a horse and buggy and in seconds was standing before her. He took her hand and the couple walked slowly from the bridge onto a patch of grass by the water's edge where they sat on a bench in the midday sun.

Anne had prepared a luncheon for two including slices of sausage, cheese, and soda crackers wrapped in oiled paper, all packed neatly into a tin with a tight fitting lid. Mildred, the Wellington family's cook, had offered to make the lunch, but Anne preferred to do it on her own.

20

"So," began Jack doubtfully, "explain to me how a high school girl is free to make luncheon dates on a school day. We didn't get that kind of a deal back when I was a senior."

"Well, Jack, that's because you weren't one of the first Holyoke High School students to be given special privileges. A small group of seniors was selected to work downtown five days a week, 12:30 to 4:30 each day. Carolyn and I were both chosen. A photographer from the *Transcript* took our picture yesterday, so you'll be reading all about it in tomorrow's edition."

"Wow," replied Jack. "That's swell. Do you get paid?"

"Well, no. But we get on-the-job experience. My assignment is at the Women's Home, working for Mrs. Calavetti. Isn't that perfect? Carolyn's working at Gregoire's Shoe Shop on High Street, just a few blocks away. We leave school and walk downtown together, then meet at 4:30 and walk home."

"Shouldn't you be at work now?" asked Jack looking at the silver pocket watch that hung by a fob from his belt.

"Well, they allow us thirty minutes to get to our jobs, but I told Miss Edwards we had to leave Senior English fifteen minutes early on Tuesdays - a little white lie. So, here I am."

"Sounds like a good deal all around," exulted Jack. "Boy, these are good," he added as he swallowed several bites of sausage at once.

Anne smiled proudly. "How are things in the sorting house? Everything going all right?"

"Yeh, everything's okay," Jack replied casually. "So tell me more about your new job. What's it like?"

"I love it, Jackie, I really do. But Mrs. C. needs so much help. What a jumble that office is. And sometimes the telephone never seems to stop ringing. I'm getting very fond of the girls and they seem to like me - at least I hope they do."

"Of course they like you," replied Jack, looking into Anne's bright emerald eyes and gazing on her pink

21

complexion and beguiling smile. Hers was a face he could never resist, could not stop looking at, even from the first day he met her, or so he told her. The truth was at least six months passed after their first meeting before Jack started to see her through the eyes of a young man rather than of a boy.

The two talked about school, work, and their families. "I wish I could see Tommy," said Jack wistfully. "Do you realize it's been nearly four months?"

Anne nodded and her cheerful demeanor faded. "Oh, Jackie. I miss him. He hardly ever writes and he never telephones. I send him a letter every weekend. I hope and pray that he's all right. I know Mother and Father worry about him, too." Then her mood brightened. "So, what about this weekend? Will you have some time for your dear, sweet Anne?"

Just then a commotion erupted across the canal. Two men had emerged from a window onto the roof of a mill building high above the street. A crowd gathered below was urging the men on as they unfurled a long banner. At first it was unreadable as it draped over the parapet. When the men finally drew the banner taut, the words *God Bless America* became visible, and cheers erupted, first from the crowd below, then from pedestrians along Race Street. At that moment a trolley rattling down Dwight Street stopped abruptly in the middle of the bridge. Men leaned out of the car windows waving flags and cheering. Others standing on the car's steps joined the chorus of cheers.

"Look, Jackie," said Anne, pointing along the canal. Only then did they realize that every building in sight was festooned in red, white, and blue bunting and every turret, window, and ridgepole was decorated with Old Glory, her forty-eight stars and thirteen stripes snapping smartly in the breeze. All of Holyoke, it would seem, was caught up in patriotic fervor as the nation mobilized for the *War to End All Wars*.

~ 4 ~

MONDAY, MAY 21

Two weeks went by without a word from the dyehouse. Then one day when Jack and Jim were loading bales of wool onto a truck on the loading platform, there was Mr. Tuttle, talking loudly to Mr. Leduc while looking his way. "Bernard," he barked. "Monday morning, first thing, in the dyehouse. Got it?"

"Thank you, sir," Jack shouted, but such pleasantries were lost on Mr. Tuttle who had already turned and lumbered off toward the dyehouse, spitting loudly on the pavement as a plume of cigar smoke swirled above his head.

The starting bell for the morning shift rang loudly at 6:30 on Monday morning, just as Jack strode across the factory yard. The air was crisp at that hour. Brilliant rays of orange sunlight splashed across the cobblestones and up against the brick mill walls.

Stepping through the heavy wooden doors of the dyehouse felt like descending into another world, a mysterious, sinister world. Inside it was hot, oppressively hot, well over one hundred degrees. A dank fog hung in the air, tiny droplets glistening like rain in the dim light cast by an occasional electric lamp and dripping from the walls, ceiling, and overhead pipes. Strange odors wafted about, acrid and pungent, unlike any Jack had ever encountered on the farm or in the sorting house. Through that steaming miasma, shirtless men moved ponderously, some pushing wagons laden with heavy rolls of fabric or skeins of yarn, others hefting bundles of wool fleeces on their shoulders. It reminded Jack of lithographs from *Dante's Inferno* or *Pilgrim's Progress* that had fascinated him in the library many years ago. But this inferno was real, all too real.

"Bernard. You're late," barked Mr. Tuttle from his office door. "I want you in here ten minutes before your shift, understand? Now get in there with Aucoin and Fredette."

"Nice to see you, too," said Jack under his breath as he hung his hat on the rack. He might have been put off by the man's gruffness, but Jack had already concluded that the disagreeable codger's bark was worse than his bite.

Wool-dyeing is a messy, difficult, and dangerous process. Wool as it is shorn from a sheep is dense and matted, its fibers coated with natural oils, perspiration, dust, and dirt. For dye to penetrate and color wool uniformly, a fleece must first be cleansed, a process known as scouring. This usually required several steps, first soaking in hot, soapy water, then in a scouring agent such as ammonia or carbonate of soda.

On one side of the dyehouse, long trough-like machines called wool washers were arranged. Workers fed fleeces in one end of a washer, removed them at the other end, replaced the fluids, then loaded the wool once again. Mr. Sullivan, the dyer, oversaw the whole process. Only when he was satisfied was a fleece finally rinsed and moved along to the next washer or to the drying room upstairs.

Jack's two co-workers were young men about his age. They gave him a few words of instruction, then disappeared, leaving Jack to the seemingly endless task of loading raw wool into the machine. Eventually Mr. Sullivan, the dyer, emerged from the mist. His face was flushed but he smiled as he spoke to Jack. "Well, Bernard, how's it going?" he asked.

Jack paused and nodded. "Okay so far, sir." For a few moments the man stood watching as Jack loaded more wool.

"You're goin' to engineerin' school, right? Well, you'll want to see how this thing works. Watch those brass teeth there." He pointed into the murky gyre of solvent and wool. "See how they move the wool back 'n forth in the solvent? That's the key, right there, son - agitation. But not too much - just enough. Too much and we got problems, understand?" Again Jack nodded. Mr. Sullivan gave him some further instruction, then faded into the mist.

By mid-morning the supply of raw wool had dwindled. Not knowing what to do, Jack looked for one of his co-workers. Just then Mr. Sullivan materialized out of the mists once again and Jack explained the problem. "Yeh, well, we gotta change out the solvent here, but we gotta let the last of this batch o' wool finish first. Come with me, son, while we're waitin', I'll show you a few things."

Jack followed his mentor along a narrow aisle past other washers being tended by other workers. Beyond the last of the machines they stopped in front of a circular, wooden tub of steaming swirling indigo dye and watched for several minutes. Big muscular men were lifting fleeces from a wagon into a net suspended by a block and tackle, running the bundle along a cable that stretched across the tub, then lowering the wool into the roiling cauldron. A vatman stood by poking the wool with a rake.

"Used to be," began Mr. Sullivan, "most dyes came from nature, you know? Deep red from a bug, cochineal, they call it, yellow and gold from thistle. This purple 'ere woulda been from the wild indigo plant." Jack nodded. "No more, son. All manufactured products today: blue vitriol, copperas, chromium. Some colors, like black, you gotta blend plant dyes and synthetics. It's a science."

Just then one of the workers emerged from the mists carrying a heavy burlap bag. Another man sliced the binding rope across the end of the bag with a long knife, revealing a crystalline powder.

"That's chrome-alum, a mordant or fixative." He looked closely at Jack to see if he understood. "It fixes the dye in the wool - so it don't fade or wash out." Jack nodded.

"Every dye needs a different mordant," continued Mr. Sullivan. "To make things more complicated, the mordant can affect the color of the dye. So you have to make adjustments."

Jack shook his head in amazement. "How do you know all this, sir - I mean, what to use and how much?"

Mr. Sullivan leaned toward Jack and looked him squarely in the eyes, his ruddy face dripping with sweat and condensation. He smiled as he tapped his temple with one finger. "It's all up 'ere, son - right up 'ere." Again Jack nodded. His father had always spoken of dyers and their work with admiration. Knowing the precise combination of dyes needed to produce a particular color or shade was a highly specialized art. That was why the job of dyer was one of the best paying jobs in the entire mill, so Charles had told him.

Just then the two men hoisted the bag of mordant over the tub and dumped the powder into the dark liquor. Jack watched as they stirred the mixture with long wooden paddles, much like alchemists of ancient times. Suddenly Jack's eyes were stinging and he groaned as he turned abruptly from the dyebath.

"Nasty business, them mordants," acknowledged Mr. Sullivan. Jack rubbed his eyes with both hands, then gradually opened them. The acrid vapors felt like searing sandpaper on his face and bare arms. "You get used to it," explained Mr. Sullivan, showing no concern about Jack's condition. "That's one thing about the dyehouse, son. Everything takes gettin' used to."

Jack returned to his post tending the wool washer, glad to be away from the dyebath and its noxious concoction. The new solvent having been added and a fresh supply of raw wool moved into position, he resumed loading the machine, a task he worked at for the remainder of the morning.

After lunch Jack was assigned to another, smaller room in the dyehouse. A new kind of scouring agent was being used here for the first time in the Wellington mill, something called coal naphtha. It was very effective at cleaning raw wool, faster and cheaper than other solvents, explained Mr. Sullivan, although he admitted there was still much to learn about how best to apply it.

As soon as he stepped through the heavy sliding doors into this room and took his first breath, Jack felt light-headed. Here the searing burning sensations he'd encountered that morning were absent, but sweet-tasting vapors overwhelmed him, leaving him dizzy and slightly nauseated. Eventually those symptoms abated, but then a throbbing began in his head; it was so bad that his vision blurred periodically. But the other men on his team didn't seem to be affected by the fumes and he was determined not to let his discomfort show.

Jack worked with several veterans of the dyehouse, Poulin, Goudreau, O'Malley, and Proulx. Unsmiling, these older men went about their business loading armfuls of raw wool into long, rectangular vats called jigs. Meanwhile one of the dyers moved from jig to jig adding the experimental scouring agent from a bail-handled can with a tapered spout. Then Jack and his co-workers stirred the brew with long wooden rakes. The saturated wool was dense and heavy and the work was hard. The older workers seemed to handle the job with ease, but Jack was struggling. His pulse was racing, his vision blurring as he labored.

The scouring process continued all afternoon, with the cleaned wool being hoisted out of the bath with block and tackle, then lowered into a long vessel on wheels for the trip to the dryer upstairs. The floor of the dyeing room was covered with a greasy slime that made walking treacherous. To make matters worse, the cement was crisscrossed with drains carrying waste water, dye, and solvent to the rear of the dyehouse where it drained into the the canal. Jack was straining to shoulder a particularly heavy load of wool when one foot slipped into a drain. He lost his footing and fell, fell hard, on the cement floor. For several seconds he lay stunned, the wind knocked out of him by the impact. Slowly he drew himself up to a seated position on the floor, the room spinning about him. Several of his co-workers approached and he thought for a moment they were coming to his aid. But they stepped around him carrying their loads.

"C'mon, Bernard, no sittin' down on the job," shouted one of them, and they laughed and continued on their way. Determined not to be labeled as lazy or inept, Jack struggled to his feet smiling. He had bruised his right hip and it ached badly, but he resumed his work. It was clear that there would be no sympathy for anyone who couldn't take the rigors of the dyeing room, not even from his fellow workers.

It's only for a few months, thought Jack as he fought to keep his equilibrium, *only a few months.*

~ 5 ~

Charles Bernard had a way with all things mechanical. There wasn't a loom or spinning rig at Wellington Textiles that didn't show his handiwork: an oak plank sistered against a weak harness beam to guide the warp threads more consistently; a misshapen shuttle restored with a few strokes of a knife or rasp to travel faster and straighter, the better to carry the weft thread back and forth. Such were the precise, often ingenious remedies that he accomplished by the dozens each day.

Perhaps Charles's greatest gift was his ability to determine merely by the look or the feel of the cloth which of dozens of fine adjustments was required to correct a malfunction: the driving belt too tight or slack, too dry or jerky, the picker timing too rapid or slow, the shed too small or tall. An adjustment once made was not forgotten when Charles Bernard was on duty. The loom operator knew that Charles would return later in the day to see that the problem had been corrected.

When gasoline-powered trucks replaced horse-drawn drays on the shipping and receiving platform, Charles was often called away from his normal duties to diagnose a problem when younger men had nary a hint as to how to make an unreliable engine do their bidding.

But more than three decades in woolen mills had taken their toll on Charles's constitution. At forty-five his thick, lustrous hair, once black as coal, was steely gray. His brow was deeply wrinkled, his eyes only occasionally sparkled as in his youth. He walked with a limp these days, sometimes assisted by a cane, and winced as he rose from a chair or ascended the stairs of the Bernard homestead.

For nearly a year now Charles had been at home, unable to work in the mill, doing his best to tend the farm, allowing Jack to become the family's chief breadwinner. That was a necessary change, but one he deeply regretted. Both Charles and his childhood friend, Evelyne St. Onge, had left school in Québec by grade eight to work in a woolen mill, never to complete their education. When the young couple married, they vowed that their children would not follow that sorry path to adulthood. After the birth of their son, the family emigrated to Holyoke where Charles was hired as a loom fixer at Wellington Textiles.

Charles was bending over a dilapidated delivery truck in the barn of the Bernard's farm in Westfield at mid-afternoon. The truck belonged to his neighbor, Pierre Bousquet, and Charles had promised to get it running by the end of the day. In return Pierre and Émile would help Charles and Jack with planting of corn seed by the weekend. For what seemed like the hundredth time he yanked at the starter crank. The engine gave out a few pathetic pops and sputters before it went silent once again. An oath was about to slip from Charles's lips when a welcome voice interrupted him.

"Father, I'm home," chimed Marie from the barn door. "Are you still working on that old junk?"

The discouraged look in Charles's eyes brightened a bit. "Ayeh, Pierre and Émile need it to make deliveries tomorrow - I gotta git it going." He shook his head slowly, looking defeated.

"Why don't you give it a rest for a few minutes? Come inside and let me make you some tea."

Charles couldn't resist the invitation. He sighed, dropped his wrench to the gravel floor, then walked slowly out of the barn and across the yard toward the kitchen door. Father and daughter sat comfortably at the kitchen table sipping hot tea as she recounted the events of her school day.

Marie Bernard was a soft-spoken, serious young woman with dark brown hair, green eyes, and a shy smile. She had taken on most of the duties of woman of the household when her mother passed away just two years before. Her earnestness was due in part to the circumstance of her mother's death, but in equal measure to her desire to care for her family. Cooking, mending, and cleaning for her father, brother, and sister all came naturally to her. In addition to all of that she somehow also managed to keep up her studies at Holyoke High School. And on weekends and in summer she tutored Émile Bousquet, assisting him with his speech and lip-reading. One thing entirely perplexed Marie in her new role, and just then that one thing came bounding through the door, tracking mud into the kitchen.

"Claire, please remove your muddy galoshes before you take another step," scolded Marie.

Claire Bernard was as different from Marie as a sister could be. Short, round-faced, always smiling and effervescing, she had rosy skin and reddish-brown hair like her mother's that tumbled in ringlets from either side of her face. She was entirely lacking the reserve and self-effacement of her mother and sister. There was always curiosity and calculation going on behind those big, saucer-like eyes, often regarding the affairs of others.

Tossing her book bag on the floor, Claire exhaled theatrically. "I am so exhausted. Sister Jean was plaguing me all day today. I think she hates me. I honestly don't know why, but she does. She says I talk too much, but I don't..." She paused as Marie's gaze rose to meet hers, then continued: "And when I do it's usually because I have something to say. Can I have a snack, Marie?" And she lunged across the table toward the cookie jar.

"Claire, mind your manners," replied Marie evenly. Moving the jar out of her sister's reach, she peered intently into her eyes in an effort to calm her. "You must learn - you're almost thirteen and it's time you learned to act more ladylike." But Claire was out of the room and gone before her sister's admonition had a chance of being heard, much less heeded.

Marie could sense that her father's eyes were seeking hers. She turned and he smiled gently. "Let her be, dear, let her be. She's just a girl, ya know, like you were once, remember?"

"But Father, I was never like *that*," replied Marie, shaking her head. Charles smiled, nodded in agreement, then took another sip of his tea.

"I'd best be starting supper now," said Marie, then she paused. "We'll be eating a little late tonight. Jack won't be home until seven or so." With that she turned quickly and headed into the pantry in hopes of avoiding any questions.

"I'll get back to work, then," replied Charles from the kitchen. Marie was just relaxing when her father leaned around the corner and added, "Why's Jack gonna be late?"

Marie hesitated. "Oh, he said something about an errand he had to do on High Street - I'm sure he'll be along as quickly as he can." This seemed to satisfy him, but Marie was uneasy. She knew her brother well and she was not entirely convinced that he had told her the truth.

It was nearly 7:30 when Jack finally came through the kitchen door. He stopped and leaned against the door jamb while removing his tattered leather boots, then set them on the boot rack. Marie was stirring a pot of stew on the black and chrome Glenwood stove as her brother fell heavily into a chair at the kitchen table.

"Phew, sorry I'm so late - the cars were running slow. I had to wait nearly twenty minutes on Sargeant Street."

"That's okay, the stew only gets better the longer it cooks. Would you call Claire and Father while I serve it up?"

"What's new at the mill, Jack?" began Charles as he took his seat. "Jim still working with you guys in the sorting house?"

"Yeh - yeh - Jim's still there. But he's takin' an apprenticeship with a blacksmith in Aldenville this summer."

"That's good for him - nice boy, Jim. You'll miss him, eh?" Jack nodded, then abruptly changed the subject.

"Big doin's at City Hall tonight, Dad. Hundreds of people wavin' flags and flyin' banners for President Wilson and the Declaration of War. They were singin' and cheerin' and the mayor gave a patriotic speech. I can't imagine why they're so all-fired excited about goin' to war. I mean, we have to help our allies, and we have to defend our country, but why all the hoopla? What's there to celebrate?"

"Well, son, war does that to some people, 'specially the old guys that don't have to do the fightin'." As he spoke Charles thought he saw a cloud, a wave, pass across his son's face. Was it doubt? Was it fear? He couldn't tell.

Just then Claire darted into the room and reached for a slice of bread. Marie placed her hand on her sister's, then raised the breadboard. "Sit down, Claire, please."

"I have so much homework to do - I'll just have a slice of bread..."

"Claire, dear," said her father slowly, "your homework can wait. Relax and have some stew. No one can learn on an empty stomach, you know." Grudgingly Claire sat, accepted a serving of beef and turnip stew, then began to eat noisily.

"How come you're so late, Jackie? Cars running slow?" inquired Charles, referring to the streetcars that operated on many of Holyoke's main thoroughfares.

33

"Yeh," replied Jack. "They say the motormen are dragging their feet, holdin' out for more pay."

"Those guys're always belly-achin'. They oughta spend a day in the mill - see what hard work is really like," said Charles, shaking his head.

His meal complete, Jack rose to carry his plate and cup to the sink. As he brushed past his father, Charles sniffed several times. "What the deuce? You smell like Wednesday night at the Ladies of Sodality meeting. You wearin' perfume or something, Jackie?"

Jack turned to the sink, his back to his father, and began pouring hot water for the dishes. "It's just soap. I washed up at the mill before I left and the soap in the washroom was smelly." Then he changed the subject. "How's Mr. Bousquet's jalopy comin'? Any luck?"

"Yeh, finally. Had to tinker with the throttle a good bit but she's goin' now. They'll be plantin' corn soon so they're gonna need it, I guess."

When the dishes were done, Jack started toward the stairs. "Jackie, can you help me? I'm trying to learn the names of the presidents - please?" shouted Claire from her first floor bedroom. "Sister Jean will kill me if I don't..."

Jack turned and walked slowly toward his sister's bedroom, then peeked in the partially opened door. "I'm kinda tired, Claire. Couldn't you get Daddy or Marie to help you tonight?"

Claire looked up into her brother's face. "You look awful, Jackie. You better get to bed early. Maybe that new job is too hard on you."

Jack bristled, looked around to see if his father or Marie were within earshot, then stepped into Claire's room, closing the door tightly behind him. "How do *you* know about *that*?" he whispered angrily.

Claire was undaunted. Even though her brother loomed nearly a foot over her, she knew how to handle him.

"Madeleine Trottière told me in school. She heard it from Jim. Don't worry, Jackie, your secret's safe. But that place - everyone knows it's a death trap."

Just then there came a tap on the bedroom door. Jack shot a baleful look at his sister. "Shhh." Then he turned and opened the door. Marie was standing in the hallway.

"I'll help you with your homework, Claire." Then she turned to Jack. "You should go to bed. You look a fright."

A few minutes later Jack sat on the edge of his bed. His father appeared at the bedroom door. "You all right, Jack? You seemed kind of withered at supper. They workin' you harder 'n usual at the mill?"

"Naw," replied Jack, trying to appear indifferent.

"Well, get a good night's sleep. It'll do you good." Charles turned toward the door.

"Dad." Charles paused and looked back at his son's face, gaunt and ashen in the dim lamplight. "Those crowds, all that flag-wavin' and patriotism..." Jack paused.

"What about it, son?"

"I guess I understand how people feel...after the *Lusitania* and now the *SS New York*. But some of those men were yelling and cursing about foreigners, practically accusing them of being disloyal. One of the banners read *Bolsheviks go home*. They were burnin' flags, I think they were Polish or Lithuanian or Russian flags. Like those people that work with them in the mill were traitors or somethin', you know?"

"Ayeh, war does that to some guys. It's not pretty, son, but it's kinda to be expected."

Jack shook his head and exhaled loudly. "Good night, Dad."

"Sleep well, son."

~ 6 ~

The next morning Jack stepped through the dyehouse door at 6:20 under the watchful eye of Mr. Tuttle. He was already feeling slightly nauseated just anticipating the stench of fumes he knew would confront him. But when he entered the dyeing room where the coal naphtha was in use, the odor was much less intense than on the previous day and he began to relax. They were experimenting with a dilute mixture today, explained Mr. Sullivan. Jack worked all morning with only a mild headache and an occasional lightheaded feeling.

At the noon bell he raced out of the dyehouse door and in minutes stood before Anne by the canal. She kissed him on the cheek, then wrinkled her nose. "What is that smell?"

"Oh, it's a cleaner they're using - in - in the sorting house. It's really strong, isn't it?"

"Since when do they clean *anything* in *that* place?" asked Anne shaking her head. The pair sat in the usual spot, a bench by the water's edge, enjoying another luncheon prepared by Anne.

"We still on for Saturday night, Anne? There's a Charlie Chaplin moving picture at the Bijou that starts at eight."

"Well, let's see, I think my calendar is still free for Saturday evening," teased Anne. "Yes, I'd say we're still on, Jackie. That would be very nice. Oh, but there's something I

36

want to tell you." Anne's pretty smile suddenly turned serious.

"Yeh, what's that?"

"It's about Tommy. He called last evening. Mother talked to him. He's coming home - Wednesday or Thursday."

"Wow, that's wonderful news, Annie, that's great. It'll be so good to see him again."

Anne nodded and smiled weakly. Her brother and Jack had been best friends since they met at Forestdale Grammar School in grade eight. There were no two better friends in Holyoke. They fished, played ball - they were inseparable. Even when Tom went off to the Dorchester School, a private school in Greenfield, in grade nine, the two were still thick as thieves.

"But I thought he was gonna be at that - that place in Williamstown 'til the end of June. What's goin' on? Is he okay?" Jack looked into Anne's eyes as he asked the question.

"He says he's fine. He told Mother he hasn't had a drink since he left Holyoke." Jack looked reassured, but Anne wasn't. "He called from Boston."

"Boston? Tommy's in Boston?" Jack was surprised and concerned.

"I guess he's been visiting Digsy for the last week or so." Digsy was Tom's roommate at the Dorchester School. Tom's schooling took an unexpected turn when he had an automobile accident while gallivanting with Digsy in his parents' Packard. Digsy was a nice enough chap, Jack thought, but somehow he couldn't help but wonder if some of Tom's troubles began with his association with Chester Arthur Digsworth the Third.

Anne looked briefly into Jack's eyes, then away across the street. "I'm worried, Jackie," she said softly. Suddenly her complexion reddened. "He promised us - when he left."

Jack put his arm around Anne and stroked her hair. "I'm sure he'll keep his promise, Anne. He will, I know he will."

Jack's lunch hour was almost over and he had to hurry back to the mill. The couple stood holding hands. "Thanks for the lunch, Annie. You're the bee's knees. I'll see you - and Tommy - on Saturday, okay?"

Anne reached up and kissed Jack lightly on the cheek, then smiled sweetly. "Okay." Jack turned and ran off down Dwight Street.

That evening Jack lay in bed exhausted, his arms and legs aching. Once again he had rebuffed Claire's request for help with her homework, explaining that he was too tired. What he had not admitted to was a pounding headache that made it nearly impossible to concentrate on anything. Only when he lay down, closed his eyes, and remained very still did the throbbing abate. He was stretched out on his side, his back toward the window. A few gentle taps sounded on his bedroom door.

"Who is it? I've gone to bed."

"Jackie, are you okay?" asked Claire through the closed door.

"I'm fine, Claire. I'm just tired." The door opened a crack. Jack looked up, squinting into the light from the hallway.

"Are you sure, Jackie? I'm worried about you - and that place."

"Shsh, I'm warning you." Claire's rosy cheeks paled, her head dropped, and she whimpered softly. Jack sat up in bed and reached out his hand to his little sister.

"I'm sorry, sweetie. I'm gonna be fine. I'm only workin' there to make a few extra dollars, that's all. It's for us, can't you understand? Please don't tell Daddy or Marie, huh?"

Claire nodded and Jack kissed her on the forehead. "Okay, let's hear the Presidents."

Claire stood, hands clasped in front of her, squinting as she concentrated on her task. "Washington, Adams, Jefferson,

Madison, Monroe, John Quincy Adams," and on to "McKinley, Roosevelt, Taft, and Wilson."

"Excellent, Claire, excellent. Sister Jean will be very impressed." Claire rolled her eyes. "Now I have to get some sleep, okay? Goodnight, Claire." Claire backed out of the room, closing the door silently. Soon Jack fell into a restless sleep.

⚜ ⚜ ⚜ ⚜ ⚜ ⚜

It was a dark, moonless May night and the air was perfectly still. Suddenly Jack was awakened by a sound, a dull thud. Just then his father's steps could be heard on the stairs outside his bedroom door and he quickly fell back to sleep. Sometime later he was awakened once again by what seemed like another muffled sound. He lay in bed, willing himself to go back to sleep, knowing that 4:30 would come all too soon and he would need every bit of sleep he could get. The throbbing in his head increased a bit, then was transformed to a soft shushing, like wind through pine trees. Jack closed his eyes and tried to ignore the sound, but it persisted.

All at once through closed eyelids Jack sensed bright light. He opened his eyes and gazed on the faded wallpaper beside his bed. The design seemed to be moving, swaying to the shushing. Then he realized that on a dark night he wouldn't be able to see the wall, not unless there was light shining through the window behind him. Confused, he slowly rolled over onto his back, his eyes following an arc across the bedroom ceiling toward the window. As he turned, the intensity of both light and sound increased.

Suddenly Jack turned his head and looked directly at the window. It seemed to be on fire. The muntins between the glass panes formed a dark grid through which an impossibly bright light shone. The light pulsed, throbbing in synchrony with the pounding in his head. As he stared at the window in confusion, he could feel himself slipping away, spinning,

39

falling helplessly. Then they appeared - two dark orbs in the middle pane, at first dull and diffuse, then more distinct. They were eyes, fierce eyes, eyes that glowed eerily as they stared directly into Jack's eyes. The pounding in his head grew worse; the rushing sound enveloped him. His head jerked violently to one side, then back. Then there was nothing.

~ 7 ~

WEDNESDAY, MAY 23

"Jackie - Jackie - it's nearly five. You'd better get up," called Marie as she tapped softly on Jack's bedroom door. She waited for a few groans of acknowledgement from her brother, but none came. "Jackie - Jackie." Gently she lifted the wrought iron latch, then opened the door just enough to speak again. "Jackie?" In the half light she could see her brother's motionless form on the bed, the covers lying on the floor.

Marie stepped into the room, reached down, and touched her brother's arm. "Jackie - wake up." There was no response. She repeated his name louder, alarm sounding in her voice. "Jackie - come on, Jackie." Still there was no response. She shook him harder and rolled him toward her. A muffled croak came from Jack's lips. His eyes were open, staring blankly at the ceiling.

"Jackie - oh my God, Jackie, what's wrong?" called Marie, her voice cracking. "*Father*," she shouted loudly.

At the sound of his sister's voice Jack's eyes moved and met Marie's. He groaned, lifted his head briefly, then spoke: "Wha - what time is it? Where...?"

"Jackie, are you all right?" asked Marie. Just then Charles appeared at the bedroom door. The fear etched in his daughter's face shocked him.

But at that moment Jack got his bearings, sat up, looked at his father and sister, and spoke. "What's the matter? Why are you..."

"Jackie, are you all right?" asked Marie again, only barely keeping herself under control. "You - I thought you w..."

"I'm okay, I'm fine. I guess I just had a nightmare..." He winced as he rubbed his neck, then reached for the silver pocket watch on his bureau. "I gotta get going." Slowly he stood up. "I can't be late for work."

"Jack," said his father, "maybe you should stay home today. You look wretched."

"I'm all right - really," answered Jack. He looked into his father's eyes, trying to reassure him, then into Marie's eyes. "Can you excuse me? I have to get dressed."

Charles and Marie left the bedroom. Minutes later they were standing in the kitchen speaking in low whispers. When Jack entered they were suddenly silent.

"Here's your coffee - and I made you some oatmeal with maple sugar," said Marie. "Why don't you sit down, relax, and have a leisurely breakfast, Jackie?"

Looking at his watch again, Jack gulped his coffee, took a few spoonfuls of oatmeal, then dashed out the door.

Exhausted, weak, and still a bit nauseated, Jack struggled through his workday. Even one of his co-workers observed that he didn't look well. He left the mill directly when the ending bell rang, walked slowly up Dwight Street, and was thankful to catch a car to Westfield without a wait.

Jack's father had been worrying about him all day and was pleased to see him home at a more reasonable hour. "Sit down, boy, and rest your bones. Marie will have supper on the table shortly. You look badly, Jackie, you still sick?"

"I'm all right, Dad, I just need to get caught up on my sleep - that's all. I don't think I can eat anything. I'm going up to bed."

Marie was just setting a platter on the kitchen table. "Before you go, I have a message that should cheer you up. Tom Wellington called on the telephone."

"Tommy? When? Where is he?"

"About an hour ago. He's at home. It was so good to hear his voice, Jackie, he sounded like - like the old Tommy, you know?" Her eyes met Jack's in silent understanding. "He wants you to telephone him this evening."

Jack's face brightened at the news. Rising slowly from his chair, he crossed the kitchen to the living room door where the telephone hung on the wall. Lifting the handset, he leaned against the door jamb and spoke to the operator. "Holyoke three-two-five, please." There was a long pause, then he heard his old friend's voice. Jack spoke loudly into the mouthpiece. "Tommy? Is that you?"

"Yeh, Jack, it's me. How's my old buddy?" said Tom enthusiastically.

"I'm okay, Tommy, I'm okay. I can't believe it's you. When'd you get home?"

"This afternoon, about four. I would have met you outside the mill at the bell but Mother insisted I be here for supper. Uncle Richard and Charlotte came by and we had a little bit of a celebration."

"Wow, that's great, Tommy," responded Jack with genuine excitement.

"It's so good to be home, Jackie. I missed my parents, Annie, and my old chum."

"How long are you home for? Do you have to go back to Williamstown soon?" asked Jack. There was another pause, then a burst of static on the line. "Tommy - are you still there?"

43

"Yeh, Jack, I'm here. I'm - I'm all done with the clinic. I'm not goin' back. Annie said she told you, right?"

"Naw, I don't think so," replied Jack, "first I'm hearin' of it. So is everything okay, Tommy?"

"Yeh, Jack, everything is fine. Listen, I have to go, but I wanted to ask you something. I know Anne and you have a date for Saturday night, right?"

"Saturday?" Jack was confused. "Do we? I guess so..."

"She told me you two were going to the movies downtown, remember?"

"Oh, yeh - yeh," replied Jack vaguely. "Saturday - the pictures - yup."

"Well, I thought maybe we could go fishing at Hampton Ponds in the afternoon, then you could come here and the three of us could go downtown, have a bite to eat, then go to the theatre. Would that be okay, Jackie? My treat."

"Oh, sure," replied Jack, still trying to get his bearings. "Fishing, then supper, then the movies. That'd be grand, Tommy, just grand." The thought of seeing his old friend and doing what the two of them used to do so often, fishing at Hampton Ponds, was reviving his spirits.

"How about noon, Jack? That way we can have a few hours of fishing. Bring a change of clothes so you can be fresh as a whistle for a night on the town, okay buddy?"

"Yeh, Tommy, and I'll bring some crawlers for bait."

"Okay, Jackie, I'll see you Saturday."

Hearing Tom's voice had rejuvenated Jack's spirits and he forgot about the confusion over his Saturday plans with Anne. He sat by the stove in the kitchen, telling Marie and Charles of his conversation with Tom.

When he finally climbed into bed, Jack fell off to sleep almost instantly. But by midnight he was wide awake and staring at the bedroom ceiling. The excitement over his conversation with his old friend had begun to wear off. His thoughts drifted, unbidden, to the terror of Monday night, the

44

throbbing, the sound of rushing water, and those eyes, those glowing, malevolent eyes. Every time he thought of them he shuddered and beads of sweat popped out on his forehead.

Finally he lit the oil lamp on his bedside table, opened a library book, *The New Onion Culture,* and tried to concentrate on reading. After a time his eyelids drooped and the book slipped from his hands. He placed the volume on the table, extinguished the lamp, rolled over, and closed his eyes. Shortly the memory of that dream - that nightmare - brought him back to full consciousness. Again he lit the lamp, raised the book, and resumed reading.

The next morning Jack and his team were moved to a different area in the dyehouse where a backlog of pieces awaiting dyeing had accumulated. By mid-morning he was encouraged; the weakness in his arms and legs had abated and his stomach was settling.

At noontime Jack sat on a wall in the mill yard with Jim Trottière and Leo Lacroix from the sorting house eating the lunch Marie had prepared for him. As the three talked Jack caught sight of several of his co-workers from the dyehouse engaged in a quiet conversation some distance away. These were older men, dyehouse veterans, men who seldom conversed much either during work or on breaks. Something about their slumped postures and furtive glances struck Jack as a bit odd. He pretended to be listening to Leo and Jim while keeping an eye on the suspicious group beyond.

"De Papermakers playin' at de fiel' Saturday," began Leo, referring to Holyoke's semiprofessional baseball team. "You goin', *Jacques?*" But Jack's attention was elsewhere. "*Jacques?*"

"Huh? Goin' where, Leo?"

"De Papermakers - Saturday - you goin'?"

"Uh, no, Leo, I don't think so. I got things to do."

After lunch Jack was assigned back to the dyeing room and the now familiar weakness and queasiness returned almost immediately. He struggled through the long afternoon, trying hard to keep his footing on the slippery floor. Several times he stumbled briefly, then caught himself. Each time the other men looked on him with annoyance. Jack's face turned scarlet with embarrassment and by the end of the day he felt silly, like he didn't belong among these older, far more capable workers. He was convinced that seeking out this job, the job he had hoped would be such a boon for him and his family, was a terrible mistake and a humiliation.

As he was leaving the mill that evening he caught sight of one of his dyehouse co-workers, one of the trio he'd been eyeing at noontime, bent over in a corner of the mill yard, retching on the grass.

~ 8 ~

By Friday afternoon Jack was exhausted from lack of sleep and it was beginning to show. His skin was gray, his normally bright eyes were dull. It felt like a great mass was pressing down upon him, making every movement difficult. He refused to give in, though, and labored gamely alongside his co-workers in the dyeing room right up until quitting time. When the ending bell finally rang, Jack felt a wave of relief. He just wanted to go home.

"You comin' to the meetin', Jackie?" asked Bill Fredette as soon as they had stepped out of the dyehouse onto Race Street.

"What meeting?" replied Jack. "There's a meeting?"

"Yeh, it's a union meeting down on Canal Street. Some bigwigs from Boston gonna be there to talk about organizing all the workers of Holyoke - textile, paper, rail - all together. You musta heard about it, Jackie, everyone knows."

Jack shook his head. Union activity was never discussed while on the job or anywhere in the mill; that was an infraction guaranteed to get a worker fired on the spot. And Jack rarely spent time with his co-workers outside the mill, so there were few opportunities for him to learn about such things.

"You gotta go, Jackie. This is big - this is really big. Come on, let's go."

Reluctantly Jack followed Bill through the dark streets along the Third Level Canal close to the river. After several blocks they turned into a narrow alley, then descended a flight of stone stairs and stepped through heavy doors into the basement of an old factory building. Dozens of other workers had already arrived and were standing in the dimly lit room smoking and talking excitedly.

Jack was surprised to see a group of genteel young women in immaculate white dresses huddled together by the door, looking very much out of place in the decrepit surroundings. He guessed they might be from the silk mill. Silk was a refined product and that mill insisted that its operatives, nearly all of whom were women, be equally refined both in dress and deportment. They were taking a great risk attending this meeting; if anyone in management at the silk mill got wind of it, they'd be fired at once. But then, the same could be said for everyone present in that room, thought Jack.

A buzz of excitement filled the air as Jack and Bill stood quietly watching the activity around them. Nearly ten minutes went by when finally a voice could be heard from the front of the room announcing that the guest speaker would be arriving shortly. Jack was not in the mood to linger and he finally spoke to Bill. "I gotta go, Billy, I'm feelin' - I got a lot of work to do this weekend."

Bill nodded and Jack started to leave. But just as he approached the door, it swung open and three men surged into the room dressed in long, dark coats and fedoras that looked out of place in Holyoke in May. Jack stepped aside as the men swept past but he caught a brief glimpse of the face of the tallest of the men as he tipped his hat to the women. His skin was dark, his hair dark brown with a distinct wave. The crowd parted as the men strode the length of the room and stepped up onto an elevated platform.

Jack's curiosity was piqued and he paused to watch the proceedings for a few minutes. One of the guests, introduced as Mr. Grant, spoke first. He in turn introduced the dark-haired man, a Mr. Garfield, who stepped up onto the improvised stage. Cheers, whistles, and applause rippled through the crowd. The man smiled warmly and looked out on the audience, appearing to recognize and acknowledge several workers with a nod or wave. When at last the boisterous greeting had abated, he began to speak.

"Thank you, my frrriends," he began. "It is good to be here in Holyoke, my hometown." With that the crowd erupted once again. Garfield smiled and paused until the shouts and applause had once again quieted, then continued. "We come today bringing you greetings from your bruthahs - and sistahs - in Boston, Providence, Lowell, Lawrence, and Haverhill - to urge you to consider the importance of organizing all the workahs of Holyoke." The man spoke like a seasoned orator, a style of speech quite unfamiliar to folks in Holyoke.

As impressed as he was by Mr. Garfield's eloquence, Jack turned and left the assembly hall after ten minutes or so, stepping into the cool night air. He caught the next trolley on Sargeant Street and walked through the Bernard kitchen door thirty minutes later. As much as he would have liked to ask his father about this Mr. Garfield, he did not mention it. For his father, and most of the older generation of French Canadian mill workers, anything having to do with unions and worker activism was suspect.

~ 9 ~

SATURDAY, MAY 26

Hampton Ponds felt like an old friend to Jack Bernard. Some of his earliest memories were of this spot, his father teaching him how to cast, how to hold his line very still, how to think like a fish. It was here that Jack and Tom Wellington spent so many Saturdays beginning in grade eight, swapping stories of adventures real or imagined, dreaming of tomorrows unknown.

Much like a human friend, Hampton Ponds had its moods, one day bright, shining, alive with wind and sunlight, the next day muted and somber. One day its waters rippled with cat's paws reflecting the deep blue sky, the rich hues of autumn foliage, the massive bulk of the distant hills. Another day mists hung over the water, obscuring views, turning the observer in on himself, alone with his hopes and dreams, his doubts and fears.

The last time Jack had fished here was on a sparkling day the previous autumn and it had felt like a soothing balm for his aching heart. He'd been missing his mother who had died a year and a half earlier, feeling her memory slipping from his grasp. In those glistening waters he had imagined she appeared that day, her loving smile and quiet eyes shining up at him again. Even her voice seemed to materialize as he stood on the bank, and he took it as a sign. He knew that it was probably nothing more than a mirage conjured up by his heavy heart, but it didn't matter, it was real to him all the same.

From that day forward, thought Jack, his fortunes had begun to improve. His sisters seemed to be thriving. He and Anne were of one heart. He had been admitted to one of the finest schools of engineering in the country for the following September. The shadow that had hung over Tom had been lifted and his best friend seemed to be trying to get his life back on track.

On this May morning the waters were perfectly smooth and glasslike. A dense mist hung over the surface of the pond like filmy drapery. In fact it was difficult to tell where the waters ended and the mists began. The sun was shining not far above and it lent an eerie opalescence to the diaphanous shrouds hanging over the water.

Jack chose a spot on a grassy embankment that sloped steeply to the water's edge. Setting his tackle box and rucksack on the grass, he baited a hook, secured a cork float to the line, then gently cast into a deep pool not far from the shore. After a few minutes of casting and repositioning, he reeled in his line to make adjustments, adding another sinker and moving the float up to allow the baited hook to hang lower in the pool. He cast his line once again, then stood stock still.

Several minutes went by. As Jack looked intently at his float, the milky mist seemed to brighten. The sun's rays began to penetrate, lending a pearlescent sheen to the thinning fog. Jack saw it first reflected in the waters around his float. As he looked up into the haze, he could hear rushing water, though there was no stream anywhere nearby. The sound swelled and seemed to come from all directions. A feeling of dread gripped him. The curious gaze in his blue-gray eyes became a blank, expressionless stare and he collapsed on the embankment.

51

"*Jack* - hey - *Jack*," shouted Tom Wellington as he approached along the shore. He could see his friend lying on his side on the grassy bank facing away from the direction of his approach.

"Jack, it's me, Tommy, wake up, buddy," called Tom as he drew nearer. He reached down and shook Jack's arm. "Jack, are you okay?" He pulled on his arm and Jack rolled slowly onto his back. Tom looked into his friend's face, unable to make sense of what he saw.

Just then Jack blinked, looked up at Tom, and spoke. "Hey, Tommy. When'd you..." He paused, looked around momentarily confused, then stood up shakily. "Hey, it's great to see you, Tommy. Really...great." He took his friend's hand and shook it vigorously.

"Are you okay, Jack?"

"Oh, yeh, I'm fine," replied Jack confidently. "Just fine."

"But you - you seemed - I called your name - but you..."

"I just fell asleep, that's all. There was nothin' bitin' and I guess I just nodded off."

Tom was clearly shaken by what he had just witnessed. "But Jack, you - you..."

"I'm fine, Tommy, fine. Hey, you look good, pal. Maybe put on a few pounds since I saw you last," observed Jack while looking intently at his friend whom he hadn't seen in some time. Tom was just a bit taller than Jack and walked with a certain swagger. He had black, wavy hair that was carefully coiffed and groomed. Dark eyebrows and a slender nose made his a classically handsome face. He exuded self-confidence with all he met. Perhaps it was his good looks, or the self-assured smile, that invariably caused the eyes of young ladies to pause and stare, briefly. Jack had always wondered why Tom was so much more popular and at ease with the fairer sex than he.

For the next three hours the pair fished on the banks of Hampton Ponds. Again and again Tom cast his line out to where it landed with a gentle plop amongst the ripples. But just as the line came to rest, Tom would reel it in, move a few feet to left or right, then cast again. Meanwhile Jack would stand motionless for many minutes at a time, his eyes intent on the floating cork affixed to his line.

"It's a death trap, Tommy, a lousy death trap. Animals in the slaughter house get treated better than the guys in that place," argued Jack. He was referring to the dyehouse.

"I don't know," replied Tom. He paused just long enough to reel in his line and make another cast. "I've been in there a few times and I don't see what the big deal is."

"Yeah, Tommy, but all you ever did was walk in and walk out. I dare you to breathe that air for just ten minutes. You'll start sneezing and coughing, I guarantee."

"Well if it's so bad, why do you wanna work there, Jack? Why don't you just quit and go back to the sorting house?"

"Well," replied Jack, "I - we need the extra money. The other guys are okay and Tuttle, he pretends to be mean, but he's not too bad. You just have to learn to ignore his insults and his foul tongue, that's all. Besides, I'm off to college at the end of the summer." He paused, as if contemplating that day, then continued. "What's sad to think about are those guys that'll spend the rest of their lives in that hell-hole. I just think the company ought to do something," added Jack. "Like put electric fans in there to ventilate it or something. Anything, it's indecent."

"I admire your idealism, Jack, I really do. But that's business. If the workers don't like it, they should look for other work. Folks talking about men getting sick from working in the mill are just trying to rile up the workers, that's all, just scaremongering." Tom moved a few steps and cast again into deeper waters. Just then his line went taut. He jerked impulsively on the rod and the baited hook flew out of the water, over his head, and into the trees behind him.

"You gotta take it easy," scolded Jack. "When you think you got a nibble, just pull gently until you're sure you've got something. Give 'im time to get the bait, then you've got a better chance of hookin' 'im. I swear you forgot everything I ever taught you about fishing, Tommy - you gotta be patient," said Jack mockingly.

"I know, but patience isn't my strong suit, Jackie," said Tom as he looked at his friend and smiled. Jack nodded in agreement. After another long, quiet interlude, Jack spoke to his friend in a low voice.

"So, how come you're home so soon, Tommy? I thought that - that thing was supposed to go to the end of June."

"It was just a lot of talk, and I didn't need any more talking. I'm clean, Jack, I haven't had a drink since Christmas, I swear."

"That's great, Tommy, that's really great. I'm glad, and I know Anne is, too. We were really worried about you, ya know?"

"I'm okay, I'm okay. Let's just drop it, okay?" replied Tom, a note of annoyance in his voice.

Tom's sharp retort startled Jack. He turned and stared out at the still waters, as if concentrating on his line, but his thoughts were of the past. The close friendship between the two young men, forged right there at Hampton Ponds, had been fractured a year and a half earlier while Anne was in South America with her father. Much against his better judgment, Jack had agreed to attend a social at Mount Holyoke College with Monique Fleury, one of Tom's ex-girlfriends. Monique was an unapologetic flirt, and Jack should have known when he spurned her advances that evening that there was a price to be paid. Monique used a much-embellished account of the evening to infuriate Tom. Under the influence of too much liquor, Tom had written a letter to his sister exaggerating Monique's story, thus ending Jack and Anne's alliance.

The following summer, Tom was seen at the scene of a mill workers' rally in Holyoke where a riot broke out and a deadly fire ensued. Several months later, during Tom's first semester at Harvard, he was arrested and charged with arson and murder. Tom had been within seconds of pleading guilty to the charge of manslaughter in the fire and death, a charge that would likely have earned him a long prison sentence. It was only thanks to Jack and Anne's efforts that evidence planted to incriminate Tom was revealed.

Finally Jack spoke. "So what's next, Tommy? You goin' back to Harvard?"

"Well, Jack, I've got some big news. Monday I'm starting a new job in the accounting office at the mill. I'll be assistant bookkeeper."

"Wow, Tommy, that's great, really - great," replied Jack.

"It's mostly sorting bills and paying invoices," added Tom. "Sounds kind of dull, I know."

"Well, you have to start somewhere, right?" observed Jack.

"Right. I had a long talk with Uncle Richard. He says he's grooming me for better things. Who knows? Maybe I'll work my way up to be Vice President of the company, maybe President one day, just like he did." Tom turned as he said those words, watching for Jack's reaction. Jack nodded but his eye never left his float.

"You know, I never realized 'til now the kind of guy my uncle is. He's so devoted to the company - his work. He doesn't let anything stand in his way. That's what it takes to be a success in this world, you know, Jack? You gotta be tough. That was my father's problem, he was never tough enough." Jack nodded but continued to watch his line. Tom's father was a mild-mannered man, quite the opposite of his brother.

"So, Jack, rumor has it there's some union organizers in town stirring up trouble."

"Oh? First I'm hearin' of it, Tommy."

"...had a meeting just last night, so they say."

"Oh?"

"Come on, Jack. You know the guys on that Committee, don't you?"

La Comité, as it was known, was a small group chosen by the French workers at Wellington Textiles to represent them. They were responsible for bringing suggestions, concerns, sometimes complaints, of their fellow French workers to the mill managers. But the workers of Holyoke who were most vocal about unions were the Irish, English, and Italians, groups with which most French Canadians had little sympathy. Many of the French operatives had come to Holyoke directly from their family farms in Québec, ready to work, grateful for their jobs, and not inclined to make demands of the hand that fed them. Back home in Canada, parish priests and bishops preached frequently of the evils of unions, of the dangers inherent in a society slipping into godless socialism. Being a good, respectful, compliant employee was, they were told, as important as being a good, respectful, compliant Catholic.

"Naw, they're old guys, most o' them come from Canada thirty, forty years ago, been working at the mill ever since. Guy Letourneau, George St. Pierre, old man Proulx, Cloutier, couple others. My dad knows them all."

"Uncle Richard knows them, too, Jack, real well. Talks to them like they were old buddies. From what I hear."

"Yeh, well, like I said, they're old guys. The younger workers, they're not so chummy with the boss."

Tom looked warily at his friend. "Come on, Jack. Just between us - what's up?".

"I swear I don't know a thing, Tommy. But then, even if I did I wouldn't be tellin' the - the management."

Tom was stung by Jack's words, but at that moment Jack's line went taut. "I've got a little nibble here, Tommy, just a nibble. See? I'm just watchin', waitin', tryin' not to spook him..." Just then the float was yanked beneath the surface. Jack pulled sharply on the rod and a long slender pickerel arced out of the water, hook in mouth. Jack let the fish carry his line out a short distance before he gave another tug, then reeled it in.

"That's a beaut, Jack, a real beaut."

"I don't know - respectable," replied Jack modestly as he drew the line toward him, grasped his catch firmly, and turned away from the water's edge. The two boys stood admiring the slender, glistening fish as it lay lifeless on the sand.

"So, you and Anne, what's the news on you two? She won't tell her big brother a thing. Come on, Jack, spill the beans."

"Nothing to spill, Tommy. She's graduating in June - then she wants to go to work full-time at the Women's Home. I'm off to Worcester in September. End of story."

"Have you two talked about that? I mean, for real?"

"Sure, we've talked, a little," replied Jack. Then he sat down on the bank, his hands pawing disconsolately at the sand in front of him. "Not really, I guess. It's just, you know, a sensitive subject. The last time we were apart, well..."

Tom didn't have to be reminded. When Anne left with her father for a year in South America, she and Jack had agreed to socialize, to see other people, a plan that ended in disaster for the young couple. It was nearly a year before they were reconciled.

"But we're going to make the best of the next three months," added Jack. "You know, eat, drink, and be merry." As soon as he said it he wished he'd chosen his words more carefully. "Speaking of being merry, Annie and I were hoping maybe you'd want to go to the Senior Formal with us, you and…"

Tom interrupted his friend. "Wait. Let me guess. You want me to ask Carolyn, right?" Jack said nothing, pretending to focus all his attention on his line. "Well, forget it, Jack. I graduated a year ago and I'm not going to be seen at some high school dance. And I'm definitely not asking Carolyn Ford." Tom looked directly at Jack as if demanding a response, but Jack stood silently, his eyes still trained on his float. "Besides, I'm sure she's already been asked."

That ended the conversation about the Senior Formal. Tom had once been sweet on Carolyn, his sister's best friend. And the four had spent some good times together. But that was in the past. Tom had gone off to the Dorchester School in grade nine where he had enjoyed a very active social life that didn't include Carolyn Ford.

By mid-afternoon both young men were ready to call it a day. Jack had several pickerel and a bass to bring to the Wellingtons, Tom had nothing to show for a day's fishing. They walked slowly along the dusty path toward the trolley line, then waited by the tracks for the next car to approach. Eventually a Holyoke-bound car clattered up the tracks, sparks flying from the wires overhead. Tom smiled at his friend and the two boarded. They sat together near the back of the car as it rumbled off through Rock Valley toward Holyoke.

"By the way, you're right," said Jack after several minutes of silence. "Carolyn has been invited to the Formal - by a couple a guys, according to Anne. But she turned them down. Who knows? Maybe she's waiting for an invitation from someone - in particular."

For a moment their eyes met. Tom turned and looked out the window and the subject was dropped.

~ 10 ~

Isn't this grand?" offered Anne as she, Jack, and Tom strode down Appleton Street. "Just like the good old days of the Fearsome Foursome."

"Yeh," replied Tom with a wide smile. "Hey, Jack, remember Jerry's Soda Shoppe - and the revues at the Victory Theatre - and the carnival down at Riverside Park? We always had a jolly time, didn't we?"

"The only thing missing is Carolyn, you know?" interjected Anne. "I tried to talk her into coming with us but she wasn't able. Where shall we dine, boys?"

"How about O'Shaughnessy's?" suggested Tom. Moments later the three were seated in a booth at the popular restaurant on High Street. As they ate, conversation ranged over past adventures of the two boys, school dances, and summer vacations.

"We gotta do this a lot this summer," said Tom. "Make every minute count, you know? Right up until the day Jack leaves - ow." Anne may have been a petite young lady but she nevertheless was capable of administering a painful kick under the table.

Tom paid the bill and the trio stood up to take their leave. Once outside the restaurant they started along High Street toward the theatre. Suddenly a long, gleaming coupe pulled up to the curb next to them, its engine roaring. Smiling from behind the wheel was a stunningly attractive young woman with long dark hair. She poked her head out the window and called to the three: "Yoo-hoo. Hi, all."

It was Monique Fleury. She parked the motorcar and climbed out. As she approached, the boys' eyes nearly popped out of their heads. She was wearing a tight, red satin dress covered with sparkling sequins and cut very low in front, red heels at least four inches high, and a scarlet hat accented with a long, white feather. Curled eyelashes and brightly painted lips gave her face a dramatic, almost comical look.

"Hey, baby," said Tom as he grasped Monique firmly in his arms and kissed her squarely on the lips, right there on High Street - in broad daylight! Jack appeared stunned by everything he saw; Anne looked annoyed. "Anne, Jack," said Tom, "you remember Monique - Monique Fleury? Monique, Anne and Jack."

"My, my, how are you two these days?" she asked in a sassy, dismissive tone.

"We're fine," began Jack. But Monique wasn't listening. She was looking intently into Tom's eyes.

"Hey, Monique, we're headed to the theatre. Why don't you join us?" asked Tom enthusiastically. The expression on Anne's face suggested she did not share her brother's enthusiasm.

"Gee, I'd love to, but I gotta be somewhere. Tommy, could I speak to you - in *private*?"

Tom nodded to Anne and Jack. "Go ahead - I'll catch up." The couple turned and walked along High Street, happy to put some distance between themselves and that girl.

"I can't believe her. She's no good - no good - and my brother better be careful." Anne's face was bright red.

Jack took Anne's hand. "Come on, let's forget about her. We're gonna have fun, remember?" And the pair walked slowly hand-in-hand down the busy thoroughfare until they reached the entrance to the Bijou Theatre. Several minutes later Tom rejoined them and the trio entered the theatre.

The evening's program began with a Burton Holmes travelogue, *La Belle France*, depicting breath-taking scenes of

Paris, the chateaux of the Loire Valley, and the turquoise waters of the *Côte d'Azur*. The irony was not lost on the audience that evening. Nearly everyone had a son, brother, husband, or friend who would soon be fighting to save France from the Kaiser's invaders. Jack was thinking about Stephen Bousquet.

A short silent film, *Sue the Sleepwalker*, followed the travelogue and elicited more catcalls than laughs from the audience. Finally the main show began, *The Immigrant*, starring Charlie Chaplin. Everyone was amused by the antics of America's favorite movie star as he lampooned a poor, helpless European just arriving in America, a story that was familiar to all present but did not fail to provoke much laughter at the hapless immigrant's expense. Somewhere out of sight a honky-tonk piano played, lending a rollicking, festive air to the evening.

After the show the trio walked up Dwight Street laughing and recounting the funniest moments of the movie. Jack and Tom took turns imitating Chaplin's walk, much to the entertainment of onlookers. Back at the Wellingtons' home, Tom went to the garage for the Reo to take Jack back to Westfield, the last trolley having departed at least an hour earlier. Jack and Anne stood together in the shadows of the mansion's entrance.

"That was swell," said Jack, "great fun." Anne nodded. "The three of us together - you, me, Tommy - it's been so long since..." Anne nodded once again but there was a look of uncertainty in her eyes as they followed her brother.

"He's the old Tommy, I swear he is," said Jack in a reassuring tone.

Again Anne nodded, but then she paused. "I guess so." She put her arms around Jack's waist and looked up into his eyes. They kissed, then held each other in a tight embrace. "Good night, Jackie," said Anne sweetly. "See you Tuesday?" Jack nodded, smiled, and walked toward the Reo that was just pulling up to the portico. Anne watched the pair laughing as the sporty car roared down the driveway and off into the city, hoping and praying that Jack was right.

~ 11 ~

SUNDAY, MAY 27 – MONDAY, MAY 28

Jack was up early the next morning. He had slept poorly every night that week and he was feeling the cumulative effects of fatigue. But he had his regular chores to do and he wanted to get to them early so that he could tend to the gardens.

He downed his breakfast hurriedly, then stepped out into the yard. The morning was cool and fog hung over the fields that stretched into the distance behind the Bernard home. In the barn he mucked out the animal stalls, fed the chickens, then climbed into the loft to get hay for the family's one dairy cow, *Angélique*. He hauled the heavy bales to the edge, then dropped them to the barn floor far below. The air in the loft was stuffy and filled with dust. Jack coughed repeatedly as he labored.

Finally he clambered down the ladder and began breaking up the hay bales, tossing several flakes into each stall. He was breathing hard and sweating heavily despite the chilly air. Then he felt faint. A rushing sound began to rise in his head and he staggered, leaning on a hay bale. The sound grew louder and more intense. The pressure in his head became unbearable. He gasped and fell heavily, face down, into the hay.

Just then Marie entered the barn. "Jackie - Jackie - are you up there?" she called, looking up at the loft. She heard a sound

63

in one of the stalls and peered over the rail. Jack was sprawled in the hay, his arms and legs thrashing violently.

"Oh my God, Jackie..." Marie was unable to move, so horrified was she at what she was witnessing. She wanted to kneel next to her brother, to hold him and reassure him, but his movements were violent and she was afraid to get near. She turned and ran out of the barn, yelling for her father. Minutes later Charles and Marie were crouched on either side of Jack in the hay. The thrashing had ceased but Jack's breathing was irregular and his father and sister were frightened.

"Go get Pierre and Émile - they're unloading the hay wain," said Charles as he knelt next to Jack. "I'll stay with your brother." Moments later the two neighbors appeared in the barn door with Marie. In the workshop they found a wide plank and placed it next to Jack in the hay, then gently lifted him under his arms and legs and placed him on the plank. The four then carried him into the house where they moved him onto the bed in Marie's first floor bedroom.

Marie tried to reassure Claire and enlist her help in drawing cold water to apply to their brother's fevered brow. Charles telephoned Dr. Gibson, the family's physician of many years, who gave Charles instructions and promised to be there as soon as he could. But fifteen minutes later an ambulance pulled into the Bernard driveway, two attendants climbed out and raced across the yard to the kitchen door. Moments later Marie was seated in the ambulance next to her brother as it sped down Southampton Road toward the hospital. Charles reassured Claire, sent her next door to stay with the Bousquets, then started the Model T and tore down the road after the ambulance.

The next twenty-four hours at the Westfield hospital were frightening and confusing for Charles and Marie. Jack had been sedated and was quiet, but his skin had a ghostly pallor that worried them. His breathing was shallow and the nurses were checking his vital signs constantly. Grim-faced doctors came and went from his room frequently, but no one was willing or able to provide a diagnosis or prognosis. Pierre and Madeleine Bousquet arrived in the evening to pick up Marie and take her home. Charles stayed with Jack all that night.

By the next morning Jack was awake and able to speak to his father. When Pierre arrived with Marie and Claire, the girls were relieved to see their brother sitting up in bed, looking more himself. He even marshaled a weak smile for Claire who bravely fought back tears as she grasped his hand in both of hers. The three visited for a few minutes, then the nurse ushered them out of the room so that Jack could be washed and his bedding changed.

Charles, Marie, and Claire walked hand-in-hand down a long hallway to a glass-walled solarium where they sat in wicker chairs. Marie had been trying her best to maintain her composure for her younger sister's sake, but finally Claire began to cry.

"Now, now," began Charles, "don't cry. I talked with Dr. Gibson early this morning and he says Jack's gonna be okay. He says these things happen and sometimes never happen again. And they have some new medicine that helps. So let's just keep our chins up, eh?" He looked into Claire's eyes and she nodded.

Marie sat with her face buried in her hands, breathing heavily. "Father," she began, "What if - if he has another one, at work, or driving the car, or..." She was shaking her head.

"Don't you worry, dear, don't you worry. He's not goin' to work again for some time, I can tell you that. I'll call the mill in the morning and tell them not to expect him in the sorting house."

Claire looked up and into her father's eyes, then began to cry again.

"Come on, child, be brave. Everything's gonna be okay, I promise." But the look in his daughter's eyes told him there was something more on her mind. "What is it, honey?"

"Daddy, is it wrong to break a promise you make to someone, even if there's a real good reason?"

"Now there, what are you talkin' about?"

Marie spoke up. "What Claire is trying to say is that there's something you should know about Jack's work. He's not in the sorting house any more. He's been working in the dyehouse since last Monday. She found out at school. She just told me this morning."

"What?" Charles looked at his eldest daughter with disbelief.

"I'm sorry, father, I should've told you. But I knew you'd be angry."

By midday Jack was looking better and his father and sisters sat in his room talking in low voices with forced smiles for the patient. Everyone was buoyed by the news that the doctor thought Jack could go home the next morning. He would have to remain in bed and take the medication, something called Luminal, on a very regular schedule, so work at the mill or even on the farm were out of the question. But Jack would be home!

There had been some memory loss, the doctor explained to Charles. Jack could not recall any of the events of several days prior to his seizure. Charles was stunned at this news, but the doctor reassured him that it was not uncommon and that some of the lost memory might eventually be recovered. "It's probably just as well, Mr. Bernard," explained the doctor. "Some things are better forgotten."

"Oh, Jackie, I'm so relieved. We were so - we're very happy that you're doing well," exclaimed Marie. Jack smiled weakly.

Later in the afternoon the Bousquets returned and Marie and Claire prepared to say their good-byes to their brother. "As soon as I get home I'll telephone the Wellingtons, Jackie," said Marie.

"No, no, don't, Marie." replied her brother.

"But Jackie - Anne, Tommy, Mr. and Mrs. Wellington - they would want to know."

"No. Don't tell them. Don't tell anyone."

Claire spoke up. "Jackie, they're your friends, they can help."

"No, I forbid it," said Jack as forcefully as he could.

"Okay, Jackie, okay, don't get upset," replied Marie anxiously, "we won't tell them."

Then Claire added with a twinkle in her eye, "Now you get some rest. And do what the nurses tell you."

With that Jack's sisters left. Charles stayed with him until after his supper, then gave him a few words of reassurance before departing. "It's gonna be all right, boy, you hear me?"

As Charles Bernard walked down the long corridor his heart was heavy. He was thinking of his wife, Evelyne, wishing she was there by his side about now. But as he thought about it, he felt some relief that she was not alive to witness this bitter turning in the fortunes of her first-born, her son Jack.

~ 12 ~

Holyoke three-nine-one, the Women's Home. May I help you?" asked the bright-eyed young receptionist, speaking slowly and distinctly into the telephone mouthpiece. She pressed the handset tightly to one ear, trying to discern a man's voice over the noisy line.

"This is Miss Wellington," she replied. Again she listened, struggling to hear the caller's next question.

"No, I'm sorry, Mrs. Calavetti is out. She is attending a meeting in the mayor's office. Perhaps you could telephone again in an hour or so?" She paused once again, listening intently.

"All right, Mr. Smith, I'll tell Mrs. Calavetti you called. Thank you. Good-bye." In her precise hand she recorded the message on a clean sheet of paper and placed it atop the pile of papers on her boss's desk.

This was Anne's first week as an employee of the Holyoke Women's Home, but the surroundings were quite familiar. For four years she had volunteered at the Home with Carolyn Ford whose mother, Nina Calavetti, was the Home's director. They served meals, washed dishes, and sometimes entertained the young residents with board games, knitting bees, even dramatic readings in the large living room on the first floor.

Anne returned to the task of sorting the stacks of manila file folders on the counter. Mrs. Calavetti had many talents, but keeping orderly records was not among them. That chore had been assigned to Anne and she was quite capable and very pleased to carry it out.

The work of the Holyoke Women's Home seemed terribly important to Anne. Young women just arriving in Holyoke to work in the mills could find temporary accommodations here. The rooms were Spartan, the meals just adequate, but it offered companionship, support, even a certain amount of camaraderie among the residents and staff. Some of the girls were very young, younger even than Anne and Carolyn. Some were overwhelmed, even frightened, by the city. The Home was an island of security for its residents, many of whom were away from their families for the first time.

Anne loved school, especially literature. And she had thought of continuing her studies at Mount Holyoke, Smith, Wellesley, or Massachusetts Agricultural College, as several of her closest friends would be doing. But the Women's Home held a special allure for her. It all began on a snowy January afternoon some four years earlier, the day that she and Carolyn met Clara.

Barely sixteen, Clara Hudson was a resident of the Home, and Anne would never forget those lugubrious eyes and the loneliness they bespoke. Clara would soon be having a baby, they learned, and yet she had been abandoned, both by her parents and by the father. Carolyn and Anne adopted her, brought her gifts, held a party for her, and shared with her the excitement of the approaching birth. They succeeded in bringing friendship, joy, and a ray of hope into Clara's sad life. And then, without warning, Clara was gone, having died in childbirth. That was the very day, Anne later realized, that working at the Women's Home had become her career goal.

It was late afternoon and a group of residents came through the front door, having spent the day applying for work in the city's mills. Anne greeted them cheerily, then resumed her task. A few moments later Mrs. Calavetti returned.

"Everything all right here, Anne?" Nina inquired. Looking at the clear counter, an expression of surprise spread across her face. "My goodness, don't tell me you finished all those files, Anne?"

"Yes, ma'am, it was easy. It was just a matter of concentration."

"Well, you must be exhausted, dear - and it's 4:30, so you should be on your way. See you at 12:30 tomorrow?"

"Yes, ma'am."

"Are you and Carolyn..."

"Yes, I'm meeting her at Gregoire's in ten minutes. We'll walk home together."

"Well, thank you, Anne. I'll be attending the Ladies' Temperance Union meeting at five. Please remind Carolyn that I will be home by seven o'clock."

A few minutes later Anne was strolling along High Street feeling exhilarated. *My first job*, she was thinking, *and what a perfect place to work.* As she stepped through the entrance to the women's side of Gregoire's Shoe Shop - the store was divided into two sections, one half devoted entirely to footwear and accessories for women and children, the other half to men's shoes and boots - a jingling bell over the door announced her entry.

The aisles were like canyons lined with dark walnut shelves rising fully nine feet on either side. Wooden ladders mounted on iron wheels rolled along tracks the full length of the store, thus allowing the sales staff to climb high in search of a special brogue or a dainty slipper or dress shoe. The aroma of fresh leather filled the air.

Positioned between the men's and women's sections was the service counter where a clerk rang up each sale and wrote out a receipt. Purchases were wrapped in wide sheets of brown paper drawn from a long roll at the end of the counter. The clerk then reached up and pulled a length of twine off a large spool suspended several feet above the counter, and with a dramatic flourish tied the parcel with two loops, a knot, and a bow. The wrapping and tying were all achieved with a certain casual flair that fascinated customers young and old.

Mr. Gregoire was a kindly old gentleman. He walked slowly with a pronounced stoop, but he had a smile for every customer and each worker. He knew all there was to know about footwear of every type and style, but his hearing was fading and he relied increasingly on his two senior employees, Miss Halliwell and Mr. Barton, and their helpers to deal with the customers.

As soon as Anne entered, Carolyn Ford emerged from the back room. She was slender with long black hair tied in a tight bun against her head. Her eyes were large, almond-shaped, and usually downcast; her olive complexion was lovely but her slender lips seldom betrayed a smile. She and Anne were perhaps unlikely friends, Anne being much the more sociable and bright of mien. But they had been friends for over ten years and there existed between them the closest of bonds. Only a year or so earlier, Carolyn had revealed to Anne the truth about her father, details she had never shared with anyone, some of which her mother had only recently made known to her.

"I'll be on my way now," said Carolyn softly to Miss Halliwell, only raising her eyes briefly toward the stout, gray-haired woman.

"We will see you tomorrow at 12:30 sharp," replied Miss Halliwell formally.

A light rain was just beginning to fall as the two young ladies made their way up Appleton Street toward the Highlands, each holding a small umbrella. "How was your afternoon, Carolyn?" asked Anne. "Everything going well?"

Carolyn sighed. "Yes, Anne, pretty well - I guess. It's just that there's so much to know about shoes. I don't believe I'll ever understand everything about sizes, fitting, vamps, insteps, lasts. My goodness, Anne, there are London lasts, English lasts, Astor lasts, Healey lasts. The ladies and children are usually nice and very patient with me, but it's embarrassing when I have to ask Miss Halliwell for help with nearly every customer."

"And what about the men?"

"I haven't worked on the men's side as yet. I honestly don't think I want to; they make me nervous. And Miss Halliwell warned me not to act too friendly or they'll think I'm - flirting." Carolyn paused nervously. "I just want to stay as far away from them as possible."

"You'll get accustomed to it in time, Carolyn. This is only your second week. Once you know your job, I'm certain you will feel better about dealing with the customers - all of them."

Despite the encouraging words, Carolyn's face betrayed serious misgivings. "Everything okay with you, Anne? Did Mama get under your skin?" she probed, looking tentatively into Anne's eyes and displaying a slight smile.

"Everything is just fine. You know, it's all pretty familiar to me. And there's plenty for me to do. I must have sorted through about a thousand files today. They were completely disheveled."

The pair walked slowly side by side up Appleton Street, Anne doing most of the talking. Finally they reached Carolyn's house and stood facing each other on the sidewalk. Anne looked off into the distance, trying to choose her words carefully. "Carolyn, won't you please reconsider about the Senior Formal?"

Looking down at the concrete sidewalk, Carolyn spoke softly, shaking her head: "I don't think so, Anne, I'm sorry."

"But why? It would be so much fun - imagine, the Fearsome Foursome, together again, just for one night. Please? I'd be with you every minute." Carolyn stood quietly, now looking up the street. "Dearest Carolyn, this is the social event of your senior year. I'm afraid if you don't go you'll regret it."

Again there was a long pause. Carolyn was not a skilled conversationalist, even with her closest friend, and the subject clearly made her uncomfortable. She shook her head slowly.

"Is it Tommy? Listen, I know he hasn't always been well behaved, but he has changed, Carolyn, he really has. Give him a chance, please. You'll see what I mean."

Another long pause ensued. Finally Carolyn replied. "Anne, there's something else..."

"What, Carolyn? You told me you'd already been asked by Billy Corcoran and Aaron Peasley, and you turned them down. Is that what you mean?"

"No - well, yes, I mean."

"What is it, Carolyn?" Anne was perplexed by Carolyn's reticence. Her friend was always slow in conversation, but even Anne's patience was beginning to wear thin.

"I've been meaning to tell you that - I've - I've been seeing a boy for a while now."

Anne turned and looked on her friend with astonishment. "Carolyn - since when? Who?"

Carolyn's complexion turned deep red. "His name is Jan, J-A-N, Jan Krawczyk. He's Polish - the J is pronounced like a Y. He's twenty. He lives in Willimansett and works at Schofield Paper with my cousin Anthony. That's how we met. Anthony introduced us when Mama and I were visiting a while back."

"Carolyn, that's wonderful. But why so secretive? I thought we were bosom buddies, you and I? Well, come on, tell me all about Jan."

Carolyn blushed and a faint smile crept across her face. "Well, he has blond hair, and he's big - I mean, you know, tall and stocky. He's very strong; I guess you have to be to work in that mill. But he's kind, he's very polite - and he has a wonderful sense of humor."

"And you have spent some time together, just the two of you?"

Carolyn blushed. "Just a few times, in Chicopee. We met in the park, with Anthony, one Sunday a while back. And he treated me to college ice last Saturday. He asked me to come to Sunday dinner at his house but I said no. Mama would never..."

"So your mother hasn't met Jan yet?"

Carolyn shook her head. "She doesn't know." Suddenly she looked up at Anne with a panicked expression. "You won't tell her, Anne, please."

"Of course not, Carolyn, of course not. But sooner or later you'll..." Carolyn shook her head. Then Anne had an idea. "Carolyn, maybe Jan could escort you to the Formal," she said, her eyes shining and her voice rippling with excitement.

"No, I don't think so. He's not that type, and Mama..." Carolyn stood quietly, her eyes lowered, looking quite dejected.

"Oh, Carolyn, don't give up. We'll figure out something, I promise."

Finally Carolyn managed a weak smile. "Thanks, Anne, but it's all right. Really, I'd just as soon not go at all."

The two parted, but as Anne walked the several blocks home alone, she was determined to help her friend.

~ 13 ~

Yes, size six, just as you wanted. Can I help you try them on?" It was after four o'clock the next day and Carolyn was being as courteous and helpful as possible with Mrs. Flynn, mother of one of her classmates. Mrs. Flynn was tall and buxom with unusually large feet for a lady, and Carolyn was trying her best to accommodate her wishes. She knelt on the floor, cradling a white satin shoe in both hands, attempting to force it onto one of Mrs. Flynn's pudgy pink feet. The lady was grunting, squealing, and expostulating under her breath, not wishing to draw attention to their struggle. But the foot was not even close to fitting into the delicate dress shoe.

"May I assist you, Carolyn?" asked Miss Halliwell. Carolyn looked up into her supervisor's face with a shy smile, then moved aside without a word.

"Ma'am, that shoe is at least two sizes too small. Carolyn, find Mrs. Flynn an eight, won't you please?"

As soon as Miss Halliwell had turned her back, Mrs. Flynn resumed her efforts. "Nonsense," she sputtered under her breath so only Carolyn could hear. Carolyn suspected the shoes were to be worn to graduation, only two weeks away now, and she also knew Mrs. Flynn well enough to let her have her way.

Finally with aid of a tortoiseshell shoehorn, Carolyn managed to get the shoes to cling tenuously to Mrs. Flynn's feet, though they threatened to slip off at any moment. Standing with some effort, the lady took several painful steps. Then she looked at herself with obvious satisfaction in a floor-length mirror. "You see, Carolyn? That woman doesn't know from Adam about shoes. Wrap them up for me, won't you, and I'll be on my way."

At the counter Carolyn pulled a long sheet of brown wrapping paper from the roller, tore it carefully, and wrapped the shoes. She pulled confidently on the dangling twine end and in one quick motion had the parcel tied securely. She wrote out a sales slip, rang up the sale on the cash register with a musical *dddring*, then made change for her customer. "Thank you, dear," replied Mrs. Flynn. "See you at graduation, hmmm? Mary's so excited."

Carolyn smiled and nodded. Mrs. Flynn cast a reproachful glance toward Miss Halliwell, then turned in the opposite direction and started for the door. Carolyn watched her walk away, then pivoted toward the women's section where there were several other customers to be attended to before she finished her shift.

But at that moment there appeared at the counter before her, as if out of nowhere, a tall, distinguished looking man with dark, wavy hair and swarthy skin. He looked squarely into Carolyn's eyes long enough to make her feel uncomfortable. She would have turned away and retreated quickly but he was not about to let her. "Miss, excuse me, I wonder if I could have some assistance?"

Carolyn looked past him, hoping to be rescued by Mr. Gregoire or Mr. Barton, but neither was in sight. The man spoke again. "I wonder if you could show me your dress hosiery for men?"

Carolyn was standing behind the long counter and she was determined to keep that formidable barrier between her and the dark haired man. She looked down the aisle to her right. "Just there, sir, you'll find an assortment of hosiery."

She started to turn away but the man was too quick. "Could you help me, please?" He looked into Carolyn's eyes again, but sensing her unease he quickly turned in the direction she had indicated. "Uhh, if you could just show me where they are, that would be fine."

Reluctantly Carolyn took a few steps along the back side of the counter, but when she reached the end she stopped and gestured. "Right over there, sir. Mr. Barton will be at your service in a moment." The man thanked her and began to walk down the aisle away from her.

Relieved but still shaken, Carolyn returned to the lady's department where she quickly came to the aid of an older woman whom she hoped would require her attention well out of view of the sales counter and the men's section. Fully fifteen minutes later when the woman had chosen a pair of black brogans, Carolyn led her to the sales counter to wrap her purchase and ring up the sale.

Again the dark-haired man appeared, this time holding several pairs of men's hose. He placed them on the counter, then carefully positioned a dollar bill next to them. Seeing no alternative, Carolyn took the stockings, folded them, and quickly laid them in a long, brown box. She tied the box in the usual manner and placed it on the counter in front of the man, taking pains not to look into his face.

"Thank you, Miss," he said, smiling. And he took his parcel, turned, and walked toward the door. Relieved once again, Carolyn reached for the bill. Beneath it was a small envelope. She paused, staring at it for several moments. Then cautiously she picked it up. She paled as she read the inscription written across the envelope in a studied hand:

Miss Carolyn Teresa Ford

At that moment the bell jingled indicating that a customer was entering the front door on the men's side of the store. Carolyn looked up. The dark haired man was standing next to the door, looking directly at her. The customer who had just entered walked past him and toward her smiling. It was Tom Wellington.

"Hello, Carolyn." She was startled and momentarily flustered, her eye shifting from Tom to the man and back to Tom. "How are you, Carolyn?"

"Why, Thomas, what are you..." She paused in mid-sentence, glancing nervously toward the man, then back to Tom. "It's very nice to see you, Thomas. Uh - I - I'll be just one minute - I'll just gather my things and I'll be ready to go." She threw several brief glances toward the man and back to Tom, trying to convey to Tom a sense of urgency.

"Oh, all right. No hurry," replied Tom, perceiving something was amiss. In less than a minute Carolyn had retrieved her belongings, said her good-byes to Miss Halliwell in the back room, and reappeared. She walked directly toward Tom, took his arm, and pulled it gently toward the exit. Stepping quickly, Tom opened the door, allowing Carolyn to exit, and with the briefest of glances toward the man, followed her out the door. As soon as they were on the sidewalk Carolyn retracted her hand.

The couple walked quickly along High Street, then turned onto Dwight. Carolyn stayed close to Tom's side but set a brisk pace, as though she couldn't get away from the shoe store fast enough. Finally she spoke. "I'm sorry, Thomas, to be so abrupt, but I had to get out of there." She was breathless and she paused, only then looking squarely at Tom. "Could I ask you to walk me to the Women's Home so I can talk to Anne? She was to meet me at the shoe store in ten minutes."

"She can't, Carolyn, she has to stay until five - some delivery she has to sign for. She called me at the mill and asked me to come by and walk you home."

"Oh, I see. Well, that was very kind of you."

"But what was that all about at the shop?"

"What? Oh, nothing, I just - nothing. But thank you for coming for me."

"But that man, you acted like you were afraid of him. Who is he? What was…?"

"I don't know, just a customer. It was nothing, really." Abruptly she changed the subject. "How are you, Thomas? What are you doing these days?"

"Well, I've been away a while. I just got home last Wednesday. Yesterday was my first day at my new job in the mill office, in accounting. I'm the accounts payable clerk."

"Oh, that sounds interesting - and very complicated. You'll do well at that, I'll bet."

"Well, thank you. I'm sure I will. And you? I guess you must be excited about graduation, hmm? Are you hoping to stay on at Gregoire's after you get your diploma?"

"Maybe for a while. I've applied to the Agricultural College in Amherst to study business, but I don't know if that's what I want to do, or even if I'll be admitted."

"I'm sure you will, Carolyn, of course you will. That's wonderful. I'm very happy for you." They were walking at a more leisurely pace, climbing Appleton Street toward the Highlands. They reached Carolyn's house and stood on the sidewalk. There was a long pause and Tom was looking carefully at Carolyn's face, though she had turned and had one eye on her front door. Finally he spoke. "Are you sure you're all right, Carolyn? You looked a little harried in the shop back there, and you seem upset about something."

After another lengthy pause Carolyn finally spoke as she looked away from Tom toward the house. "That man - he bought some things and when he paid, this envelope was

79

under the dollar bill he placed on the counter. It has my name on it, my full name, even my middle name that hardly anyone knows..." She drew the envelope from her purse, holding it lightly between her thumb and index finger.

"Well, aren't you going to open it?" queried Tom.

"I guess - I don't know - I'm afraid. Maybe I shouldn't. I don't know."

Tom thought for a moment. "Do you want me to open it? I could look at it and..."

"Would you?" Carolyn handed the envelope to Tom.

He opened the envelope and read it, then looked up into her eyes and spoke softly.

"Carolyn. That man. He - he says he's - he's your father."

Carolyn sat on a chaise on the front porch, her face flushed, her fingers holding the letter nervously. Wisteria vines that twined around the porch railing and posts were laden with lavender and white blooms, their sweet scent filling the late afternoon air.

Tom sat opposite Carolyn, not sure what he should say. He knew nothing about her father except that he had never before been the subject of conversation with Carolyn, with Anne, with anyone so far as Tom knew. "When did you last see him?"

"I've never met him, ever. He left when mother was - expecting, and he never came back, never even wrote us. I didn't even know if he was still alive, or where he was. Mother never told me his real name. When I was born she chose the name Ford for me - to hide the truth."

"How did he seem to you? In the store, I mean."

"Well, he was nice looking, neat, you know. But he made me nervous the way he stared at me. I didn't really stop to pay attention. And when you came along, well, I just wanted to get away, that's all."

"It sounds like he wants to see you, Carolyn."

"I don't know..."

"Maybe you could, just once, I mean, give him another chance. Everyone deserves a second chance, don't they?" Carolyn looked up and their eyes met. Briefly she found herself thinking about the past, of her and Tom. She shook her head slowly and a pained expression spread across her face. Tom leaned forward, touched her hand, and spoke softly. "Carolyn, perhaps you should talk to your mother about this?"

"No, no, I couldn't. Oh, Thomas, please don't tell Anne, or my mother, or anyone, please. Swear to it, won't you?"

"Of course, of course, my lips are sealed." As Tom was speaking he was admiring this quiet, unassuming girl. He had known her for years and yet he was seeing a side of her that was new to him and that he liked. It was unusual for Tom who was often attracted to bold, brazen young women. But there were qualities in Carolyn that appealed to him.

"Well, I'd better be going inside now. I'm supposed to be preparing supper for Mama and me." She withdrew her hand and stood.

Tom nodded, rose, then stood aside to allow Carolyn to step to the front door. "Carolyn..." She turned and looked up shyly into Tom's face. "If there's ever anything I can do, I mean, if you want someone to accompany you to meet with your - uh - that man, I would be very willing."

Carolyn nodded, reached into her purse for the key, then turned toward the door. Tom spoke again. "Say, Carolyn? The Senior Formal, it's Friday, isn't it?"

Carolyn froze, her eyes fixed on the wooden porch floor, and nodded again. "Are you planning to attend? I mean, are you engaged for the evening? If you are, that's wonderful, but if you aren't, perhaps we could go with Anne and Jack, if you..."

Carolyn stood perfectly still. Then, ever so slowly, she raised her head and lifted her eyes to meet his. She spoke barely above a whisper. "Thank you, Thomas. That would be very nice."

"Swell, then. I'll come by about seven."

"All right."

"And Carolyn, I meant it, if there's ever anything else I can do, please don't hesitate to ask."

~ 14 ~

The Wellington home stood grandly atop a hill on Beech Street, as if looking down imperiously on the city of Holyoke. It was one of the largest, most elegant homes in the city, a symbol both of the success of its owner, Thomas A. Wellington, and of the vitality of the city below. The edifice rose four stories high above a broad, sweeping lawn, its distinctive mansard roof, inspired by a French design, declaring it a structure apart from all below - original, grand, a bit ostentatious perhaps, but a declaration of one man's ambitions fulfilled. The more than twenty rooms included a grand parlor for entertaining, several smaller sitting rooms for more informal gatherings, a library, a dining room, a sunlit breakfast room, a music room, and eight bedrooms for the family and their guests. Half a dozen small rooms on the top floor housed the family's domestic staff.

Anne was sitting comfortably on a velvet chesterfield in the parlor, book in hand, her stockinged feet drawn beneath her, when her brother appeared at the door. "Guess what, sis?"

"I don't know, Tommy, what?"

"I've got some news, big news. Prepare yourself."

Anne placed the book on the seat beside her, turned and looked at her brother, then rolled her eyes as if she was prepared to be bored by whatever he had to tell her. "Let me guess, you paid some bills in the office at the mill today. That *is* big news, Tommy, congratulations."

"Carolyn Ford is going to the Senior Formal," blurted Tom. Then he stood looking at his sister with a self-congratulatory smirk on his face.

Anne was suddenly interested. "And how would you know that?"

"Well, gee, I don't know. Maybe because she's going...," Tom paused for dramatic effect, "*with me.*" Then he posed triumphantly before Anne, his chin thrust forward in self-adulation.

"Quit your fooling," replied Anne, a look of genuine astonishment illuminating her face.

"No fooling. Tommy asked, and when Tommy asks, well, you know what the answer will be."

"I can't believe it. When did this happen?" Tom described his conversation with Carolyn, minus the part about the letter.

"But what about - did she mention Jan?"

"What?" replied Tom. "Mention what?"

"Never mind. Well, brother, that is news. I'm very happy for you, both of you. Does Jack know? Have you told him?"

"No, I thought I'd give you the pleasure."

"Well, I will telephone him this evening. He'll be very pleased, I know he will." All at once the smile on Anne's face faded and she stood up, confronting her brother with a determined expression. "But in the meantime you and I must have a little heart-to-heart. Carolyn is my best friend and I will not let you mistreat her."

Tom was still smirking, but when he saw the stern expression on his sister's face, his smile disappeared. "I know - I know."

Carolyn was busy preparing supper when her mother finally arrived home. Nina Calavetti was tall and slender, her gray hair drawn back and done up tightly in a bun at the back of her head and secured with a single hairpin. Her brown eyes were set close together, her nose aquiline, lips thin, her chin sharp, determined.

Nina was well known in Holyoke for two causes that were close to her heart, the Women's Home and the Ladies' Temperance Union. Her sympathy for young girls and their plight in that male-dominated city was well known, as was her belief that alcohol was the root of most if not all the evils of society. It was a credo learned at a young age, watching her father swing from mild and warm-hearted to harsh and abusive after a few drinks.

In the few hours that had elapsed since accepting Tom's invitation, Carolyn had turned over in her mind a hundred times how she would tell her mother. She and Tom's mother worked together daily, Helen Wellington as President of the Board of Trustees of the Women's Home, Nina as Director. But Carolyn had taken pains to hide from her mother every detail of her few male friendships. She knew each would be scrutinized, probably to her complete humiliation, and so the occasional assignation was accomplished without her mother's knowledge.

In the past Tom has been presented as nothing more than Anne's brother, even though there were many times when he and Carolyn had been in each other's company. As to Tom's weakness, that was a matter kept in strictest confidence by his family and by Carolyn. Had Nina ever learned of Tom's drinking habit, it would have severely tested her working relationship with Helen. It would also most certainly have ended any prospect of an association between Tom and her daughter.

Carolyn's life consisted largely of allaying her mother's overly protective tendencies, avoiding conflict, and hiding the secret longings of her own heart. But the Senior Formal was only four days away and there were preparations to be made.

She needed to tell her mother, and that daunting task had to be accomplished soon.

"How was the Temperance Union meeting, Mama? Any news?" asked Carolyn at supper.

"Well, we're gaining many recruits. Two ladies from Aldenville attended this afternoon. They would like to organize a new chapter in Chicopee; they say there is a good deal of interest there. And the plans for our speaker series at the YMCA are coming along well. The next is this Sunday, a Professor Dillard, all the way from New York City. He's a well known advocate of prohibition." She paused briefly. "I was hoping you might attend."

"I would very much like to do so, Mama," replied Carolyn, seeing an opportunity. "I always enjoy the Temperance Union speakers." Then she added, "They are so - inspirational," even as her inner voice was saying *deadly dull.*

Nina's lips stretched into a tight smile. "Yes, I agree."

"It's going to be a busy week ahead, what with work, graduation rehearsals, and all. But I will definitely attend." She paused. Now is the time, she thought. "By the way, Mama, Anne asked me to go to the Senior Formal on Friday with her and Jack - and, uh - Thomas. I told her I would go. I felt certain you would approve."

"Anne is a lovely girl. Young Thomas - I haven't heard anything from Helen about his whereabouts since all that unpleasantness last fall. Did he return to Harvard?"

"I - I'm not sure. I think perhaps in September."

"Well, all right, you may go, but don't be late, do you hear?"

"Yes, Mama. And I really am looking forward to hearing Professor Dullard - uh, Dillard - really."

86

That evening the telephone rang at the Bernard residence. Claire raced from her room, crossed the kitchen to the living room, and lifted the handset to her ear. "Bernard residence. Oh, hello Anne," bubbled Claire cheerily. She always enjoyed talking to Anne. But suddenly her tone changed. "Uh - no, he's - well, yes, he's here but he's gone to bed. He - uh - he was really tired." She listened for a moment, then replied. "Yes, I'll tell him you called."

"Oh, Claire. No need to trouble him tonight. I'll be seeing him for lunch tomorrow anyway."

The normally ebullient Claire stuttered. "Oh - um - Marie didn't call you? Jackie said to let you know he won't be able to have lunch tomorrow. Something - something came up..."

"Marie, Marie," whispered Claire at her sister's bedroom door. "That was Anne asking to talk to Jack. I told her he was already asleep. And that he couldn't have lunch with her tomorrow. Marie, what are we gonna do?"

"I don't know. I don't know," replied Marie. "She needs to know, and so does Tom. I'll talk to Jack in the morning."

~ 15 ~

Jack had been awake repeatedly in the night but was asleep by the time Marie prepared to leave for school the next morning. Her father had insisted that she go, assuring her that he would get Claire off to school and tend to Jack himself. So Marie headed out the door shortly before eight o'clock.

At mid-morning Marie and Anne were huddled in a corner of the girls' lavatory in the high school basement. Anne was crying and Marie was trying her best to console her. "I wanted to call you on Monday but Jack was so insistent. He's going to be cross with me when he finds out I told you, but I knew you'd want to know."

"But I have to see him, Marie, I need to see him. Could I visit this afternoon after school? I'll ask to be excused early from work. I'll tell him I heard it from someone else if that would be better."

"No, Anne, I'll go straight home after school and I'll tell him you're coming. He has to accept it - he can't keep this a secret - he's got to - to realize." Marie broke down and started to cry. Just then Miss Edwards, the girls' English teacher, appeared in the door. She was shocked to see Anne and Marie in such a bad way. Jack had been a favorite pupil of hers and she was clearly shaken by the news of his condition.

⚜ ⚜ ⚜ ⚜ ⚜ ⚜

"Ooooh, aren't those pretty?" said a rosy-cheeked young woman to her five-year-old daughter. "How do they feel, Margaret, hmm? Do they pinch your toes?" Carolyn was fitting the girl for silk party slippers. Meanwhile the girl's brother had disappeared around the end of the aisle and was eyeing men's work boots on the other side of the store. Carolyn followed after him and led him back to his mother, trying gamely to interest him in dress shoes but to little avail.

"Let's see if we can find you a nice pair of Sunday bests, Jerome," said Carolyn, pulling boxes of shoes from the shelves. "Look - there's black leather, brown leather, suede, high-tops, strapped, side-buttoned." Still the boy showed little interest and started wandering away once again. As Carolyn spoke she was aware of another customer, a slender woman with golden hair and fair skin, watching her and smiling sympathetically at her dilemma. Again Carolyn gave chase, took the boy by the hand, and led him back to his mother.

Eventually the mother and two children made their purchases and left the shop. Carolyn was sorting through a mountain of tissue paper, carefully rewrapping a dozen pairs of shoes, then returning them to their boxes and placing them back on the shelves. As she worked the golden-haired woman approached her with a pair of leather pumps. Carolyn looked up and saw the woman smiling down at her.

"You must be exhausted. Those two, they were a handful, no?" Carolyn nodded, returning the woman's smile. "You handled them very well, my dear. You have a real knack with leettle ones, did you know that?"

Carolyn blushed, shrugging her shoulders dubiously. "Did you find what you wanted, ma'am?"

"Yes, I theenk so. But please, finish what you are doing. I am in no hurry."

Quickly Carolyn finished reshelving the children's shoes, then led the woman to the sales counter to wrap her purchase and ring up the sale. "Carolyn," said Mrs. Halliwell who was seeing to another customer not far away. "When you're finished there, could you help me over here?" Carolyn nodded to Mrs. Halliwell, then turned back to the blond woman. She wrote up a sales slip and the woman paid her.

"Thank you, Carolyn, you have been very helpful." Their eyes met briefly and the woman smiled warmly. "I must be on my way now, my dear. But I weell be back."

Marie hurried home after school and spoke to her father in the kitchen. Jack had slept most of the day and seemed to be a bit better, Charles explained in a whisper.

"Father, I told Anne at school. I just had to. How could I see her in class or pass her in the corridor and just pretend everything was fine?" Charles nodded. "She wants to see him. She's coming in just a while." Again Charles nodded. "But I don't know how Jack is going to react. He's going to be awfully angry when he finds out. He asked me - he *ordered* me not to tell her."

"I'll have a word with him, dear, before she comes."

Just then Marie heard a sound from the driveway and looked out the window. "You better have that word, Father. That's Anne - and Tom."

"You make them some tea and talk to them here," replied Charles. "I'll go upstairs and wake your brother."

Jack and his father were talking in muffled voices when soft footsteps could be heard on the stairway followed by a light tap on the door. Jack lifted himself up, wiped his eyes, and briefly rearranged the bed covers.

"Come in," he said weakly. And then, in an instant, Anne was at his bedside, eyes gleaming, hair sparkling in the light of the gas lamp on the wall, a faint scent of rosewater wafting about her. Charles held the antique rocking chair, Evelyne's rocker that he had brought in from the other room especially for Anne. She sat, thanked him, and smiled at Jack.

"Let us know if you need anything," said Charles as he backed out of the bedroom and climbed tentatively down the stairs. When his footsteps were no longer audible, Anne reached out and took Jack's hand, then leaned over, kissing him lightly on the forehead.

"How are you?" she asked sweetly, looking softly into his eyes. She was trying very hard not to reveal her alarm at his sickly pallor and obvious loss of vigor since their last encounter only a few days earlier.

"I'm okay," replied Jack slowly. His voice cracked as he spoke. He turned and looked toward the bedstand. Anne lifted a stoneware pitcher decorated with a blue floral design and poured water into a tin cup. Jack struggled to sit forward, allowing Anne to hold the cup to his lips. Then he slumped back against the pillow. Anne could read only one emotion in his face, despair. But she gamely picked up the conversation.

"You look good, Jackie. And Marie tells me you've made a lot of progress already." Jack did not respond. "Why didn't you tell me you were working in the dyehouse, Jackie?"

"Didn't want you to worry, that's all," replied Jack.

"But that place, it's horrible. Everyone says it's the worst place in the mill," said Anne.

"It's not that bad. It's dark and smelly, sure, but you get used to it after a while. They got this new solvent, coal naphtha they call it. It smells awful, but it's really good for scouring the wool."

"Maybe that's what..." began Anne. Jack shook his head.

"Other guys, they can take it. They're just fine. Just a matter of gettin' used to it, that's all."

91

"Tommy and Mother and Father - they asked me to say hello." When Jack didn't respond Anne continued. "Tommy - that Tommy - you know what he told me last night? He asked Carolyn to the Formal. And she said yes. I can't believe it. Just a few days earlier each was adamant that..." She shook her head and smiled at Jack. "Well, who knows, in matters of the heart? Do you know what I mean, Jackie?"

"Who knows anything?" replied Jack, his voice now cracking with emotion. "One day everything's just ducky, then it's all gone to - to hell." With one hand Anne squeezed Jack's hand, with the other she brushed the hair off his forehead. She spoke softly, tenderly.

"But things get better, Jackie, don't they? Remember?" She wasn't sure she should go on, but she did anyway. "After your mom, and our troubles, and Tommy's?"

Jack nodded but looked away. "I guess we won't be goin' with Carolyn and Tommy."

"Well, no, I don't suppose we will, but that's okay. They are adults now. Well, one of them is, anyway." And she looked brightly into Jack's eyes and smiled. Jack managed a weak smile in response.

"Anne..."

"Yes, Jackie?"

"I'm - sorry," said Jack in a whisper, his eyes glistening in the dull lamplight.

"Jackie, there's no need to apologize, it's just a dance..."

"I don't know what's gonna happen - to me - to us," he interrupted.

Anne was shaken by his words, especially the words *to us*, but tried to conceal it. "Only good things, Jackie, I promise - only wonderful things. Believe me, trust me..."

Jack looked briefly into her eyes, then away. "Aren't you supposed to be working this afternoon?" asked Jack.

"I left a telephone message for Mrs. C. I'm sure she'll understand. I'm not all that essential. Anyway, it's been kind of quiet around there this week. Yesterday there was practically nothing for me to do. I just sat at the front desk…"

She looked up. Jack's eyes were closed and he was breathing loudly. Anne sat for several more minutes, then rose quietly, kissed him on the forehead, and left the room, closing the door softly behind her.

Tom was standing in the kitchen speaking quietly with Marie and Charles when Anne entered the room. He turned and looked at her hopefully. "How's he doing?"

"He's sleeping." Anne's eyes shifted to Marie's.

Marie took Anne's hand. "Come, sit down, have some more tea."

"Thank you, but we'd better be going," said Anne, her voice shaking.

Marie shot a concerned look at Tom. "Okay, let's go," said Tom to his sister. Then he looked at Marie and Charles. "Thank you for the tea. We'll come back, maybe tomorrow. Please call us if there's anything you need - or any news." Tom stood and shook Charles's hand. The elder Bernard was looking very frail and tired, Tom thought.

Anne sat quietly as she and Tom rode back to Holyoke, sniffling and dabbing at her eyes with a lace handkerchief. Finally she spoke. "What's this all about, Tommy? What causes those terrible fits - or seizures - or whatever they are? I feel so lost - and frightened."

"I talked to Miss Beldon before we left home. She says it's called epilepsy and that it's a very mysterious condition. Sometimes people have one and never have another. Sometimes they have them again and again."

"So maybe this could be his only one?" She turned and looked at her brother who was deliberately keeping his eyes fixed on the road. "Maybe, Tommy? Do you think?"

"Annie..." Tom steered the Reo onto the grassy shoulder, slowed it to a halt, then shut off the engine. He was grasping the wheel with both hands and staring through the rain-spattered windscreen.

"What, Tommy, what?"

Tom shook his head, then turned and looked glumly at his sister. "It wasn't his first. Last Saturday, the day we went fishing at Hampton Ponds? I came along the path and I saw him lying on the bank. I thought he'd fallen. I called to him and he didn't answer. And when I got up to him he - he was out - out cold." The usually poised Tom Wellington was shaking and pounding his hands against the steering wheel. "His eyes - they were open but they were - they were empty. It was like he was in some kind of trance." Tom turned away from his sister, then quickly regained his composure. "But then he opened his eyes, looked right at me, and acted like nothing had happened. He was the old Jack. He just said he'd fallen asleep. But Annie," continued Tom in a whisper, "he was *not* sleeping."

Anne dissolved in tears and her brother placed his hand awkwardly on her shoulder. Several minutes went by without a word. Anne was thinking. Finally she spoke. "You know, he told me a while back how one day he went fishing out at Hampton Ponds alone. He swore he saw his mother's face in the water. Oh, Tommy, you don't think he's going cr - I mean losing his..." She began to sob. Tom put his arm around his sister's shoulder and drew her to him, gently stroking her hair.

"He'll be all right, Annie. I know he will. He has to be."

~ 16 ~

Trade was slow at Gregoire's that afternoon and Miss Halliwell had asked Carolyn to rearrange some shelves in the back room. "Carolyn, there's a customer asking for you out front," Mr. Barton informed her. She stood up, straightened her pinafore, looked briefly in a mirror while arranging her hair, then emerged through the curtained passage into the sales room.

At the counter stood the fair-haired woman who had spoken so kindly to her the previous day. "It ees me again," began the woman, smiling, then pausing. "How are you today, Carolyn?"

"Very well, thank you."

"I am very sorry to trouble you, but you were so helpful yesterday, I wondered if you might help me again? Perhaps a purse and a waist-belt?"

"Yes, of course," responded Carolyn. She turned and led the woman to the last aisle on the women's side. A row of shelves separated them from the rest of the store. Carolyn stepped behind a glass-topped counter. "These are our finest purses and handbags, ma'am. Satin on the top shelf, leather below. Waist-belts are right behind you there."

"Oooh, you have a wonderful selection. Maybe, if I could see that one, there." Carolyn bent over, slid open the cabinet door, and reached for a delicate purse of rose satin with green brocade trim. She straightened up and presented it to the woman. "It ees exquisite, ees it not, Carolyn?"

"Yes, it's my favorite. Every time I walk past I can't help looking at it."

"Well, dear, maybe it weell be yours one day." Carolyn blushed and smiled. The woman smiled again, then briefly cleared her throat. "Carolyn," she began in a low voice. "I have a confession to make. I didn't come here today just to shop." Carolyn paused, gazing into the woman's kind eyes. "I came to speak to you."

"To me? What about? Why me?"

"About - about your father."

Carolyn froze. "What do you know about - him?"

"Well, dear, I - he asked me to come to see you."

Carolyn was suddenly tense and clearly uncomfortable. She looked down at the purse, absently stroking the shining fabric. Then she looked anxiously toward the end of the aisle where another customer was examining some merchandise.

"John - your father - he wishes to meet you, Carolyn. He came to see you the other day heemself. He tried to give you a letter. Did you get it?" Carolyn nodded. "But he thought perhaps you were frightened, or suspicious, and rightfully so. A young lady cannot be too careful in thees day and age. He understands that." The woman paused, waiting for a response. Finally Carolyn looked up and into her eyes. "He ees a good man, Carolyn, a wonderful man, an honorable man. And he wants to meet his daughter."

"How did he find me?"

"John has been in Holyoke for several days on business. He saw the photograph of you and several of your schoolmates in the *Transcript*. It said you were working here."

Carolyn was listening intently, all the while fingering the satin purse. "But who are you? How do you know him, ma'am?"

"I am Adrienne - his wife."

Carolyn hesitated. "His - wife?"

"Yes. I came to Boston from Paris with my sister ten years ago. That ees where I met your father. We have been married seex years. A finer man I have never known, dear, I can tell you that."

"You live in Holyoke?"

"No, we leeve near Lowell. We are just visiting for a few days..." At that moment Miss Halliwell's voice could be heard in the next aisle, but Adrienne continued. "He was hoping he might see you after work today. Perhaps in Hampden Park? Please do not be afraid, dear. I can be there, too, if you like."

Miss Halliwell appeared at the end of the aisle. "Carolyn? Oh, well, dear, when you're done there, would you assist this lady with a pair of boots?" Carolyn nodded at Miss Halliwell, then turned back to Adrienne, a confused expression on her face.

"Please say yes."

Carolyn looked into Adrienne's eyes, then down at the purse. When she looked up again her lips betrayed a slight smile. "All right. I have a - a friend. Perhaps he can accompany me to the park."

"Very well, then, we weel meet you near the entrance on Maple Street." She smiled warmly, then began to turn.

"Oh, ma'am - did you want the purse?"

"Of course, silly me, I almost forgot. And, please, call me Adrienne." They walked to the sales desk where Carolyn placed the lovely rose and green purse in a small white box and wrapped and tied it in the usual Gregoire's fashion.

"Carolyn, Carolyn," yelled Tom from across High Street. It was nearly five o'clock, the busiest time of day in Holyoke. Carolyn had telephoned the mill office and spoken to Tom, telling him about the meeting with her father and asking him to meet her at four-thirty. He dashed across the busy thoroughfare, prompting horns and shouts from motorcars and omnibuses and clanging bells from two trolleys rumbling past in opposite directions. Carolyn stood watching the mayhem with alarm. Finally Tom emerged on the sidewalk before her.

"Hello, Thomas," said Carolyn with a shy smile.

"Sorry I'm late. Things were busy in the mill office and I had to get the accounts settled before I left. I telephoned Anne at the Women's Home like you asked me to tell her I'd be walking you home today. Shall we?" Tom held out his arm and nodded toward Hampden Park. Carolyn took his arm but was silent as they walked, while Tom more than compensated with a constant line of chatter about work, the weather, and the frantic pace of the city at this hour. When they stepped through the gates at the park entrance, Carolyn paused. "Well, where do you suppose he is?" asked Tom. "Let's have a look around. I'm not sure I'd recognize him but you…"

Carolyn squeezed Tom's arm to silence him. Her eyes were fixed on a couple sitting on a bench further along the walkway. Tom turned and followed her gaze. The couple rose, smiling, and walked toward them.

"Hello, dear," said Adrienne. She smiled warmly as she extended both hands to Carolyn's arms, then leaned in and kissed her lightly on the cheek. Carolyn smiled weakly, her eyes wide and fixed on the pretty face before her. "Carolyn," Adrienne continued softly, "thees ees your father."

Carolyn turned slightly toward him, raising her eyes slowly to meet his. He was, as she remembered from the shoe shop, a handsome man with a kind face. He was looking intently into her eyes as he had that day, and it unnerved her. She looked down.

"Carolyn," he said softly but formally, as if reciting carefully studied lines, "thank you for agreeing to meet me." Then he seemed to be groping for words. "I fear - I'm afraid - well, perhaps I shouldn't have come to see you in the shoe store like that. We saw your photograph in the *Transcript* and I just - I had to see you. I'm sorry if I frightened you." Carolyn shook her head very slightly. Her lips parted as if she was about to reply, but there was just an awkward silence.

"Carolyn, dear," interjected Adrienne, "won't you introduce us to the young man?" Tom had been standing several steps behind Carolyn, watching her carefully.

"This - is - Thomas - a friend. Thomas, I'd like you to meet - Adrienne - and - John." Each word seemed to take an eternity to emerge from her lips as the others stood waiting.

John extended his hand. "How do you do, young man? May we call you Tom?"

"Oh, yes, yessir, please do. It's so very nice to meet you both. Carolyn has told me all - eh - about you. Are you enjoying your stay in Holyoke?"

"Yes, indeed," John replied. "It's so full of life."

"Carolyn, Tom, won't you sit down?" Adrienne gestured toward the bench.

Tom took Carolyn's arm but she seemed anchored to one spot. He turned and faced her, taking both her hands and looking into her eyes. "Shall we?" And he drew her gently toward the bench where they were seated together. Adrienne sat on her other side, John remained standing.

"How do you enjoy your work, Carolyn? Adrienne tells me you are a natural for the job." Carolyn blushed and shook her head slowly. "I don't know about that. I'm just learning about shoes and fitting and everything."

"Oh, my dear, you are much too modest," offered Adrienne with a twinkle in her eye. "She ees very good. She listens to her customers and tries very hard to please them - all of them - even little monsters." As she said *monsters* her eyes widened in mock horror. Carolyn smiled, then laughed.

"And you graduate soon, " added John. "Congratulations, that's quite an accomplishment." Carolyn blushed. "What's next, then, will you be staying on at the shoe shop?"

"She's going to college," interjected Tom. "She has applied to Massachusetts Agricultural College in Amherst, the business program. Isn't that ripping?"

"Ripping. Yes, ripping, indeed, Carolyn," he replied.

"Well, I don't know if I'll be admitted."

"With your work experience," added Tom, "you're a shoe-in." Only after he'd said it did Tom realize the humor in his words and he laughed loudly. Adrienne and John laughed along with him and a slight smile crept across Carolyn's face.

"And what's on the horizon for you, hm?" asked the man, casting an appraising but good-natured glance at Tom.

"I've just accepted a position in the office at Wellington Textiles. I'm only an assistant bookkeeper, but I'm headed up," added Tom with his usual bluster. Again everyone laughed. Even Tom was amused at his own boastfulness.

"Well, that's wonderful, young man. I'll bet you are. I can tell you're a man with prospects," said John. "Wellington Textiles, eh? That's a big operation. Quite an accomplishment, a young man like you securing a position like that."

Carolyn quickly interjected. "How - how long are you staying in Holyoke?"

"Well," responded Adrienne, "John has business to attend to for a few more days. I must return home. The children..." At the mention of children Carolyn suddenly looked wide-eyed at Adrienne. "Oh, yes, I'm sorry. I should have told you sooner, we have two leettle ones: John, Jr., is five. Little Adele is just three." Carolyn was struggling to digest this unanticipated news.

"Yes, dear, you have a brother and a sister," said John proudly. There was another long silence. "And how long have you known my daughter, Tom?"

"Oh, for ages. She and my sister have been best friends since grade one." Carolyn was blushing again. "We're going to the Senior Formal tomorrow night, aren't we, Carolyn?" Carolyn's face turned still redder as she nodded.

100

"Well, isn't that wonderful, young man. Quite an honor, to be escorting the prettiest girl in Holyoke."

"Yes, sir, it is that. An honor, a real honor." And Tom turned to Carolyn smiling, again grasping her hand in both of his. "And we're going to have a wonderful time, aren't we?"

The warmth of Tom's smile and of his hands on hers and the beaming faces of the couple before her were finally having an effect. "Yes, we will," replied Carolyn, noticeably more at ease. "Well, we must be going. Mama will be expecting me..."

"How is your mother, Carolyn? I hope she is well." asked John.

Carolyn looked briefly into his eyes. "Yes, she is well, thank you."

"Carolyn, dear, shall we have a chance to meet you again during our stay?" asked Adrienne.

Carolyn smiled. "Yes, I hope we will."

101

~ 17 ~

THURSDAY, MAY 31

How's Jackie doing?" asked Marie as soon as she arrived home from school the next afternoon. Her father was repairing the electric water pump that he and Jack had installed only three years earlier. It was losing its prime and Charles lay on his back on the pantry floor, trying to reseat the old, worn rubber seal between the pump and the water line. He'd chosen this day for the project so that he could be within earshot of his son.

"No different, I'm afraid. He just lies there in bed in the dark with the curtains drawn. I look in on him every so often, but he's not eatin' much and he's hardly speakin'. Looks the death, too. Why don't you bring him some tea? Water's on," said Charles, nodding toward the stove.

A few minutes later Marie tapped on Jack's bedroom door. "Jackie? May I come in? I made you some tea." There was no reply. She tapped and spoke her brother's name again, then pushed the door open and stepped into the darkened room. In the dim light from the hall she could just make out Jack's form beneath the bedcovers. She placed the cup of tea on the bedside table, then pulled up a chair and sat. "Jackie," she spoke softly as she gently lifted the covers that were drawn up over his head, revealing his ashen, mask-like face. "Jackie." Slowly Jack's eyes opened. "I brought you some tea - and Oneida biscuits." She could hear breathing but it was so weak she could scarcely believe this was her brother she was gazing upon. "C'mon," she continued softly, "sit up and I'll plump your pillow." She stroked his arm as she spoke, as if coaxing the blood to start circulating in his veins again.

Jack groaned weakly, then ever so slowly drew himself up onto one elbow. He blinked several times. "Wha - what time's it? How long you been home, Marie?"

"I just got home. Father's working on the pump. C'mon, sit up and have some tea. You'll feel better." With effort Jack turned and straightened up, placing his bare feet on the cool floorboards. Marie handed him the cup. He had to use both hands to steady it, then sipped the tea carefully. "Feeling any better?" Jack shook his head slowly but made no reply. "I talked to Anne at school. She wants to visit with you again. I told her I would telephone her. Shall I suggest she come now? Or this evening?"

"I'm just spent. Can't do a thing. Tell her I can't have visitors right now, okay?"

"Okay," replied Marie. "Maybe a good night's sleep tonight will help you feel better, Jackie."

"That's the thing, Marie. I can't sleep at night. And when I do begin to nod off I wake up again in two minutes. All night long. I just can't seem to sleep."

"Maybe the doctor can give you something to help you."

Jack wagged his head as if shaking off the very idea. "I can't, Marie, I just can't. The night..."

"What about the night, Jackie?" She was looking into Jack's eyes as she asked, and she got her answer.

"She's just about had it, Pierre," said Charles Bernard to Pierre Bousquet with a note of regret in his voice. "Maybe you better think about a new truck." They were leaning against the fender of Pierre's derelict pickup truck that had been a frequent visitor to the Bernards' barn in recent weeks.

"Yeh, I 'spose," replied Pierre. "Still, I hate to part with 'er. And I don' know where the money'd come from for a new one. With Stephen gone we're havin' to tighten the belt, and it was already cinched up pretty good, eh?" The two men exchanged knowing glances and nods. "How's yer boy doin'?" asked Pierre.

"Uhh, not too good. He's pretty much down in the dumps. Guess I can't blame him, poor kid. Doc's comin' tomorrow. Maybe we'll know more then. So what's goin' on at the mill? I read in *La Justice* that there was a lot of grumblin'."

"Best I can tell's folks are het up 'bout the pay. With the war and all, business is booming, so I guess they figure they deserve a increase."

"Somethin' 'bout a walkout?" probed Charles, his voice lowered.

"Waal, ya know, somma those guys talk big, mostly the Micks. But they're not gonna get nowhere without the Frenchmen and, I dunno, most guys I know don' 'ave the stomach for it - prob'ly just get theyselves fired, eh?" Charles nodded in agreement. "Some talk about better workin' conditions, too. Weavin' and spinnin' rooms too crowded, guys gettin' hurt. And girls. Just lass week this little girl, barely sixteen, got her 'air caught in the works."

Charles grimaced. The two men stood in silence for several minutes, gruesome images of the injured girl barely kept at bay. Just then Claire Bernard and Elaine Bousquet came walking up the gravel driveway, the late afternoon sun shimmering on their flaxen braids. The two fathers waved and smiled at their daughters, then turned and exchanged glances laden with irony. "*Bénis-nous Seigneur*," said Charles softly. "Bless us, oh Lord."

Pierre stood up. *"Alors, mon voisin,* be on my way," he said with a sigh of resignation. "Émile, Thor, an' me, we get this 'eap outta 'ere tomorrow. T'anks for tryin'."

"He's frightened, Father, he's scared to death. Scared of the dark, of the night. I've never seen him like this. It's like he's a little child again," said Marie to her father.

Charles was standing in the side yard, a pipe wrench in one hand. "Doc's comin' tomorrow, maybe he can give him somethin' to help him sleep."

Marie paused. "But it sounds to me like he doesn't want to sleep, not at night. That's why..." Her voice trailed off as she looked up at the curtained window of Jack's room.

"Well, maybe it's 'cause a those so-called miracle pills."

"Father, has Jackie said anything to you about the seizures? I mean, what it feels like?"

"Well, no, not really. But the Doc says people sometimes forget all about 'em, like they never happened."

"I don't know, Father, I think maybe he *is* remembering things. Maybe that's the problem." Her voice was shaking as she turned abruptly away from her father.

~ 18 ~

Doctor Gibson arrived late the next morning. He stood at Jack's bedside questioning him, all the while scrawling notes on a notepad. He had never discussed a diagnosis with Jack and made no mention of it this day.

"All right, young man. You're coming along well. Your father tells me you have been staying in bed. I think it's time to get yourself up and moving around. Nothing strenuous, mind you, but you need to get up and about every day. A little walk outside in the cool of the day would not be a bad idea, all right?" Jack nodded. A few minutes later the doctor made the same recommendation to Jack's father in the kitchen. Charles nodded, then hesitated.

"But - could he have another one of those - spells, Doc?"

"Oh, sure, it's possible," responded the doctor cavalierly. "But that's a risk he'll have to take. And Luminal has a pretty good record of controlling seizures. No guarantees, mind you, but your son needs to accept that and start being more active."

Around noon Jack finally arose. His father helped him down the stairs and he sat in a cushioned chair in the living room sipping coffee. Charles tried to engage him in conversation but Jack offered no response. His color had improved somewhat but he had little appetite. Only after much urging did he accept a bowl of hot oatmeal, but after eating two small spoonfuls he left the serving unfinished.

"I've got to tend the animals, son. Why don't you step out into the yard, hmm? Sit on the glider, maybe?"

"I don't think so, Dad, not today. I'll be fine right here." Charles suspected that Jack couldn't bear to face the barn, the animals, and most of all the gardens, knowing he couldn't do anything about them. This was a boy who ever since he was able to walk was a doer, a worker, a fixer. To be unable to put his hand to productive pursuits was as good as taking his life away. It just ran contrary to his nature, thought Charles, for Jack Bernard to sit idly by while the chores - the world - went on without him.

"Well, you call if you need anything, okay?" Jack nodded as his father stepped out of the kitchen door. Barely twenty minutes had passed when Charles returned, anxious to keep a close eye on his son. Jack was sitting exactly where he had left him. Charles pulled up a chair opposite Jack and waited. For many minutes the two sat in silence. The clock on the mantle ticked lightly; steam hissed gently from an iron kettle on the stove. Finally, without raising his head, Jack spoke to his father.

"What's wrong with me, Dad? What happened? I don't remember a thing."

"Don't worry, boy, don't worry. The important thing is that you're on the mend now."

"But I have to know. I mean, I remember having a headache when I got home from work that night. And going to bed. Next thing I recall I was lying in the hay and you and Marie were next to me. Did I faint?"

"Well, yes, son, you did. You were working in the barn and you must have just - passed out. Maybe you were overtired."

"But why did they take me to the hospital? It must be something else."

"Well..."

"What is it, Dad?" Jack paused, then continued. "Please tell me."

Charles wished he didn't have to answer. "Well, you had a - an episode - a bad spell, that's all. And the doctor was afraid you might - hurt yourself."

Jack was taking the information in, trying to understand. Suddenly he looked up and directly into his father's eyes. "Did I have a - a fit? Was that it?"

Charles winced, looked away, gathering his strength, then turned and looked into Jack's eyes. He knew his son and he knew that there was no point in trying to sugarcoat things. "A seizure, son, that's what the Doc says. But not a bad one."

"Is it - epilepsy? I was reading about that in a magazine at the library last week. Is that what it is?" Jack swallowed and looked into his father's eyes awaiting a reply.

Again Charles cringed. "Well, they're not sure, son. It's hard to say. And they think you're makin' lots of progress, so maybe it's not. And they have this new medicine that's bound to help. So don't you be thinkin' about that, Jack, just leave it up to the docs. Okay?"

"Okay," replied Jack. He closed his eyes and laid his head back against the cushion. "Maybe I'll just have a little nap."

Marie came home from school early that afternoon. The Senior Formal was only a few hours away and there was much to do in preparation for the biggest social event of the school year at Holyoke High School. She was resigned to wearing a black silk dress with a velvet sash that had been her mother's. It was a nice enough dress, she thought, but she secretly envied her classmates who had purchased new dresses, colorful dresses in smart new styles at Besse Mills Clothing Store on Suffolk Street or Steiger's on High Street. Then there was the matter of petticoats, one of which required a small repair. For shoes she had received her father's permission to purchase a new pair of black leather pumps with slender straps from Gregoire's. She wished she had a brooch or necklace suitable for the occasion but her jewelry collection was woefully inadequate. She would have to do without.

A few minutes later Marie stood before the kitchen stove about to lift a large black kettle of boiling water. Just then Jack appeared, stepping in from the yard. Seeing his sister struggling with the heavy kettle, he intervened. "Marie, let me help you with that." She gratefully stood aside and watched as her brother hoisted the kettle and poured the contents into an enamel washbasin set on the kitchen table. "When's Herbert coming for you, then?"

"Seven-thirty. His father's driving us; Herbert doesn't drive yet."

"Well, that'll be cozy, eh, just the three of you?"

Marie blushed. "Please, Jackie, don't you start. I've been getting quite enough teasing about this from Claire. Now if you'll excuse me..." Jack left his sister alone to wash her hair over the basin of steaming water.

Charles and Claire prepared supper that evening although much of the work had been done by Marie before she left for school that morning. After the meal, they started the dishes while Marie retreated to her room. She spent nearly half an hour re-arranging herself, flouncing her petticoats, fussing with her hair. Then she stood before the long mirror in the hallway. It would do, she was thinking, but how she wished for some little touch that would transform her otherwise unremarkable appearance. At that moment she was aware of her father standing behind her, gazing at his daughter with a melancholy smile.

"What's the matter, Father?"

"It's just - in that dress - you remind me so of your mother."

Marie smiled. "Thank you, Father. That's the nicest thing you could say."

"Let's have a look, eh?"Charles stood behind his daughter and turned her toward the mirror. As she gazed glumly at her image, he hesitated, then spoke. "How about this?" In the mirror she saw her father's face and a string of pearls dangling from his fingers. Each bead glowed softly in the dim light.

"Oh, my g… Father, where did you get those?"

"They were your mother's. She never wore 'em much - a little too showy for Westfield, she used to say. But maybe they'd be suitable for Holyoke and such a special occasion, eh?" He handed them to Marie who clasped them around her neck and arranged them carefully against the black dress.

"They are perfect, Father, just perfect." She turned and kissed his cheek lightly. A few minutes later a motorcar pulled into the gravel driveway. It was time.

~ 19 ~

*T*ropical *Paradise* read the banner suspended above the entrance to the Holyoke High School gymnasium. The cavernous, dimly lit space had been transformed nearly overnight into a South Pacific island, the walls decorated with palm trees silhouetted against white sand beaches lapped by aquamarine waters. Centerpieces of coconuts, pineapples, and tropical blossoms, many from the Wellington family's glasshouse, decorated dozens of tables surrounding the dance floor. On an elevated platform at one end of the hall a small orchestra played dreamily as the first couples entered. A basketball hoop, cleverly disguised as a crescent moon, hung overhead. The affair was indeed formal, the young ladies sporting long, flowing dresses of crinoline, lace, satin, or velvet. Some of the young men wore tuxedoes with vests or cummerbunds, while others settled for dark suits, double-breasted waistcoats, starched white collars, and black bow ties.

As the orchestra gamely struck up the first chords of *Yellow Bird*, several couples stepped out tentatively onto the floor and began to dance. Others remained on the perimeter watching the dancers enviously, but soon dozens of couples were moving more or less gracefully to the music and the atmosphere became livelier and more relaxed.

Just then Tom Wellington appeared beneath the palm tree arch over the gymnasium entrance looking dapper and smiling proudly. On one arm was Carolyn Ford wearing a long, pale green organdy dress. She appeared uneasy and avoided meeting the eyes of her classmates. On Tom's other

111

arm was Anne in a pink silk dress, smiling bravely and looking around with curiosity at the other attendees. Friends knew that Anne's expression was as much of bravado as of pleasure, for her heart was truly aching. Tom led the two young ladies to a table near the back of the auditorium where they quickly sat together, as if trying to offer mutual aid and succor.

Tom leaned in and spoke into Carolyn's ear. She blushed and nodded. He turned and whispered to Anne who seemed to be in agreement, then disappeared through another palm tree arch that led to the refreshment tables.

"Are you having a good time, Carolyn?" asked Anne as soon as Tom was gone. Carolyn smiled weakly. Anne took her by the hand and looked into her eyes. "Relax - and just have fun."

Carolyn managed a slightly more convincing smile. "Oh, Anne, I'm trying, but, you know..." Soon Tom returned with three pastel-colored fruit drinks - Tropical Delight is what they called the punch - each glass sporting a tiny paper umbrella. As he placed the glasses on the table in front of the girls, they all laughed at the image of a Polynesian paradise in gritty, industrial Holyoke.

The three sat watching the dancers for several minutes before Tom turned, smiled at Carolyn, then nodded toward the dance floor. Blushing profusely, she took his hand, rose slowly, and was led away. The pair danced to *Avalon* and *Moonlight Bay* and by the end of the second dance Carolyn was smiling at Anne over Tom's shoulder. *She's having a good time,* thought Anne, *miracle of miracles.* When the couple turned and Tom was facing Anne, he gave his sister an exaggerated wink. The couple danced for several more numbers before returning to their seats.

Two young men had approached Anne during that interval and asked her to dance, but she had declined each with a smile. When Carolyn and Tom returned to the table,

Anne accepted her brother's invitation and danced a single dance with Tom. "Carolyn looks like she's having a wonderful time, Tommy."

"Of course, Tommy knows how to make the ladies happy."

Anne raised one gloved hand and pinched his cheek. "Don't be like that, Tommy. Just be yourself. You know, you are really at your best when you aren't putting on airs." After one dance Anne thanked Tom as he led her back to their table. Carolyn smiled at Anne as her friend seated herself.

Just then Tom's eyes drifted toward the far end of the gymnasium. "I'll be right back, okay?" Anne glared at her brother but Carolyn nodded approvingly as Tom disappeared across the dance floor.

"He's being really sweet, Anne. You were right; he has changed. As usual I have you to thank. You always know what's best for me." Anne put on a smile for her friend. Just then Marie appeared on the arm of a boy who was not familiar to either Anne or Carolyn. Her dress was simple but contrasted beautifully with her mother's string of pearls glinting softly against her alabaster skin.

"Marie, you look lovely," said Anne softly.

Marie beamed. "May I introduce you to Herbert Miller? Herbert, I'd like you to meet Anne Wellington and Carolyn Ford."

Herbert was tall and lanky and seemed ill at ease. He barely looked at the two young ladies and managed only a mumbled "How do you do?" Marie and Anne spoke quietly together for several minutes while Carolyn sat expectantly and Herbert stood fidgeting. Finally the couple moved along.

After fifteen minutes elapsed with no sign of Tom, Anne was worried. Finally she caught sight of him at the refreshment table. She rose, offering to get another glass of punch for Carolyn, then walked the length of the gymnasium toward the spot where she had seen her brother. By then he was standing in the doorway to the outer lobby, his back to her, talking animatedly to someone. As she approached she recognized that someone - it was Digsy.

"Hello, Anne. How are you this evening?" asked Digsy glibly. "So nice to see you again."

"I am well, thank you, Digsy. What are you doing here?"

"Tommy invited us." He turned and gestured toward a young woman next to him. "Anne Wellington, this is Gloria - Gloria Parker. I think you've met."

"Oh?" replied Anne. "I don't know as I recall."

"Oh, yeh, it was at the Dorchester School - ages ago," replied Gloria. Anne was remembering an unfortunate weekend when Jack had come to Greenfield for a visit. It involved a wild automobile ride to the top of Poet's Seat, one of Tom's childish pranks, and a flask of whiskey.

"Yeh," continued Digsy, "she lives in Northampton. I told Tommy I'd be out here this weekend, so he invited us. Isn't that a hoot?"

"Yes," replied Anne coldly, "a hoot, indeed." Just then another figure appeared out of the crowd of young people. It was Monique Fleury. Anne turned and stared at her brother, her chin set stonily.

"Thomas, someone's waiting for you. Don't you think you'd better get back to her?"

"I'll be right there," replied Tom sharply. Then he resumed his conversation with Digsy, Gloria, and Monique. Anne returned promptly to Carolyn with more glasses of punch and made an excuse for her brother. Soon she and Carolyn got to talking with another classmate.

After at least ten more minutes, Tom reappeared, his hair rumpled and his tie askew. He swooped into the chair next to Carolyn, took a sip from her drink, then grasped her hand. The two stepped onto the floor and started to dance. Anne was watching her brother intently and he was aware that his every action was being scrutinized. Soon he managed to lead

Carolyn beyond a replica of a Polynesian temple and out of his sister's sight.

Just then Marie and Herbert returned and once again Anne's attention was diverted. She was talking to Marie, her back to the dance floor, when Marie's eyes were suddenly raised in alarm. Anne turned to find Carolyn standing before her, tears streaming down her face. "Anne, I have to go - now," said Carolyn, her voice thin and cracking.

"What's wrong, Carolyn dear?"

"Please, take me home." Marie and Anne took Carolyn's arms and walked her out of the gymnasium. Herbert followed along looking bewildered. In the foyer Carolyn dissolved in tears, broke away from her two friends, and ran toward the outside entrance. The others rushed after her and out into the mild June evening.

"Let me talk to her," said Anne to Marie. And she followed Carolyn down the front walkway of the school and out onto the sidewalk on Hampshire Street. After several minutes Anne gestured to Marie and Herbert and the trio walked Carolyn home.

Anne and Carolyn sat on the porch speaking in whispers so as not to alert Carolyn's mother.

"When he came back to the table, he was a different boy, Anne. Out on the dance floor he was rude and he - he started holding me, squeezing me - and then he said some things that were very - that he shouldn't have said to me..." Then Carolyn paused, sniffling.

"Carolyn, what is it? What did he say?"

"No, Anne, that wasn't it. He, he had - liquor - on his breath."

Anne's heart sank. Tears filled her eyes and she buried her face in her hands. Then she took Carolyn's hand in hers and spoke without looking up: "Oh, Carolyn, I'm so sorry - and ashamed." And the tears began anew.

~ 20 ~

SATURDAY, JUNE 2

The following morning Anne sat alone at the breakfast table sipping a cup of tea. Soon her mother entered the room. "Good morning, dear. I didn't hear you and Tom come in last night. You must have been late, hmm?" She sat across the table from her daughter while the waitress poured her tea.

"No, Mother, actually I returned quite early. I wasn't feeling well and…"

"Oh, my, what's the matter? Are you ill?" Anne shook her head. "Worried about Jack, I presume. Well, I'm sure you will find him much improved today. You and Tom are still planning to go to Westfield this afternoon, aren't you?"

"I don't know, Mother. Maybe if Bromley can take me. I'm not sure Tom will be going."

"Do you think he and Carolyn had a good time?" asked Helen. Anne shrugged her shoulders. She was trying her best to keep her composure, but Helen Wellington knew her daughter. She rose from her seat, came around the table, and knelt beside her. "Honey, what's wrong? Did things not go well last night?" Anne began to sob. "What happened, Anne? Please, dear, tell me."

"Mother," began Anne, struggling to catch her breath, "it's Tommy. He invited Digsy and a couple of friends to the Formal."

"What? Well, that's not allowed. The Formal is for students and their escorts only. Oh, that boy, I'm going to have a word…"

Anne was looking into her mother's eyes and Helen was startled at what she read in her daughter's expression. "Mother, they were drinking. Digsy, his friends, and Tommy. Liquor." A pained expression spread across Helen's face. "I should have realized by the way he was acting. You know, he was a perfect gentleman at first and he and Carolyn seemed to be getting on just fine. She was smiling like I've never seen her smile. She was thanking me for - for encouraging them. Then he disappeared for nearly half an hour and when I finally found him he was with those - *friends*." Her normally angelic face contorted as she spoke the word, as though a bitter, repugnant taste had crossed her lips. "When he came back to the table he was rude and ill-mannered and - God knows what he said - or did - to Carolyn. She was in tears in minutes and we had to take her home. It's all my fault, Mother, I should never…"

"No, dear, it's not your fault. We both know whose fault it is." She shook her head and bit her lip, all the while gently stroking her daughter's hair. After several more minutes, she excused herself: "I am going to wake your brother right now. Thomas and I will have words."

"Maybe you'd better let him sleep a little longer, Mother, he's probably…" But her mother was out of the room. Anne sat, head down, poking disconsolately at a poached egg with her fork. The waitress had spoken to Mildred, the cook. Mildred had known Anne since she was an infant and the two were very close. She entered the breakfast room and knelt next to Anne, speaking softly to her. Just then Helen returned.

"Well, Thomas's bed hasn't been slept in. Apparently he never came home last night."

118

Tom called later in the morning and spoke to his mother, explaining that he had spent the night at Digsy's friend's house in Northampton. He apologized and promised to be home later in the day. Helen managed to keep her worry and fury at her son at bay and thanked him for calling.

Anne was preparing to leave for Westfield when the morning mail arrived. She looked briefly at the letters on the table in the library. One was addressed to her and she recognized the handwriting; it was from Jack. She picked up the envelope, stared at it, then seated herself in a cushioned chair. Carefully she broke the seal on the envelope and pulled out a single sheet of stationery. She read the short letter, tears welling in her eyes, then sat quietly, her head bowed.

"Annie, Bromley's waiting for you out front," called her mother from the hall. Hearing no reply she stepped through the library door. "Annie?"

Anne looked up at her mother and spoke softly. "Please thank Bromley for me, Mother, but I won't be needing a ride after all."

⚜ ⚜ ⚜ ⚜ ⚜ ⚜

A few minutes later Anne was lying face down on her bed sobbing. Her mother was seated next to her reading Jack's letter.

> *Dear Anne,*
> *Thank you for coming to see me on Wednesday but you really shouldn't trouble yourself with me anymore. You have so much to live for and you don't need an invalid like me holding you back. Please don't worry about me, I will be fine.*
> *Always,*
> *Jack*

Helen Wellington was a strong, determined woman, but this was turning into a Jonah day if there ever was one, and it was taking its toll on her. Her husband had to be spared all of this for the sake of his heart. It was clearly up to her to save her children from more sadness, more tragedy, but she was not at all certain that she could do so.

"Annie, don't take this too hard, dear. Jack's a wonderful boy - a wonderful young man. But he's having to adjust to a very difficult situation. Give him time, honey. I'm sure he'll think better of this. One day soon he'll probably show up at the door smiling, asking for you. After all, dear, he did sign the letter *Always*."

Just then footsteps could be heard on the carpet in the hallway. Helen looked up to see her son standing in the half open door. She waved him off and Tom quickly disappeared. Anne was still lying face down, sobbing, and Helen couldn't think of what else to say.

"I'll ask Mildred to bring you some chamomile tea and honey - how about that?" Anne's head nodded slightly. Helen rose and left, closing the door gently behind her.

Helen was exhausted by the trials of her children at this moment and went to her favorite retreat, the glasshouse. Seated on a wrought iron bench, she was cheered by the colorful and exotic blooms around her. The gentle patter of water flowing over rocks provided a badly-needed balm for her heavy heart. A ruby-throated hummingbird was darting from bloom to bloom before her when a familiar voice came from the glasshouse entrance: "Mother? I thought I might find you here."

Helen looked up as Tom approached. She always took pleasure in the sight of her son. Even when he was misbehaving, she found reassurance in his face and his stance - so like his father when he was young, filled with confidence and purpose. *How ironic*, she thought to herself at that moment.

"Thomas. Come, sit here, won't you please?"

Tom approached but remained standing. "I can't, Mother, I've got to get going."

"Going?" she replied softly. "But you just got home." She looked into her son's face, hoping to see some trace of remorse, of regret, for the damage he had wrought the previous evening - to Carolyn, to Anne, to his entire family. But what she saw was something quite different, a steely determination that frightened her.

"To Onset on Cape Cod. Digsy's parents have a summer place on an island. He has invited me to stay there for the summer and I've accepted the invitation."

"But what about your job?"

"It's not for me, Mother. It's just not right for me."

"I see. Well, what is right for you, Thomas? I'd like to hear."

"I don't know, Mother, but I need some time."

"Digsy and you, how will you two get along? And isn't he going back to Harvard in the fall?"

"Nope. He left Harvard. He's planning to take a job with his father's company at the end of the summer. It sounds like a good situation for him."

"Ah, I see. Well, I'm happy for him, then. But I'm not sure that spending the summer with Digsy is the best situation for you."

"I've made up my mind, Mother. I'm going. I'm eighteen and I don't need your permission."

"Thomas," replied Helen in the gentlest tone she could muster. "Were you drinking last night?"

Tom's face became rigid, mask-like. "No, what makes you say that? I was fine."

"I have two very reliable sources who say otherwise."

"Well, they're lying. I've had enough, Mother. I'm going," he snapped. He turned to leave.

"Before you go, Thomas, I hope you'll speak to your sister. She - she really needs her brother right about now."

Tom stopped. Slowly he turned toward his mother, paused, then nodded. "Okay, I will."

"Promise?"

"Yes, Mother, I promise."

Several hours later Anne was seated in the shade of a graceful copper beech just beyond the rose garden. She was remembering the times that she and Jack had spent together on the lawn, playing badminton with Tom and Carolyn, sipping lemonade, talking about the future. And she was thinking about Jack, how they had once shared their first dance right beneath that tree. It all seemed so distant and unreal to her now. Never in her life had she felt so blue.

"Annie?"

She looked up and saw her brother standing tall and straight before her dressed in a pinstriped shirt with a monogram on the pocket, sharply creased trousers, and shining cordovan brogues.

"What are you all gussied up for, Tommy?" She wanted to add *Got a couple of dates lined up for tonight?* but she restrained herself.

"I've come to apologize. And say good-bye."

"Good-bye? Where are you going?"

"To Cape Cod. I'm spending the summer at Digsy's parents' vacation house. Sailing, swimming, tennis - it should be grand."

"Well, Tommy, that's quite a - a sudden change. What about your new job?"

"I'll find something in Boston in the fall. We'll see, something will come up."

Anne looked briefly into her brother's eyes, then beyond into the dense foliage that hung around them like verdant drapery.

"And the apology, what did you have in mind?" she asked with unabashed scorn.

"Come on, Annie, I made a mistake. I just slipped, that's all. I'm not perfect, you know. I'm no Jack Bernard." As soon as he said those words he wished he hadn't.

"Well, Tommy, I fail to see how moving in with Digsy is going to help you get yourself right. But you know better than anyone else, don't you?" There was another long, awkward pause. Anne was very angry with her brother but she knew that if she started to let it out she would lose control and probably dissolve in tears. Finally she continued.

"Well, I'll accept your apology, Tom. But I hope you know who really needs to hear it."

Tom nodded. "As soon as I get settled in Onset I'm going to write her a letter. I promise."

"I hope so, Tommy, but I've heard too many promises from you to keep my hopes up for long."

Tom hung his head, unable to reply. Finally Anne spoke again.

"You'd better get going." She looked briefly into his eyes, then turned away.

"Weren't you planning to go to Westfield today to visit Jack?"

"Change of plans," was all Anne could say in reply.

"Say hello for me when you see him, okay?" Tom leaned down and kissed his sister on the head, then straightened up, turned, and walked across the lawn toward the house.

In just three hours, thought Anne, she had lost her two favorite boys.

~ 21 ~

Tom stood on the platform at the Holyoke railroad station waiting for the train that would carry him to Boston to meet Digsy. He was feeling some relief at this new turn in his life, the chance to make a new beginning, to leave some bad memories behind. That's what he needed, he was convinced, a fresh start. Just then a familiar figure emerged from the station.

"Carolyn."

"Hello, Thomas," said Carolyn weakly, her eyes, those almond eyes, darting left and right uncomfortably.

"I - I didn't expect to see you here," stammered Tom.

"I was checking the train schedule - for a friend." As she spoke she slipped a small piece of paper into her purse. "I understand you're leaving Holyoke. Your mother telephoned me."

Tom nodded. "Onset, Cape Cod. Just for the summer. Then maybe Boston. We'll see. Look, Carolyn, I'm sorry about last night. I - it just - I'm sorry."

Carolyn looked sullen. "I - I have to be going along, Thomas."

"Please, just listen to me - just for a minute?" He took her hand and directed her to a bench. Once they were both seated, he continued. "I want you to know I was having a real nice time. You looked very pretty. I mean, you always do, but you looked especially pretty - and happy - last night. And I - I ruined it - I know I did. Can you ever forgive me?"

Suddenly Carolyn's demeanor was altered. She spoke with uncharacteristic force and confidence fueled by anger and hurt. Her voice quavered with emotion. "I don't know, Thomas. I don't know. I guess I can forgive you for what you did, the way you acted, last night. It was the liquor, I suppose." Tom looked away, his face red with shame. But Carolyn wasn't finished.

"But what I don't know as I could ever forgive you for is what you're doing right now." Tom looked into her eyes, confused. "Leaving your sister when she needs you the most? I'd say that is, well, unforgiveable."

"She'll be fine," replied Tom. "Jack'll get better and they'll be hunky-dory. She doesn't need her big brother to take care of her."

Carolyn was astonished. "Didn't she tell you? Didn't your mother tell you?"

"Tell me what?"

"About the letter."

"What letter?"

"Jack sent Anne a letter. He pitched her. He said he's going to be sick and in bed the rest of his life and he doesn't want to be a burden to her."

"What? When did he do that?"

"It came in this morning's mail."

"I saw her just before I left the house. She didn't mention it."

"Maybe - maybe she figured you wouldn't care. Obviously you've decided to leave all that behind."

Tom was stunned by Carolyn's words.

"I have to go. We have practice for graduation at five o'clock, and, on top of everything else, my father's coming to graduation. No one else knows. It's going to be a big day."

With that Carolyn got up to leave. "Good-bye, Thomas, and good luck." And she walked down the platform toward Lyman Street.

The late-afternoon sun was still searing as it hung over the Berkshire Hills beyond the Bernards' farm. Charles was shuffling slowly along the dusty path from the river to the farmhouse. As he approached the house he could see one of the Wellington automobiles in the driveway. By the time he reached the end of the barn, Tom was just emerging from the kitchen door into the side yard.

Inside Tom had received a less than enthusiastic reception from the two Bernard girls. Marie had nothing but a curt hello for him. Claire, having been unable to get any specifics about the Formal from her sister, had consulted a classmate for details. She greeted Tom with a scowl and a few sharp words: "What are you doing here - trying to mend fences?"

Tom had asked to see Jack. Marie pointed to her father as he approached across the back lawn.

"Ask my dad."

"Hello, Thomas. How are you?"

"I'm all right, Mr. Bernard. I was hoping I could talk to Jack. Is he out in the barn?"

"Nah, he's down by the river. I walked down with him but he wanted to be left alone. I didn't feel right about leavin' him there, but he can be awfully stubborn. Maybe you could go down and bring 'im back?"

"Yeh, oh, sure, I would be happy to." The route was familiar to Tom, a winding path that skirted the sunny edge of the Bousquets' corn field. Raspberry and blackberry bushes sprawled along the border, their canes arched as if bowing in tribute to the sun. Soon the path plunged into the deep, brooding shade along the river's edge.

The first summer he and Jack were friends, nearly five years past now, Tom had visited the Bernard family for several days. The highlight of that visit was swimming in the river. It was a day much like this one, Tom recalled, steamy and still.

A few minutes later Tom was standing atop a sandy embankment that sloped steeply to the river's edge. An old cottonwood, likely the same tree that hung over the river five years earlier, was now slumped and mostly submerged. At the river's edge sat Jack, his feet in the shallow water, his shoes beside him on the sand. Tom could see that his friend was holding something small and shiny in his fingers. It looked like he was about to throw it into the water.

Tom spoke softly, not wanting to startle his friend. "Remember the rope swing, Jackie? Summer before grade nine?"

Jack looked up, nodded, and spoke flatly: "Yup, I remember."

"You grabbed the rope and climbed up the bank, then jumped off into space like it was the easiest thing in the world. Remember?" Again Jack nodded, then cracked a slight smile as Tom sat beside him in the sand. "I was scared, I can tell you," admitted Tom. "I just wasn't sure I wanted to try it."

"But you did."

"Yeh, yeh. But only because of you." Jack shook his head. "Yessir. I was chicken and you could have called me on it, but you didn't. You said to go up part way and try it from there. And I did. Then you said go up a little more. And I did. Pretty soon I was climbing to the top, running and swinging way out into the blue, just like you." Tom was grinning and laughing at the memory. "Isn't that right, Jackie, huh? Isn't it?"

Jack nodded. "Yeh, I guess so." Both boys looked out across the water that shimmered in the sun just as it had years before.

Tom chuckled, then sighed. "Those were good times, eh? Everything was just a barrel of laughs." Jack nodded again. Tom turned and looked at his friend. It was hard to see him like this, thin and pallid. Both boys looked out across the shallow river, the only sound the water's gentle riffles.

"What're you doin' here, Tommy?" asked Jack at last.

"Visiting with my buddy. I came with Anne the other day but thought I'd let you and her be for a while. Today I decided to come on my own, Tommy and Jack - just like the old days."

Jack nodded slowly, gazing across the water that formed two eddies as it flowed around the trunk of the dead tree.

"So, how was the Senior Formal? You have a good time?"

Tom surmised that Marie and Claire had chosen not to tell their brother about the previous evening's fiasco. "Yeh, pretty good. Everyone was sorry you couldn't be there."

Jack continued to stare at the rippling water, then turned and looked at his friend with a slight smile. "You and Carolyn, eh? Weren't you the guy that said he was darned if he'd be seen at a high school dance with her? Guess you had a - a..."

Tom laughed. "Annie told me I *doth protest too much.* I swear she's got a line from Shakespeare for everything, that sister of mine." At the mention of Anne the smile on Jack's face dissolved and he turned and looked out across the water again. Tom knew what he wanted to say but he wasn't sure how. Several minutes went by. Finally Tom spoke softly.

"She's pretty upset, buddy. She's been crying and going on. It's not like her, you know? She's usually on top of things. I've never seen her this way."

Jack pulled a handkerchief from the pocket of his overalls and blew his nose loudly. "I - I'm really sorry, Tommy, but it can't be helped. I'm sick - damaged goods - it wouldn't be fair for me to keep - to keep seeing her - it wouldn't be fair to her."

Tom thought about this. He wasn't known for tact or diplomacy and he knew it. So he just let Jack's words settle for a moment before he replied. "You know, that sister of mine, well, she cares a lot about you. I don't know exactly why. Personally, I think you're a pain in the arse," said Tom with a twinkle in his eye, "but she - she loves you."

Suddenly Jack was breathing with difficulty. For a moment Tom was worried, but he quickly concluded that it was emotion obstructing his friend's lungs, nothing more.

Maybe that was not a bad thing, he thought. "You've done a lot for me, Jackie, since that day here. You believed in me when - when even I didn't. Not just swinging from that rope. You taught me so much by the way you got on after your mom passed. Heck, you and Annie saved me from going to prison." Jack was shaking his head. "I just wish - I wish I could do the same for you, you know? Help you get over this."

"It's not something you just get over," replied Jack angrily. "It's epilepsy. It's a terrible disease and it can strike any time. I could have another fit - seizure, I mean - right here, right now, and fall in the water and drown in a minute. Don't you understand?"

"Yeh, Jack, I understand. But you don't know that's what it is. It might be something else. And anyway, I heard they have some new miracle cure." Again he paused, then continued. "Everyone has their - their, you know, challenges. No one's perfect."

"You're the one who's had challenges, Tommy. And look how you've faced them. I mean, losing your brother, getting arrested, then look how you decided to go to that place in Williamstown for help." Tom was thankful that his friend wasn't looking at him as he said those words, for fear that the shame he felt was emblazoned across his face.

"We'll see, Jackie, we'll see." Tom sat down in the sand next to Jack. "Don't you wish we could just turn back the clock? Five years ago - Jackie and Tommy - right here on this very spot - not a care in the world?"

"Yeh," replied Jack wistfully. "You know..." Jack paused, remembering, then continued. "I was wishin' and prayin' to grow up so fast. If I only knew what lied ahead, I woulda never wished for that."

"Hey, Jack. If you want to go back to the mill - I mean, when you feel up to it - I know there's a job for you in the sorting house this summer. Just say the word. You said you needed to save for college."

Jack shook his head slowly. "Forget about that."

"Whataya mean, Jackie? You're still going, right?"

"I doubt it, Tommy. I really doubt it. This thing could hit again anywhere, anytime."

"But Jack, maybe it's not - that. Maybe it's something else and won't ever happen again. Don't give up everything."

"But the doctors..."

"What do they know? Jack, you can't live the rest of your life in bed. That's not like you. It's not like you at all. Jack, I believe in you, Anne believes in you, your family - you should, too, Jackie, I mean, believe in yourself." Jack didn't respond for several minutes. He was fingering the shiny object. "Whatta you got there, Jackie?" Jack held it up.

"It's my St. Christopher medal. They tell you it'll protect you from harm," said Jack shaking his head. "And I believed it. Hell of a lot of good it did me."

"Don't say that, Jackie. You know, that's what makes your family different from others." Tom nodded at the medal. "You - you have a - kind of like an anchor, keeps you from drifting. You have to keep a hold of that, you know what I mean?"

Another minute went by. Finally Jack turned, looked briefly into his friend's eyes, and nodded. Then he opened the chain and secured it around his neck again.

"Let's walk back, okay?" The two stood up, climbed the sandy embankment, and made their way back to the farmhouse. On the way Tom surprised Jack with the announcement that he was leaving for Cape Cod. When Jack asked about Carolyn's reaction to his departure, Tom's answer was curt. "She'll get over it - girls always do." Jack didn't press his friend on the matter, but he had the distinct feeling that there was more to Tom's sudden departure than he was willing to reveal to his friend.

Once back at the farmhouse, the pair walked to Tom's motorcar, then stood talking for several minutes. Charles watched from the barn door, relieved that at least Jack was talking to his best friend. Finally they shook hands. "Well, good luck, Tommy. Have a good summer on Cape Cod. And say hello to Digsy for me."

~ 22 ~

SUNDAY, JUNE 3

The next morning was a typical Sunday morning in the Bernard household, at least as far as Charles and his daughters were concerned. There were the usual chores to be done, feeding the animals, pressing of Sunday clothes, the ritual shining of four pairs of shoes at the kitchen table. Marie stood at the sink preparing vegetables for a stew. Having completed polishing the footwear, Charles rose from the creaking Windsor chair and placed the shoes on the floor by the back door. "I'll go up and wake Jack. He's gotta turn up the steam if he's gonna be ready for Mass."

"I don't think he's going, Father. He told me last night," replied Marie.

"Well, let me see what I can do." Charles limped across the room to the narrow front hallway and called up the stairs. "Jack? You up?" There was no response. "Jackie?" Still no response. Charles grasped the rail that Jack had installed the previous winter and climbed the stairs slowly and with effort. He rapped lightly on the bedroom door. "Jack? You okay?" He heard a faint groan, then the creaking of the bed.

"Yeh, Dad, I'm okay."

"Well, you best be gettin' dressed. We leave for Mass in about half an hour." Charles waited for a reply. When none was forthcoming, he lifted the latch and opened the door a crack. "C'mon, boy, get a move on."

Jack was sitting on the edge of the bed looking dazed. He shook his head slowly. "I can't, Dad. I - I feel sick."

Charles opened the door and stepped into his son's bedroom, speaking softly. "Now, there, why don't you give it a try? Once you're up and dressed and had some breakfast, you'll feel better."

"I - I don't think so."

"That new priest, Father Bertin, gonna be saying Mass today for the first time. He'll want to meet the whole family. You missed Mass two weeks runnin', now. Whataya say?"

Jack shook his head. "I don't think so. Next week, maybe."

"Suit yourself, son. But I think it'd do you a world o' good."

A few minutes later it was Marie's turn to implore her brother. But Jack could not be swayed. "I just don't feel up to it, that's all, I'm sick. So just leave me be, please?"

"You were well enough to walk down to the river yesterday. And you seemed to be having a good chat with Tom when you came back. So why not go to Mass? It will be good for you - for your spirits, you know?"

Jack turned away from his sister. "Yeh, well, like they say: spirit's willing, flesh's weak."

"If you're not going to Mass, then maybe you could do your devotions, Jackie." She handed him a prayer book, a gift from her mother many years before.

Jack took the book but did not reply. Standing at the bedroom window, he watched as this father and sisters climbed into the Model T and departed for Mass. For several minutes he stood holding the book in both hands, his thumbs stroking the intricately engraved cover. He pulled gently on the several silk ribbons sewn into the binding, ribbons that his mother used to mark her favorite prayers or passages.

May was *Le mois de Marie*, the month of Mary, he thought, and he'd let it slip by without recognition. When she was a child back in Québec, his mother and her family went to church practically every evening in May to pray. Even farmers working in the fields would pause from their labors to offer prayers to the Blessed Virgin every day in the month of May.

Jack looked down at the prayer book, then slowly descended the stairs and turned into the narrow hallway. The family shrine was nestled in a shallow alcove off the hallway. It consisted of a gate-legged mahogany table and an upholstered *prie-dieu*, a kneeling stool on which his mémère had carefully embroidered the words *Je vous salue, Marie, pleine de graces.*

Kneeling on the stool, elbows resting on the table, hands clasped tightly, head bowed, he recited the words he knew so well:

> *Hail Mary, full of grace. The Lord is with thee.*
> *Blessed art thou amongst women,*
> *and blessed is the fruit of thy womb, Jesus.*
> *Holy Mary, Mother of God, pray for us sinners,*
> *now and at the hour of our death.*
> *Amen.*

Gently he lifted a string of rosary beads from an emerald crystal dish. Holding them in the fingers of one hand, he crossed himself with the other. Then he whispered the Apostle's Creed, *I believe in God the Father, Almighty, Maker of heaven and earth…,* then *Our Father who art in heaven…,* then the devotional to the Blessed Virgin, *Hail Mary, full of grace,* and, finally, *Glory be to the Father and the Son and the Holy Ghost.*

As his lips moved and the familiar words tumbled out, the beads slipped singly through his fingers, carrying him through the fifteen Mysteries, each followed by a repetition of the *Our Father, Hail Mary,* and *Glory Be to the Father.* He concluded with:

Hail, Holy Queen, Mother of Mercy,
our life, our sweetness and our hope!
To thee do we cry, poor banished children of Eve;
to thee do we send up our sighs,
mourning and weeping in this vale of tears.

As the last words crossed his lips he dropped the rosary beads into the platter and hung his head, tears streaming down his cheeks.

Charles, Marie, and Claire arrived home after Mass to find Jack standing by the fence overlooking the garden he had planted to onions a few weeks earlier. Claire crossed the lawn in her Sunday best and approached her brother.

"How was Mass?" Jack asked.

"The usual - boring. Oh, the new priest wants to meet you, Jackie. Daddy asked him to come by for a visit." Jack snorted, then shook his head. "What's the matter with you, Jackie?"

"I just don't feel like having some priest inquiring after my soul, that's all."

Claire could tell that the subject of Mass and Father Bertin was not getting them anywhere. She looked out on the onions for a moment, thinking. "Need help with the garden? 'Cause I could give you a hand, Jackie. Just tell me what to do."

"Well, there's lots of weeding to be done, Claire, but it ain't a job for a little girl. It's hard work."

"Okay, okay, I'm just trying to be helpful."

"Well, thank you, Claire, but it's not helpful." Claire's bright face darkened and she started to turn away. "I'm sorry, sweetie. I know you're trying - I know. It just doesn't help, always being reminded of what I can't do."

"I thought the doctor said you were improving and could be a little more - active."

"Yeh, well, it's not possible. It's just not possible. So please, just leave me be."

Claire started to walk back toward the house, then stopped and turned. "We saw Father Lévesque in church. He asked about you - wanted to know how you were doing. He's leaving for Québec this afternoon." She turned and continued to the house, not waiting for Jack to reply.

It was late afternoon and Jack lay on his bed staring at the bedroom ceiling when a soft knock sounded on the door. "Uh-huh," mumbled Jack. The door opened slowly.

"'ello, *Jacques*."

"Father Lévesque, what are you doing here? I thought you'd be on your way to Montréal by now," said Jack.

"I decided to wait a few days, my boy. No rush. I'm only being put out to pasture, you know. No reason to 'urry that, eh?"

"But..."

"*Jacques*, I wanted to see you, to talk to you. I thought you might be at Mass today." Jack shook his head but diverted his eyes. "Father Bertin - he wants to meet you, you know? I told 'im I'd ask you about cutting the grass in the cemetery again like you did last summer. When you feel up to it, I mean." Again Jack shook his head but offered no response. "So, 'ow are you doing, *Jacques*?"

"I'm okay, Father."

"Okay? Just okay?" replied the priest with a twinkle in his eye. "That doesn't sound like the *Jacques* Bernard I know. That *Jacques* was always busy gardening, fixing, building, doing things for others. That's the *Jacques* I remember."

Jack emitted a muffled laugh and shook his head. "Haven't you heard, Father? That Jack is gone. All that's left is - a - an invalid."

"But he looks like the same old *Jacques*," replied the priest, sadness etched in the lines on his face.

"Yeh, on the outside, maybe."

Father Lévesque leaned toward Jack, staring intently. "And on the inside?"

Jack looked briefly into the priest's face. He saw caring and kindness behind his gray eyes, but worry in his wrinkled brow. "Inside he's hollow, Father, like an empty chest. There's nothing left inside."

He grasped Jack's forearm. "Have you talked to Him about this, *Jacques*?" Jack looked up and watched as the priest's gaze turned slowly skyward. "Maybe He can help."

Jack looked down at his hands, turning them over as if examining them. "I don't know, Father. I think He's given up on me."

The priest seated himself. For a moment his head was bowed in prayer. Then he looked up and into Jack's eyes. "You know, *Jacques*, many years ago back in Sherbrooke there was a young man just about your age. He 'ad a - a growth - in his groin. It was very painful. The doctors told his parents it was cancer and it was getting larger - that there was no 'ope."

Suddenly Jack was listening intently. "What happened to him, Father?"

"He thought that God had abandoned him. He told his parents he didn't believe in God any more, that he wanted to die." The old priest's voice dropped to a whisper, but a whisper filled with emotion. "He was angry, *Jacques* - so angry."

"Did he die?"

"He prayed that night. 'e told God that 'e didn't believe in Him anymore, that 'e didn't deserve this. He told Him to go to hell." The priest's moist eyes looked squarely into Jack's eyes as he spoke the word *hell*.

"So what happened to him, Father? He died, right?"

"The next day a new doctor came to see 'im. He was young, just out of medical school in Toronto. He told the boy about a new treatment. The boy doubted it would do 'im any good, but 'e decided to risk it anyway."

"And?"

"They did an operation and removed the growth."

"So, what happened to him?"

"It never came back, the growth." There was a long pause. The priest took several deep breaths. His eyes glistened. "He asked God to forgive 'im for 'is lapse of faith. He promised never again to doubt Him."

"So - so what happened to him, Father?"

"He decided to go to seminary…"

Jack nodded, then paused, then turned and looked into the old priest's eyes. "You mean it was you, Father?"

Father Lévesque nodded. "That was almost fifty years ago, son. But I remember it like it was yesterday."

Jack lay back, tears welling in his eyes. There was a long pause as he tried to find the right words. "I - I think I've given up on Him, too, Father. I tried sayin' the Rosary this morning." He paused and swallowed hard. "You know how the Rosary's supposed to bring you closer to God?" The priest nodded. Then Jack spoke slowly, his voicing cracking with emotion. "But Father, this morning - I never felt so alone."

"*Jacques*, believe me, my son, you are *not* alone. *The Lord is my shepherd, I shall not want.* Remember that?" Jack nodded. "*Yea, though I walk* - Say it with me, son, come on." And they recited that familiar line of scripture in nearly perfect synchrony: "*Yea, though I walk through the valley of the shadow of death, I fear no evil, for thou art with me.*"

The old priest looked beseechingly into Jack's eyes and whispered. "Trust in Him, my boy. Believe in Him."

Jack nodded. Father Lévesque was about to rise and take his leave, but he detected something in the young man's expression, doubt, confusion, perhaps fear. "Is there something else, *Jacques?*"

"Father." Jack's jaw twitched as he tried to formulate the words. "Do you believe in the Devil?"

The priest sat back and sighed. His eyes met Jack's, then looked down at the floor for what seemed like an eternity. Finally he spoke, still looking down. "I do *Jacques*, yes, I do." Then his eyes rose to meet Jack's. "Do you?"

"Maybe, I don't know. But, Father, I've - I've been seeing things."

"What kinds of things, *Jacques?*"

"Eyes, Father, deep, horrible eyes, staring..." Jack's face was ashen and he closed his eyes tightly as if trying to rid his mind of the memory.

The priest was shaken by Jack's words and the deep wells of fear and dread they evidenced. He whispered to Jack: "When do you see these - these things, *Jacques?*"

"Right before a - a seizure."

The priest listened to Jack's testimony in silence. Then he took his hand and spoke softly but firmly. "*Jacques*, my son, listen to me. You must fight him, resist him, cast him out, just as God cast him out of heaven, in *Revelations*. The next time those eyes appear, *Jacques*, you must fight back, do you understand me?"

"I don't know if I can, Father, I'm just not sure."

"Yes, *Jacques*, you can. If anyone can, you can. It may be difficult, it may be the hardest thing you have ever done, but you must resist him. Understand?"

"I will try, Father, I will try, I promise."

Father Lévesque saw the old prayer book on Jack's nightstand. He lifted it, opened it, and gently turned the pages. Carefully he placed the silk ribbons to mark several pages. "I want you to read these pages, *Jacques*, every day, to build up your strength. You're an athlete, right? You know how the body needs to be strengthened to compete, right?"

Jack nodded. "So does the soul, *Jacques*, so does the soul." Then he handed the book to Jack.

Jack looked up. "Thank you, Father." The priest stood, said a silent prayer, then turned to leave. "Father?" The priest stopped and turned back toward Jack. "What will you do with your time once you're settled in Montréal?"

"Oh, I don't know, read, go for walks, pray. *La Refuge*, it's called. It was a cloister some years ago, but it's been converted to a 'ome for old priests like me. There's gardens, paths, benches. I plan to walk every one of those paths every day that I'm able, and sit on those benches. We still have our differences, He and I, you know? But we'll talk, the two of us, in the gardens. Lots of time for that now."

"I - I'll miss you, Father, we all will."

"Thank you, my boy. I'll miss you, too. But remember, you are not alone. Godspeed."

~ 23 ~

Carolyn stood at the end of the second floor corridor of Holyoke High School the next morning waiting expectantly. This was the place where she and Anne met every morning, where they exchanged greetings and made plans for the day. When the bell rang announcing the start of classes and Anne still had not appeared, Carolyn reluctantly turned and mounted the broad stairway to the third floor where her civics class was about to begin.

Later in the morning Carolyn sat in class waiting for Senior English to begin. Surely Anne would appear for this, her favorite class, especially as they would be starting *King Lear* today. But Anne never appeared.

Shortly after noon Carolyn left school and started down Hampshire Street in the direction of Gregoire's Shoe Shop. As she was about to cross Maple Street she looked to her left and spotted Anne ascending the steep stone steps of the Women's Home.

"*Anne*, oh *Anne*." As she called, Anne looked briefly in Carolyn's direction, then quickly turned away, and disappeared inside. Carolyn hurried down the sidewalk, climbed the steps, and entered. Anne was standing in the office in conversation with Nina.

"Hello, dear," said Nina to her daughter. "Aren't you supposed to be at the shoe shop?"

"Yes, Mama. But I needed..." As Carolyn spoke Anne disappeared into the storage room adjoining the office. "I just need to speak to..." began Carolyn, taking a step toward the storage room door. "Anne?" said Carolyn softly, tentatively. Her friend was standing with her back to the door. She turned and briefly met Carolyn's gaze, then looked away and began rearranging supplies on the shelves.

"Oh, hello Carolyn," Anne replied, her back to her friend. "How are you, dear?"

"Anne, I've been worried about you. You weren't in school today."

"Uh, no, I - I was feeling poorly this morning and I - I told Mother I couldn't go to school."

"Oh, I'm sorry," replied Carolyn sincerely. "But should you be working if you're feeling ill?"

Still Anne did not look up. "I - I knew your mother needed me here this afternoon. You know, the Temperance meeting and all."

"Well that's very kind of you, but you mustn't overdo."

"I'm all right, Carolyn, really. I'm fine. Please don't worry."

"Well, all right, I'll go along. But I'll see you later?"

Anne nodded but made no reply. Carolyn left, still feeling uneasy about her friend. When her shift at the shoe shop had ended, she returned to the Women's Home only to find one of the residents sitting behind the front desk. Anne had left early, the young woman explained. "She wasn't feeling well. Mrs. Calavetti had to go to the Temperance meeting at the YMCA. She asked me to sit at the desk and answer the telephone."

Now Carolyn was alarmed. She had the distinct feeling that Anne was not exactly ill. She left the Women's Home and headed up Appleton Street toward the Highlands and home. When she reached her front walk she was surprised to see Anne seated in a wicker chaise on the porch, her face flushed, her expression glum. "Anne, what are you doing here? Are you sure you're all right?" Anne remained seated and nodded slightly. Her voice shaking, she spoke.

"Carolyn, dear, I am sorry for being so abrupt with you this afternoon. I just wasn't feeling..." Then she stopped and looked up squarely into Carolyn's eyes. Her lower lip quivered.

Carolyn's expression suddenly turned very serious. "Oh, dear, you're ill. Is it - your monthlies?"

"No, Carolyn, It's not that. I'm not ill. I'm just so - so ashamed."

"Anne, please, don't be."

"But I am, Carolyn. It was all my fault. I pleaded with you to go to the Formal, and..." Just then a neighbor stepped out onto the porch of the house next door and began hanging laundry on a line that stretched the length of the porch. Anne paused, then continued, her voice lowered. "I promised you that he had changed, and I let you down."

"Anne, you are my best friend, and yes, you pleaded with me. But in the end it was he that asked me and I who agreed, so I have no one to blame but myself. You had no way of knowing..."

"I couldn't believe - I didn't want to believe he could be that way. And he had pledged to me that he was reformed, that he was - a new Tommy." She barely mouthed her brother's name. Her voice broke as she continued: "Carolyn, dear, please believe me, I am so very sorry." Carolyn shook her head. "He told me," continued Anne, tears now streaming down her cheeks, "before he left - he promised me he would apologize to you. I'm sure - well, I hope he keeps his promise."

"He already has, Anne. I saw him downtown on Saturday. He apologized, Anne, he did. He was very contrite - it's hard to stay angry with him when he's so sweet, even after..." Anne was dabbing at her eyes with a handkerchief. "Any news about Jack?" asked Carolyn after a moment. Anne shook her head. "Well we certainly are at their mercy, aren't we?" said Carolyn, reaching out and gently stroking Anne's hand. Anne allowed herself the slightest laugh and smile, then dabbed at her eyes again. Carolyn smiled back.

A look of astonishment was on Anne's face. "Carolyn, dear, I am surprised, frankly, that you are taking this so well. If I were you I'd be fit to be tied. You seem so, well, so chipper."

"But Anne, aren't you the one who's fond of saying, *It's always darkest before the dawn* and *When one door closes another opens?*"

Just then Mr. Boudreau, the postman, appeared on the front steps. "Afternoon Carolyn, Anne," he said, smiling and tipping his blue-visored cap. The man knew everyone in Holyoke - man, woman, and child - by name, or so it seemed. Some said his knowledge of folks went well beyond names. He handed Carolyn a single letter, tipped his hat again, turned, and retraced his steps to the sidewalk. Carolyn looked down at the letter and froze.

"Carolyn, dear, what is it?"

"It's a letter - for me - from - from the Agricultural College."

"Oh, Carolyn, could it be?" Carolyn stood looking at the long, official-looking envelope, her hand shaking. "Well, open it, for goodness sake."

"Oh, Anne, I - I can't. Would you?" And she placed the unopened letter in Anne's hand. "Please?"

"Are you sure?" replied Anne. Carolyn nodded. Slowly, gently, Anne broke the seal and removed a long sheet of vellum. Carefully she unfolded it and scanned it, her face entirely devoid of expression. Then she looked up and into Carolyn's eyes. "Carolyn, dear," she began flatly, "you have been - *admitted.*" On the last word her voice ascended to an exultant shriek, her eyes danced, and she leapt to her feet, embracing her friend. Carolyn let out a shrill yelp of joy, as

144

loud as any she had ever produced in her life, and the two friends hugged, swirled about, then hugged again and again.

"Oh, Carolyn, dear Carolyn, I am so proud of you. What an honor. I believe you are the first of our class to be admitted to MAC." Finally Carolyn took the letter, sat next to Anne, and read it aloud. "Imagine, Carolyn, you are going to college. How exciting to be in Amherst. New horizons will unfold for you, new worlds, new…"

"Yes, Anne, it will be so exciting." Then her expression changed abruptly from exultant to grim. "But Anne."

"Yes, Carolyn?"

"There's - just one - problem."

"What is it, dear?"

At that moment a figure approached on the sidewalk. Carolyn quickly folded the letter, re-inserted it into the envelope, and placed it on the seat beside her just beneath the edge of her skirts. "Hello, Mama," said Carolyn brightly. "How was the Temperance Union meeting?"

~ 24 ~

TUESDAY, JUNE 5

I t's men, Anne. That's the problem," whispered Carolyn at school the next morning. She and Anne were standing in their usual meeting place in the second floor corridor before their first class. "In Mama's mind men are the root of all evil. That's why I could never tell her about Jan, or Thomas, or anyone. She doesn't trust them, not a one. Worse still, just last week we attended a lecture at the Temperance Union. The speaker went on and on about the evils of colleges today. He said all they teach young men is how to drink, as if it is a special skill to be learned and practiced, day and night, when they are away from home for the first time. He said colleges are like Sodom and Gomorrah, breeding grounds of evil. I knew that day that Mama would never agree to allow me to go away to college, even just ten miles away."

Anne couldn't help but think about Tommy and the Dorchester School that he attended beginning in grade nine. That was, she had to admit, precisely when his troubles began. "But surely your mother realizes not all boys become drinkers. And you would never associate..."

"It's more than that, Anne. Like I said, it's how she is about men. She just doesn't trust them, none of them." The two friends stood facing each other and looking sullen. The bell rang for the start of classes, but the pair seemed oblivious to the harsh metallic clangor a few feet above their heads. "I think it all goes back to - to - my father. He…"

Anne was surprised - shocked was more the word for it. Carolyn hardly ever spoke of her father. Only once before in ten years had a word ever been exchanged between the two friends about him. "Mama thinks he is…" She paused, then began again. "If she would only try…"

Anne was listening intently to her friend's halting words, searching her eyes for some glimmer of insight. She thought it was about to come, that Carolyn was about to reveal something important about the mystery of her father, when Carolyn looked up at the clock. "We'd better get to class."

That evening Helen was working at her desk in the drawing room when Anne appeared at the door. She reported the good news about Carolyn's letter. "I wish you could have seen her, Mother. She was so happy, so excited. I've never seen her like that before, ever." Then she revealed to her mother Carolyn's predicament. Helen watched her daughter's face and listened intently to her words. Finally she replied.

"Honey, I've known Nina for a long time, a very long time. And I count her among my best friends in Holyoke. You know, we work together almost daily. But more than that, we share a dream - for the Women's Home, for Holyoke, for young girls everywhere." Helen paused, shook her head, then sighed. "But when it comes to men and alcohol, well, dear, we simply have our differences. But we never let them get in our way. Do you see what I mean? Friends aren't always of one mind. Sometimes they have to put aside their differences and concentrate on what they have in common. I'm sorry, dear, but I really do not feel it is my place to interfere."

"But Mother, think what a wonderful opportunity this could be for Carolyn - to attend a fine school, to further her education, to expand her horizons. And her only obstacle is her mother and her - her prejudices."

"Now, dear, you don't know that. Remember, there is also the question of cost. Maybe Nina feels she cannot afford to pay tuition, room, and board for her daughter for two years. Even the Agricultural College is getting expensive. Just the other day I read an item in the *Transcript* about how tuition is going up to $125 next year. That's a lot of money for anyone to pay these days. And Nina's salary at the Women's Home - well, I can tell you it's not very generous. Of course, every time the Board tries to give her an increase, she declines it. She prefers that every extra penny go to the Home and the residents."

Anne shook her head, her delicate chin set in anger. "It's a shame that she can be so generous to girls she barely knows, yet so - so *penurious* when it comes to her own daughter."

"I'm sure that Nina believes what she is doing is best for Carolyn. Please try to understand."

~ 25 ~

WEDNESDAY, JUNE 6

Tom and Digsy had just finished a busy day of sailing and tennis at Digsy's family home on Cape Cod. The two friends were seated in wrought iron lounge chairs on a manicured lawn that sloped gently away toward Buzzards Bay. The late afternoon sun shimmered on the water. In the distance waves crashed along a sandy beach. Far out on the bay dozens of small pleasure boats plied the bay, their white sails reflected in the dark waters.

"What time do we pick up the girls?" asked Tom.

"About eight - plenty of time. Here." He handed Tom a fizzing gin and tonic in a hobnail glass. "Bottoms up."

Tom took a sip, then paused, his eyes on the sea. "I have to say, Digsy, this is the life: swimming, sailing, girls. Too bad I beat you so bad on the court today. Better luck tomorrow."

"Yeh, well, I'm out of practice, you know. Not much time for tennis at Harvard this past year."

"So why are you leaving school? You never explained."

"Not for me, too much work. My dad's got this spot for me with his company whenever I want it. It's the perfect deal. How could I pass it up?"

"He doesn't care that you're quitting school. I mean, that's a big step."

"Yeh, well, my grades weren't that good. Harvard kind of encouraged me to consider my options."

"You mean they pitched you?"

"No, no, not at all. I just decided it wasn't worth it. I figure if I can get a good job with my dad's company without a college degree, why waste four years?" Digsy lit a cigarette. "Smoke?" Tom shook his head. "What about you, buddy? Any plans? Your father's company? That high school gal, Carol what's-her-name?"

Tom smiled. "Carolyn, you mean Carolyn."

"You two still...?"

"Naw," replied Tom flatly. "Had to break it off."

"If you ask me, she wasn't your type. Pretty enough, but not a Tom Wellington kind of girl, I'm guessing."

"I don't know," replied Tom, gazing into his glass and swirling his drink into little eddies. "I just don't know."

Digsy picked up the morning edition of the *Boston Herald* that lay on a glass-topped table between their chairs. "The Red Sox - they sure gave Cleveland a shellacking yesterday. Eleven to four. They're on their way to a pennant this year, I'm sure of it. Long as Babe Ruth and Ernie Shore stay healthy, they're a good bet, I'd say." When Tommy didn't respond, Digsy handed him the newspaper.

"So, sounds like Wilson's gonna get his way, huh?" continued Digsy. Tom was still lost in his own thoughts. "What, you still thinkin' about that Holyoke gal?"

Finally Tom shook his head, then smiled vaguely. "What were you saying about Wilson?"

"Haven't you heard? It's his proposal for the draft. He wants to start calling up eighteen-year-olds. If he gets his way, it'll start next month."

Tom's attention returned abruptly to his friend's words. He took the newspaper from the table and began to read the story on the first page, his eyes suddenly dark and penetrating. "Digsy, I never thought they'd do it, at least not so soon. Everyone said they wouldn't call up boys under

150

twenty-one, not for a while, anyway, not unless they really needed them."

"Yeh, well, now they need them. Haven't you been readin' the papers? Things are going to hell in Belgium. General Haig and his forces are getting pounded by the Krauts. American troops are already landing, but they need more. It's a real mess over there, Tommy."

"But does that mean - us?"

"Yeh, it does, buddy. That's exactly what it means. You and me." Digsy paused, looking out on the bay. "Unless, of course, you've got a plan." Then he turned and looked at Tom. "You do have a plan, Tommy, don't you?"

"Well, what do you mean? What's your plan, Digsy?"

Digsy took one last, long drag from his cigarette, tossed it into the grass, then cast his gaze out across the bay. "Well, whenever they start calling up guys our age, I go on the payroll at my father's company. When I get my notice, he calls one of his old buddies on the draft board and takes care of it. You know: essential industry, employee with unique skills, that kind of blather. Or maybe he works out a special deal for the friend and my name suddenly disappears from their files. Just like that, I'm in the clear."

Tom's gaze drifted across Buzzards Bay. The sky was cloudless and steel blue, but suddenly all he could see were storm clouds gathering.

~ 26 ~

"Ⅰn the name of the Father, the Son, and the Holy Ghost, Amen." The final benediction echoed in the sanctuary of St. Agnes Church that Sunday, then the organ swelled with the recessional hymn as a smiling Father Bertin, followed by two cherubic acolytes, walked slowly down the center aisle and out of the church. A few minutes later members of the congregation emerged from the church onto the front steps to be greeted by their new pastor. The Bernard family eventually appeared. Father Bertin shook hands with Charles, then with Claire and Marie. Next in line stood Jack.

"Well, this must be *Jacques*, eh?" Jack blushed, then shook the priest's hand and smiled weakly.

"Jack, Father - he likes to be called Jack," interjected Charles.

"Ah, Jack, I see. Pardon me. Well, it is a pleasure, young man, a real pleasure. And your health is improving, I trust?"

Jack shrugged. "About the same, I'd say."

"Well, these things take time, you know."

"Have you heard anything from Father Lévesque, from Montréal? " Jack inquired.

"No, son, not a word. I trust it will take time for 'im to get settled. Then, perhaps, he'll write. You know what, my boy? I bet he'd appreciate a letter from you and your family, what do you think? They'll have his new address in the church office."

Jack nodded. As he was talking to the priest, Jack spied Jim Trottière and his parents waiting in line to greet Father Bertin. Briefly Jack's eyes met Jim's, but at that moment Claire pulled on his sleeve, reminding him that they needed to get home quickly.

That afternoon Jim Trottière ambled up the Bernard's gravel driveway. Charles was standing in the open barn door as he approached.

"'Lo, Jim. How're you these days?"

"Middlin', Mr. Bernard."

"Jack tells me you're gonna try your hand at smithin'."

"Yep. Start in a couple weeks."

"Well, you'll make a fine blacksmith, Jim."

Jim flashed a grin revealing several missing teeth. Then he looked away toward the house. His face was angular as was his frame. His long muscular arms bulged beneath the sleeves of a faded gray work shirt. His hands were huge, his thumbs hooked around a pair of brown suspenders that held up tattered duck trousers. A rumpled wool cap was perched precariously atop a mop of thick, ungainly black hair. His speech was slow and awkward, as if every word required an effort. "Jack 'round?"

"Ayeh, in the shop." Charles turned and called into the barn: "Jackie, you got a visitor." Then he looked into Jim's eyes. "I know he'll be glad to see you, Jim," he added, nodding toward the back of the barn. Jim shuffled past the animal stalls, then stepped through the shop door. Jack was seated at the workbench.

"Jack," said Jim. Jack turned and their eyes met.

"Jim."

"Ha - how - how you been?" There was a long pause as Jim waited for a reply. He and Jack had been schoolmates at

St. Agnes School, then co-workers in the sorting house at the mill for several summers as well as much of the previous year.

"Been better, Jim. You?"

"Okay - okay."

"Started smithin' yet?"

"Naw, pretty soon, though."

"Your folks, sisters okay?"

Jim nodded. "Ayeh."

Just then a familiar voice came from the barn. "Jay-Jay." A smiling Émile appeared at the shop door, a tangle of leather harness in his arms. "Hey, Jay-Jay," he said brightly as he stepped through the door. Only then did he see Jim and the smile was quickly replaced with an anxious grin. "Oh, hey Jim." Then Émile stood silent, nervously rearranging the rat's nest of lines.

"'Mile," said Jim, casting only the briefest glance toward Émile. The pair knew one another from St. Agnes School. Jim and several grammar school friends often entertained themselves on the playground by taunting Émile with questions like *Hey, deaf boy, how come you so dumb?* and laughing. Émile would pretend not to understand.

Jim looked nervously at Jack, then at an iron anvil bolted to the workbench. He grasped the handle and tightened it, then loosened it, then tightened it again several times, appearing distracted. Finally he spoke. "Jack," he began. He tossed a furtive glance toward Émile, then lowered his voice. "Leo, Hank, t'other guys at the mill been askin' 'bout you. They was thinkin' maybe you'd come back to the sortin' house in time."

Jack shook his head slowly. "Don't think so, Jim. But tell 'em I said hey."

Jim nodded, then grasped the vice handle and turned it hard, tightening the jaws against themselves. "That Tuttle, he's a crotchety ol' bastard, that un," said Jim.

154

Jack shrugged his shoulders. "Just a lot of hot air's all. Why?" Jim never engaged in idle chatter. When he brought up a subject, there had to be good reason. Jack looked directly at Jim. Émile was also watching Jim's face intently as he spoke. "What about Tuttle, Jim?"

Again Jim paused, his eyes darting nervously from Jack to Émile and back to Jack. His voice dropped still lower. "Ehh - couple men in the dyehouse quit t'other day, jus' like 'at. Said they had better offers. But there's hardly any jobs now. Truth is they was gettin' sick, headaches, bilious. One of 'em, Poulin, he clapsed on the dyein' room floor. Had to be drug out."

"Poulin - Maurice Poulin?"

"So they say," answered Jim with a slight nod.

"He's as strong as a bull - been working there for years." Jim nodded again. "When was this, Jim?"

"Wednesday last. He come in again Thursday mornin' but Tuttle told 'im ta git out. Fired 'im - jus' like 'at. All the guys is fightin' mad. Gonna be a confab er somethin' - tomorra."

"Tomorrow?" replied Jack in a whisper.

"Ayeh, noon tomorra. Don' tell anyone I said so. I need my job - least for 'nother few weeks."

"Sure, Jim, sure."

"Well, I gotta be goin', Jack." Then he turned toward Émile and spoke loudly: "See ya, 'Mile." Jim turned and walked toward the door.

Jack stood and grasped the vice handle. He tried to turn it. "Hey, Jim?"

Jim turned and looked at Jack, then at the vice. His face contorted into a crooked smile. "Sorry, Jack." replied Jim. Stepping up to the vice, he grasped the handle with one hand and loosened it like it was a child's wind-up toy. "Guess I wasn't thinkin'. See ya."

Jack's eye met Émile's as Jim departed. "Never get on that guy's bad side, 'Mile, he could do some real damage." Émile chuckled and nodded, but he kept his thoughts to himself.

~ 27 ~

MONDAY, JUNE 11

Anne was seated at the reception desk of the Holyoke Women's Home at mid-day on Monday. Her assignment: to reconcile the cash box. Nina had departed for her weekly Temperance Union meeting at the YMCA a few blocks away, assured that the office was in good hands. Of all Nina's considerable talents, keeping the Home's financial records up to date was not her greatest, and she had enlisted her very capable young assistant to undertake the task on a quiet afternoon.

As much as Anne loved working at the Women's Home, her heart was burdened this day with worry about Jack. Despite their youth, she and Jack had endured a number of crises since they had been courting. But now there was a wall, it seemed, an impenetrable barrier that threatened any possible future for the young couple. What was worse, she feared, a fine young man with so much to live for seemed to be discounting any chance for an education, a career, a life, because of his condition.

Several of the Home's new residents were seated in front of the long windows in the drab front parlor doing needlework. Otherwise the place was entirely without activity on this June day, and activity, distraction, these were the very antidotes Anne needed most for the ache in her heart.

She was carefully logging dozens of expenditures in a heavy, leather-bound ledger, when the front door rattled, seemed to open briefly, then shut again. When it happened once she credited it to the wind, but after a second and then a third time, she finally rose from her seat and stepped into the hallway. Through the frosted glass in the door she observed the outline of a figure. She opened the door and peered out. "Émile, what - what are you doing here?"

Émile blushed as he removed his cap and held it before him with both hands. "Miss - Miss - Well - I - uh…"

"What is it, Émile? Come in, please, come in." She held the door and gestured for him to enter, but he seemed incapable of moving, of stepping through the door. Anne had never seen Émile anywhere other than on the farm in Westfield, save for the one encounter at St. Agnes Church. She suspected he was uncomfortable in the bustle of downtown Holyoke; not surprising, she thought, the city had that effect on many new arrivals. Finally she stepped onto the front stoop, pointed to a wrought iron bench beside the entrance, and gently corralled the young man toward it. Then she sat beside him.

"Émile, is something wrong? Is it about the Bernards? About Jack?" Her face went suddenly white anticipating what possible news Émile might be bearing.

"Iss Jay-Jay," he began.

"Jack? Is he all right, Émile? Please tell me he's all right." Émile nodded. "He so-kay, Miss, he so-kay."

"Thank goodness for that. But what is it, then?"

Émile needed time to gather his thoughts, to find the words, amidst the commotion of Maple Street. Just then a team of horses clomped past hauling a loaded coal wagon and he was momentarily distracted. But finally he began to speak. "Iss Jim, Jay-Jay's frien' - from the mill."

"Jim Trottière? Yes, I know him. He worked with Jack in the sorting house. What about him, Émile?"

"He 'as talkin' ta Jay-Jay - 'bout the mill - yestady." Émile's round hazel eyes suddenly grew larger. "'Bout the dyehouse."

"The dyehouse? Jim was talking to Jack about the dyehouse?" asked Anne. Émile nodded. "What did he say about it, Émile?"

"'e sayin' the guys thayas quits. Two - tree."

"Two or three of the men in the dyehouse quit?"

Again Émile nodded. "Said they get beddu jobs. But Jim - Jim - sayin'..."

"What, Émile, what did Jim say?"

"He say they go' sick. Upchuckin' 'n such. Couldn' take it thaya n'more. Ole Tuttle, 'es sayin' they's fired, but they's quit..."

"What are you saying, Émile?"

"Miss - Miss - one uv 'em, Poulin, they say he had a fit."

"You mean, a seizure?" Émile blushed, then nodded once. He was looking at Anne, his saucer eyes the very picture of innocence, and in that meeting of gazes an unspoken but mutual understanding formed.

From the pocket of his overalls, Émile drew several sheets of paper. They were yellow, faded, and wrinkled. He fumbled with them, unfolding and arranging them, then handed them to Anne. "What's this, Émile? Some kind of medical journal?" Émile nodded. "Where did you get this from, Émile?"

"The lib-ry, Miss. The lib-ary."

"But Émile, you mustn't tear pages from a library b...," began Anne. Then she saw the title and read it aloud: "*The Neuropathology of Benzene and Benzene Derivatives, Dr. James Whittemore, Johns Hopkins Hospital, Baltimore, Maryland.*" Anne looked into the boy's eyes, confused.

"What, Émile, what about this?" Émile then pointed to a sentence in the first paragraph of the scholarly article. Anne read it aloud. "*Benzene...also known as coal naphtha.*" Anne was stunned.

"Jay-Jay, he tol' me 'bout it - in the dyehouse."

"Émile," asked Anne, holding up the pages. "Have you shown this to Jack?" He shook his head slowly. For several minutes Anne sat silently, trying to assimilate this startling information. Émile was staring at her, looking confused, wondering if he had said something wrong or inapt. Finally he spoke.

"I sorry, Miss, I shouldna - I bedda go." His words seemed to bring Anne back from some distant place.

"Oh, no, Émile. Don't be sorry. You - I - I'm very, very grateful that you came. Émile, is there something else?"

Émile paused, looked anxiously around him, then spoke. "Jim - 'e say they walkin' out - 'cuz o' it."

"The workers in the dyehouse, Émile, they're walking out?" Émile nodded, wide-eyed. "When, Émile? When are they walking out?"

Émile's eyes grew still wider. "T'day - ri' now..."

"Émile, I have to go there. Will you go with me, please?" Émile nodded. "One minute, okay?" Anne rose and disappeared into the Women's Home to speak to one of the residents and leave a note on the desk for Mrs. Calavetti. Moments later she and Émile were rushing down Dwight Street toward the mill.

A small crowd was already assembled in front of the dyehouse; news always traveled fast in Holyoke, especially news of worker unrest. Dozens of operatives were spilling out of the mill, from the dyehouse, the sorting house, the carding, weaving and spinning rooms, the power house, and the warehouses, and gathering on Race Street by the canal. As Anne and Émile crossed the bridge they became aware of a surge of others, workers, tradesmen, shop-keepers, arriving from all directions, hurrying to see what was seldom witnessed in Holyoke, workers taking action on their own behalf. Young men were shinnying up lampposts to get a better view. Two trolleys were stopped on Dwight Street; half a dozen passengers had climbed onto the car roofs to look down on the scene.

A dozen or so workers stood shoulder-to-shoulder on the top step of the dyehouse entrance. Anne recognized one or two whom she had seen leaving the mill with Jack at lunch hour in recent weeks. One of them was trying to speak above the clamor, but there was no chance that he would be heard, not with the growing din. Anne could make out just a few isolated words: *management - united - strike*. People closer to the front of the crowd apparently understood what was being said and erupted in frequent, boisterous cheers.

Within ten minutes the crowd numbered in the hundreds as workers streamed up Race, Main, and Lyman Streets, all converging into a single mass on the dyehouse steps. Émile touched Anne's elbow. "We bedda go, Miss," he said, a look of alarm in his eyes.

"No, Émile, not yet. I want to find out..." Just then a long, black motorcar appeared, making its way slowly through the throng. At the dyehouse entrance the car halted, the doors swung open, and three tall men in fedoras and long dark coats emerged. The crowd roared still louder as the men ascended the steps of the dyehouse and came into view of all.

One of the men raised both arms in an effort to quell the din. In one hand he held a megaphone. Some in the crowd appeared to recognize the man and the roar of the crowd suddenly abated. The man spoke through the megaphone. "Ladies, gentlemen, citizens of Holyoke." The crowd cheered at the mention of the city's name. Again the speaker raised his arms. "My name is Garfield." Another brief explosion of cheers erupted and he paused once more, then continued. "We come from Lowell, birthplace of American industry, to offer

160

our support for the workers of Holyoke." Another roar rose from the crowd.

"In every industrial city, every mill town in the Commonwealth, in New Hampshire, Maine, Rhode Island, Connecticut, and across America, workers are uniting. Men and women, young and old, English, Irish, French, Italian, Polish, Lithuanian, all united in a common cause: justice for the workingman, freedom from oppression of mill owners, higher pay, shorter hours, better working conditions. It is their God-given right as men, as citizens of this great nation, to be treated with humanity, not merely as tools of the capitalists." The crowd cheered wildly, but briefly, then the speaker continued.

"Nowhere is this struggle, this battle, more important than right here in Holyoke, Massachusetts, and nowhere is the need for reform greater than in the textile mills of this great city. When my colleagues and I visited Holyoke just a few weeks ago, we warned that the working conditions in this city's mills were deteriorating. How ironic it is that, in this era of great progress in science and medicine, industry strives only to make more money without regard to the welfare of its workers." More cheering erupted.

"The textile industry, including Wellington Textiles and many other of this city's largest mills, has been particularly lax, uncaring, and downright negligent, adopting new methods that serve only one purpose." He paused, then spoke forcefully: "To line the pockets of the rich." The crowd roared.

"And in the process they permit their workers, on whose backs those riches have been accrued, to suffer egregious harm. Workers have been subjected to dangerous, life-threatening conditions, caustic materials splashing on them, hideous fumes invading their lungs. Men - and women - sickened, fainting, some who have worked in those same jobs for decades, now suddenly unable to work in the fouled air of these hell-holes." Again the din from the crowd swelled, but the speaker continued.

"Why? Because it is cheap, my friends, because it saves the mill owners parting with their coin." The crowd roared still louder and the noise was sustained for several minutes while the men on the dyehouse steps conferred. "This outrage against workers, against their families and loved ones, must cease." Again the crowd roared.

"And so we call on all the workers of Wellington Textiles, and of all this city's industries - fiber, paper, construction, rail - to unite. Let us put an end to this travesty, this inhumanity, once and for all." Another sustained roar rose from the crowd. Garfield's voice then dropped and the crowd became still.

"In this brave endeavor, I can assure you that you are not alone. You enjoy the support of workers in dozens of other cities near and far, many now organized as members of the Textile Council, the Amalgamated Textile Workers, and the IWW."

With the mention of the three large unions, none of which had established itself as yet in Holyoke, the crowd roared once again. But just as the din was easing, a rhythmic chant could be heard from a separate, smaller body of men standing on the Dwight Street bridge. *Go home - go home - go home* was the thin but unmistakable cry rising from that group and echoing off the mill buildings on all sides.

The larger crowd seemed to be aware of the dissenters for the first time, and those in a position to see them could discern several large signs and banners held above them reading *Bolsheviks go back to Russia* and *Death to Traitors*.

Again Émile grasped Anne's elbow. "Miss, please Miss, c'mon." At that moment several dozen men burst from the larger crowd and rushed the bridge. Mayhem erupted. Sticks, boards, and baseball bats swung violently; stones flew in both directions.

Suddenly a shrill whistle could be heard from far up Dwight Street. A mass of blue uniforms was emerging from Police Headquarters and descending the hill toward the bridge. At the sight the crowd broke up, people running wild-eyed away from the approaching echelon. Amidst the confusion, the dark-coated men slipped into their automobile which rushed away down Race Street toward the County Bridge and South Hadley.

Anne and Émile found themselves caught in a surging mass of humanity racing south on Main Street. All traffic on the busy thoroughfare - trolleys, motorcars, omnibuses, buggies, and carriages alike - had come to a halt as men, women, and children ran down the street, between the vehicles, and along the sidewalks.

Suddenly a young man collided with Anne sending her sprawling on the pavement in front of a stationary trolley car where she lay motionless. Émile ran to her side.

"Miss - Anne - Miss." But there was no response. Émile turned her onto her back. "Miss Anne..." Her eyes opened. "Miss..." In one quick motion he grasped her, one arm under her back, the other beneath her knees, and lifted her effortlessly. She wrapped her arms around his neck and he ran, carrying Anne's small frame, racing around the corner onto Appleton Street. The crowd had thinned and he was able to run along the sidewalk. Just then an elderly man appeared in front of them.

"Miss Anne? Miss, my dear, what has happened?"

Before Émile could find the words to reply Anne spoke up. "Take me home, Bromley, please." Bromley led Émile across the street to where the Wellingtons' motorcar was parked. He opened one of the back doors and Émile carefully placed Anne on the wide seat, then climbed in beside her. The car made an abrupt turn and raced off up the street. In less than a minute it pulled up to the portico at the Wellington house.

~ 28 ~

TUESDAY, JUNE 12

I'm all right, Mother, please don't fuss," begged Anne at the breakfast table the next morning.

"It was a riot, dear. It must have been awful. What were you doing down there? Who knows what might have happened to you?"

"Émile heard one of Jack's friends tell him that the workers in the dyehouse are getting sick. And that there was going to be a walkout. I had to find out what was going on. And I did. They're trying out some new way to scour wool and it is making the workers ill, Mother. We have to talk to father and Uncle Richard about it."

"Well, your uncle has his hands full right now, dear. I don't think he has time. And I don't want your father involved."

"But if they're really using that - that coal naphtha - it's deadly, Mother. It's been proven. Richard would want to know." Her mother seemed doubtful. Anne stood and left the dining room.

Jack sat at the kitchen table sipping steaming black coffee from a graniteware cup. His sisters had already left for school and his father was working under a tractor in the barn when

164

the harsh jangle of the telephone sounded. It rang three times before Jack rose, gingerly making his way to the door into the living room. He raised the handset to his ear and leaned to speak into the mouthpiece.

"Hello?"

"Jackie?"

"Anne?"

"How are you, Jackie? Feeling any better?"

"Well, I guess a bit. Why are you...?"

"Jackie, I need to talk to you."

"Anne, aren't you s'posed to be at school? Marie said there's a graduation rehearsal this morning."

"Yes, Jackie. But I'm not going. I - I had things to do at home. And I needed to talk to you."

Jack hesitated, leaning against the wall, struggling for words. "Annie, listen. I'm sorry - I mean, for the way things have gone for us. It's just - I can't - I don't want you to - it wouldn't be fair..."

"Jackie, please, just listen to me, okay? There's something I need to tell you, something very important." She paused, then continued. "Monday afternoon, at the mill, there was a walkout."

"I know. Well, I heard. Pierre Bousquet was telling me 'n my dad. Sounds like things got outta hand for a few minutes there."

"I'll say. The workers poured out of the mill and gathered on Race Street right in front of the dyehouse. They were joined by many others - from the silk mill, from American Thread, from the New England Mill. It got to be a huge mob. They were shouting slogans, waving signs and banners. Oh, Jackie," Anne's voice trembled, "Jackie, it was so awful."

Jack chuckled. "Gee, Annie, you talk like you were there. It's not..."

"I was, Jackie."

"What?"

165

"I said I was - I was there. Émile came to the Women's Home and told me about it. He said he heard - that Jim told you there was going to be a walkout."

"Huh? 'Mile went all the way to Holyoke to tell you? Why'd he go and do that? That boy had no right..."

"He did it because he knew I'd want to know. Not just about the walkout but about the dyehouse."

"What about it?"

"Jackie, remember that new scouring solution you told me about, coal something? It's making the men sick. Didn't Jim tell you about it?"

"Yeh, but..."

"The men have been nauseated and light-headed, several took falls, bad falls. Big men, Jackie. Strong men."

"Well, he said Poulin got sick, and he's an ox, it's true. But what of it?"

"Jackie, Émile heard that Poulin had a - a seizure - at home that night after he collapsed in the dyehouse. He went in the next day thinking he'd be able to work and Tuttle gave him the sack, right there."

"Well, Tuttle's an ass."

"But Jackie, don't you see, it's that coal stuff, it has to be. Don't you see?"

"Yeh, I guess so."

"Jackie, you're the chemistry expert. Isn't that dangerous?"

"Well, it's an aromatic hydrocarbon - it produces fumes."

"It's also called benzene, Jackie, *benzene*. Émile read about it at the library. It's dreadful, Jackie. Some scientist from Baltimore figured out that breathing the fumes can trigger seizures. They're caused by the solvent and they stop when the fumes go away."

"Émile knew all that?"

166

"Don't you see, Jackie? That's probably what happened to you. You had only been working in the dyehouse for a few days when it happened, right?"

"Yeh, I guess so."

"But Jackie, it means that maybe it's not - that maybe you don't have - epilepsy. That it could be the benzene."

"That's interesting, Annie, but..."

"Jackie, don't you see? This is wonderful news." There was just silence. "Jackie?"

"Yeh, yeh, wonderful. Thanks, Annie. But I gotta go..."

"I don't understand, Jackie. This is the best possible news. You should be relieved. Aren't you?"

Again there was only silence. Finally Jack replied. "Listen, Annie, maybe so, maybe so. But nobody's gonna believe it. They're still gonna think I'm - I'm crazy or..."

"Why, Jackie, why would they think that?"

"They just *will*, that's all. It's like a stamp, a label - Jack Bernard, the cripple - Jack Bernard, the guy who has fits."

"Jackie, no one will think that. And besides, you'll show them. You'll go to college, you'll have a career, you'll - you'll get married some day and have a family. All good things, Jackie, I promise."

"C'mon, Annie, who'd hire me after all this? And what girl would..." His voice trailed off into silence.

At first there was no reply. Then Anne's voice broke through the silence, thin but steady. "This girl, Jackie - this girl would." As she spoke Anne heard her own words echoing back along the telephone line as if she was saying them again. She was stunned and embarrassed at her outburst.

Finally Jack spoke. "Annie, you're the greatest gal in the world. You deserve more." Another long pause occurred. "Listen, thanks for calling. But I - I can't talk right now."

"Jackie? Will I see you at commencement tomorrow?"

"I don't think so, Annie, I'm not well enough. But Dad, Marie, and Claire will be there."

"Jackie," replied Anne softly, the ache in her heart nearly palpable in her frail voice.

"I'm sorry, Anne, I really am. Good-bye, Anne."

Later that morning Jack was leaning on a fence post at the end of the yard, looking down the length of the garden and the rows of thousands of bright green onion tops now six inches high and pointing skyward. But the fields were dry and the crops were in desperate need of water. The Bousquets and Bernards shared an irrigation system that, when in operation, pumped water from the river through iron pipes to the fields. Several days were required to set it up, work that could normally wait until July, after the planting and weeding had been tended to. Drought in June was unusual.

Émile, Pierre, and Elaine Bousquet were moving slowly along the rows, hoes in hand, weeding, working the soil between the plants. Marie stood on the kitchen doorstep watching her brother. She spoke to her father through the closed screen door. "He's fuming, Father, I just know he is. Letting the neighbors tend his garden, do his work, it's got to be churning his insides, just the sight of it."

Charles nodded. "It doesn't set right with that boy for anyone to be doin' his work for 'im, that's for sure."

"He says he's not going to graduation. He's got to, for Anne, for Carolyn. Can't you talk some sense into him?"

"Let 'im be, dear, let 'im be. He's got enough crosses to bear 'bout now." The weeding complete, Pierre and his daughter waved to Jack as they crossed the yard, hoes shouldered. Émile carried two bushel baskets of weeds to the compost pile beyond the barn, then approached Jack smiling, an empty basket dangling from each hand.

"Thanks, 'Mile." Jack nodded to his neighbor, then shifted his gaze to the fields beyond.

168

"So-kay, Jay-Jay, so-kay. Me 'n Pa be geddin' the pum' goin' tomorra, too." Jack nodded but looked away.

"You feelin' beddu tuday?" asked Émile, though he knew Jack well enough to gauge how he was feeling.

"About the same, 'Mile. Just the same. I'm useless."

"You be beddu, Jay-Jay, real soon. Why don' you read in summa them collesh books, ya know, gedda head star?"

Jack shook his head. "No college, Émile, not for this boy. Not now - maybe never. I can't remember things, I get confused, I'm a wreck, Émile, a wreck."

Émile set the two baskets on the ground, then stood up straight and looked squarely into Jack's eyes.

"Don gif up, Jay-Jay. You can do it. You ga lots o' frens, you papa and sistas, an' Anne. They c'n hep ya."

Jack shook his head. "They don't understand, Jay-Jay. I keep tryin' to tell them but they don't understand." Jack paused, poking a willow branch into the grass at his feet.

"It's so maddening, 'Mile, trying to make people understand what I'm saying, what I'm goin' through. Do you know what I mean?" He looked up into his friend's face.

Émile took a step forward. His dark eyes grew round, his voice soft. "Ayeh, ayeh. I know washa mean, Jay-Jay, I sher do." Then he turned and ambled away, a bushel basket swinging from each arm.

High School, Holyoke, Mass.

~ 29 ~

WEDNESDAY, JUNE 13

*H*olyoke High School - 53rd Annual Commencement *Exercises* read a purple and white banner hung over the stage of the high school auditorium. Beneath those words was the school motto in Greek, Αἰέν ἀριστεύει, *Ever to Excel.* It was a Wednesday evening in mid-June and family and friends of the graduating seniors were streaming through the wide doors, milling in the aisles, talking excitedly.

Helen Wellington and Nina Calavetti were among the first arrivals. In the foyer they smiled warmly at Marie Bernard as each accepted a commencement program. Helen paused and extended her hand to Marie. "Thank you, my dear, for everything," she said, looking gratefully into the young woman's eyes. "Will we see the rest of your family today?"

"Just Father and Claire, I expect," replied a blushing Marie. The two women quickly claimed seats near the front of the auditorium. Anne's father had wanted very much to attend but his poor health made it impossible. His brother, Anne's Uncle Richard, and his wife Charlotte arrived shortly and were seated next to Helen and Nina.

Soon the auditorium was nearly full and the school band struck up a medley of patriotic songs including *America the Beautiful, Battle Hymn of the Republic,* and *Stars and Stripes Forever.* As they played, Helen turned to greet friends nearby but her eye was also scanning the auditorium. She had been resisting the temptation to hope that Tom might appear to see his sister graduate. She was more hopeful of seeing Charles and Claire Bernard to whom she was determined to speak.

Just then the opening strains of *Pomp and Circumstance* echoed off the auditorium walls. The audience stood in unison and turned toward the rear as the class of 1917 entered the auditorium, black robes and mortar boards lending a note of solemnity to the occasion. They were proceeding up one aisle very slowly, some still struggling with the special step they had been practicing for weeks. When she caught sight of Carolyn just entering at the rear, Helen touched Nina's arm. Several minutes went by before Anne, the next to the last graduate in the procession, appeared. Riveted on her daughter, Helen's eyes glistened, then shifted to the doors that had closed behind the last graduate.

At that moment Helen observed Claire and Marie Bernard opening and holding the other set of doors to the auditorium. Her heart leapt when she saw Charles and Jack stepping through the entryway into the auditorium. She watched as the family took seats in the back row next to the aisle down which the graduates would exit. She could see that Jack was holding a bouquet.

When all the graduates were seated across the front of the auditorium, their backs to the audience, the ceremony began. In his invocation Reverend Curran, rector of St. John's Episcopal Church, called upon all present to thank God for this opportunity to honor such an outstanding group of Holyoke's youth assembled before them. Mr. Donahue, Jack's track coach and chemistry teacher who was now principal, rose to welcome all and to praise the graduating class. The choir sang an anthem, *Their Native Land*, then the class salutatorian read a poem in honor of the occasion, *Gladden Our Hearts This Day.*

Soon it was time for the presentation of awards. Carolyn was named outstanding student in the Commercial course. As she accepted the bronze medallion, she smiled to the presenter but did not look up as applause rippled through the auditorium. Miss Edwards then presented the Literature Award to Anne. The emotional and well-liked teacher momentarily violated the formality of the occasion, kissing Anne on the cheek and hugging her. Claire, Marie, and Charles all turned and smiled at Jack at that moment and the young man permitted himself a grin and nod toward his family.

Following the awards the choir sang another anthem, *Oh Italia, Italia, Beloved*. Then the mayor of Holyoke stepped to the podium and delivered a lengthy, self-congratulatory speech about his city and his graduates about to be sent off into the unknown. He made mention of events in Europe and the need to honor the many young men, including several of the graduates, who would soon be shipping out. The class valedictorian followed the mayor, reciting a poem he had written entitled *Answering the Call*.

At last the moment came for conferring of diplomas. The audience sat in silence as each student strode across the stage, received a diploma, and shook the hands of the principal, the mayor, and the chairman of the school committee. Only when Olivia White, the last student, had received her diploma, did Mr. Donahue speak the words: "Ladies, gentlemen, families, friends, I present to you the Holyoke High School graduating class of 1917."

With those words the audience rose as one, beaming, cheering, and applauding. The graduates turned toward their families and friends, a mixture of pride, delight, and relief illuminating their faces. For a moment Anne's eyes were squarely on her mother's, but then they rose toward the back of the auditorium and brightened suddenly. When she looked back at her mother there was relief in her expression. Carolyn was looking a bit dazed by the noise and excitement but managed to smile weakly at her mother and Helen.

Finally Father Kaplinksy, Pastor of the Parish of Mater Dolorosa, gave a spirited benediction, asking God to watch over His children, one and all. With that the band once again played the familiar strains of *Pomp and Circumstance*. The graduates exited by the aisle closest to Helen and Nina and the two mothers smiled warmly to all the graduates while saving a special smile for their daughters.

Jack, who was standing next to the aisle, brightened momentarily and nodded as familiar faces marched by. He was looking first for Carolyn. When he finally spotted her a dozen rows from him, he tried to catch her eye. Their eyes met briefly, but as she passed Jack could see that her attention was diverted past him to the doors at the back of the auditorium. He turned to see where she was looking and there in the foyer, just beyond the opened doors, stood a tall, dark-haired man wearing tinted eyeglasses, smiling warmly, and looking directly at Carolyn. As she passed the man spoke to her and handed her a single, long-stemmed rose. Then he turned and left. Jack was surprised and curious about this brief encounter that seemed to have been noticed by no one else.

Just then his father tugged on his arm and Jack turned. Anne was approaching and she was on his side of the aisle. In a few seconds she was walking toward him, beaming. She paused in front of him, waiting for him to act. There was an awkward moment. Then, as if he'd forgotten, Jack produced the bouquet of pink and white carnations, much like those that Anne had presented to him at his graduation a year earlier, and Anne's face lit up. "Congratulations, Annie. These are for you," he said smiling.

Anne took the bouquet with a wide smile and kissed him on the cheek. "Thank you, Jackie," she said. She turned and smiled at Charles, Marie, and Claire, then rushed off to catch up with the rest of the procession which had already exited the auditorium.

Moments later the audience was pressing through the exits into the foyer, then out the main entrance onto the lawn where they mingled with the graduates. For a moment the four Bernards stood quietly on the sidewalk. Then Claire took Jack's hand and pulled him toward Anne, Carolyn, and their mothers. Marie and Charles followed docilely. Claire kept pulling on Jack's arm until he and Anne were face to face. Jack blushed, momentarily scolded his sister, then turned to Anne.

"So, the Literature Award, huh? No surprise there."

Anne and her mother laughed. "Well, I do like to read, Jackie - as you know."

"*There is no frigate like a book...,*" began Jack.

"*...to take us lands away,*" continued Anne. "Emily Dickinson, a true kindred spirit." Then Anne stepped up close to Jack and spoke softly into his ear.

"Thank you, Jackie, for coming today. It means a lot to me."

"Yeh, sure," replied Jack.

"What made you decide to come, Jackie?"

Jack hesitated, then spoke softly.

"It was you, and Émile. I realized that, well, we have to make do, don't we? Everybody does, one way or another."

Anne smiled and nodded, but her smile quickly faded. Her face was scarlet. "I - I am sorry about what I said this morning - on the telephone. I should never have..."

"Don't be sorry, Annie. You were right. I've been a fool. I got a lot to live for. And like you said, I'll just have to show 'em." Then he looking squarely into Anne's green eyes and smiled.

"*We'll show 'em.*"

~ 30 ~

THURSDAY, JUNE 14

Nina rose at the usual time the following morning. In the kitchen she started coffee in a gray graniteware pot on the stove. As she turned toward the ice box she saw it, a note propped against the salt shaker in the center of the kitchen table. She reached down, picked it up, and stood stiffly as she read. Then she looked up and out the window into the small backyard where the morning dew glistened on the thin grass. She gasped, tears welled up in her eyes, and her entire body shook as the note dropped to the floor.

Several gentle taps on her bedroom door woke Anne from a deep sleep. "Anne, dear." It was her mother. She pushed the door open and spoke to her daughter. "Anne, may I come in?"

Anne began to stir, rolled over to glance at the clock on her bedside table, then straightened her hair.

"Yes, Mother, come in." Helen entered and looked gravely at her daughter.

"I'm sorry to wake you, but honey..."

"What is it, Mother?" She could see her mother was upset.

"It's Carolyn - she's gone."

"Gone? What do you mean?"

"She's disappeared. Nina just telephoned. She's in an awful state. Apparently Carolyn left early this morning. She took some of her clothes and a valise."

"Carolyn? She left? Why? Did they argue?"

"No, I don't think so. But she left a note. She just said she had plans, that she would be all right. Not to worry, it said."

Helen's face suddenly contorted and her eyes filled with tears. "Not to worry? Oh, my God, how could she?" And Helen grasped her daughter and held her in a tight embrace.

~ *31* ~

Jan Krawczyk stood at the front door of a large, rambling farmhouse on a gravel road outside Lowell, Massachusetts. Removing his cap, the strapping young man nervously arranged his shag of blonde hair, then pressed the doorbell. Several seconds went by with no response. Finally a voice could be heard.

"*Oui, oui, un moment,* please."

At last the knob turned, the door swung open, and an attractive, middle-aged woman with light hair done up in a bun smiled at the visitor. "'Allo."

"Hello, ma'am," began Jan, smiling nervously.

"May I 'elp you?"

"Yes, ma'am. My name is Jan - Jan Krawczyk." He paused.

"*Jean?*"

"No, ma'am, Jan," he repeated, carefully pronouncing his first name. "I'm from Holyoke." Then he glanced nervously to his right. Carolyn Ford stepped into view.

"Carolyn, *mon Dieu,* Carolyn. Where - how?"

"Hello, Adrienne, it is so nice to see you again," began Carolyn.

"My dear, it ees wonderful to see you. I am - astonished. Please, please, come in." And she led them into the sitting room off the foyer. "What brings you here? Is everything all right at home, dear? Your mother?"

"Yes, yes, everything is fine. I'm sorry to arrive unannounced, but there wasn't time to write. And Father said to come anytime."

"It is no matter, my dear, it is so lovely to see you. And this young man - Jan - it is a pleasure. Weel you have some tea?" Jan and Carolyn sat in soft, comfortable chairs gazing at the elegant furniture and charming decorative touches that surrounded them. The small fireplace was framed by a brass screen. The polished marble hearth shone as though no fire had ever burned there. After several minutes their hostess returned with a silver tea tray and served her two young visitors.

"Now, tell me, what brings you two to Westford?"

Jan caught Carolyn's eye. She looked shyly toward Adrienne, then spoke softly. "I - I was hoping - wondering - if it would be all right if I were to visit - for just a few days. Jan has been kind enough to accompany me on the train, but he is going on to Lewiston."

Adrienne looked at Carolyn. "Of course, my dear, of course." Then she turned to Jan. "Lewiston - where is that?"

"In Maine, ma'am. I'm hoping to find work in a paper mill. I just got laid off from the Schofield Mill in Chicopee and there's no other work around Holyoke right now, so I thought I'd try Maine."

"Well, eet is very brave of you, young man, to strike out on your own like thees. And when you find work, I presume, this young lady will be joining you?"

Jan blushed. "Oh, no, ma'am. I just offered to help her get here. I'd better be on my way..."

"Now? Nonsense, Jan, you will at least stay the night, eh? You look as though you could use a good night's sleep."

"That'd be very kind of you, ma'am. We been on our way since before sunup."

It was nearly ten o'clock when Jan shouldered his rucksack and retired to the sun porch where Adrienne had made up a daybed for him. Adrienne and Carolyn sat in the parlor speaking in hushed tones for the sake of Jan and the children who were fast asleep upstairs.

"He seems a fine young man, Carolyn, this Jan. You are fond of him?"

Carolyn blushed. "Jan is a friend, a good friend, that's all. It just happened that we were both traveling this way and he was kind enough to accompany me. He needs to find work and I hope he succeeds. He's a very good worker."

Adrienne chose her words carefully. "And, er, *Monsieur* Thomas, what about heem?" As she asked the question she looked intently into the eyes of her young guest, suspecting there would be more to learn from her face than from her words.

Raising her delicate chin slightly, Carolyn spoke softly, trying hard to maintain her composure: "Thomas has left Holyoke. He is spending the summer - with an old school chum at a family house on Cape Cod."

"Oh, my, what a nice way to pass the summer. But hees job?"

"He has quit his job. It wasn't for him - so he said."

"Ahh, I see. So young Thomas has the luxury of doing *what* he wants, *when* he wants, *with whom* he wants, eh?" Carolyn's eyes grew large and moist. She drew a quick breath.

"Ooh, he has hurt you, my dear?" asked Adrienne. As she spoke she knelt next to Carolyn's chair. Carolyn bit her lip, then looked away. Adrienne took Carolyn's hand. "He ees a fool, Thomas, if he gives up a good job and such a lovely young girl for one summer by the sea." Carolyn turned and looked into her eyes. "Carolyn, dear, have you talked to your mother about thees - thees hurt?" Carolyn looked down and shook her head slightly. There was something in her voice that told Adrienne that she had probed as much as she should, at least for now. "But she knows that you are here, right?"

Carolyn nodded. "Your father, he weel be home in a few days. He weel be so very pleased to see you."

"I don't understand," Nina was saying through her tears. "Why would she do this? What has gotten into her?" She was seated on an upholstered divan in her parlor, dabbing at her cheeks with a lace handkerchief. Helen and Anne sat on a cushioned settee opposite Nina, not sure what to say to console her.

"Nina, dear," began Helen, "maybe you should start by sending cables to some of your family. Wouldn't that make sense?"

"But I have practically no family," said Nina tearfully. "My parents are gone and my only sister, Maria, and her husband are visiting with his people in New York City. If they knew anything about this, they would surely have contacted me. And their son Anthony still lives with them. Other than that, there's no one."

"Does Carolyn have any friends that might know something?" inquired Helen.

"Anne is Carolyn's best friend, of course. There are just a few other girls at school that she is acquainted with, at least that I know of." She turned to Anne. "Can you think of anyone, Anne, dear? Anyone at all?"

Anne knew more about Carolyn Ford than almost anyone, yet she was at a loss. She shook her head slowly, her gaze cast downward. Suddenly she looked up into Nina's eyes.

"What about Anthony's friend, Jan?"

"John? John who?" retorted Nina. "I don't know of any friend of Anthony's named John."

"No, Jan. Jan something. He's Polish and works at Schofield Paper in Willimansett," recalled Anne. "Carolyn told me she met him through Anthony and they had - they went out to the soda shop once or twice. That's all I know."

Nina looked at Helen and began to cry again. Helen stood, then went to Nina's side, knelt next to her, and took her hand. "There, there, dear, don't jump to any conclusions. I'm sure nothing has... Why don't you telephone Anthony? He'll know about this young man, how to reach him." Nina asked the operator to ring her sister's house but there was no answer. Anthony also worked at the Schofield mill. He probably didn't return from work until evening. She would try to call him then.

Helen and Anne walked the several blocks back to the Wellington home. "I'm sure this has nothing to do with that boy, Mother. She only met him a few weeks ago. Mrs. Calavetti shouldn't be worried about him."

"Well, dear, she is, and I can understand why."

"What do you mean, Mother?" As she spoke, Anne could see fear in her mother's eyes.

"Because Nina is worried that Carolyn is going to end up like Nina did at her age."

Anne's eyes met her mother's in silence. "Oh, Mother, she would never..." Suddenly they were both worried anew for Carolyn.

That evening Nina telephoned Helen. She had reached Anthony, she began, her voice breaking as she spoke. Jan had lost his job at the paper mill nearly two weeks earlier. Unable to find other work in Holyoke, he had left for Maine early that morning promising to send word when he was settled. Neither Anthony nor Jan's family had heard from him yet.

181

Was anyone traveling with him? she had asked. No, Anthony had explained, Jan had left alone. He had seen him off at the train depot in Chicopee himself.

"Well, that at least is a relief, Nina," offered Helen optimistically. But she knew that her friend was not convinced and was imagining her daughter following the young man to God knows what kind of life in Maine. Helen thanked Nina for calling, urged her not to worry, and promised to speak with her the following morning. When she hung up the telephone she stood in silence, her back to Anne.

"Mother," Anne said cautiously. "Do you think we ought to try to reach Tommy at Digsy's summer place? I don't mean that he would know her whereabouts, but maybe he should be told."

"Oh, I don't know, dear. Your brother…"

"I know what you're thinking, Mother. But Tommy isn't entirely self-centered - I mean, not when he's thinking clearly. You know, he really cares about Carolyn. He told her - well - in his way."

"Anne, are you telling me that your brother and Carolyn - that they had some kind of - of understanding?"

Anne looked at her mother, then down at her hands. "No - I don't know - it was hard to tell. She is always so timid, and he is always so, well, Tommy. I just think he might want to know, he might care, that's all."

Helen sighed. "Oh, honey, I really do wish that were true. That boy has so much to offer, if he would only stand up and face his - his demons." Helen turned away from her daughter abruptly. "Would you try to reach him, dear?"

❧ ❧ ❧ ❧ ❧ ❧

It took almost an hour for a long distance operator to return Anne's call. Anne was waiting by the telephone in the library. It had been nearly two weeks since Tom had left and

182

Anne was not sure what to expect. "So, how are you doing? Having a good time with Digsy?"

"Oh, yeh, ripping, Annie, ripping. We played tennis all morning and this afternoon we're going sailing out on the bay with Gloria and a friend of hers."

"Wow, Tommy, it sounds like you are really rusticating."

"Yeh, it's great." There was a long pause. "Although, I've been doing a lot of - of thinking, lately."

"About what, Tommy?"

"I don't know, it's all so confusing. It's - it's like everything is getting out of control..." His voice trailed off.

"Tommy?"

"So, how's Jack doing?"

"About the same, Tommy. But actually there's something else I wanted to talk to you about. It's - Carolyn."

"Carolyn? What about her? I apologized to her, honest I did."

"She's gone, Tommy. Carolyn has disappeared."

"Disappeared?"

"Well, I mean, she's run away. She left yesterday, the morning after commencement. She just left. I guess she took some of her clothes and a couple of valises. She wrote a note to her mother saying she had plans but not to worry. Nina is fit to be tied, Tommy, and so are Mother and I." Her voice cracked. "I'm worried, Tommy, and scared."

She waited for her brother to reply, but heard nothing. Finally she continued. "I was hoping maybe - maybe you'd know something, or perhaps you might have a thought about what this is all about." Still there was no reply. "Tommy?"

"Yeh, I'm thinking, I'm thinking."

Anne continued. "She seemed really happy at graduation, she smiled and laughed a lot, and we talked after the ceremony and she didn't give me any hint. I thought - I thought we were, you know, best friends. And she's gone. I can't imagine what her mother is thinking. Tommy?"

183

"Yeh, I'm - I..."

"Her mother is afraid that she's run off with some boy. Tommy, if you know anything, anything at all, please tell me. We're all worried sick about her."

"Well, if you think she's with me, forget it. She's not. She'll probably never talk to me again."

There was another long pause. "Tommy?"

"Yeh, yeh. Listen, Annie, I gotta go. We're meeting the girls in just a few minutes."

Anne was chagrined. "Oh, I see. You don't have time for your sister, or your mother, or Carolyn. You only have time for yourself."

"That's not it, Annie. I'm worried, too. It's just that I really don't have any ideas. But I'll - I'll do some thinking. I promise. I just don't..." His voice trailed off again. It was hard to tell whether he was truly concerned about Carolyn or distracted by other matters.

"Well, Tommy, you go ahead. But think about it, won't you? Please?"

"I will, Annie, I am..."

Anne might have been distressed at her brother's response, but there was something in his voice, something in the usually unflappable Tom's voice that left her wondering whether he might know more than he was letting on. She decided to cling to the hope that either his conscience or his concern for Carolyn would elicit some response. She just hoped it wouldn't be too long in coming.

~ 32 ~

FRIDAY, JUNE 15

Awaiting Carolyn and Jan the next morning was a sumptuous breakfast of oatmeal, a soft-boiled egg, strong black coffee, and a flaky pastry Adrienne called a *croissant*, the likes of which neither of her young guests had ever tasted before. Upon finishing this feast and thanking Adrienne repeatedly, Jan said his good-byes, promising to write to Carolyn when he had some news about a job and asking her to write him. Then he was off, ambling down the dirt road, his rucksack slung over his shoulder.

"A fine young man, eh?" asked Adrienne as she and Carolyn stood on the porch watching him disappear around the bend in the road.

"Yes, he is. I hope he can find work."

Just then a small commotion could be heard from above. "Well, my dear, the children are awake. Would you like to meet them?"

"Yes, very much," replied Carolyn, her eyes sparkling with anticipation.

Colleen, the Wellingtons' maid, rapped lightly on Anne's bedroom door. "Miss Anne, you've had a telephone call from

Master Thomas, all the way from Cape Cod. He said he would call again at half eight, Miss."

Anne thanked Colleen, looked at the clock on her bedside table, then rose and dressed hurriedly. She was seated in the library waiting nervously when the telephone emitted a piercing jangle.

"Annie, it's Tommy. I was up half the night thinking about Carolyn and, well, there is something I know of that might - might be a clue. But she swore me to secrecy. That's why I don't feel right about…"

"What, Tommy? Tell me, please. She could be in trouble, don't you see? You must tell me."

"Remember the day you asked me to meet her at the shoe shop?"

"Yes, I remember."

"There was a man in the shop and he was making her very uncomfortable. He gave her a note."

"A note? What kind of note?"

"Well, when she saw me she asked me to walk her home. Actually she pretended like she was expecting me and took my arm and we rushed out of the place."

"Did he follow you?"

"No, no, I don't think so. But when we got to her house she handed me the note and asked me to read it."

"What did it say?"

"I swore to keep it a secret, Annie."

"Tommy, you've got to tell me. She could be in trouble and we need to help her. Please."

"He claimed he was her father."

"What?" replied an astonished Anne. "What did she say?"

"Nothing, really, she was just very nervous. He said he wanted to meet her."

"So what happened? Did she agree to meet him?"

"I offered to go with her, I mean, to go along if she decided to see him, you know, just to keep an eye on her. A

186

few days later she called me at the mill and asked me to go with her to Hampden Park after work. He was there - with his wife. He seemed very nice. They both seemed very nice. I think Carolyn began to take to him - to both of them. The last thing they asked was if they could see her again and she said yes. She seemed really happy, Annie. You should have seen her smile."

Tears were streaming down Anne's cheeks as she listened to her brother. This was the Tommy she remembered, that she had missed so the last few years.

"Annie, are you still there?"

"Yes, I'm here. Oh, Tommy, I'm so scared for her. And Mother and Nina are beside themselves." Suddenly Anne got herself under control. "And that was the last you heard about her father?"

"Well, yes. But then I saw her at the train station, you know, the day after the Senior Formal. She mentioned that he was coming to graduation."

"You saw her - that Saturday?"

"Yeh, I was waiting for the train and she was just coming out of the Depot. She said she was checking the schedule for a friend. It looked like she had a ticket in her hand."

"Oh my Lord, Tommy, she must have already been planning her escape - I mean her trip. Did she tell you what her plans were?"

"No, and I didn't ask, I wasn't really sure that it was a ticket and she was telling me about you and about Jack and..." He paused. "But just before we parted she told me that her father was planning on attending her graduation. *It's gonna be a busy day*, I remember her saying."

"Tommy, it was the morning after graduation that she disappeared. You don't think that man took her away? Or that she followed him somewhere?"

"Maybe, I don't know, maybe. But he seemed nice, Annie, like he really cared about her."

187

"I'd better be saying good-bye, Tommy. I need to talk to Mother about this. And to Nina."

"No, Annie, you can't. I promised Carolyn I wouldn't tell anyone."

Anne was furious with her brother. "Do you care anything about her?"

"Of course I do."

"Well, then, you have to understand. She could be who knows *where* with who knows *who* doing who knows *what*? One more thing. Did she mention Jan, Jan Krawczyk? From Chicopee?"

"Never heard of him. Who's he?"

"Well, Tommy, Jan is Carolyn's boyfriend. And he's disappeared, too."

There was silence on the line but Anne waited for a reply. She knew she might be overstating the facts, that there might be no connection between Jan's and Carolyn's disappearance. But she thought it might prod her brother just a bit more.

"Listen, Annie, I've gotta go. But call and leave word as soon as you hear anything, please."

~ *33* ~

Nina and Helen spent several hours at the Holyoke Police Station with Chief Hanrahan and a detective. Anne had offered to go along but Helen had insisted she stay at home in case there should be a telegram, telephone call, or other message. Nina tearfully described her daughter and tried, with Helen's assistance, to answer their questions.

Nina had been stunned at the news that Carolyn's father had contacted her. Carolyn's father had been completely absent from their lives since the day he left, nearly nineteen years earlier. Never a letter, a card, a visit, although Nina admitted that she did not try in any way to encourage him. She explained that he was simply not a suitable father for a child to have any contact with. She would not elaborate except to say that he had been associating with some unsavory and disreputable men. She believed he had moved shortly thereafter to Lowell. Beyond that she knew nothing.

The detective was taking careful notes. He promised to make some inquiries with the Lowell police in hopes of locating Carolyn's father in that city. Then Chief Hanrahan, as gently as he knew how, raised the question of whether someone might be pretending to be Carolyn's father. It was true, admitted Nina, that she had never shown her daughter so much as a photograph of him nor given her the least little information about him. The less said, the better, she believed. Unfortunately, she realized, that might mean that someone could have tried to impersonate Carolyn's father, but it seemed an unlikely strategy. Most daughters would know their own father.

"Did it ever occur to you, Mrs. Calavetti, that your daughter might have been curious about her father? Might have wished to know something about him?"

"If she was," replied Nina haltingly, "she never made her wishes known to me." She paused, her expression turning stolid. "But then, she would know how I felt about that, I presume." She dabbed her eyes with a lace handkerchief.

The chief and the detective also spoke at length about the young Polish man, Jan Krawczyk.

"Sounds like a suspicious character," said the detective. Nina knew nothing about him beyond what her nephew had told her. Again the detective assured her that the police in several of the larger manufacturing cities in Maine would be contacted and asked to make inquiries. Both men tried to be reassuring about all that would be done to locate Carolyn.

Later that day Helen and Anne were seated in the family's library, hoping so that the telephone would ring with news that Carolyn had returned or had contacted her mother. They were making lists on long sheets of paper, lists of every possible clue to Carolyn's whereabouts, every friend or acquaintance, no matter how remote, who might have some information. They agreed that Anne should visit the high school and try to speak with several of Carolyn's teachers, including Miss Edwards, on the chance that one of them might know something, might have overheard something, might have observed something that could be a clue.

Suddenly there came the rattle of the front door. Anne rose and ran from the library into the foyer. Standing in the doorway was Tom carrying a single valise and looking uncharacteristically tired and unkempt.

"Tommy." Anne ran to him and hugged him.

Helen came to the library door and looked on impassively.

"Thomas. Welcome home. What brings you this way?" she asked in a reserved tone.

"Carolyn." He paused, looking expectantly, first into his mother's eyes, then into his sister's.

"Any news?"

"No," replied Helen. "Nothing." But as she looked into her son's face, she observed a certain softness in his expression, a slight tremor in his lips.

"But thank you, Thomas, for coming home. Mrs. Calavetti will be very glad to hear of it."

"Well, honestly, I don't know what I can do. But I couldn't sleep last night after talking to Annie, and I had to come back, for Carolyn - I - I..." The normally verbose young man was unusually taciturn. He hung his head in silence.

"Yes?" said Helen softly. But she hesitated to press him. Her voice attenuated. "Thomas, you must have had an exhausting trip. Why don't you go upstairs and freshen up? I'll have Moira draw you a hot bath."

Helen and Anne stood and watched as Tom climbed the broad stairway to the second floor. Mother and daughter stepped back into the library, now speaking in whispers.

"I barely know my own son," said Helen softly. "He seems a stranger. What is going on, Anne, do you know?"

"I think maybe I do."

~ 34 ~

SATURDAY, JUNE 16

The following day Claire walked up the driveway, returning from the Saturday Confirmation class at St. Agnes Church, her bookbag slung over one shoulder, skirts dragging in the gravel. She was carrying the afternoon edition of the *Holyoke Daily Transcript*, looking at the front page as she walked. Marie was about to scold her sister for not watching where she was going.

"Another story about union men in Holyoke. What're they doin' there, Marie? And what's a *Bull-shuv-ik,* anyway? " Marie took the paper from her sister.

"No concern of ours, Claire. Now go in and get out of your good clothes. Maybe you can tend to the chickens - you forgot them this morning." Marie passed the paper to her father who was seated at the kitchen table.

"Go easy on her now," advised Charles. He opened the paper and spread it on the table. Even though he was no longer working in the mill, news of union activity always attracted his attention.

Nearly a half hour went by and Marie was still busy over a kettle of soup simmering on the stove when she heard the creak of a chair in the living room. Peering around the corner she found Claire seated next to the telephone, the handset to her ear. She grabbed the handset out of Claire's hand and placed it gently on the hook as Claire protested.

"You are not to be listening in on other peoples' conversations, Claire. Do you hear me? Father, Claire has been listening in on the party line again."

"But that man has the funniest way of talking..."

"Claire, dear," said her father, "those are private conversations. You wouldn't want someone eavesdropping on you, would you?"

"What a funny word - eavesdropping. Is it like the side of a house falling down or something, Daddy?"

"It means listening to things you're not 'sposed to, Claire, and it's wrong. Now no more of that, understand?" Charles reached out and drew his youngest child close to him. "Claire, honey, would you do your father a favor?" She nodded. "Would you try to cheer up your brother? He needs a little lift, okay? He's out back." Claire nodded again and stood up. "Take the paper out to him, too. That'll occupy him for a while."

Claire preferred talking to her brother these days. *At least he's not always criticizing me like Marie*, she thought. She stepped out into the yard and walked barefoot across the cool grass. Jack was seated in the glider he and his father had built for their mother some years back.

"Jackie, why is Marie always scolding me?" asked Claire, dropping onto the bench next to her brother.

"She's just trying to help you, sweetie. You know that, don't you?"

Claire's expression, usually bright and animated, was dreary. "I suppose, but Sister Jean does that to me all day in school. When I get home I need a rest from being scolded. I deserve it, don't you think?" She looked up into her brother's eyes. "You're on my side, aren't you?" With her lips she formed an exaggerated self-pitying pout, an expression she knew was certain to put a smile on her brother's face.

Jack laughed. "Always - and so are Marie and Dad..."

Claire was not convinced but seemed to be relaxing. Just then she remembered the newspaper and handed it to Jack. "Jackie, what's a *Bull-shuv-ik*? Can you explain it to me?"

"Well, it's a Russian revolutionary who - why do you want to know that?"

"Didn't you hear? The Bureau of Investigation, in Washington - they're looking for three *Bull-shuv-iks* who were in Holyoke last week. There's pictures of them in today's paper." Jack was looking idly out at the hills to the east, barely hearing Claire's words. "Garfield, Grant, and Taylor were their names. Isn't it funny how they have presidents' names?"

He turned abruptly and stared at his sister, a confused look on his face.

"What's the matter?" asked Claire.

"Where did you see that? Show me." Claire held up the newspaper, pointing to a story on the first page. FEDERAL AGENTS PURSUING UNION ACTIVISTS read the headline. Jack drew the paper from his sister's hands and began reading the article.

"What is it, Jackie?"

"Nothing, sweetie, I - I just thought - those names, they - they sound familiar." Jack looked at the headline, then unfolded the paper and saw the photograph.

"Sweet mother of mercy," he whispered. "I have to make a telephone call."

"Well, good luck. That man on the party line's been talking for an hour," Claire was saying as Jack broke into a run toward the kitchen door.

"This is Jack Bernard. May I speak to Anne, please?"

"Miss Anne is not in right now, sir. Would you like to speak to Master Thomas?"

194

"Tommy? He's home? Yes, please, may I?" A minute later a familiar voice greeted him.

"Hello, Jack? Hey-hey, old chum, how are you doing?"

"I'm okay, Tommy, when'd you get home?"

"Just this afternoon. I - I had to see if I could do anything, you know? Anne and Mother are just so worried about Carolyn."

"Worried? What about Carolyn?"

"No one's told you, Jack? Carolyn's gone - she's missing."

"Missing? What do you mean? When?"

Tom recounted Carolyn's disappearance to his friend, the note, Jan Krawczyk, the police, everything he knew. He explained that Anne had called him on Cape Cod and how he had traveled by train that morning. "Anne and Mother are visiting with Mrs. Calavetti right now. They're going mad with worry. I've been trying to figure out where Carolyn could be, Jack."

"Tommy, have you seen today's *Transcript*? Look at the front page." The afternoon paper lay unopened on the library table next to Tom.

"You mean that business about the union organizers? Yeh, so?"

"I was there, Tommy, the night they held a rally, down in the Flats, after my shift. I forgot all about it, somehow, but when Claire read the names of those guys it suddenly came back to me."

"But Jack, what does that have to do with...?"

"Look at the picture, Tommy," interrupted Jack. "That guy in the middle, Garfield. He was at Commencement, I swear. He was wearing dark glasses and had a hat pulled down over his face, but I saw him near the door. I don't think anyone else saw him, but I did - I swear it was him."

"So what if you did?"

"He gave Carolyn a flower, and she smiled at him like she knew him, and she seemed so happy. Tommy, I think that's Carolyn's father."

"Her father?" replied Tom. "I don't know, Jack. I don't think so."

"How would you know, Tommy?"

"Well," replied Tom, hesitating. "I - I met him - just a couple weeks ago. He asked to meet Carolyn and, well, she asked me to go with her. He and his wife - they were in Hampden Park. We talked with them for a while. Real nice folks. The picture's pretty grainy - it doesn't look much like the guy."

"Well I got a really good look at him, twice. Once at the union meeting, then at commencement. But I never made the connection until now."

"If that is her dad, maybe that's where she's gone - to live with him."

"Tommy, the Feds are after him. If she's with him it could be bad business - she could get caught up in a raid. She could get hurt, Tommy. We've got to find her and get her away from him." Through the handset Jack could hear noise in the background.

"That's Anne and Mother, Jack, they're just coming in. I better talk with them. I'll call you later."

"Mother and I and Mrs. C. went through Carolyn's things. It felt very strange, you know?" explained Anne to Tom a few minutes later. "As if she had d..." Suddenly Anne's face blanched.

"So did you find anything that might give us a hint? Anything at all?" pressed Tom.

"Not much, really. Mostly school papers and some needlework patterns and instructions. I know she kept a diary, but I suppose she took that with her. The only thing that I could see that might be a little hint was this."

Anne showed her brother a blank sales slip from Gregoire's Shoe Shop. It had been torn from a pad, but the tear was uneven as if it had been removed in a hurry. Written in a scrawl across the pad was an address:

150 Main St Westfld

Anne and Tom looked at it together, each thinking about its possible significance.

"Tommy, you don't think this could be where Carolyn is? Right in Westfield? Maybe that's where her father lives."

"I have to go there, Annie, first thing tomorrow."

"Shouldn't we talk to Mother and Mrs. C. first?"

"No need to get their hopes up. It'll probably prove to be just nothing - a fool's errand."

"Tommy, why don't you talk to Jack first? Westfield's not so very large. He might even know who lives at that address."

"Yeh, I will. I'll take the trolley so no one will have to know where I'm going. But you have to help me by making up a story for Mother. Just for a few hours."

~ 35 ~

SUNDAY, JUNE 17

Tom and Jack stood in the Bernard kitchen late the next morning. Tom had taken the trolley from Holyoke to Park Square in Westfield, then changed cars at the Trolley Centre where the Holyoke-Westfield line met the Springfield line. Less than a mile from the square he had disembarked in front of an old farmhouse.

"It's just a shabby old farm, kind of long in the tooth," explained Tom. "These old folks - Bascom was the name on the door - they were nice and friendly. They even offered me tea. But they didn't know anything about Carolyn, and I don't think they were hiding anything, Jack, I really don't."

"Yeh, my dad knows them from the Grange. Not the kinda folks to be caught up in anything shady."

Tom looked dejected and beaten. "I really thought we were onto something there, Jack. I don't know what to do..."

"Don't let it get to you, Tommy. Trust me, we'll - I mean you'll find her." Tom was uncharacteristically somber, not at all the old Tom that Jack knew. He was shaking his head.

"I don't know, Jack, I feel like maybe I'm responsible. Like maybe Carolyn took off because of me."

"No, Tommy, I'm sure that's not true. You know, things haven't been that easy for her. Mrs. C.'s pretty severe from what I hear."

"So many times I've let her down - taken her for granted. Now that she's gone, I'm worried about her and I'm kicking myself for the way I treated her. And now, the way things are going for me, I just hate to think…"

"What do you mean, the way things are going for you? What's got you so down, Tommy? This isn't like you."

Tom stood, turned away from Jack, and looked out the kitchen window toward the fields.

"Okay, Jackie, but just between us, huh?"

A few minutes later Claire came in from the barn. Just as she entered the kitchen Jack was exclaiming: "Wow, Tommy, that's - great - really great."

"What's so great?" asked Claire as she stepped through the door into the kitchen.

"Tommy's - uhh," began Jack. Then Tom interrupted him.

"I was telling Jack about my new fishing rod. It's really - great."

Claire stood expressionless. She was still angry with Tom for the Senior Formal fiasco. "Any news about Carolyn?" Tom shook his head disconsolately. The sales slip with the scrawled address lay on the table. Claire saw it and picked it up. "What's this?"

"Just something Anne found in Carolyn's room. It's an address, right here in Westfield. We thought it might lead us to her, but Tommy just went over there. Nothing."

Claire was holding the note, her eyes scanning it. Suddenly she cocked her head and looked sharply at her brother, then at Tom. "What makes you think it's Westfield, Massachusetts? There's other Westfields, I'll bet, maybe in Vermont, or Connecticut. Did either of you geniuses ever think of that?"

Jack's eyes met Tom's. "She's got a point, Tommy. How do we know it's Westfield, Massachusetts?"

"By the way," continued Claire, "there's another story about those *Bull-shuv-iks* in today's *Transcript*. They think they're hiding out in Lowell. They're searching the city. There's a reward - a thousand dollars - for anyone who can lead them to the guys. I guess they really want them bad."

"Uh, well, Tommy, you'd better be gettin' back to Holyoke, right?" said Jack awkwardly, nodding toward the door. "I'll walk with you to the trolley stop." When they were outside and beyond earshot of Claire, Jack spoke in a whisper.

"Just a minute, Tommy." He opened the door of the family's Model T and fumbled around inside. He pulled out a ragged map printed on oilskin showing roads, rail and trolley lines in Massachusetts and spread it on the hood.

"Let's see, there's Lowell, up toward New Hampshire - uh, Lawrence, Chelmsford - Westford. Look at that, just a few miles from Lowell. Maybe that's where he lives, Tommy - Westford, not Westfield."

"But if she's with him and the Feds raid the place she could be in big trouble, Jack, real big trouble." Tom looked directly at Jack. In his friend's eyes Jack saw resolve, determination, things he hadn't observed in Tom lately. "I'm going to Lowell, Jack, or Westford, wherever I have to."

"Tommy, wait a minute. Are you sure that's a good idea? It could be nasty. It could be dangerous."

"Yeh, it could be - for Carolyn."

"When are you goin'?"

"Right away. I'll just go home to get the car and a few things."

"Where'll you stay?"

"I don't know, maybe in a guest house, or a hotel, maybe I'll just sleep in the car."

"I wish I could go with you. I feel so useless."

"No, Jack, stay here. I'll be okay." At the trolley stop the pair stood peering at the map.

"Are you gonna tell Anne and your folks where you're goin'?" asked Jack.

"I don't know. They'd probably just try to stop me. I'll make up something about visiting an old school chum." Jack looked directly into Tom's eyes.

"I hope you know what you're doin', Tommy. Don't go takin' any chances."

"Don't worry, Jack, I'll be fine. And remember, not a word about what I told you, okay? I want to tell them myself when I get back."

~ 36 ~

MONDAY, JUNE 18

Early the next day Tom Wellington stepped onto the sidewalk of a busy thoroughfare in Lowell, Massachusetts. He had driven from Holyoke in his family's Pierce Arrow. It was nearly two in the morning when he stumbled bleary-eyed up the steps of the YMCA. The front door was locked but a night watchman allowed him entry and issued him a key for a dingy, sparsely furnished room on the fourth floor. Carrying only a small traveling case, Tom had struggled up the eight flights of stairs, found his room, collapsed on the bed, and immediately fallen asleep.

A few hours later the clanging of a trolley woke him. He lay dazed, looking up at a gray ceiling. Slowly he rose to a seated position, his head hung, long bony feet on bare wooden floorboards. On the bedside table lay his wallet, the road map, and a few papers including a photograph of Carolyn, the one that would appear in the *Purple and White*, her high school yearbook. She was smiling in that photograph, but in her eyes Tom saw weariness and melancholy that no makeup or hair styling could disguise.

Tom washed in a bathroom at the end of the corridor, dressed, then hurriedly stuffed his few belongings in the small travel case. A few minutes later he was drinking coffee at a lunch counter across the street while looking intently at the road map. Just then a boy entered the shop with a stack of the

Lowell Sun, the city's daily newspaper. Tom bought one and spread it on the counter in front of his coffee cup. The headline sent a chill up his spine: FEDERAL AGENTS SEEKING UNION AGITATORS IN CITY.

He asked the clerk for directions to Westford. Soon he was speeding along a country road. He slowed only slightly at a small intersection where he saw a sign with an arrow, *Westford 6 miles.* He turned and stepped heavily on the gas pedal and the long car tore off in that direction.

The road was lined with small, neat farmhouses, each with a large barn and several outbuildings at the rear. Shortly he passed a sign reading *Entering Westford.* Within minutes he entered a small commercial center with brick two- and three-story buildings lining both sides of a wide, gravel main street. The trolley line from Lowell ran down the center of the street. He proceeded several more blocks until he saw the number 138 on one of the buildings. In the next block he pulled up to a granite curb and stopped. A single story building numbered 150 bore a large wooden sign reading *Westford Print Shop.* In the window was a display of books, flyers, and circulars of various sizes and styles.

Tom was surprised and mystified; this did not look like anyone's home. He stood studying the display in the window for several minutes, then stepped to the door, opened it, and entered. A bell affixed to the door frame announced his entrance as he stepped up to a long counter.

"One moment - right with you," came a voice from the rear of the shop. A single door was half open revealing a dimly lit work room where Tom could see several small presses and stacks of paper. Nearly a minute passed and he could hear some movement in the back room. Eventually a man emerged wearing a long oilcloth apron covered with black ink. He was middle aged, slender, with short black hair and sharp facial features. He smiled at Tom.

"Yes sir, what can I do for you?"

Tom was unsure whether he was in the right place and a little reluctant to reveal the purpose of his visit. "I'm looking for a friend. He told me to look him up next time I was in Westford. He gave me this address, 150 Main Street."

"You lookin' for Charles August? Or Norbert Latour?"

"No," replied Tom. "Nope."

"Well, it might help if you could tell me the name of this fella, don't ya think?"

Tom hesitated. "John's his name, Johnny we call him."

"Ah, Mister Garfield. He's the proprietor. He gets his mail here but he lives out on Chipman Lane. Left a half mile, yellow house on the right." The man pointed up the main road. At that moment the jangle of a telephone could be heard in the back room. The man shook his head in apparent annoyance. "I'm sorry, I can't hear myself think when that damned thing starts a-ringin'. A botheration. I'll be just a moment."

Tom stood nervously as the clerk disappeared into the back room. He could hear him talking on the telephone in muffled tones. Finally the man reappeared, but now his speech and manner were curiously slow.

"Well, now, I am sorry about that, sir. Some folks can go on and on when they get you on the telephone, you know how it is? My lands, I sometimes wish Mr. Bell had never invented the fool thing. Where'd you say you were from?"

"Holyoke. You were giving me directions - to Mister - Garfield's home?"

"Ah, Holyoke, yes - fine city - fine city indeed. Had a friend moved out there a year or two ago to work in one of the paper mills. Yup, big paper town, Holyoke, ayeh."

"Did you say Chipman Road?"

"Never did find work, I guess. Ended up headin' out Buffalo way. Haven't heard..."

"I've got to be going," interrupted Tom. And he turned and headed toward the door. As he opened the door two figures suddenly appeared on the sidewalk blocking his way. The men parted as if to let Tom pass, but as he stepped between them each grabbed an arm and pushed him forcefully back through the doorway.

"Hey," shouted Tom, but as he spoke a rag covered with ink was wrapped around his head from behind, knocking off his hat and covering his eyes and mouth. He struggled, managing briefly to free one arm that pushed several stacks of circulars from the counter, then caught one of his assailants a hard blow to the head. A returning punch sent Tom crashing to the floor where he lay motionless. The trio dragged his limp form through the back room and into a closet. Another rag was used to tie his hands, then the door was shut and locked.

Minutes later a streetcar rattled up Main Street, screeching to a halt a block away from the print shop. Jack Bernard stepped onto the gravel, then up onto the wooden sidewalk. He looked bedraggled, having ridden half the night by train from Springfield to Lowell with a long delay in Worcester. When Tom revealed his plan to save Carolyn, Jack had been worried, worried about Tom, his state of mind and the risks he might be taking, and worried about Carolyn as well. After several hours of deliberation, he concocted a plan. He would travel to Westford by train and try to divert Tom from what seemed like a foolhardy enterprise. But Jack's father was away, having driven the Model T nearly forty miles to Southbridge to see Evelyne's sister, Yvette, who was seriously ill. Jack had prevailed upon Anne to come to Westfield and stay with his sisters overnight. Not wanting to worry her, he made up a story of how he and Tom had learned of Carolyn's location, omitting the details about her father, the bounty on his head, or the risks that might be involved in rescuing Carolyn.

Jack hoisted his rucksack to his shoulders, looked up at the numbers over several storefronts, then began walking west past a clothier, a bank, and a soda shop. Soon he was standing in front of the building numbered 150 looking up at the sign for Westford Print Shop. He tried the door, but it was locked. He peered through the window, but saw no sign of life, just a counter with stacks of books and printed material. He rapped several times on the door and waited. He turned and looked up and down the street, hoping someone would come by who might know something about the shop. Seeing no one, he turned back to the print shop and walked the length of the dusty window, peering at the dingy interior. At the far end of the counter near the cash register he could see what looked like papers strewn over the counter and on the floor. A chair was resting on its side. On the floor next to the chair lay a man's cap bearing a familiar monogram, *TPW*.

Frantically Jack worked the knob, rapped again, and finally banged loudly on the door. Next to the shop was another small storefront, a bakery, and beyond it a narrow alleyway. He raced past the bakery entrance, turned down the alley, then turned again into another alley that led to the rear entrance of each store. The second entrance was ajar. Jack pushed it open and entered.

"Hello?" he called tentatively. "Hello?" he called louder. "Tommy?" At that moment a muffled sound came from another room. Jack pushed his way through a door and the sound grew louder still. Then he heard loud banging on a closet door down a narrow hallway. He turned the key, opened it, and found Tom lying on the floor, his head still swaddled in a bloody rag.

"*Tommy, Tommy,*" yelled Jack as he knelt next to his friend and carefully removed the rag. Tom was gasping for air and looked a fright with blood as well as several colors of printer's ink staining his face. Small puddles of fresh blood, maroon and black, marked the spot on the floor where he had lain for a few minutes.

"Jack? What the hell? Where'd you..."

"Are you okay, Tommy? What happened?" Tom sat dazed, still groggy from the blow to his head. The flow of blood had been from his nose and had stopped.

"These guys, they grabbed me and punched me, then gagged me - I guess I passed out." Then he looked into Jack's eyes, alarmed. "They must be headed to Carolyn's father's house - the reward. We have to try to find them and stop them." Tom got to his feet.

"Wait, we gotta get you cleaned up, Tommy." Jack led him to a sink, found a clean rag, and washed the blood and ink from his friend's face and hair. "Anyone see you on the street lookin' like that'd call the cops in a minute. But maybe we should call the police, Tommy, these guys are dangerous."

"No, we can't, they'll be looking for Garfield, too. Come on, my car's right outside." Before they exited through the front door onto the street, Tom recovered his cap, dusted it off, then set it back on his head.

"Do you know where we're goin', Tommy?" asked Jack as he started the engine.

"All I know is a yellow house on Chipman Road. I think he said it was the next left." They turned sharply at a battered sign reading merely *Chipman* and Tom gunned the engine. A yellow house soon came into view.

"What a minute, Tommy, wait, pull over. Let's think about this."

Moments later Tom had parked the car in a narrow lane between two fields where it would be hidden from view by a hedgerow. They ran along the lane until it entered woods, then scurried through the woods parallel to the road and behind two houses. Soon they were viewing the yellow house from the back through the dense forest foliage. The main house faced the road. Attached to it was a long ell consisting of what appeared to be a summer kitchen and a shed that connected the house to a large red barn.

Bent over, the pair scrambled along a low rise that separated them from the house. When they were near the house they stood up slowly until they could just make out the front yard through the trees. Two motorcars were parked on the gravel driveway. A figure could be seen standing on the front lawn.

"That's the guy from the print shop, Jack, the one who gave me directions," whispered Tom. "The two guys that grabbed me must be inside - with Mrs. Garfield and Carolyn. We gotta get them away from those thugs before they get hurt." Tom stood up in full view of the house. "I'm going in there, Jack."

"Wait, wait, Tommy, you wouldn't stand a chance against the three of them - someone could get hurt. Look, that guy, he's got a shotgun."

Tom quickly dropped to his knees. "We gotta do something." Jack was surveying the house and the several smaller buildings that connected it to the barn. The smaller structures were set into the rise in such a way that the rear eaves were barely six feet above the ground.

"Let's just think a minute, Tommy. Maybe there's something we can do. So they want Carolyn's father, right? If he were home they'd have him by now and be on their way. Maybe he's not there. Maybe they're thinking they'll just wait for him to come home."

"Or try to force Mrs. Garfield or Carolyn to tell them where he is," added Tom with alarm. "We gotta get them away from those thugs. Our best chance is to split them up."

"Tommy, I got an idea. What if you go back to your car, put on that driving jacket and pull that cap down over your face? Then you come drivin' down the road and pull up in front. But just stay in the car. They'll think you're Mr. Garfield seein' those strange cars in front and tryin' to decide what to do. Meanwhile I'll go round back of the barn and come through the shed and the summer kitchen. As soon as those guys step out the front door I'll sneak in and take Carolyn and Mrs. Garfield out the back and into the woods."

"Okay, but what then? Where will I find you?" asked Tom.

"We'll circle around and be in the woods near where we left your car."

"Jack, are you okay? I mean, are you feeling all right? I thought you weren't supposed to..."

Jack looked into Tom's eyes. "You can't go through life worryin'. Sometimes you just have to do what's right. Like you said, you gotta live your life, ya know?"

Tom nodded and smiled at Jack. "Okay, I guess we better move. About fifteen, twenty minutes." Tom made his way through the thick undergrowth, retracing the route he and Jack had followed minutes before. Jack watched him, then began a wide circle that would take him back into the forest well behind the farmhouse. Eventually he made his way through the woods toward the house, keeping the barn between himself and the main house.

The only entrance on the back end of the barn was two tall sliding doors that were closed. Jack noticed a chicken run off the south side of the barn with an opening for the birds to be fed from the barn. He gently lifted the latch and entered the coop. Several birds clucked softly but he had gathered a handful of seeds that had fallen outside the pen and once inside tossed them toward the birds which became distracted and began scrambling for the feed.

Jack leaned toward the opening in the barn and cautiously peered inside, assuring himself that no one was within. Then he returned to the rear of the building and slid one door just far enough to get through, but leaving it open should he need to beat a hasty retreat.

Bending below the half-wall along the cattle stalls, he moved quickly toward the corner of the barn nearest the house where he could see a small door. He skirted a ladder leaning against the loft eight or ten feet above him. Hanging on the wall next to the door was a three-tined pitch fork which he grasped in his left hand. As he suspected, the door gave access to the shed at the rear of the ell, and he opened it just a crack. Assured that all was clear, he crossed the shed toward the summer kitchen that adjoined the main house. The floor boards creaked loudly and he stepped toward the wall, correctly guessing that there would be less movement of the boards and less creaking near their junction with the building's foundation.

The door leading to the summer kitchen was half open. Jack stood listening for several minutes, his back against the wall next to the door jamb. He could hear footsteps but they were distant and muffled, probably in the main house. After several minutes he peered briefly through the door into the summer kitchen, taking in as much detail as possible in a few seconds, then pulling back. On his right against the front wall was a laundry tub resting on a low table, half full of soapy water. Next to it was a large wooden hamper filled with sheets, towels, and garments apparently waiting to be washed. Beyond the tub a door led to the yard and the driveway. On his left he could see a sink with a hand pump, a counter, and a small coal-fired stove. On the far wall hung shelves with dishware and cooking utensils. Straight ahead a wooden door with glass panes led into the main house. The door was shut and latched. Through the glass he could see a flight of narrow stairs leading up to the second floor of the main house.

Jack took several breaths, then stepped through the door and across the summer kitchen to a narrow niche in the far corner next to the shelves, gripping the pitch fork firmly in one hand. Suddenly there were loud voices, men's voices, coming from the main house. Then the latch clinked and the door opened. Jack withdrew into the niche like a turtle into its shell. He held his breath as someone stepped into the summer kitchen just out of his sight. He heard the sound of light footsteps, then a gruff voice.

"So get what they need and make it quick. And don't make a false move, you hear?"

Just then the figure stepped into view. It was Carolyn, her back to him, reaching for some wood from the woodbox next to the outside door. She grasped some small pieces of kindling, then turned toward the stove. Suddenly she saw Jack and dropped the kindling with a loud clatter.

"Watch what you're doing there," said the man's voice sharply from the next room.

Jack could see Carolyn's face blanch as she stooped to retrieve the kindling and he feared she would faint. But to his surprise and relief she recovered, gathered up the kindling, stood, and proceeded to stoke the stove. He could tell she was working very slowly and guessed by the expression on her face that she was trying to figure out what to do next.

Several minutes went by as Carolyn worked at the fire. Finally she drew a bucket of water, filled a small pot on the stove, then took a loaf of bread from the shelves and began slicing it on the counter. After several minutes Jack could hear the man's footsteps and guessed that he had moved away from the door where he had been watching her.

Carolyn finally looked up at Jack and he spoke in a low whisper. "Where is Mrs. Garfield?"

"In the parlor," mouthed Carolyn. And she nodded toward the front of the house.

"How many men are there?" he whispered. Carolyn held up three fingers. Just then the footsteps got louder and approached the door once again.

"Hurry it up, Missy, I'm givin' you five more minutes to get those children their lunch. Five minutes. And fix some coffee for me and my friends."

At the mention of children Jack's eyes suddenly popped. This complicated the situation still more. Carolyn looked at him briefly. But the man was obviously standing in full view and she couldn't speak. Just then she opened the firebox and appeared to be adding some coal. As she stoked the fire she held up two fingers toward Jack without looking at him. Then she raised her thumb and pumped it upwards several times while jabbing the fire with a poker in her other hand.

Jack nodded and mouthed, "Two children - upstairs." Carolyn nodded.

Jack stood silently, thinking, trying to visualize the layout of the house. It looked much like his home in Westfield, though bigger in every dimension. Unlike his house, he figured, it must have two flights of stairs to the second floor, one from the front, one from the rear.

He watched as Carolyn spooned coffee grounds into a pot of boiling water. She placed three cups and saucers on a decorative serving tray. After several minutes she poured steaming coffee into the three cups, replaced the pot on the stove, and lifted the tray. She looked nervously at Jack, then disappeared through the doorway into the main house. A minute later she returned to the kitchen, reloading the tray with what appeared to be food for the children.

Jack whispered: "Take it, Carolyn, go ahead, take it upstairs, to the children."

Carolyn again looked pale and unsteady, but she hoisted the tray and stepped through the door into the main house, then quickly ascended the rear stairs. At the top she turned to enter a bedroom. As she turned she saw Jack ascending the stairs silently behind her. He gestured for her to proceed.

Nervously Carolyn entered a second floor bedroom on the south side of the house. Jack followed. The children were

212

playing, apparently unaware of what was taking place downstairs. In a whisper Carolyn introduced Jack.

"Johnny, Adele, this is my friend, Jack." They smiled and greeted Jack who stood looking uneasily around the room. Then he stepped to a low window at the rear and looked outside. Just beneath the window was the sloping roof of the summer kitchen. Jack raised the sash, then looked to Carolyn and nodded toward the window.

"I've got an idea," he whispered. She approached him nervously. "I'm gonna get out on the roof and let myself down to the ground on the back. It's not a long drop. Have the children ready."

"Jack, are you sure?" But Jack had already disappeared out the window onto the roof and in seconds was on the ground at the rear of the summer kitchen.

"Where'd he go, Carolyn? What's he doin'?" asked Johnny wide-eyed.

"Uh, it's a little game. He's gonna show us how to sneak out the window - it'll be fun." Moments later she could see the top of a ladder coming to rest against the eaves below and then Jack appeared, clambering back onto the roof. The pitch of the roof was just enough to make climbing tricky, but Jack had a rope under one arm and tossed an end to Carolyn.

"Tie that end to the bed, then hand the children to me one at a time and I'll carry them down." Silently Carolyn followed Jack's instructions. Several agonizing minutes went by when Jack expected at any moment that one of the men would appear in the bedroom or below.

But finally Carolyn reappeared at the window holding Adele and speaking softly to her. "Shhh. It's okay. Just put your arms around Jack's neck and hold on tight." The child was tiny and very light and Jack was able to crawl down the steep roof, one hand around her and the other clasping the rope. In one moment he was on the ladder. In another he had placed her on the ground.

"Stay put now, honey, and I'll get your brother and Carolyn."

"Where's Mama? Is she coming, too?"

"Yes, she's coming too. Don't worry." In another minute Jack was back at the window and grasping Johnny in similar fashion. The boy was twice his sister's weight and for a moment Jack had difficulty balancing himself on the roof with the boy clutching him, but balance he did and soon Johnny stood on the ground next to Adele.

"Shhh. You two stay put, okay? I'm gonna get Carolyn now." This, Jack feared, was going to be more of a challenge, but as he emerged at the top of the ladder he was surprised to find Carolyn already on the roof, grasping the rope, and ready to descend.

"Come ahead," whispered Jack. But just as Carolyn stood up her feet slipped from beneath her and she slid down the roof toward Jack. He put out both arms and caught her, but the motion caused the ladder to slide. He released his grip on Carolyn's arm to grab the ladder and then they both began to slide in the opposite direction. Jack released his grip on the ladder and grabbed the rope which slipped through his hands. Searing pain shot up his arm as he held the rope tight and pulled the ladder toward him with his knees. By now Carolyn was grasping the eave with one hand, Jack's neck with the other. Wincing in pain, Jack slowly stepped down the ladder, Carolyn hanging on his neck. In a moment they were both standing on the ground. The children, who had been watching the acrobatics wide-eyed, clutched Carolyn's hands and looked up warily at her and Jack.

"Okay, follow me," whispered Jack. And the four crept along the back of the ell, then beyond the rear of the barn, putting as much distance as possible between themselves and the house in several minutes.

Suddenly a loud, sharp report could be heard from the direction of the house. Jack recognized it at once as a shotgun blast. A look of terror filled Carolyn's eyes as she crouched and held the children close to her.

"What was that, Jack?" she asked, her voice shaking with fear. Jack was crouched next to them but rose to try to see toward the house.

"I don't know, probably just a car backfiring. I'll go see."

"Jack, don't, there's three of them. What can you do?"

"Don't worry, Tommy's not far away. We have a plan."

"Tommy?"

Carolyn was still adjusting to that news when Jack added, "You stay here. I'll go see what's happening."

"Be careful, Jack, please."

Again Jack approached the rear of the barn, re-entering through the open door. He'd already removed the ladder to the loft but was able to climb up on the hay wagon, then jump from it to the loft. Two swinging doors on the front of the loft through which hay could be loaded were shut, but a long crack in one door afforded Jack a view of the summer kitchen, the main house, and the driveway. What he saw terrified him: Tom, lying in the driveway, face down, a dark-haired man standing over him aiming a shotgun at his head.

Jack froze, watching, thinking. He could do nothing, risk nothing, as long as Tom was in such peril. Maybe, Jack thought, if he could create a distraction that would draw one or more of the thugs away from the house, maybe Tom stood a chance, and Mrs. Garfield. As Jack watched, the man with the shotgun looked up and toward the road. Tom's car was parked in the road. At that moment another motorcar approached. The man moved, apparently in an attempt to hide the shotgun that was still trained on Tom's head. The approaching motorcar pulled up behind Tom's car. A tall man that looked like Carolyn's father stepped out and stood looking at the house, the car partially shielding him. He was shouting. Jack wasn't sure what he was saying but he heard fear and desperation in that voice.

At that moment another figure came into view, striding across the lawn toward Garfield, speaking in a lower voice that Jack couldn't hear. Garfield came around his car and approached the man on the lawn who appeared to be unarmed. Then the figure standing over Tom stepped toward the other two while still pointing the shotgun at Tom.

Suddenly Garfield lunged at the man on the lawn, shouting at him. The man carrying the shotgun turned the gun on Garfield and in that moment Tom was on his feet, diving at the gun carrier from behind. The man fell hard on the brick walkway and the force of the impact freed the shotgun, sending it hurtling across the grass.

Jack leapt down to the hay wagon, then to the barn floor. In seconds he had dashed through the summer kitchen into the main house where he found Adrienne. He led her out through the summer kitchen to the barn and beyond, heading directly to the place where he had left Carolyn and the two children a few minutes earlier.

Once they were reunited, Jack turned and ran back toward the house. As he approached three police cars came roaring up the road, pulled onto the front lawn, and disgorged half a dozen uniformed officers.

John Garfield kissed Adele, Johnny, Carolyn, and Adrienne before he was led away in handcuffs by three Lowell policemen. A gruff officer questioned Jack and Tom about their role in the confrontation, then shrugged his shoulders and walked away, apparently concluding that they were not guilty of any crime. The three Westford men insisted they were merely trying to protect the public from a dangerous criminal, an anarchist, possibly even an agent for the Kaiser or a Russian Bolshevik.

"You have to arrest these guys. They were holding Mrs. Garfield, Carolyn, the children, like hostages," argued Tom.

"And that guy had a gun," added Jack, pointing to the shotgun still lying on the grass. "He fired a shot at Tom."

"Shut up," said the officer. "They'll get their due." With that the trio were led away. It was clear that they were friends of one of the officers and Tom had his suspicions that *their due* would be the reward money - or some fraction of it. Back in the house Carolyn made tea for Adrienne and coffee for Jack and Tom. The four sat in the parlor grim-faced while the children played upstairs.

"I knew when we married that John's work could be dangerous. But I believed in him and what he was doing. And I loved him. I just prayed it would never come to this."

"What will you do, Adrienne?" asked Carolyn, "until he comes home, I mean."

"I can't live here with the children, not now, not while he's in jail. I won't feel safe. My sister and her husband have a large home in Watertown outside Boston. We visit them often. I'm sure we can stay there for a time."

"Well, we can stay with you here until you leave."

"No, no, my dear. Your mother, she must be worried terribly. I want you to telephone her immediately. And go back to her as soon as possible, do you understand?" Then Adrienne looked intently into Carolyn's eyes.

"My dear, a mother separated from her child, it is the worst form of torture imaginable. Someday when you are a mother, you will understand." Carolyn nodded tearfully.

"Once John is free, I pray we may all be reunited. And Carolyn, I pray that you and your father may one day be together again. Until that time, you must, my dear, stay by your mother's side. Please, now, go telephone her. She'll be very anxious to hear your voice."

~ 37 ~

Jack held the leather-wrapped steering wheel of the Wellingtons' Pierce Arrow with a death grip, his eyes fixed on the road ahead. He'd driven tractors and farm trucks since age ten, but navigating a long, elegant town car down a dark country road in the driving rain was a new and unnerving experience. Thankfully traffic was light, but every time another vehicle approached he slowed the car, veering toward the side of the road.

In the wide back seat sat Carolyn, still wan and shaken after the day's harrowing events, leaning lightly against Tom's arm as he spoke gentle words of reassurance into her ear. The sliding isinglass window that separated the driver's compartment from the rear seat was closed, and Jack could only guess at the conversation between the two. But he had quite enough to do just keeping the car on the rutted road.

"Why don't you try to sleep?" Tom suggested in a soft voice. "Here." And he slid to the end of the seat while drawing Carolyn's slight form toward him. With her legs stretched across the seat, she seemed to be more comfortable.

Several minutes went by and Tom thought she had fallen asleep. Then she spoke: "Thomas, I'm scared - about my father. What - what's going to happen to him?"

"He'll probably be arraigned in the morning. You go in front of a judge. And the police or the Federal agents have to say what the charge is. He might be released on bail right then. Or the judge might set a time for a hearing on bail. I bet it won't take long."

"And then?"

Tom stroked Carolyn's hair with one hand. "Listen, Adrienne said the union has lawyers. I bet they'll fight the charges and maybe get them dismissed before the case ever has to go to trial. Those unions are really good at that. I'll talk to my uncle - he might know someone in Lowell or Boston who can help him."

In the dim light of a street lamp Tom could see Carolyn's eyes filling with tears. She bit her lip. "Just when I was starting to get to know him, this happens. I don't know when - when I'll see him again, or even if I'll ever see him again - and Adrienne and the children." She looked frightened. "I hated to leave them."

"I'm sure Adrienne's sister and her husband will take care of them until your father is back home. It's gonna be all right, I promise."

Carolyn looked up and into Tom's eyes, wanting to believe him. The slimmest, slightest of smiles broke briefly across her lips. Then she closed her eyes and was soon asleep.

Carefully Tom slid the window open a few inches and whispered: "Jack, Carolyn's sleeping. Why don't you let me drive for a while?" They were approaching Worcester, less than half the distance to Holyoke, and Jack was only too happy to oblige his friend. He pulled the motorcar off the road onto a grassy shoulder. Soon they were back on the road and speeding along faster and more confidently with Tom at the wheel.

Silently Jack nudged the sliding window until it was closed. "Is she all right, Tommy?"

"I think so, for now, anyway. She was shaking like a leaf at first. She's worried about her father, of course, but I told her everything's gonna be okay." Tom's eyes met Jack's briefly. "I hope it's true, Jack, I really do."

"Did she talk about why she ran away? Why she just disappeared like that?"

"Not really. Her mother always said that her father abandoned her as soon as he found out she was having a baby - like he didn't want them to be a family - like he didn't care about Nina or the baby. All those years, Jack, that girl thought he didn't care. But it was really Mrs. C. who sent *him* away. She thought he was unfit to be a husband - or a father - that he was a socialist or some kind of anti-American revolutionary." Tom chuckled. "Well, she was right in a way, I guess he's been doing this stuff for nearly twenty years. But he believes in it - and he's no more anti-American than you or me."

Jack nodded. "Anne found out that he's been fighting for years to get mills to stop using dangerous chemicals for scouring agents. Last spring he wrote a letter in a labor magazine about how harmful some of those things can be. I suppose the mill owners would call that a lot of scaremongering, right? "

Tom nodded. "I know, Jack, I know. Tuttle - it was his idea. He thought it would save the company money. I swear Uncle Richard knew nothing about it."

"Yeh," replied Jack. "But your uncle, he's Tuttle's boss, Tommy."

"I know. I'm sorry, Jack. You were right all along about the dyehouse."

"Forget it, Tommy. I shoulda never taken that job."

Jack turned his head and looked briefly at Carolyn, then turned again and stared into the oncoming rain, thinking about the confrontation in Westford. "What made you do it, Tommy? I mean, tackling that guy with the shotgun like that. You coulda gotten hurt. You coulda got killed, you know." Tom smiled, his eyes still fixed on the road.

"It wasn't that risky, Jack. I mean, he'd already fired the shotgun and he hadn't reloaded. So I knew he wasn't gonna shoot me."

"It was a double-barreled shotgun, Tommy. He probably had another round." Tom's smile disappeared briefly, then spread across his face again.

"Oh, well, he wouldn't have shot me just for a share of the reward money, right?" Jack shook his head in disbelief. "Besides, what've I got to lose - you know?" Tom's words seemed to hang in the air, to hover over the two young men like a gathering storm cloud.

"Tommy," asked Jack in a whisper, "does she know?" nodding toward the back seat. "Have you told her yet?"

Tom shook his head as the Pierce Arrow pressed onward to Holyoke in the darkness and the rain.

The steady rain had yielded to a light drizzle as the car pulled onto Appleton Street in Holyoke. It was nearly midnight and Carolyn, Tom, and Jack were exhausted, both by the long, slow drive from Lowell and the day's exertions.

Helen Wellington saw the headlights first as the car pulled up in front of Nina's house.

"Nina, dear, they're here." The two women stood, Helen holding Nina's arm. "They must be very weary," added Helen. And she looked into her friend's eyes, hoping to calm her. As they stepped onto the front porch Carolyn emerged from the back seat of the Pierce Arrow with Tom's assistance while Jack retrieved her one valise from the trunk.

"Oh, my baby," said Nina, her voice rattling with emotion.

"I'm all right, Mama, I'm okay," spoke Carolyn softly. "Everything's okay." Nina embraced her daughter, then dissolved in tears. But Carolyn stood impassive, glum, her eyes fixed on the sidewalk. Meanwhile Helen hugged her son and Jack, then looked them both over.

"You two - no wounds - no broken bones?"

"Jack's got a rope burn on his arm. I'm fine, just a black eye. No worse for the wear, as they say."

Helen shook her head, hugged each of the young men again, then spoke to Carolyn and Nina. "Well, this has been quite a day. We all could use some sleep. Perhaps we'll go along then?"

Nina thanked Helen, Tom, and Jack. Carolyn smiled shyly at Tom and Jack, then turned and walked up the front walk ahead of her mother.

"Jack, why don't you drive the car, deliver Thomas and me, then get yourself back to Westfield? I know three young ladies who will be very happy to see you. How would that be?"

Home at last, Jack quietly let himself in the front door of the Bernard farmhouse. Slowly he climbed the stairs, hoping not to wake the occupants of the two first floor bedrooms at the rear of the house. Without lighting a lamp he sat on the edge of his bed, pulled off his shoes, shirt, and trousers, then stretched out. The bed felt warm but he was too exhausted to wonder why. Rolling onto his side, he drew his legs up and under the covers.

Jack was just getting comfortable when a slender white arm emerged from under the sheets and enfolded him. A pair of moist lips caressed his cheek, then whispered softly in his ear: "You can tell me all about it in the morning, Jackie."

~ 38 ~

TUESDAY, JUNE 19

Carolyn sat eating her breakfast in silence the next morning. Not a word was exchanged between her and her mother beyond a curt good morning - no explanation from Carolyn nor any questions from her mother.

The clink of glass meant the milkman was at the back door picking up empty bottles and leaving two quarts of fresh milk and a pint of cream. Nina opened the door, collected the newly delivered bottles, and placed them in the icebox. That task done, she proceeded to wash the few dishes and one small pan that lay in the sink.

As she dried the dishes a cup slipped from her hands and shattered. Her face became taut and her hand shook as she picked the pieces out of the sink. Suddenly she winced in pain and groaned. She had cut her finger and a trickle of blood dripped into the sink.

"Mama, here, let me help you," said Carolyn when she realized what had happened.

But her mother abruptly withdrew her hand and turned away from her daughter. "No, thank you. I - I'm all right." And she quickly left the room, then ran up the long stairway to the second floor.

Carolyn followed and stood by the closed bedroom door. "Mama, let me help you. Please." There was no reply. "Mama." Still no reply. Finally Carolyn opened the door. Her mother was standing in front of her dresser, a tissue wrapped tightly around the cut finger. "Mama, please, let me see your finger."

When her mother still wouldn't turn and face her, Carolyn looked up and into the oval mirror that hung over the dresser. Tears were streaming down her mother's reddened cheeks. Carolyn looked upon the anguished face reflected in the mirror, then hung her head. Eyes cast downward, she spoke: "I'm sorry, Mama. I'm sorry and ashamed of what I did. I know - it was thoughtless of me to go off like that. Please say you forgive me and let me help you." Nina's tears had stopped but she stood stiffly offering no forgiveness to her daughter, only silence. "Please, Mama, I'm sorry. I just wanted to get to know my father." Nina looked briefly into her daughter's eyes but turned away, shaking her head.

"Mama, please try to understand. All those years I believed what you told me - that he abandoned you. That he wanted nothing to do with us. And then one day he appeared and told me a different story - that you sent him away. Can't you see how that felt? Like I'd been lied to all my life. And now I find out he wants to know me. He cares about me. Do you blame me?"

"Coffee's ready," chimed Anne brightly as Jack entered the kitchen. "Did you sleep well?" Jack turned briefly to see if his sisters were within earshot, then spoke in a whisper.

"No, not *real* well. It took me about an hour to fall asleep after you…"

"I'm sorry," replied Anne with a conspiratorial twinkle in her eye. "I sat up in the parlor reading until I could not keep my eyes open any longer. But I needed to know you were home safely - and feel you close to me again. So I went upstairs and lay on your bed. I must have dropped off. Are you disappointed in me?"

"Yes, Anne Wellington, I am, I'm very disappointed - and shocked," replied Jack in a mock scolding tone. He was blushing profusely but there was a smile on his lips. He put his hands around Anne's thin waist, drew her to him, and kissed her. For the next half hour they sat at the kitchen table as Jack recounted the previous day's adventures. He was just completing his narrative when Marie appeared, much relieved to see her brother home and in reasonably good fettle. Over tea and oatcakes she listened to a shorter version of the same narrative. Finally Claire appeared.

"Where were you, Anne?" she demanded. "I woke up in the night and couldn't get back to sleep. I looked in to see if you were awake but your bed was empty." Anne hesitated.

"Oh, I - I couldn't sleep either, Claire. So I sat up in the front room reading for a while."

"I looked. You weren't there," protested Claire. Again Anne hesitated, blushing.

"Well, Claire, I must have been in the privy," an explanation that seemed to satisfy Claire.

An hour later Anne and Jack were preparing to return to Holyoke. Jack lifted Anne's travel bag into the trunk of the car. Claire and Marie, having made the beds and cleaned up in the kitchen, stepped into the yard to thank Anne and say their good-byes. Anne kissed each sister on the cheek, then clambered into the car.

Just then Claire stepped up to the car window and produced a pink satin hair ribbon as she spoke to Anne in a low voice. "I think this is yours, Anne. I found it while making Jack's bed. I thought you might be missing it." Claire's face was flushed, whether with embarrassment, amusement, or delight, Anne couldn't tell.

"Thank you, Claire." And the long car backed slowly out of the gravel driveway.

On the short return trip to Holyoke, Anne was chattering animatedly about how proud she was of Jack, Tom, and Carolyn, and how anxious she was to see her brother and her best friend. Jack seemed to be concentrating on driving, but the truth was that he didn't know what to say or how to say it. A block before the Wellingtons' home he pulled the car to the curb and shut off the engine.

"Anne," he began, his voice low, his eyes directed at the imposing house looming ahead. "There's one thing I didn't really tell you about that - that to-do in Westford."

"Oh, what's that?"

"It's about Tommy. How fearless he was. That guy was holding a shotgun right at Tommy's head. I was in the barn loft looking out and I just froze. I couldn't move. But Tommy..." Jack smiled and shook his head. "As soon as that thug took his eyes off him and started walking toward Carolyn's father, Tommy just tore after him. He tackled him as hard as he could. It was just plain luck that the gun went flying. The guy could've turned and shot Tommy."

Anne's face turned a ghostly white as Jack continued.

"In the car on the trip home last night I asked him about it. I said he coulda got killed."

"What did he say?"

"I have nothing to lose."

Anne looked at Jack, confused.

"That's what he said, Annie, I have nothing to lose. Listen, there's something you should know about Tommy. And the sooner the better."

"What is it, Jack? Please, tell me."

Mr. and Mrs. Wellington were glowing with pride as they sat with their son in the parlor. Tom had provided a carefully edited version of the events of the previous day so as not to upset his parents. He had glorified Jack's efforts to get Carolyn, Adrienne, and the children to safety while playing down his own role in trying to prevent John Garfield from being captured by the three thugs.

When Anne and Jack appeared, Mrs. Wellington greeted them enthusiastically, hugging her daughter and shaking Jack's hand. "And I trust you found everyone safe, sound, and fast asleep when you got home last evening, Jack?"

"Yes, ma'am, fast asleep," replied Jack. But as he spoke those words he turned and gave a discreet wink seen only by Anne.

"Thank you, both of you, for what you did for Carolyn and the Garfields," continued Helen. "I don't know what would have happened if you two hadn't appeared on the scene." She kissed Jack on the cheek, then turned and did the same to Tom. "But I'm worried about Mr. Garfield. What's going to happen to him, Tom?"

"The IWW, they'll bail him out," replied Tom. "They'll get some big city lawyers on his case. I bet he'll be all right. He's no Bolshevik, he really cares about workers and their protection." To Tom's father, union organizers were all suspect, but he was relieved nevertheless that his son, Jack, and Carolyn were safe back in Holyoke again.

"Rumors are already circulating around town about his arrest," said Helen. "You know, he is held in very high regard by the workers of Holyoke. He was once one of them. I fear what the reaction will be when the news appears in the *Transcript*."

After a few more minutes Tom stood up. "I - I'd better go - to see Carolyn." And he took his leave.

"Mother, Father, did - did Tom tell you - anything?" queried Anne after her brother had left.

"Well, he talked a bit about Lowell and Carolyn but he seemed distracted. Like there was something else on his mind. Why dear?" Helen could see that her daughter was upset. "What, dear. What is it?"

"Tommy's enlisting - in the Navy. He's leaving for training in Rhode Island in about two weeks. His ship will be sailing for England by September. He says the first units of American soldiers are already in England. They'll be crossing the English Channel to France soon. So they need to have more units ready to ship out - right away."

Helen seated herself slowly on the velvet couch, a shocked expression on her face. "I see. Of course. We are, after all, at war. I knew there was talk of drafting men as young as eighteen, but I never imagined it would happen so fast." Then her composure began to crumble. "Heaven help us," she said as she took her husband's hand.

"Why doesn't he wait to get his notice?" asked Helen.

"He says by enlisting he gets to choose when and which service. He's chosen the Navy. He always did like boats, he told Jack." Anne smiled weakly.

Suddenly Helen turned and looked up at Jack who stood with Anne, his eyes downcast. "Jack? Does this mean - you, too?" Jack shook his head without looking up.

"Jack won't be eighteen for another month," replied Anne. "But his doctor is on the Westfield draft board. He told him his - his services would not be needed."

It was early evening and Anne, Jack, and Anne's parents were just sitting down to supper. "I'm worried about Tom," Anne finally confessed. "What could be keeping him? Perhaps we should go and look for him." At that moment they heard the front door creak and footsteps sounded in the hall. Then Tom burst into the dining room.

"Tommy," said Jack brightly. "We were beginnin' to worry about you. Where have you been?"

"I was talking to Carolyn. Then I went to the station. I bought a ticket - to Boston."

"Boston?" said Anne with alarm. "Tom, you just got finished talking about how Carolyn needs you."

"That's just it. I've got to do something about her father. I mean, we can't just accept this."

"What are you thinking, Tommy, planning a jailbreak or something?" replied Jack.

"Jack, I'm serious. The man isn't what they say. And he and the others, they could get sent up - or worse." Tom paused. "I have to do something, you know, for Carolyn - and Adrienne - and those kids."

"So you're thinking...?"

"I'm going to Boston, tomorrow. I have to find out exactly what the charges are against those men and whatever else I can learn. I know it's a long shot, but I have to do something - before I - you know..." He looked nervously toward his sister.

"I wish I could go with you, Tommy, I really do. But I'm goin' back to work at the mill tomorrow."

~ 39 ~

The next day Jack returned to work in the sorting house at Wellington Textiles. The cavernous space filled with huge mountains of fleeces might have seemed daunting to anyone else, but to Jack it felt like home in contrast to the dark, sinister depths of the dyehouse. Mr. Leduc, the sorting house boss, was loud but reasonable, quite a contrast to the vituperative Mr. Tuttle. Most important, Jack looked forward to working alongside friends and familiar faces, Jim, Leo, and the rest.

What astonished Jack that morning was the frantic level of activity in the sorting house so early in the day. Several crews were just finishing an overnight shift and there would be no down time, not the least lull in the activity, with the arrival of the new shift. Wellington Textiles was on a wartime schedule now, struggling to keep pace with orders for uniforms and blankets for American troops headed for Europe.

As Jack entered, the workers from the third shift were just leaving. These men were unfamiliar to Jack and they passed without a word or even a glance as he headed to the loading platform. Within minutes Leo appeared alongside an unfamiliar worker.

"Ay, *Jacques*," began Leo. "Dis 'ere 's Raoul. 'e's new."

Jack nodded to Raoul, then turned to Leo. "Where's Jim?"

"Lef' Friday, 'im. New job."

230

Jack nodded. "Big shoes to fill, Raoul." He smiled at Raoul, then turned to Leo. "Real big." Leo laughed loudly.

"This place," said Jack, looking around wide-eyed, "it's a madhouse. What's goin' on?"

"Everyone's workin' like crazy dese days," replied Leo. "Tree shifts a day - double crews some days. Poosh, poosh, poosh." Jack shook his head in amazement.

Just then Mr. Leduc hollered. "*Bernard, Gamache, LaPierre.* Section seven, pallets one to twelve, to the dyehouse. Then they got a frame of pieces that goes up to Third Floor West. *Grouille-toi* - now."

And so began Jack's first day back on the job, back in the familiar confines of the sorting house, but a transformed sorting house where everything had to happen now and double fast. Without Jim his crew seemed weak. Every task was an effort and Jack was still not feeling as strong as he had been a month earlier. Nevertheless, it felt good to be working again, to be of use, to be occupied.

But there was tension in the air, there was no doubt about that. The news of the arrests of Garfield, Grant, and Taylor had appeared in the local newspapers the night before. Garfield had the respect of all the groups in Holyoke. His mother had emigrated to Holyoke from Québec nearly a half century earlier. His father had labored most of his life in a mill in Chicopee. John began working for the Holyoke Street Railway when he was seventeen.

Yet another burden was weighing heavily on the hearts of all the French workers at Wellington Textiles, Jack soon learned. At the noon hour he and his co-workers were sitting on the grass next to the canal, their lunch pails open at their sides. They ate in silence until one of the members of *La Comité* came by and spoke to the three. It was about Yvonne Gilbault, the girl who had been injured in the weaving room a week earlier.

"That little girl, she been bad this week," the man reported. "Real bad. But the mill's got a doc from Springfield to take care a her. So maybe dere's some hope."

After the man had moved along, Leo spoke in a low voice, shaking his head. "She jus' fourteen, so dey say. But her family, dey needs the money, eh? Who don't? Pity."

Jack nodded. He knew too well the temptation of families to send their children off to work in the mills, even in this time. Congress had enacted new, stricter laws on child labor nearly five years earlier, yet children continued to work in the mills with falsified papers. When violations became known, employers would plead ignorance, blaming the families for lying on applications. But everyone knew that the mills were complicit, accepting birth certificates that were obviously phony or had been altered.

~ 40 ~

THURSDAY, JUNE 21

High Street in Holyoke was always teeming with life, but on Thursday evenings the pace quickened noticeably. For Thursday was payday at nearly all the city's mills and factories. Wallets bulging, workers headed for the bars, clubs, and nightspots up and down the city's main thoroughfare. Single men laughed, clapped one another on the back, and ogled the young ladies who dared to venture forth on that one night of the week. Married men could be found as well, often hunched over a bar downing one more foaming lager before returning to their homes, wives, and families. The trolleys ran late on Thursdays, prepared to aid the mass exodus that began around ten. Friday would be another workday, so even the most exuberant celebrations had to come to an end before the hour grew too late.

This payday, however, would be different. Jack was leaving the sorting house with Leo and Raoul at six-thirty, the end of their shift. Because his first payday would not be for another week, Jack parted company with his friends in front of the paymaster's office, then walked another block to the trolley stand to await the next Westfield car. While he waited Jack heard shouts from the direction of the paymaster's office, but at that moment the trolley arrived and he climbed aboard, presenting his worker's pass to the motorman. As the car bumped up Sargeant Street and turned onto Northampton, he

233

was thinking about the mill, how it had been transformed, even in the few weeks of his absence: the dizzying pace of the workers, the constant noise and commotion, the nearly palpable tension in the air. He was also thinking about Tom, wondering when he would be returning from Boston. Or if he would return at all.

Back in Holyoke, workers emerged from the paymaster's office and counted up their earnings. Soon angry shouts could be heard. Groups of men gathered on Race Street hurling oaths toward the mill. The cry went out along the canal and up and down the city's streets: "*Short pay - short pay.*"

Scores of angry workers gathered at the most popular bars, only to discover that they were being shut down. The bar owners feared violence and did not wish to be found responsible for contributing to worker unruliness. High Street and the other major thoroughfares of the city were soon patrolled by the city's police aided by quickly recruited deputies.

Rumors swirled about - of rocks hurled through mill windows, maybe gasoline bombs. More police were on the way, so the stories went. And troops. Any time now the governor would call out the state National Guard. Maybe some units were already en route to Holyoke, to take up positions around the mills to prevent looting and malicious vandalism, and to round up miscreants.

The greatest weakness of the city's labor force had always been its unwillingness to act as one. The French distrusted the Irish, the Irish the Italians, the Italians the Germans, the Germans the Poles, the Poles the Lithuanians, and so on. But the mood of the workers this time was far more incendiary than in the past. It was the pay cuts that fueled the fires the most. Every worker knew with just a glance at his reduced pay what that would mean for his wife, his children, often grandparents, as well, family members already worked to their limits and getting nowhere.

As angry words of retribution spread among the workers, so did talk of a strike. Soon the word had circulated that a meeting would be held in Chicopee late that evening.

Richard Wellington sat behind his desk in the main office of Wellington Textiles. His accountant sat facing him with several large, leather-bound ledgers opened in front of him. Just then there was a knock on the door.

"Who is it?" demanded Richard tersely. The door opened and Tom stepped in.

"Why, Tom, this is a surprise. Everything okay, son?" Richard shook his nephew's hand. "Come in. Sit down. Jamison, can you excuse us for a few minutes? Family business." The balding accountant closed the ledgers, stacked them, and left. "So, your mother told me you were spending the summer on Cape Cod. What brings you back to Holyoke, son?" He was expecting his nephew to be his usual smiling, affable self, but instead he was sober and grim-faced.

"I - I have to talk to you, Uncle, it's important."

"I see. Well, Tom, I'm not surprised, really. I'm guessing I know what you want to talk about." Tom was taken aback. "I know what's on your mind, Tom, and it's been on my mind, too. You're eighteen now, right? And you want your job back, right?"

Tom sat stunned but chose not to speak.

"You want to come back to the bookkeeping office. Well, that's no problem, no problem at all. I know you've been having some difficulties lately and you gave up your job rather, well, abruptly. But while you were in that job you did well, and I have no doubt you can do so again. So let's just forget about the past and have a new go at it, how's that? First thing Monday morning?"

"Well, thank you, thank you very much, but..."

"And," interrupted his uncle, "we'll give you a new and impressive title, Manager of Wartime Operations or something like that. Something that sounds very important, that kind of thing."

Tom made no reply and Richard continued. "If you get your draft notice, we'll just write a letter, tell them how vital your job is to the war effort and so on. If anyone questions it, well, I have some friends in Boston and in Washington. I don't think there'll be any trouble."

Finally Tom spoke. "Thank you, Uncle Richard, thank you very much. But that's not what I came to talk to you about."

~ *41* ~

FRIDAY, JUNE 22

Richard Wellington was awake well before dawn at his home in the Highlands, high on a hill overlooking downtown Holyoke. As he dressed he gazed out on the city through the tall windows of his dressing room. From that vantage his gaze encompassed the full sweep of Wellington Textiles, his domain.

His face was flushed, his expression stern as he sat alone at the breakfast table drinking steaming black coffee from a delicate china cup. The waitress brought him his usual soft-boiled egg, several strips of thick, fatty bacon, and buttered toast points. He spooned a gleaming mound of strawberry preserves from a small decorative bowl and applied it to the toast.

Richard relished his work and the challenges it constantly presented. He was single-minded in his determination to maintain the reputation of his company - his father's company - as one of the largest, most successful woolen mills in the northeast.

He had been up late the previous evening awaiting visits from his two top managers. They had arrived together just before midnight with the news: the mill operatives - some of them, that is - would walk out the next morning. Sources had infiltrated a workers' meeting that evening at a social hall in Chicopee. The workers' rage at the pay cuts received that day had been fueled by reports of the arrests of Mssrs. Garfield, Grant, and Taylor. The workers would leave their posts at eleven, they had agreed, and not return until the management retracted the pay cuts. The plight of the three labor leaders, while much on the workers' minds, was not presented as an issue. So far as the workers knew, it was unrelated to their dispute with the local mill owners.

But there was more, Richard's managers explained. One of the largest unions of paper mill workers was prepared to call on its members to walk out in sympathy with the textile workers. Paper workers had grievances about working conditions and reduced pay in their mills as well. What was worse, they explained to Richard, the motormen for the Holyoke Street Railway, the company that owned and operated all the trolleys in Holyoke, Chicopee, and surrounding towns, had consented to walk with the others. This news shocked Richard Wellington. Never before in Holyoke had workers from both textile and paper mills acted together, nor had the streetcar workers ever participated.

Despite the bad news, Richard Wellington was still confident. One factor, one critical factor, had always insulated Wellington Textiles from past labor actions: the French workers. Nearly three-quarters of the company's operatives were French Canadians, and they had never, ever in his years in the business, shown any sympathy for labor activity.

"What about the French workers?" Richard had asked his managers. "Have you talked to Letourneau and the other members of *La Comité*? Are they with us?"

"Yes, sir, we have, sir. Letourneau assures us. Our French operatives were not present at that meeting - they will remain at their jobs." A self-assured smile spread across Richard Wellington's face, a smile that quickly turned to a stolid, unbending leer. As long as he had the French workers on his side, a walkout of at most one quarter of Wellington's employees, while not insignificant, could be overcome.

238

"We have to get the police out in force to protect our property - and to protect our loyal workers," added Richard angrily. "I'll meet with the mayor first thing tomorrow morning; I'll see to it that every patrolman in Holyoke is on duty around the mill by ten. Operatives who walk out will be replaced, damn it, do you hear me? Every one of them. By Monday if possible. We can get by on the weekend. We'll announce that we're cutting back to just a day shift on the weekend due to a delay in delivery of wool. That will buy us time. But Monday morning, by God, I want every job filled, by whatever means necessary. I want those looms running, every one of them, and those spinners spinning."

Jack stood by the kitchen sink sipping a cup of coffee. Marie was stirring a pot of farina over the stove. Just then Charles appeared at the kitchen door. Through the screen he spoke to his son.

"Jackie?" Jack looked up and caught his father's eye. "Before ya go, eh?" Charles nodded toward the barn. Jack hurried to finish his bowl of hot cereal. Marie handed him his lunch bucket and he stepped out into the predawn half-light. In the barn he found his father leaning against one of the animal stalls, looking absently at the pigs.

"Did you want somethin', Dad?"

"Yeh, Jack, just a word. Pierre come over last evenin' after you'd gone to bed. He got a call from one of his friends at the mill, Gervais? He's a member of *La Comité*." Jack nodded. "Could be trouble brewin', son, just wanted you to know."

"What kind of trouble, Dad?"

"At the Paymaster's Office last evenin' - things got a little hot. Seems there's been pay cuts. Everyone at the mill got a reduction, two, three, four dollars or more." Jack was surprised.

"What happened, Dad?"

"Well, all's I know's they called a meeting for late last night, in Chicopee. Letourneau and the others weren't goin' is what Pierre heard. But it sounds like everyone's on edge. Just - be careful, boy, okay? Don't go gettin' involved."

"But Dad, if they cut my pay it's gonna be bad for us. I was hopin' to save a little between now 'n September."

"Don't you worry about that, Jackie, just do your job. Maybe the Irishmen, the Italians, the Poles all feel like flexin' their muscles, but the Frenchmen 've never gone in for that stuff, ya know? We just do our job, come what may."

"You don't think there's gonna be a - walkout?"

"I don't know, Jackie, I don't know. A pay cut - that's pretty hard medicine to swallow. Just don't go gettin' yourself fired over it is all I say."

Jack nodded, turned, and left for work. The eastern sky was a dull gray as he walked along Southampton Road to the trolley stop, then waited longer than usual before a Holyoke-bound car arrived. As the car pulled away, his eyes scanned the fields of corn along the tracks. In the distance he could just make out his family's home, thin wisps of fog hanging ominously over the roofline. There was a sense of foreboding to this day, and Jack could feel it.

As he crossed the bridge over the Second Level Canal, Jack's gaze took in the full view of Wellington Textiles, nearly half a mile long. From this vantage point all seemed normal. Looms rattled, steam rose from the power plant, other workers were approaching the several entrances to the mill. Jack had feared a throng of jeering, threatening workers gathered around each door as he had heard about from past walkouts. But all seemed quiet, like any another day, as he entered the sorting house and joined his co-workers.

Just then Mr. Leduc approached. Jack expected him to bark out instructions, but instead the gray-haired man looked uneasily at the three young workers. He hesitated briefly, then gestured for them to follow him into a narrow passage between two towering stacks of fleeces.

"Jus' so you boys know," he said in a whisper, "lots of the operatives, they're walkin' out at eleven. Pay cuts, rumors, and all."

"What rumors?" Jack asked.

"Somethin' about those IWW guys bein' arrested, I guess. And that girl who got tangled up in the loom. Just a lot of things happenin' all 't once, is all." The man who was usually loud and forceful looked worried. "Listen, we got a job to do, and we got a right to do it. So jus' do ya job, boys. We'll see no harm comes to no one." Leo and Raoul seemed to be unperturbed by their boss's words, but Jack was alarmed.

"Harm? What do you mean, Mr. Leduc?"

"Don't worry, kid, like I said, jus' do ya job." Then he barked: "Fifty bales on platform two, section two; get ta work, now, ya hear?" And so the day began like any other day in the sorting house. But how it would end, Jack was not at all certain.

Jack, Leo, and Raoul had just finished clearing section two on the loading dock when they heard shouts rising from the direction of the weaving rooms in the next building. It sounded like a celebration was underway, not a sound that was familiar at Wellington Textiles. Suddenly as the three stood listening to the shouts, an even more unusual thing could be heard, quiet. For within a matter of a minute or less, every loom and spinner in the mill fell silent. The shouting had ceased as well, as if the workers were listening in astonishment to the lack of the customary roar of hundreds of power looms. Then the shouts resumed, combined with cheers and applause.

Just then a throng of several dozen operatives appeared around the end of the building, racing in their direction. Jack and his co-workers watched in stunned silence for a moment before they realized they might be in danger from the thundering horde of enraged men careening toward them.

"Get inside boys, quick," shouted Mr. Leduc. And the huge doors were hastily swung shut just as some of the angry operatives scrambled up onto the loading dock. Jack ran to shut and latch the small entry next to the large doors. He had just lowered the heavy bar on the inside when the weight of the mob fell against the door on the other side. Unable to open it, the angry workers smashed the single small pane of glass. A red face glowered through the shards of broken glass.

"We're walkin' out, boys, everyone. So get your asses out here now if you know what's good for ya."

In his right hand Mr. Leduc held a curved scythe used for breaking up bundles of fleeces, and he raised it before the window. "You can break that door down, son, but this is what'll be waitin' for yah."

The red face disappeared. Figures could be seen through the broken glass running toward the dyehouse and Dwight Street. Jack, Leo, Raoul, and a dozen other sorting house workers, all French and mostly young, stood tense and grim-faced, expecting the doors to the loading platform to come crashing in on them at any moment. But the doors didn't budge, and soon the activity outside, at least what they could see or hear, ceased.

The sorting house workers stood silently, fear and confusion etched in their faces. There was no fate more dread than that of workers who chose to work rather than walk out.

"We'll be okay," said Mr. Leduc with what seemed like forced confidence. "There's many more of us than 'em, remember, 'bout four to one. As long as the French workers

242

stick together, we're okay. I talked to one a the *Comité* just a while ago. "

The sorting house took on a peculiar atmosphere for the remainder of the morning. With the doors to the loading platforms barred, the dozens of workers had to busy themselves within, moving orders along the narrow walkway to the dyehouse or to the freight elevators. Soon the aisles and hallways leading to the carding and weaving rooms, now silent, were jammed with pallets of wool. Jack, Leo, and Raoul were then assigned to rearrange the stacks of fleeces in the sorting house according to a new system devised by Mr. Leduc, although no one could see how it was an improvement over the old system. All the while hushed conversations took place among groups of men.

At the noon hour the sorting house workers sat eating their lunches on the stacks of pallets at the rear of the barricaded sorting house. Soon they were joined by dozens of French workers from the weaving and spinning rooms as well as the power plant and dyehouse.

When the ending bell rang, Jack, Leo, and Raoul rose and prepared to return to work. But the operatives seated around them did not move. They seemed to be eating slowly, as if waiting for something. "What's goin' on?" Leo asked Jack uneasily. "Ain't it work time?"

Jack's eyes met Leo's, then he nodded toward one of the loading platforms. Guy Letourneau and two other members of *La Comité* were standing in a tight group, talking quietly. As they watched, Letourneau turned and addressed the now over one hundred workers in the sorting house.

"*Messieurs.*" He paused, then added, "*mesdames,*" nodding to a group of ladies from the spinning room who were standing together near the back. He was uncharacteristically serious and his voice shook as he spoke. "It is my duty to report to you dis day very sad news." Suddenly the room fell

243

eerily quiet. "We have only just learned that our young sister, Yvonne Gilbault, has passed on at Holyoke Hospital."

A communal sigh rose from the crowd and there was a long moment of complete silence. Then a few sobs could be heard rising from among the ladies at the rear of the sorting house. Several men seemed to be clearing their throats; others removed their hats and placed them over their hearts, then crossed themselves.

"Yvonne was fourteen years of age," continued Letourneau. "*Dieu ait ton âme*, Yvonne. God rest your soul."

For several minutes there was nothing to be heard but sobs, throats being cleared, booted feet shifting uncomfortably on the concrete. Then the silence was broken as voices erupted from around the room. Words such as *Just a child - la pauvre petite - shame -* were flung into the dust-laden air. Then one voice rose above all the others.

"*They killed her*. Wellington - and his rich bastards - *they killed her*." Guy Letourneau silenced the protests, trying to quell the emotions that were bursting forth.

"We promise, my friends, to meet with the management to discuss dis, to espress our - our outrage at the loss of dis child, and de dangerous conditions we all work in. Let us wait to hear their response, please."

Again there was silence. Without a word a small group of workers stood and moved toward the doors leading to the platform. There they lined up in twos. Slowly others joined until the line stretched the length of the sorting house. Several men at the head of the line then raised the bars and swung open the doors. Sunlight and warm summer air streamed into the dusty, cavern-like room. Then the line began to move.

"What's happenin', *Jacques*?" whispered Leo. "Where dey goin'?"

"I guess we're walkin' out, Leo." Within minutes the sorting house was empty.

Jack's father was straining to remove a wheel from a Packard delivery truck when Jack appeared in the barn door.

"Jack," said Charles, nodding once to his son.

"Dad," replied Jack, a look of despair on his face, "I'm guessin' things didn't go too good at the mill, eh?"

Jack shook his head slowly, then slumped against the tool bench, dropping his rucksack to the gravel floor. "Nope."

Charles rose slowly, tire iron in hand, and stepped to the workbench. He let the iron fall noisily to the floor. "What happened, son? I hope you didn't do nothin' foolish."

"I didn't, Dad. They walked out, everyone - every last one. The carding rooms, weaving, spinning, the dyehouse, the power plant, the warehouse - everyone. They shut the place down."

Charles looked into his son's eyes, incredulous. "What about *La Comité*. What'd they have to say about that?"

"There wasn't much they could say," replied Jack. "That girl, Yvonne, she died. Letourneau come 'round to tell everyone." A pained grimace crossed Charles's face.

"The guys, some of them were chokin' up. Ladies from the spinning room were cryin'. But then some of the men they started yellin' and cursin' and shoutin' about Mr. Wellington - and then they jus' walked out. Right out to the street. Some of the Italians, Russians, Poles were out there tryin' to get us riled up, but the Frenchmen jus' left. Jus' as well, cause I didn't want to see things get nasty. Enough of that."

"Well, you did the right thing gettin' out. I don't want no son of mine associatin' with those union guys." Jack said nothing for several moments. Finally he lifted his rucksack.

"Well, guess I'll do some weedin'." He was about to leave the barn when he stopped. "Tommy didn't telephone, did he?"

"Can't say. I been out here most of the day."

Jack left the barn and headed to the kitchen door. Charles stood staring glumly at the damaged wheel on the floor in front of him.

"*Jackie, Jackie,*" shouted Marie from the back steps. Jack was working along a row of onions, pulling weeds, the tall, straight leaves casting long shadows in the late day sun. He looked up. "There's a man on the telephone, Jackie, wants to talk to you."

"Is it Tommy?" asked Jack as he stepped into the kitchen, knocking soil from his boots. Marie shook her head as she stood by the stove stirring a pot. Jack talked only briefly, then replaced the handset. A few minutes later the Bernard family sat around the supper table.

"Was that Tom on the telephone?" inquired Charles. Jack shook his head.

"Anne?" Again Jack shook his head. Charles looked at his son awaiting an explanation.

"They're havin' a meeting tonight, in Chicopee. About a - strike."

"I suppose they want you to come, eh?"

"Ayeh. They're askin' every worker to be there. There's gonna be a vote."

"Well, just let 'em have their vote, son. You stay 'way, hear? Nothing good's comin' from that, nothin' good." Jack sipped his soup and made no reply.

Jack and Claire were seated in the glider in the backyard as the last light was fading from the sky. "Jackie, what's gonna happen, I mean about the strike? Do you think it will really happen?"

"I don't know, Claire, I just don't know. Don't you be worrying about that, okay?" Just then a motorcar pulled into the driveway. Jack turned and looked. It was the Wellingtons' Reo. "Tommy," called Jack as he rose from the glider and walked across the lawn.

"Hey, Jack."

"I was beginnin' to wonder where you were. You just get back from Boston?"

"Last night, Jack, I got in last evening."

"Everything go okay?"

Tom nodded. "But I hear the mill's shut down. What happened?"

"Everything happened, Tommy, everything at once. I couldn't believe my eyes when I showed up for work on Wednesday. Shifts running day and night, seven days a week. Shipments comin' in left and right - everyone runnin' like a dervish."

"Yeh, I know. Nothing like a war to get business booming."

"Then, yesterday, when guys went to get paid - pay cuts. Everyone. Like a bomb went off. Pay cuts yesterday, then today that girl, Yvonne, she died."

"Yeh, I heard. That's a pity, a real pity," said Tom looking down and shaking his head.

"But the workers, well the French workers, anyway, they'll be back on the job on Monday, I bet. They need their jobs, and they just don't take to striking. So, how'd your trip to Boston turn out? Any news?" asked Jack as the pair stood next to the car.

"Well, I found out what the charges are against Mr. Garfield and those other fellows."

"And?" Tom lowered his voice.

"It's bad, Jack, really bad: treason and sedition. If they're convicted they could get sent up for life - they could even get the death penalty."

"Just for tellin' the truth about what's goin' on in the mills?"

"That's about it. And - you're not gonna believe this, Jackie, but it's all Uncle Richard's doing."

"What?"

"You know my old Harvard chum, Harold Sampson? His dad is a judge in Boston. He told Harold that some mill owners from Holyoke went to see the governor. The next day, the very next day, charges were filed against those guys. It was Uncle Richard, James Ellis of the New England Mill, George Davis of American Thread, and Colonel Jenner from the silk mill, they're the ones responsible."

"I don't believe it, Tommy. All they have to do is call their friends and they can get someone thrown in jail, just like that? So what do we do? What can we do?"

"Well," began Tom.

"What about your uncle?" interrupted Jack. "Maybe you should go to see him first."

"I did, Jackie, I did. He told me to forget it, that those guys were only getting what they deserved. He said if I tried to help them it would look like I was a sympathizer, like I was being disloyal - to him, to the company, to the country." Suddenly there was a new urgency in Tom's voice.

"Listen, Jackie, we gotta do something and fast. And maybe this is the perfect time, really."

"What are you talkin' about, Tommy? What's perfect about it?"

"You said it sounds like the workers are never gonna get over their differences and act together. But maybe if they knew about Mr. Garfield and the others, I mean, why they were arrested and what the charges are, maybe that would, you know, light a fire under them. Maybe it would be just enough to get them..."

"Tommy, it sounds to me like the mill owner's son has turned into a union organizer - what's the word - instigator?

I'm beginning to suspect you of bein' one of them *Bull-shuv-iks* Claire is always harping about."

"Okay, okay, maybe I've changed my thinking. But we have to do something, and soon."

"Like what, Tommy? Like what?"

"That meeting, tonight. You could tell them about Garfield and those guys. And about the benzene."

Jack shook his head and looked toward the house. "Wait a minute, Tommy. You can't expect me - I'm not even goin'. You know my dad - he's dead set against unions and strikes."

"I'll go with you, Jack."

"Are you kidding? The son of the mill owner at a union meeting? You must be crazy, Tom."

"But you could get me in, Jack. Tell them, you know, about Garfield and the dyehouse. They'll listen to you."

"I'm not gonna go in there and give them some sob story about my - my troubles. That's nobody's business but mine. I'm not looking for their pity."

"Okay, okay, Jack. But let's go down there together. Let's see if they'll let me in."

"I don't feel right about this, Tommy."

"Jack, what we did for Carolyn, for Garfield and his wife and kids. Remember? It's all gonna be a waste if her father... Please, Jack."

Jack was uncomfortable. He looked uneasily toward the house, then back at Tom. "Okay, Tommy, but I have an idea."

Jack knew his father was in the barn. He spoke briefly to Marie in the kitchen, telling her that he and Tom were going to see a friend and would be back soon. A few minutes later Tom's motorcar was parked on a dark street in the Patch, the neighborhood in Holyoke where most of the Irish mill workers lived.

This was the gritty side of the city, a tangle of tiny shacks scattered about with narrow paths between them leading down to the river's edge. On one side was the water, on the other the back ends of several large mills roaring with activity even as night was falling.

Tom sat hunched in the driver's seat waiting nervously while Jack made his way to the home of one of his co-workers from the sorting house, Mike Murphy. Jack had helped Mike home one January day when the young man slipped and hurt his ankle on the icy loading platform. Jack knew that Mike's father was one of the leaders of workers at Wellington Textiles, but he also knew that that information was tightly held. Any worker known to the mill management as an agitator would be promptly fired.

Jack had rapped on the flimsy door of the tiny house. Mike had appeared and stepped out into the street to talk to this unexpected visitor. For several minutes they spoke in whispers, only the glow of the tip of Mike's cigarette visible in the dark.

"If it's about the mill, ya know, he's pretty careful who he talks to. Me and Ma don' even know what 'es up to with that these days. Betta that way, 'e says."

"But it's important, Mike. It's about those guys from Lowell, they've been arrested and they're in jail in Boston. They're bein' charged with treason, Mike, they could get life - or worse."

"So wha's that gotta do with my da?"

"I jus' need to talk to him, Mike. Please..." Just then footsteps could be heard coming down the path.

"Come inside, Jack." The two disappeared into the shack. It turned out Mike's father was at home, fast asleep on a dilapidated day bed in the front room.

Padraig Murphy's parents had emigrated from Ireland in 1850, fleeing from the potato famine that cost a million Irishmen their lives. He had worked nearly every job there was in the textile mills of Holyoke since he was twelve. He'd seen it all, the pain and suffering, injuries and deaths. Union activism was in the blood of most Irishmen in Holyoke, or so it seemed, and it was a matter of the greatest frustration to him that so many years had passed with so little progress to show for it.

Awakened by his son, Mr. Murphy heated some stale coffee on a small coal stove, then sat and listened to Jack tell him about the Lowell union leaders.

"Yeh, we 'eard 'bout 'em, sa shame."

"But there's one thing about them that you might not know, Mr. Murphy."

"Eh?"

"Listen, I got a friend, he's waiting in his car. He can explain it better than me. Can you talk to 'im?" Murphy seemed uneasy.

"Listen, Bernard, I gotta be careful, we all do, ya know? Any one of us could be sittin' in a jail cell too if we're not careful."

"I know, I know. But my friend has some information, some important information. It might help get the workers - it might unite them."

"Who is this friend?" asked Murphy suspiciously.

"He's okay, I promise." Jack stepped out into the dark lane and started walking toward the street when a figure came out of the shadows.

"Jackie," whispered Tom. Jack led Tom back to Murphy's shack and the pair entered. When Tom appeared in the dim light, Murphy stood and shot an angry stare at Jack.

"What the hell?"

"It's all right, sir," said Tom.

"I know you, you're the Wellington kid. Git outta here." He grabbed Tom's arm and started pushing him toward the door.

251

"Please, just listen to me, Mr. Murphy. I have to talk to you about something. In strict confidence, I swear."

Murphy was not pleased and he stood by the door, about to usher both visitors out at any moment. But he listened to Tom.

"I went to Boston yesterday, sir, and I found out about those three union men, Garfield, Grant, and Taylor? You know them, right?"

"What makes you think I do?"

"They've been in town a couple times lately. They're good men, Mr. Murphy, I know they are. Mr. Garfield has worked his whole life to get mill owners to change their ways. What I found out is that the charges against those three men were filed by federal agents in Boston by order of the Bureau of Investigation in Washington."

"Okay, so what? What's that gotta do with 'olyoke?"

"It never would have happened, sir, if it hadn't been for the mill owners of Holyoke - Ellis, Davis, Jenner, and Richard Wellington."

"Yeh, well, the mill owners always get their way - nothin' new there. But Wellington, he's your uncle. So why do you care?"

"Mr. Garfield lived in Holyoke when he was younger. He has a daughter. She's my - my girlfriend. It's breaking her heart, sir, that her father's in jail. He's got a wife and two little ones. I want to do something for her - for her family."

"We were thinking, if the workers knew all this, on top of the accident with that little girl, and the pay cuts, it might bring them together, you know?" Murphy sat down, thinking. Tom, Jack, and Mike stood anxiously awaiting his verdict.

"Well, I'll pass it along, boys, 's all I kin promise. I'll pass it along." He turned to Jack.

"Bernard, it's your people that really need to hear about this, ya know?"

~ 42 ~

Hundreds of French workers from the Wellington mill converged on the dingy social hall on a side street in the Flats that night. The mood was tense and the scene was eerily quiet as men stood in small groups around the hall. Several groups of women could also be seen gathered at the back, just inside the entrance to the hall. A single American flag hung from a rope suspended over the small stage at one end of the room. The few electric light bulbs dangling on cords from the ceiling cast harsh shadows on the dusty wooden floor.

Jack stood with Leo and several other sorting house workers near the back of the room. He was feeling uncomfortable, knowing that his father would not approve of his attendance. At the same time he was painfully aware of the consequences of the pay cuts for him and his family. Tom waited in his motorcar on the dark street a block away from the meeting place.

Periodically a door at the rear of the stage opened and a grim-faced worker appeared, looked intently about as if searching for someone, then disappeared, closing the door behind him. Each time the figure appeared, voices were raised in the crowd - anxious voices, angry voices - calling for the meeting to begin.

Finally, nearly a half hour after the meeting was to have commenced, the single door opened and the six members of *La Comité* appeared. They were dressed in suits and ties in stark contrast to the overalls and faded work shirts of most of the workers present. They arranged chairs in a line across the stage and were seated, unsmiling and nervous.

Guy Letourneau remained standing, cleared his throat, then spoke to the suddenly hushed audience. "*Mesdames et messieurs,* ladies, gentlemens." He turned and looked anxiously at his fellow committee members, most of whom were staring down at their shoes. "We are 'ere tonight to discuss - decide - on our response to the walkout of our comrades - at Wellington Mills. As you know, we..." He turned and nodded to his colleagues seated on the stage. "We, members of *La Comité,* was selected by the French workers to represen' chyou, to speak for you, to the mill owners and managers. The last election took place in dis hall about tree years ago. And I believe we have served you well."

A wave of murmurs rose from the assembled workers, then settled back down. Letourneau continued, his voice louder. "Remember, my fellow Frenchmen, dat we were chosen by you. We work 'long side you. Jus' like you we 'ave families and we 'ave to feed our children and pay da rent jus' like you."

Again a wave of voices rose in the audience and again Letourneau tried to speak with more force to stifle the rabble. "We don't take the matter of a labor action lightly. We need our jobs jus' like you, we 'ave to tink about our wives and our little ones whatever we do."

"Let's have the vote," cried one worker from the rear.

"Call the vote," shouted another. Guy Letourneau raised his arms.

"Please, please, wait a minute. Now, we talked with the managers dis aftanoon, all of us. They assured us that our jobs are secure if we return to work Monday morning, that there would be no disciplinary measures taken for dem dat walked out today. And dey told us that the cops'll be out in force to protec' all loyal workers who return to their jobs."

The murmur from the crowd rose once again, but this time punctuated by a hail of derisive epithets: "What about the pay cuts? Will the pay cuts be reversed? We want full pay."

"Well, no, the pay cuts have to stand. It's the government contracts, dey say. To win those jobs the mill has to bid against lots a other mills from 'round the country. We got the jobs but with very small profit. The mill can't meet dose contracts without cuttin' our pay. Otherwise the company 'ill go under, dats what they're sayin'." Suddenly the crowd was silent.

"It's our patriotic duty, my friends, to work for less," continued Letourneau. "We are at war, and we all mus' do our part."

"I'll bet Wellington, and Pierce, and the other bigwigs ain't takin' no pay cut," shouted one worker.

Letourneau shook his head. "Listen, everyone's doin' their part. We're all lucky to have our jobs."

"What about the little girl, Yvonne?"

Letourneau glanced toward his fellow committee members, then looked out over the crowd. "The mill it's payin' all the expenses includin' the burial. They been very generous." Again words of scorn rose from the workers. Several of the women at the rear could be heard among them.

"So," concluded Letourneau," La Comité, every one of us, urges you to vote against a strike and to go back to work on Monday. But we promise to keep talkin' with management about all dese matters the French workers care about."

The mood of the crowd seemed to be turning. There was another wave of voices, but they were low and seemed favorable to the recommendation of La Comité, to return to work on Monday.

"Are we ready to vote, den?" asked Letourneau, sensing a shift in the mood. Heads nodded throughout the crowd.

Just then a scuffle broke out near the main doors. "May I speak, please? I have some important information," came a voice familiar to Jack. It was Tom, shouting from the entryway at the rear, waving over the heads of several burly workers determined to exclude him. Letourneau looked startled, but proceeded.

"Let us have our vote, den, eh? You all have received a ballot..." Tom broke away from the men trying to restrain him and pushed his way through the crowd shouting.

"Wait, wait, you need to know something." Suddenly all eyes were on Tom and a hush came over the crowd. "Garfield, Taylor, and Grant. You all know who they are. They're good men, men devoted to workers, men who believe in fairness for all workers. As some of you know, Mr. Garfield, Mr. John Garfield, grew up in Holyoke. His family came to Holyoke from Montréal when he was just born. Garceau was his family name. He attended school here, then went to work for the Holyoke Street Railway Company. He's been fighting for the workers of this city, of this nation, for over twenty years. He's a loyal American, as patriotic as any of us." The crowd was hushed. "Just five days ago, John Garfield was arrested, in Lowell. That same day Mr. Grant and Mr. Taylor were also arrested in Boston."

"We know all this. What about it?" asked Letourneau impatiently.

"What you should know before you vote tonight is what those men are charged with and why. They're charged with sedition, sedition and treason." The crowd reacted in astonishment. "That's right, sedition and treason. According to the court papers they have been undermining our country, compromising national security, giving critical information to the Germans. All, of course, ridiculous charges. But if they are found guilty they will be put to death for those crimes."

Cries and shouts of anger arose from the crowd.

"And who was responsible for the arrest of those men and for the charges filed against them?," continued Tom. "Some of Holyoke's wealthiest, most powerful men: James Ellis, George

Davis, Colonel William Jenner, and Richard Wellington. That's right, the owners of Holyoke's largest textile mills, with the assistance of the Governor and the Attorney General in Washington, DC."

The crowd fairly exploded with outrage. Fists were raised and shaken, curses rang out, threats and vituperation of all sorts rose in the dusty hall like a wave. The members of *La Comité* sat quiet and grim-faced. Several looked at one another, heads shaking. Soon the chant - *Strike, strike, strike* - rang out in the hall. An attempt was made to distribute ballots but to no avail. Workers began streaming from the hall onto the street, the decision having been made. The French workers of Wellington Textiles were, for the first time, on strike.

A number of workers surrounded Tom, shaking his hand enthusiastically and slapping him on the back. Jack watched from a distance, then left the hall.

~ 43 ~

Jack was up early the following morning loading tools, several lengths of iron pipe, and cans of kerosene and engine oil onto the wagon in front of the barn. The water level in the river was dropping fast as the drought entered its third week. The intake pipe for the irrigation pump needed to be extended to ensure a constant supply of water for the gardens, and Jack was hoping to spend the morning on the project. One added benefit of his plan was avoiding his father, but just as he mounted the tractor Charles emerged from the kitchen door looking in Jack's direction. Jack sat limply in the tractor seat as his father approached.

"Need help with that, Jackie?" With his back still to his father Jack shook his head.

"Naw, I can get it, Dad." He reached for the starter lever.

"I waited up for you last night long as I could. How'd the meetin' turn out, son?" Jack dropped his hand and sat back in the seat, his eyes focused on the western horizon. He exhaled loudly. "Not good, I'm guessin'," Charles replied. Again Jack shook his head.

"Nope. Not good."

"I suppose everybody's het up 'bout that little girl, eh?" asked Charles.

"Ayeh, pretty much so," replied Jack.

"Pity 'bout her. I worked with her father some years ago at the mill. Lost another child to diphtheria, they did. That and the short pays, I guess I can see how things were gettin'. So, they're joinin' the walkout?"

"Ayeh," replied Jack solemnly. "Place is just shuttin' down today, I s'pose. I'm sorry, Dad. It was the arrests, though, that turned them around. Garfield and those guys."

"Yeh, well, John Garfield's always been well liked in town. One of our own, I guess. But I'm surprised a bit, why folks held that 'gainst the mill owners of Holyoke." Jack stood and jumped to the ground next to his father.

"Well, I don't guess they did, least 'til Tommy spoke up."

"Tom? What's he got to do with it, Jack? Surely he wasn't..."

Jack nodded. "Yeh, he was there. Had to fight his way in the doors, a course. But fight he did. And when he talked, they listened."

"To what, son?"

"It was his uncle, Richard, and the owners from the New England Mill, Franklin, and the silk mill that got those guys arrested." Charles stood silent, dumbfounded. "They got the governor to call Washington right after that rally last week. Day later the arrest warrants were issued for those three. Claimed they were traitors."

"And they believed that, the workers?"

"Heard it practically from the horse's mouth. Tommy told them he went to his Uncle Richard and he admitted it. Told Tommy the guy was a socialist, a Red. Said he deserved to be hanged." Jack paused, a grim smile on his face. "When the meeting heard that, well, it turned the tide." Jack shook his head.

"That Tom, he's got a lot o' guts, I give 'im credit," said Charles. "But Jesus, Jack, it's like he's burnin' his bridges with his own family."

"A few months ago he was talkin' like he was a union-buster. All of a sudden, he's practically a Bolshevik," replied Jack. For a brief moment their eyes met.

"Well, the die is cast," said Charles.

"I'm goin' down to the river to work on that intake line," replied Jack. Charles watched as Jack mounted the tractor again, started it, and headed off.

Silence hung over Holyoke like a heavy woolen blanket that day. Nearly every mill lay quiet. No plumes of smoke rose from the brick stacks along the canals and riverfront. Trolleys and omnibuses that normally scurried along the city's streets were nowhere to be found. An occasional buggy made its way down High Street, the resonant clip-clop of the horses' shoes on the cobblestones echoing off the brick buildings on either side.

WALKOUT read the bold headline of one newspaper displayed on newsstands; MILL WORKERS ON STRIKE read another. Small groups of men gathered in shops and at newsstands conversing in hushed voices. They spoke as if there had been a death. Holyoke, Massachusetts, quiet on a workday? The atmosphere was nothing short of funereal.

~ 44 ~

SATURDAY, JUNE 23 – SUNDAY, JUNE 24

Jack spent several hours that morning on the irrigation pump. It was now working well, but the water level in the river was dropping several inches a day. At that rate the pump would be out of water within a week and the onion crop would once again be at risk. Nevertheless he spent the remainder of the day weeding and fertilizing the onions. The mid-afternoon sun was scalding. Sweat was streaming from his head and neck as he shoveled manure into the wagon behind the barn.

"How about some lemonade, Jackie?" called Marie from the yard.

"I'll be in shortly," replied Jack without slowing his pace the slightest bit. A half hour later when Jack still had not appeared in the kitchen, Marie came walking carefully along one of the garden paths, a tin cup in one hand and a crockery pitcher in the other.

"Here, have some lemonade, Jackie. You're going to wilt in this heat if you don't take a breather."

"I gotta - get these onions - mulched - try to keep the water - keep it from evaporating - much as possible," explained Jack breathlessly. He paused, leaned on his rake, then wiped his forehead and eyes with his handkerchief. Squinting in the bright sunlight, he took the cup offered by his

261

sister and held it while she poured, then gulped it down in a single swallow.

"Can't you take a break, Jackie, for just a bit? I mean, until it's a little cooler."

Jack shook his head. "Nope - gotta do this now - but thanks for the lemonade," he added, still trying to catch his breath.

"I 'spect he's compensatin', Marie," said Charles a few minutes later in the kitchen. "If he can't work at the mill, he's gotta do double duty at home is the way his mind works."

"But I worry about him, Father. The heat - all that exertion - you know."

"Ayeh, I know. I worry, too."

The evening was not much cooler than the day. The four Bernards sat on wicker chairs in the back yard, trying to derive some benefit from the meager breeze that rose sporadically. The sun was dropping through a few thin clouds just above the horizon, streaks of vermilion and tangerine radiating out across the western sky.

"Maybe those are rain clouds, Jackie. Maybe there's a storm comin'," said Claire hopefully. "It says in the *Farmer's Almanac* that we're gonna have rain soon." She looked at her brother, hoping to spark some enthusiasm. But Jack was not to be encouraged.

"Yeh, maybe, but the *Almanac* also predicted June was gonna be a 'specially wet month, Claire." He stood slowly. "I'm bushed. Goin' a bed. Night all."

Jack's bedroom was still warm and he lay on top of the sheets wearing only his pajama bottoms. Sleep had been coming easier for him of late, to the point that he had nearly forgotten how, just a few weeks earlier, the mere approach of nightfall brought a surge of dread from deep inside.

This night the heat made sleep difficult, and Jack lay for the longest time looking up at the ceiling. First he reviewed in his mind the principles of onion culture he'd been reading about. Soon thoughts of the mill intruded, of Leo and Raoul smiling, then of Guy Letourneau's grim expression as he told the workers about Yvonne Gilbault. Then it was Anne, her smile, the smallness of her hand wrapped in his, the softness of her body pressed against his in that very bed a week earlier. Now he was wide awake, breathing hard, heart pounding.

Jack rose to his feet, the old floorboards creaking loudly under the weight of his steps. He descended the steep stairs as quietly as he could and stepped through the front door onto the lawn. The moist grass felt good on his bare feet and the cool night air was like a balm for his face and chest. He stretched out on his back on the hammock in the side yard and within minutes was sleeping soundly.

Some time, maybe minutes, perhaps an hour or more later, he was awake and looking up at the starry summer heavens. For a brief moment he heard chickens cackling from the barn, then the soft shush of a breeze through the needles of the pine tree over his head. He was just drifting off again when the shushing sound suddenly grew louder. And it seemed to originate not just from the pine needles hanging above but from all directions. Suddenly he could feel fear, feel it surge through his body. His arms and legs seemed electrified, every muscle tense, and an aching sensation rose at the back of his head and spread over him like a monk's cowl.

Eyes now wide open, his gaze focused on the sky above. But there were no stars now visible, no constellations, nothing but a light, a single white light, a ferociously, balefully intense light, that seemed to be growing and intensifying as he watched. The shushing sound got louder with every beat of his heart, and Jack tried to get to his feet, to shake off this - this dream - this apparition - this nightmare - but despite his efforts he could not move.

Just then there appeared out of the ball of intense, fiery light, two eyes. They shone darkly, fiercely, malevolently upon him. Jack felt himself slipping, falling backwards. Then the faces of his mother and father, his sisters, and Anne appeared before him, one at a time, first in focus and close-up, then blurred and retreating, fading. He was struggling, trying to reach them. *Wait - wait - wait* he called to them, but they didn't seem to hear. The smiling, familiar faces receded still further, finally disappearing completely. Now all that remained was one pair of eyes, hideous and glowering. They drew nearer as a current, a virtual river of noise seemed to surround him and enclose him.

But in that moment another face appeared, a man's face, an old man's face. It was a sad visage, but wise and loving. Jack couldn't place it at first as its features were only visible spottily, but slowly, gradually they resolved themselves and he was able at last to recognize the face. It was Father Lévesque. He was coming closer and his lips were moving slowly, though Jack could not make out his words over the cacophony in his head.

Jack's eyes locked on the old priest's eyes and held them for what seemed like a long time. Slowly, ever so slowly, the priest's facial features became clearer. And as they did Jack realized with amazement that the shushing sound was fading. Those fierce, frightening eyes were dimmer now, further away, and dissolving as he watched.

And then, as abruptly as it had begun, it was over.

Jack lay on the hammock. Slowly he opened his eyes and looked up at the sky. The stars were fewer now, the constellations different from earlier. And there was a glow in the eastern sky. It was morning, he suddenly realized - a new day. The realization swept over him like an ocean wave running up on a sandy beach. It felt good, refreshing, cleansing, as if he was somehow renewed.

A few hours later the Bernard family sat in a pew at St. Agnes Church. Mass began like any other, and yet for Jack there was something different. His memories of the previous night were fragmentary but powerful. At the start it had felt very much like a seizure building inside his head. And yet, somehow, it had been different. It had taken a turn, he knew that. He'd seen those terrible eyes, but he'd seen the faces of those he loved the most. And he'd seen the face of Father Lévesque clearly, heard his voice. Most importantly, when it was over, he had slept, slept for hours, he figured. And when he awoke, it had felt like something important, something monumental had occurred.

After the opening of the Mass, the Old Testament reading, and a hymn, Father Bertin stepped to the lectern. He greeted the congregation with a smile and offered a prayer. Then his expression grew stern and his voice cracked.

"Welcome, my friends. It is very good to see you all on this summer Sunday." He paused, looking down at his notes, then back up at the congregation, then he continued. "Normally on this day we celebrate *Saint-Jean-Baptiste*, patron saint of French Canada. But on this normally joyous occasion, dear hearts, I am afraid I have some very sad news to share with you." The congregation fell utterly silent. "Last night, in Montréal, Father Lévesque passed away."

The old priest had been in good fettle that day, retiring at the usual time, Father Bertin had learned. Then some time in the night, no one knew just when, he had died. There was, they said, no sign of any illness, of any pain or distress.

"Jackie, I'm so sorry," said Anne softly. They sat together under a shady arbor in the Wellingtons' rose garden that afternoon.

"He told me he was looking forward to his retirement, Anne. To walking in the gardens at that home, *La Refuge*. He said he and God needed to spend some time together, just the two of them." Jack recounted Father Lévesque's crisis of faith when he was younger. "I hope he got the chance to set things right, I really do."

Then Jack told Anne about the events of the previous night. "I can't figure out whether it was a dream, a nightmare, or - or what. It felt so - so real. And it was as if Father was right there in front of me, again."

"Was it disturbing? Jackie, were you frightened?"

"Well, for a while I was, but in the end, it felt like - like I - like I fought it off, whatever it was. It feels different now, Anne, like I've moved forward. And Father dying, well, I'm sorry to hear it, but maybe, maybe he'd just finished his work, you know? Maybe it was his time. But..."

"What, Jackie, what is it?"

"From what Father Bertin said, it sounds like he died just about the time I saw him in that - dream." Anne held one of Jack's hands and caressed it gently with the fingers of her other hand. "It's eerie, you know?" Jack continued. "I suppose it was just a coincidence, but then I wonder."

"What, Jackie?"

He gazed out across the garden and the rows of snapdragons, peonies, and dahlias nodding in the afternoon sun. He reached out and plucked a fading rose from a stem, sniffed it, then handed to Anne. "I don't know if I really believe all those Bible stories about spirits, miracles, visions. I figure it's in our minds. Do you?"

Anne sniffed the rose, then held it gently in her hand at eye level, as if examining it in minute detail, then she spoke:

"There are more things in heaven and earth, Horatio, than are dreamt of in your philosophy."

Jack looked puzzled.

"It's a line from Hamlet. He's saying that despite all our study, all our learning, all our so-called wisdom, there is more to this world than we know. More than we can know. It's a mystery, Jackie, a mystery no one has ever solved and never will."

Jack nodded. "I guess I'll never know exactly what happened last night. But I'm thinking maybe now I'll be able to sleep - you know, be at peace."

"You know what I'm thinking?" asked Anne with a twinkle in her eye. "I'm thinking, perhaps, if I were lying next to you, holding you, you holding me, every night, maybe that would help you to fall asleep."

Jack looked into Anne's eyes and flashed a crooked smiled. "I doubt that, Anne Wellington, I doubt that very much." Their eyes met, shining brightly. Jack leaned toward Anne and they shared a kiss, a slow, tender, lingering kiss.

~ 45 ~

SUNDAY, JUNE 24

Helen and Charlotte sat on a wrought iron bench in the garden house behind Richard and Charlotte's home later that afternoon. Storm clouds were moving in, offering hope that the drought would finally be broken. "How is Anne enjoying her new position, Helen?" inquired Charlotte.

"She's very content, I'd say. It suits her, working with the young women that come to the Home. She's leading a play reading group on Wednesday evenings. The girls just love it. Some who have moved on still return each week just for Anne's group. They're reading scenes from *The Merchant of Venice* this week - it's her favorite."

"And young Thomas? Richard tells me he's back in Holyoke."

Helen hesitated. "Tom..." She smiled briefly before a mask of pain descended over her round face. "Tom will be leaving us - soon, very soon, I'm afraid." Tears welled up in her eyes as she spoke.

"Helen, what is it, dear?"

"He's decided to enlist, Charlotte. He's headed to Newport on Wednesday - the Navy."

"Oh, dear. Well, you - we're all going to miss him." Charlotte knelt next to her sister-in-law. "I'm sure he'll do just fine, Helen, dear. They say the tide is already turning in

France and Belgium." Helen nodded, then wiped her eyes with a handkerchief just as Richard appeared in the entryway.

"Everything all right, dear?" he asked Charlotte.

"Helen was just telling me about young Tom. Did you know, Richard? He's enlisting - in the Navy. He leaves on Wednesday." Richard stood stiffly and turned away from his wife, gazing across the expanse of green grass toward a row of weeping mulberry trees.

"Well, we're all very proud, I'm sure." Then he paused. "Helen, I want you to know that I tried to - I offered young Tom an opportunity." She looked up and into Richard's face, surprise and curiosity in her expression. "I told him we could reinstate him in the front office - give him some special assignment related to the war effort so that he..."

"When was that, Richard?" interrupted Helen. "When did you see him?"

"Just the other evening, he stopped by, directly when he returned from Boston."

"And how did Tom respond to your offer?" she asked, certain she knew the answer.

"He wouldn't even consider it. All he wanted to talk about was that Garfield chap and his fellow socialist travelers."

"Yes, well, as it turns out Mr. Garfield is the father of Carolyn Ford, Tom's girlfriend. Her mother is Nina Calavetti at the Women's Home."

Richard's face reddened. "I wish that young man would not get tangled up in such matters. It could affect his future. And I dare say it reflects poorly on the company - on the family, as well."

Just then his brother Thomas appeared, moving across the lawn in his wheelchair with the assistance of Miss Beldon. Helen, Charlotte, and Richard stepped out onto the grass to greet him. The nurse turned and walked toward the street.

"Why, Thomas, what are you doing here?"

269

"Miss Beldon and Bromley helped me," replied Thomas, gesturing toward the Pierce Arrow parked at the curb. "I telephoned you, Richard, more than once. I left messages with the maid and with Charlotte. But you never..."

"But your health, brother, are you sure you should be gadding about in your condition?"

"I've been feeling stronger of late, Richard. And frankly I've been concerned about this - this strike. Are you sure what you are doing is wise - for the company?"

"Dear, please, don't get overwrought," said Helen anxiously.

"What I'm doing is ensuring that Wellington Textiles meets its obligations, Thomas. We have dozens of contracts with the War Department - dozens. They are depending on us as one of the major suppliers of uniforms and blankets for our troops and our allies' troops. It is our duty..."

"I realize that, of course. But turning out our own workers, when we need them most? Really, Richard, I ask you, how is that going to help us do our duty?"

"They are the ones who have walked out, Thomas. On strike when the company, when the nation needs them most. They are traitors, pure and simple."

"Richard, listen to yourself," said Thomas. "These people you call traitors, many of them have been with the company for decades, *decades*. Fifty-five, sixty hours a week. Year after year. Through good times and bad." Richard shook his head and laughed scornfully. Thomas continued. "I'd say they're far from traitors, Richard. I'd say they've shown extraordinary loyalty. Especially the Frenchmen, who never - until now - registered so much as a complaint about their work, their pay, the conditions they must work under."

"Dear, don't you think we should be going along?" interposed his wife, shooting looks of concern at both Richard and Charlotte.

"Well, they picked a fine time to change their ways. Turncoats, that's what they are, turncoats and riff-raff," replied Richard, his face now scarlet.

"But young Bernard says he's never seen the mill so busy, never known the workers to be so pressed: three shifts, weekends, holidays."

"Of course it is busy, Thomas. We have contracts to fill, that's what I'm saying."

"But why cut their pay at such a time? When everyone is working so hard just to keep up."

"We need to keep our payroll costs down if we hope to show a profit. These government contracts, you know, we had to outbid many other firms from across the country to land these."

"Richard, I may be feeble of body but I'm not a fool. I see the financial statements that you bring to the Board meetings every month. Our profit margin has been rising ever since we got those contracts."

Then Helen spoke up. "I seem to recall your saying not too long ago that War Department work was a goldmine for Wellington textiles. That's the word you used, as I recall, Richard, *goldmine*. Now you seem to be saying they're a liability?"

"It is a good deal more complicated than that, Helen," replied Richard, a note of condescension in his tone.

"Well, I may not know the details of the company's position," replied Helen hotly, "but I fail to understand how turning out our entire workforce, every last operative, and hiring new workers from Boston and Fall River and Manchester, people you know nothing about, is going to help matters."

"We need workers who are loyal, reliable, Helen."

"We already had such workers, Richard, until you did everything to - to betray their loyalty."

"I'm betraying them? Helen, dear, I think you have it reversed. And speaking of betrayals, did you know that your own son spoke against me, against the company, at that meeting the other night?"

"Yes, Richard, I am aware of that fact."

"How about that? My own flesh and blood turning on me. You know, that boy quit his job in Accounting without a moment's notice. He just left - no apology, no explanation, not to me, not to Mr. Drury. Not a word."

"Yes, I know. And I'm sorry about that. I won't try to make excuses for him. Tom has been, well, wrestling with some personal troubles, Richard, ever since his brother passed..."

"And then he came back and had the audacity to argue to me that Garfield and company were all-American boys and that the charges against them should be dropped."

"Well, Richard, he knows the man, he respects him, and he is very fond of his daughter. He and Jack Bernard risked life and limb to try to protect her when the Lowell police descended on his family home."

"And I told him we'd take him back - I don't know what got into me - that we would set him up in a job that would keep him out of the service - and he declined. All he wanted to do was plead for those three *union agitators*." Richard spat out the last two words as if the very speaking of them was distasteful. "He should have snapped up my offer. Why in heaven's name didn't he?"

"Maybe because he has principles, Richard," replied Helen loudly and angrily. "Principles and pride. Carolyn's father is in need, and he tries to help. His country needs him, and he answers the call. Don't you see, Richard, he's not being disloyal, he's trying to do what he believes is right."

"Well, maybe so."

"Perhaps you..." She paused and started again. "Perhaps *we all* may learn a lesson from that."

"Why don't you give your nephew a going away present?" suggested Thomas to his brother. "Get those men out of jail. Maybe then the workers will reconsider."

"If I did that, they'd see it as weakness," replied Richard, glowering.

"Believe me," replied Thomas. "No one ever accused Richard Wellington of being weak. Think of it as a gesture of good will, to your loyal operatives."

~ 46 ~

Charles Bernard was bent over the fender of a farm truck when he heard the voice of his neighbor, Pierre Bousquet.

"Charlie? You here?"

"Ayeh," came the reply as Charles straightened and peered up at his neighbor.

"Didn' I see Jackie out in the garden jus' now?"

"Yeh, dressin' the onions."

"Ain't he got the word, yet? 'Bout the mill?"

"What about it?"

"Strike's over. Everyone's goin' back to work."

"Since when?"

"Las' night, late."

Charles breathed a sigh of relief. *"Merci, mon Dieux,* I am glad to hear that, Pierre. Very glad. What happened?"

"Ol' man Wellington, he tol' *La Comité* the pay cuts were some kinda bookkeepin' error. And those three men - Garfield and all - charges were dropped. That's all they had to hear."

"What about the others?"

"I don't know. My guess is they'll have to go along, like it or no, eh?"

"I'd better go tell Jack. That's one boy's gonna be very happy, I'm bettin'."

~ 47 ~

TUESDAY, JUNE 26

Pequot Park was a popular destination for young and old on warm summer days. Situated on the shores of Hampton Ponds, its wide shaded lawns and sandy swimming beach offered city dwellers from Holyoke and Westfield a welcome respite from the summer's heat. On Saturdays and Sundays it bustled with activity as trolley cars disgorged couples, families, and groups laden with gear and bursting with excitement.

But on this languid Tuesday afternoon the setting was serene. Just a few families sat at picnic tables in the shade or waded in the shallow waters as a long, graceful wooden canoe slipped smoothly, silently away from the dock. Tom Wellington sat in the stern dressed in a white linen suit, a straw boater with a jaunty blue band perched on his head, drawing his paddle gently through the shallow waters. Carolyn Ford was seated in the bow, her flouncy white skirts filling the canoe around her, only occasionally extending her paddle into the water.

"This is so lovely. It's surprising how peaceful it is just a few miles from town. I'm surprised there aren't more people out here today enjoying all of this." Carolyn turned toward her companion. "Thank you, Thomas. I needed this about now; this is just what I needed."

Tom smiled and nodded. The sun sparkled and shimmered on the clear waters as he guided the canoe toward a small island a short distance along the shore from the park. As it approached the island the craft glided through a patch of water lilies, their pink and white blooms lending a sweet perfume to the warm summer air.

The prow was still several feet from the shore when the canoe came to a sudden halt against the sandy pond bottom. Tom rolled up his trousers and stepped into the shallows. Then he helped Carolyn as she too stepped into the cool water, holding her skirts just above the pond's surface. Once on dry land she watched as Tom dragged the canoe ashore, then muscled a large wicker basket out of the craft and onto the grass.

Then began an elaborate picnic preparation. First Tom unfolded a woolen blanket and spread it carefully on the grass. From the basket he drew a pair of linen placemats and napkins, shining enamel utensils, graniteware plates of various sizes, and two glass tumblers. Carolyn watched in astonishment as he arranged all this into two neat place-settings. He laid out an expansive feast: finger sandwiches of sausage and cheese, cucumbers sliced artfully and delicately, deviled eggs arranged in a perfect wheel design on a decorative platter, a bowl of strawberries topped with a dollop of whipped cream, and a tin packed tightly with molasses cookies. When everything was arranged to his satisfaction, he uncorked a carafe and poured lemonade into each tumbler.

"Milady," he said with a mock English accent as he handed a tumbler to Carolyn. "I should like to propose a toast: *To Miss Carolyn Teresa Ford, in honor of her graduation, her award, and her admission to Mass Aggie.*"

Carolyn blushed. They clinked their glasses, then winced as they took small sips of the tart beverage. For several minutes the couple sat in the warm sun clasping their drinks and gazing across the still waters. Just then a mallard and her dozen downy young approached among the water lilies, each producing a faint *wahn-wahn, wahn-wahn, wahn-wahn.* Individually barely audible, in combination they created a veritable avian chorus that was both entrancing and hilarious. The fluffy ducklings looked up at the two picnickers as if waiting for something. When Tom tossed a handful of bread crumbs over their heads into deeper water, the feathered family made haste in the direction of the feast, their patience rewarded. The young couple watched and laughed.

Then Carolyn spoke. "Thank you, Thomas, again - for everything."

"Carolyn," replied Tom. "We've known each other for, let me see, ten years now?" Carolyn's expression suddenly became serious, but Tom was grinning. "Perhaps it is time you started calling me *Tom.*" He looked her square in the eyes as he spoke, his eyebrows lifting suddenly on the word "Tom," as if to punctuate it.

Carolyn blushed once more. "All right, I suppose I could do that - Tom." They laughed together as Tom slid across the blanket and took her hand. She looked briefly into his eyes, then down at the grass, then out at the ducklings now engaged in a noisy feeding frenzy. For several moments they watched the ducklings parrying and dodging among the floating bits of bread. Finally Carolyn spoke, her voice suddenly thin.

"What time is your train tomorrow?"

"Eight a.m.," replied Tom. "Holyoke to Hartford, then on to Providence. I should be in Newport by evening." Two tears formed in Carolyn's eyes, then trickled down her cheeks. Her chin began to quiver.

"Don't cry now," said Tom gently, wrapping his arm around her narrow shoulders and drawing her to him. "I'll be fine. And I'll be back in no time, I promise. Things over there are gonna turn around real quick once all the American forces arrive. Real quick." He reached out and touched her cheek, then turned her head toward him. "So don't you worry about old Tommy, do you hear?"

She nodded, smiled, then spoke softly. "Okay." Tom retracted his hand and looked out across the water.

"About that, when I get back, I mean, I was thinking, you know..." The normally glib Tom Wellington suddenly found himself struggling for words. "Until I get back..." Carolyn froze, her gaze fixed on the ducklings. "Carolyn, until I get back, would you - would you wait for me?"

Carolyn sat motionless, her eyes now focused far across the water. Several seconds passed. Tom watched her intently. Finally she replied. "Will I wait for you? Wha - what do you mean, Tom?"

"I mean, Carolyn Ford, if I come home - that is, when I come home, would you consider..." Tom swallowed audibly. He was looking directly at Carolyn, holding her hand tightly. Slowly, ever so slowly, she turned and looked into his eyes. "When I get home, Carolyn - would you be my wife?"

Slowly Carolyn's eyelids closed and her brow knitted in confusion. "Your - wife?" she asked softly, turning to Tom and opening her eyes wide as her lips formed the word "wife." The first thing she saw was Tom's face and broad smile, then she saw the ring. It was small but exquisite, a single diamond of many facets glinting in the bright sunlight.

"Whattaya say?"

"Oh, Thomas," she began wondrously.

"Uhh," Tom reminded her with wide eyes.

"Tom - I mean Tom." She was looking intently at the ring, mesmerized by its simple beauty. Each facet reflected a different color, all sparkling in the sunlight. Finally she looked up into Tom's eyes that shone nearly as brightly as the ring, and his smile, filled with anticipation. Briefly she returned his smile, looked again at the ring, but then quickly turned and looked out on the water. Mother mallard and her progeny were approaching once again and Carolyn seemed to be watching her intently.

Finally after what seemed to Tom like an eternity, she spoke. "Tom," she began, looking at his lips and chin and not into his eyes, "dear Tom, this is wonderful, magical. It's like a dream..." Tom was beaming and nodding expectantly. "...and I am flattered beyond words." She paused, then continued. "But..."

Suddenly Tom's smile vanished. "I can't, Tom. I am so very sorry." She hung her head and began to cry.

Tom was stunned. His sun-burnished face turned ashen. "But Carolyn, I love you, I swear I do. And I promise to cherish you, always. Don't you believe me? I thought you felt the same." Her face now sunk in her hands, Carolyn sobbed. Tom's face suddenly regained its color and his chin projected with anger. "It's that Polish boy, Jan? That's what this is all about, isn't it? You promised yourself to him. I knew it all along."

Carolyn shook her head, then through her sobs she spoke. "Jan is just a friend, Thomas, please believe me. He has been very kind to me and I have tried to be a friend to him. Please try to understand."

"All right, all right, okay. But what is it then? Why can't you just say yes?"

"Tom, I've just graduated from high school and I need to think about my future, my career. Maybe in business, or something. I'm just getting started, don't you see? And you - you're going away."

"But if when I get back we got married, well, you wouldn't have to worry about a - career." He spoke the last word dismissively. "Why would you?"

"Tom, that's what girls are doing these days, getting an education, planning a career. Even if they intend to marry eventually. Don't you see?"

"But why? I'll get a job at the mill and you won't have to go to work."

"Well, maybe I wouldn't *have* to go to work, Tom. But did you ever think that maybe I might *want* to work? That I might *want* to have a career? The world is changing, Tom, right before our eyes. Surely you can see that. Girls are taking jobs in the mills left by boys who are shipping out. Some girls are even enlisting. And we'll be voting soon. When the war is over, everything will be different. It will be a new world, Tom. Please try to understand."

Tom nodded but looked glum. "So you don't want to marry me, ever," he said angrily.

"I didn't say that, Tom. I said no such thing. I just think we should wait and see."

Tom's face was a mask of despair. "It's your mother. That's it, she's the reason, isn't she? She hates me. She thinks I'm a drunkard, a derelict. She thinks I'm not worthy of you."

Carolyn remained silent and her silence confirmed Tom's fears more surely than any words could have. He was crushed. His skin was once again pale, all vestiges of that handsome, smiling face erased by the painful realization.

"You know, Carolyn, that I have my faults. But I am trying to change my ways. I tried to save your father and you and Adrienne and the children. And I helped to get your father out of jail. Don't those things matter a whit to her?"

"They matter to me, Tom, believe me. And I will be forever grateful. But as far as Mama is concerned, Papa does not exist. She hasn't changed her mind about him in eighteen years. She's not going to change now."

Suddenly Carolyn's breathing became labored, her speech halting. She took Tom's hand in hers and pressed it gently. "I have fought her about that, and I have fought her about my college plans, to the point where..." She looked into his eyes, worry and fear creasing her brow.

"What, Carolyn, what are you saying?"

"This." She looked down at the ring. "I can't - I just cannot do this to her. Don't you see, it would be too much. It would just be too much. What more can I say to make you understand?" Tom sighed. The look of dejection on his face was enough to break Carolyn's heart. "Tom, dearest Tom, I'm sorry, but I cannot accept this lovely ring. And I cannot pledge my troth, at least not now. But even though I'm not saying yes, Tom, I'm not saying no. Because I..." She looked sweetly into Tom's eyes once again. "I love you, Tom Wellington." Her voice began to crack. "And I have loved you for so long."

Tom nodded, still looking glum. Carolyn turned and faced him. She grasped his face between her small hands, then kissed him squarely and firmly on the lips. They embraced and Tom buried his face against her neck and shoulder until she felt his tears on her skin.

Finally Tom released her from his grasp and looked away. The mallard family was gone and there was utter, complete silence to match the utter disappointment in Tom's heart.

"We'd better head back," said Tom flatly. "I have to go home and pack."

~ 48 ~

Anne was helping Mildred prepare a special feast in Tom's honor. Pork roast was his favorite, especially the way Mildred cooked it, slowly, gently, swaddled in a rich broth with crisp vegetables. Just then Helen appeared in the kitchen doorway holding the evening edition of the *Daily Transcript*.

Anne looked up at her mother. "Doesn't the roast smell wonderful, Mother? Mother? What is it?"

Helen turned the paper toward Anne and Mildred. "Congress just this morning voted to approve the Emergency Draft Bill. That's the bill President Wilson has been pressing them to act on. He's signing it this afternoon."

Anne sighed. "Well, that was expected, wasn't it?"

"No, darling, not at all. You see, they amended it. At the last minute they made some changes. Eighteen-year-olds are not to be called. Only men twenty-one and older. At least for a year. Thank God for that."

Anne was stunned. "Wha - what? Does that mean Tommy doesn't have to enlist?"

"Yes, dear. That's precisely what it means." Anne ran and hugged her mother, then they both hugged Mildred.

"I'm going upstairs to tell your father," said Helen. "He'll be so relieved. We all will be, I dare say. Where is Tommy? Do you suppose he knows yet?"

"He took the motorcar," replied Anne. "Something about going over to see Carolyn." Mildred knew about the outing he had planned, of course, but chose not to mention it.

Preparations for the good-bye dinner continued, although now it was turning from a bittersweet occasion to a celebration. Anne ran off in search of streamers to decorate the living room while Mildred promised to change the inscription on the multilayered cake she had created for the event.

It was nearly five o'clock when Anne heard the rumble of the Reo in the driveway. She walked briskly, calmly, across the lawn, then abandoned all restraint and made a full-out dash for the garage.

"Tommy, Tommy, have you heard?" She didn't notice, she couldn't have noticed in her haste and exuberance, the expression of complete and utter despair on her brother's face.

"Heard what, sis?"

"Congress, in Washington, they voted just this morning. They're not going to draft eighteen-year-olds, not now, maybe never." Tom stood staring blankly at his sister. "Tommy, did you hear what I just said? You don't have to go. You don't have to worry about being called up."

Finally Tom seemed to brighten. "Wow, that's a surprise. I - how do you know?"

"It's in the paper. I'll show you." Anne threw her arms around Tom. "I can't believe it, Tommy, I can't believe it."

"N - neither can I."

"Isn't this wonderful, Tom?"

"It is, Anne, it certainly is." Finally Tom smiled and hugged his sister back. He drew the large wicker basket from the trunk and carried it by the handle with one hand. Anne took his other hand and led him, practically dragged him, up the driveway to the house.

"Tommy, you must call Carolyn immediately." Tom nodded but seemed distracted by the unexpected news.

The planned event began at seven sharp. By now everyone had heard the news and the atmosphere was festive. Jack came directly from the mill carrying a change of clothes in his rucksack. The rest of the Bernard family arrived shortly after Jack. Charles and Marie stood awkwardly while Claire struck up conversations with everyone she saw. Tom's father and mother were seated on a long couch and Charles and Marie shyly approached them and congratulated them. Eventually Richard Wellington and Charlotte arrived as did several of Tom's old Holyoke friends whom he hadn't seen in a long time, Bill Peterson and Pete Buchanan, and their families.

A few minutes later Carolyn and Nina arrived. Nina sat next to Helen and the two talked quietly. Carolyn received hugs from Anne, Marie, and Claire and a warm smile and handshake from Jack. At the last minute Anne had created a banner of muslin with large letters made of hastily crafted calico that spelled out what everyone was feeling at that moment: *Congratulations, Tommy!* The meal was ready and about to be served when Helen spoke to Mildred.

"We can't have our meal until the guest of honor arrives. I'll be right back." She excused herself and went to the foot of the stairs. "Thomas, are you ready? Everyone's here."

"I'll be just a minute, Mother, just another minute." Helen returned to the living room and stood talking with Richard and Charlotte. The room was large and spacious but the crowd was boisterous and the noise level high.

Suddenly a cheer went up. All eyes turned toward the hallway door. Just as suddenly the cheers ceased, replaced by a stunned hush. The guest of honor was standing stiffly in the doorway, smiling and looking around at the many friends, family, and of course Carolyn, his Carolyn. He wore a dark blue jacket with long sleeves and matching dark blue trousers that flared at the ankles. Atop his head sat a flat blue cap with a white ribbon. When he lifted the cap from his head and held it before him in both hands, gasps could be heard. That dark, wavy hair - hair that had been carefully groomed by barbers on High Street ever since Tom was five - had been eviscerated, shorn, reduced to an abrupt crew cut, revealing a white scalp and nearly naked temples.

"Hello, everyone, and thank you for all this. You really shouldn't have, but thank you anyway." There was still silence in the room and confusion on everyone's face. Hanna, Mildred, Bromley, Moira, and several other members of the Wellington household staff were standing at the rear, wondering what was going on. "I have an announcement to make. I know that the eighteen-year-old draft has been abandoned for now. So by rights, I should be free as a bird. But - I've decided - I'm shipping out tomorrow anyway. There's a job to be done and, well, I want to do my part."

After the meal Victrola music played in the grand parlor. Several of the young couples paired off and danced to familiar songs, most of the selections dreamy and romantic. Eventually some of the adults joined in, Charlotte and Richard, Mr. and Mrs. Peterson. Helen was nervous when her husband rose from his seat, took her hand, and led her to the dance floor.

Jack and Anne had found a quiet corner behind a potted palm. Anne smiled sweetly to Jack at first, but when they played *Till the Clouds Roll By* her eyes teared up and she clung tightly to Jack's slender frame, her head on his shoulder, not wishing him to witness her pain. "Are you - disappointed, Jackie? That you're not joining up, too?"

"Not so much disappointed, Annie, but embarrassed, I guess. That these guys are going to do a job and I'm gonna be back home studying - and growing onions." He chuckled dismissively, then shook his head. "I'm really proud of Tommy, though. You know, I never thought of him as a real

285

patriot, especially about going to war in Europe. He always seemed to be, I guess you'd say, indifferent. And he never had a good word to say about President Wilson, ever. But all of a sudden he's rarin' to go." Anne raised her head, turned, looked into Jack's eyes, and nodded as Jack continued. "I guess I'm kind of - surprised - I mean, at him going when he doesn't have to." He looked into Anne's eyes. "Ya know?"

"Yes, I know what you mean - I am a bit perplexed myself," replied Anne. She paused and at that moment the music stopped. Jack looked down into her eyes as she spoke. "I wonder, perhaps, if Tommy feels - well - that he has to prove himself. You know what I mean? That he's got what it takes, that he's not a - a boy anymore."

"Prove himself? To who, Annie?"

"Maybe to Mother and Father, and..." At that she glanced over to where Tom and Carolyn were seated. The two had been watching, only occasionally exchanging words, as the dancing continued. But just as Anne looked their way, Tom extended his hand and they rose and joined the other dancers.

Tom gazed down on his partner's face often, but Carolyn could offer him only an occasional shy smile. To do more, it was clear, would have caused her calm demeanor to be shattered, a charade she was determined to maintain.

It was nearly eleven when the guests began to leave. Tom stood in the front hallway as each person spoke to him, shook his hand, wished him well, then departed. The Bernards were near the head of the line, first Charles, then Marie, then Claire. Finally Jack stepped up to his friend, but Claire was standing very close as if prepared to join the conversation.

"I'll be right along, Claire. I just wanna speak to Tommy for a minute - alone." Claire was about to protest when Jack caught her gaze and looked meaningfully into her eyes, at which she retreated. Then he turned to his friend.

"Well, Tommy, I guess this is it, huh?" His eyes glistened as he spoke. "I'm sure - I know you'll..."

"Hey, Jack, don't worry about old Tommy, huh? I'll be fine, just fine."

Jack was fumbling in his waistcoat pocket. "There's something I want you to have." He produced a shining silvery disk on a delicate chain. "It's my St. Christopher medal. Catholics believe he protects us from harm, especially when we're traveling. It belonged to my *pépère*, my father's father. But I want you to have it, Tommy."

"Wow, thanks Jack, but I'm not Catholic."

"That's okay, it'll still work for you, I know it will. I'll get myself another one."

"Thanks, Jack. First thing I come home, let's go fishing, okay? Just us two."

Jack smiled and nodded. "That'll be swell. Let's plan on it. Well, I better be goin'. Godspeed, Tommy." The two friends shook hands and smiled one last time. Jack rejoined his family outside, thankful that the darkness would conceal the tears that were trickling down his cheeks.

Back inside Carolyn and her mother were greeting Tom. "Congratulations, Thomas," said Carolyn formally. And she shook his hand. Their eyes met in a brief, knowing conjunction, but just as quickly were diverted.

"Thomas, young man, we wish you well," said Nina with unaccustomed feeling in her voice as she shook his hand. "You know, my father served in the Navy. We were all very proud of his service. And we're very proud of you: Carolyn and I, your family, your friends, all of Holyoke, we all wish you godspeed."

Tom and Carolyn were stunned by the heartfelt tone of Nina's words. For a brief moment they exchanged looks of astonishment. Tom started to thank Nina but she had already turned, grasped her daughter's arm, and headed for the door. Carolyn tried to throw Tom a parting glance, but her effort was in vain as her mother led her briskly out the front door and into the June night. When the two were well along the flagstone walkway to Beech Street, Carolyn halted abruptly.

"Oh, I'm sorry, Mama, I promised Anne I would give her some - some skin cream." She held up her purse. "It contains aloe and I am sure it will be perfect for her delicate skin. I'll just run back and give it to her. I won't be but a moment."

~ 49 ~

Tom rose early the following morning. Mildred and Anne were already up and about preparing a special sendoff breakfast. The last thing Tom had told his parents and sister the previous evening was that he didn't want them to come to the train depot with him. It would be too hard, he explained, and besides, he wished to remember them gathered at the front door of their home, not at the station. The final good-byes were tearful, but Tom was in good spirits as he trudged off down the walk, duffle bag slung over one shoulder. Although wearing civilian clothes, his severe haircut left no doubt where he was bound.

He arrived at the station several minutes early and stood looking about. Several other young men were similarly dressed, no doubt embarking on like journeys, families and friends clustered around each. The train bound for Hartford arrived right on schedule and Tom stood anxiously on the platform. But his eyes were not on the train; they were directed toward Dwight Street. Just then she appeared wearing a flowing white chiffon dress, smiling bravely.

"You made it," said Tom with relief.

"I promised you, didn't I?" replied Carolyn.

"Yes, you did." Tom nodded toward the end of the platform where shipping crates were stacked high. The couple slipped behind one of the stacks, then Carolyn turned and embraced Tom. They shared a long, tender kiss.

"What made you reconsider?" asked Tom.

"Like Anne says, it is always a woman's prerogative to change her mind." Tom nodded and reached into his pocket. Carolyn looked up into his eyes and smiled. He said a few words. Carolyn nodded. Then he slipped the ring on her finger and they embraced again.

"I'll miss you, Tom, you know that? And I'll pray for you every day until I see you, right here, one day soon."

"What about your mother? What's she going to say?"

Carolyn gazed at the ring, then at Tom. "She's not going to say a thing because I'm not going to tell her, nor anyone else. It will be our little secret. I'll keep it on my necklace, close to my heart. No one will know it's there but me."

They embraced one last time. The train whistle blew. Tom stroked Carolyn's hair, gazed into her almond eyes, and kissed her. "Good-bye, Carolyn. I'll see you soon. I love you."

"I love you, too," she whispered. Then she put on a brave smile and stepped out into plain view as Tom ran down the platform toward the train. She stood in the early morning sun watching him board the train. He stood on the step, waved, and blew her a kiss. He was about to turn and disappear into the car when he saw another familiar face approaching on the platform. He blew another kiss to her before stepping inside.

Carolyn was still waving toward the train when Anne appeared at her side. She seemed surprised to see her friend. They hugged, then turned and waved toward the departing train together. Between waves, Carolyn discreetly removed the ring and held it tightly in her left hand.

"We all promised Tom we wouldn't come to the station," explained Anne. "But I just couldn't bear it. I had to see him one more time."

"Me, too," replied Carolyn as the train chugged off toward Hartford. "Me, too."

~ 50 ~

THURSDAY, JUNE 28

"Hello, Holyoke three-nine-one. May I help you?" asked the serious young lady in a buff twill suit seated behind a large desk at the Women's Home. It was mid-day on Thursday. As she spoke on the telephone she looked up at her office window as large raindrops splattered against the panes. At last it was raining in Holyoke, the first heavy rainfall in weeks, a badly needed soaking for dusty streets and parched fields.

"No, sir, Mrs. Calavetti is not in right now. This is Miss Wellington. May I help you?" Anne listened carefully to the caller's inquiry. "Yes, Mr. Emmons, I am sure we could arrange that. We have had a number of new arrivals this week, most seeking mill work. May I call you back later today after I have spoken with them?"

Anne made some notes at her desk, thanked the caller, and returned the handset to its cradle just as Carolyn entered the office. "Ready for lunch?" she said brightly to Anne. Anne nodded and smiled to her friend. Carrying a pink umbrella over one arm and a small satchel in the other hand, she pulled the office door closed behind her. The frosted window in the door had been freshly painted. It read *Miss Anne Wellington, Assistant Director*.

The two friends walked together, sharing the umbrella. At Hampden Park they sat on a rustic wooden bench under a covered pavilion. Before them the grass that had been parched and brown a few days earlier was already showing signs of new life. From her handbag Carolyn removed a purse of rose silk and green brocade trim and placed it on the bench between them.

"Carolyn, dear, what a lovely purse," said Anne admiringly. "Is that new?"

"Yes, Anne. It was a belated graduation gift, from Adrienne and Papa. Adrienne gave it to me just as we were about to leave Westford that night. Isn't it lovely?" She stroked the brocade gently, then looked up and into Anne's eyes. "Congratulations on your new job, Anne. How's it going?" Anne smiled and blushed.

"Well, it's really just my old job with a new title, but your mother insisted on giving me an office of my own. And she fussed so about getting the painter in immediately to put my name on the door. She's making me feel like, well, like I belong. It's very exciting. And, of course, now - I'm getting paid." Anne and Carolyn exchanged wide-eyed expressions of delight.

"I'm very happy for you, Anne. It's perfect for you, and for the Home, and for Mama. She pushes herself so, it worries me sometimes."

"Carolyn, I am determined to do whatever is needed to lighten her load." Anne took a small bite of her cucumber sandwich. "How are things going between you two? Getting along better, I hope?"

"A little better," conceded Carolyn. A look of despair emerged in her delicate features. "Oh, Anne, I don't think she's ever going to forgive me for - for leaving like that. And I suppose I can't blame her. I should have told her, I should have explained to her about Papa and Adrienne. I fear that one mistake has done damage that can never be undone."

"Don't think that, Carolyn, please. Remember, *Thou art thy mother's glass, and she in thee calls back the lovely April of her prime.*"

"Anne Wellington, a true romantic. I wish I shared your optimism." Carolyn shook her head. The rain had dwindled to a light drizzle now.

"What about your college plans? Is there no chance?"

"Well, Anne, I do have some news about that." Carolyn's eyes brightened and her cheeks glowed. "I received a letter from Papa yesterday. He's back home with Adrienne and the children now."

"That is wonderful. You were so worried about them - we all were."

"And - he and Adrienne have offered to pay for me to attend Mass Aggie - tuition, room, board, everything - for this year and the next."

"Oh, Carolyn, that is wonderful news," said Anne as she took Carolyn's hand, leaned over, and kissed her on the cheek. "Wonderful."

"Yes it is, and I am absolutely beside myself, Anne."

Anne looked into her friend's eyes. "And your mother?"

"I told her last evening. In her heart I know she doesn't approve. But ever since I got my letter of acceptance, she's been saying that we can't afford it. I know there's more to it than that, much more, but that was the reason she gave me, again and again. So when I told her about the gift from Papa and Adrienne, well, she really had to agree."

"Well, perhaps it is best this way, dear Carolyn. Maybe in time the two of you can settle things." Carolyn looked dubious. "But Carolyn, does this mean you'll be living in Amherst?"

"Yes, Anne. They've just completed a new residence hall for girls. But I have promised Mama I will come home every weekend. It's less than an hour by trolley."

"Oh, Carolyn, I will miss you so. At least I will know that my dearest, closest friend is furthering her education, pursuing her dream. But that means you'll be missing all those college socials and parties I read about in the *Transcript*. I'm betting there will be many handsome young college men about, especially on weekends." Carolyn laughed and smiled, but it was a weak smile, not at all convincing to Anne. A nervous silence descended on the two as they sat finishing their lunches.

"Any news, Anne - I mean, from Newport?"

Anne shook her head. Her eyes grew wide and fluid, then she looked away. "Nothing yet, but they'll keep the new recruits very busy, I'm sure. We don't really expect to hear much, not until Tommy gets his orders." Carolyn nodded and their eyes met briefly.

"Sooo, you and Tommy seemed to patch things up there, just before he left. All that whispering on Monday evening in the foyer, and then the train station. Anything going on there that you want to tell me about?"

Carolyn shook her head. "I just wanted him to know how - how proud - we are of him. And that he would be missed, that's all." They were looking across the glistening park lawn where russet-breasted robins were harvesting a bounty of earthworms that had emerged from the sodden soil. But their thoughts were far away.

"We'd better get back, hmm?" said Anne. As she said the words she turned toward her friend, but in so doing thought she observed something small, something very small, probably inconsequential. It was Carolyn's hand, pressed against her blouse just below the neckline, as if her fingers were touching something unseen. But the hand was withdrawn so quickly, Anne almost wondered if she had actually seen anything at all.

"Yes, we'd better. Miss Halliwell watches the clock like a hawk," said Carolyn wryly. The two friends parted ways at the corner, Anne heading back to the Women's Home and Carolyn to Gregoire's Shoe Shop. There was, after all, work to be done.

~ 51 ~

SATURDAY, JUNE 30

The Wellingtons' Reo pulled into the Bernard driveway on Saturday morning. Anne sat beaming from the driver's seat as Jack approached.

"Wow. Anne Wellington driving a motorcar," said Jack, "now I've seen everything."

"Bromley has been giving me driving lessons. I'm still a little nervous behind the wheel, but I have decided that the only way I'll get over that is with practice." Jack opened the door and Anne stepped onto the gravel driveway. She was wearing a loose white poplin blouse tucked in at the waist. But what caught Jack's eye was what else she was wearing.

"My stars, I never thought I'd see Anne Wellington in trousers. That is a sight." He kissed her lightly on the cheek.

"We call them slacks, Jackie, not trousers. Do you like them?" Jack grinned broadly as he looked her up and down.

"I'll take that as a yes, then?" added Anne.

"Whatever you wear, Miss Wellington, I will like."

"Well, good. I am, after all, a thoroughly modern girl. And modern girls are wearing such things these days, in the factories, in the fields, even on the streets. You'll get accustomed to it, Jackie. Times are changing."

"I suppose so. But those trousers, they make you look like a fellow, you know, like one of the boys - especially with your hair cut so short."

"Well, Jackie, I'll have to try to disabuse you of that notion." And she drew him toward her and kissed him firmly on the lips.

Jack pulled away and looked around nervously. "You may be a modern girl, Annie, but I'm still an old fashioned boy."

"Well, we'll just have to work on that, won't we?" she replied with an impish grin. The pair walked together across the back lawn to the edge of the garden. "My goodness, Jackie, you've got lots of onions, haven't you?"

Jack smiled proudly. "Ayeh, nearly two acres. They seemed to stop growin' there for a time with the heat and drought, but they revived real quick with all that rain."

"What are you planning on doing with them, Jackie? Sending them to the troops?"

"Well, I already have three buyers lined up: Mr. Aucoin at the Westfield Market, Mr. O'Connor at the West Springfield store, and a Mr. Mason from Windsor. He's a wholesaler. He's got dozens of stores he delivers to as far away as Hartford. We'll start harvesting end of August, Dad and me. Maybe Claire, too. It could be a boon, Annie, a real boon. If they all turn out, we stand to make nearly five hundred bucks. Five hundred dollars. Imagine?"

Anne was watching Jack's eyes shine, his proud smile stretching nearly from ear to ear. "I don't know which suits you better, Jackie, farming or engineering."

"Well, surprising, they have a lot in common. You might not think so, but they do. Planning, ciphering, keeping records, all that."

Jack and Anne stood together at the fence, gazing out on thousands of apparently happy onion plants, their long leaves waving in the breeze. "So, how's the new job, Miss Assistant Director?" asked Jack.

Anne smiled ruefully. "It's just the same old job, answering the phone, opening the mail." Then her face brightened. "But I have my own office, aaand - I'm getting paid."

"Wow, Annie, you are a modern girl, aren't you?" Jack paused, looking out on the distant hills, then back at Anne. "I'm real proud of you. We all are, you know." Anne smiled and blushed. "Any word yet - from Tommy?"

Anne paused but refused to let her concern for her brother spoil the mood. "Not yet, probably not for a while. They work them pretty hard, you know, especially in training."

"Imagine, Thomas P. Wellington, Apprentice Seaman, United States Navy," said Jack.

Anne shook her head and smiled. "You never know, do you? You just never know."

"So what was all that about the other night? Carolyn and Tommy, I mean. All that whispering and..."

Anne nodded. "...and conspiring?"

"Yeh, and the next morning, at the station?"

"Like I told you on the telephone, they were behind some freight pallets at the end of the platform. If you ask me there was more than mutual admiration going on there. We had lunch on Thursday at Hampden Park and I asked Carolyn - tactfully, of course."

"Uh-huh," said Jack with more than a touch of irony in his voice.

"I was tactful, Jackie, very tactful. But she was playing it coy. She says she was just telling him how proud we all are of him. I don't know, Jackie, maybe there's hope for those two yet."

"And she's off to Amherst in September?"

Anne nodded. "Yes, can you imagine?" Then her composure began to crack. She had promised herself she wouldn't lose control, but that was precisely what was happening. "Everyone's leaving," she began tearfully. "Tommy, Carolyn, you." I know I should be happy, but it's going to be lonely, so lonely."

"You're not going to be lonely, Annie. Not a bit. I predict you're gonna get so wrapped up in the Women's Home you won't have time to be lonely. And Marie and Claire are gonna be here, and Dad. They want you to come to dinner at least once a week."

Anne nodded and laughed. "Yes, Claire has already informed me - she practically *ordered* me to be here every Thursday night for supper. She and Marie have even started planning the menus."

"See what I mean? You won't be lonely for a minute. And I've got a little news on that front, too."

"News?"

"It's actually a good thing you wore those trousers. Wait here."

Anne was mystified, but she stood leaning against the fence, gazing out on Jack's onions. As she watched, a horse and rider approached across the fields. Suddenly a series of loud bangs and sputters could be heard from the barn. Anne turned to witness a plume of bluish smoke rising from the barn. Then there was an ear-splitting clatter and from the barn emerged a smoking, sputtering, gasping two-wheeled machine. It careened jerkily down the driveway, turned slowly, then roared as it accelerated the length of the drive. It flew past the barn and across the lawn, then through the break in the fence. As it streaked past Anne, Jack flashed a wild, maniacal grin as he doffed a motoring cap. In seconds a plume of smoke had encircled Anne and she was coughing and clutching a lace handkerchief against her face. The machine tore down the lane between the gardens, circled slowly, then returned. It pulled up in front of her and stopped. Jack extended his arm.

"Miss Wellington, have a ride?"

"But why is it smoking so, Jackie?"

"Oh, that's normal. It's a two-stroke engine."

With some trepidation Anne climbed on behind Jack, wrapping her arms around him and pressing herself against his back as tightly as she could. Her eyes were closed and she winced at the ear-piercing whine as they shot off again down the lane and into the distant field. They circled again and again, then slowed as they approached the horse and rider.

Riders, that is. Émile was sitting bareback on Thor, riding impossibly high, sporting a smile as wide as a mile. Thor's head was raised high as well, so high in fact that it was difficult to tell who was the prouder, Émile or Thor. Seated sideways in front of Émile was Marie in her flouncing skirts. Émile's arms were wrapped around her and she was smiling. Jack shut off the motorcycle and a welcome silence surrounded the four young people.

"Anne?" called Marie from her high perch.

"Hi, Marie. We'll have to get you a pair of these," said Anne pointing to her slacks. "A modern woman mustn't be without them these days, you know." They all laughed.

"Hey, Jay-Jay, you finally got 'er goin', eh?" said Émile grinning.

"Yep. Thanks to you. Still needs some work, though. She smokes a bit."

Anne rolled her eyes at Marie. "It has a two-stroke engine," she said sardonically.

"Where did you get this thing, Jackie?" asked Anne.

"Mr. Mason. It was part of the deal we made for the onions. It's called a *Near-a-car* 'cause it's near..."

"Wait," interrupted Anne, "let me guess. Because it's nearly a car?" Everyone laughed.

"Yep. But don't laugh, Annie. It's gonna get me home every weekend starting in September."

Émile gave a gentle kick and Thor walked on carrying his two riders across the fields toward the river.

"Did Marie tell you about Émile?" asked Jack. Anne shook her head. "He's goin' back to school. It's a special school for the deaf in Northampton. And not just for doin' busy work, either, a full academic program. That boy's gonna go somewheres, I predict."

"Wow, Jackie, it is a new world, isn't it?" replied Anne as she hugged him.

Jack smiled and they sat astride the Near-a-car, looking out across the onion fields to the mountains beyond.

Jack nodded. "Ayeh, it is that."

THE END

Bibliography

Benoit, A. W. 1920. *Organization and Construction of Dye Houses.* Chemical Age 28:470-474.

Blewett, Mary H. 1990. *The Last Generation: Work and Life in the Textile Mills of Lowell, Massachusetts, 1910 - 1960.* University of Massachusetts Press, Amherst, MA USA.

Greiner, T. 1904. *The New Onion Culture: A Complete Guide in Growing Onions for Profit.* Orange Judd Company, New York, NY USA.

Hartford, William F. 1990. *Working People of Holyoke: Class and Ethnicity in a Massachusetts Mill Town, 1850-1960.* Rutgers University Press, New Brunswick, NJ USA.

Hubka, Thomas C. 1984. *Big House, Little House, Back House, Barn: The Connected Farm Buildings of New England.* University Press of New England, Lebanon, NH USA.

I. C. S. Staff. 1905. *Wool Scouring.* International Textbook Company, Scranton, PA USA.

Kilborne, Sarah S. 2012. *An American Phoenix: The Remarkable Story of William Skinner, A Man Who Turned Disaster Into Destiny.* Free Press, New York, NY USA.

Krawitt, Laura (ed). 2000. *The Mills at Winooski Falls.* Onion River Press, Winooski, VT USA.

Moran, William. 2002. *The Belles of New England: The Women of the Textile Mills and the Families Whose Wealth They Wove.* Thomas Dunne Books, New York, NY USA.

Radcliffe, J. W. and C. E. Clarke. 1915. *Woolen and Worsted Yarn Manufacture Part VI.* The Textile American 23:20-37.

Russell, H. S. 1982. *A Long, Deep Furrow: Three Centuries of Farming in New England.* University Press of New England, Hanover, NH USA.

Zack, C. S. 1919. *Holyoke in the Great War.* Transcript Publishing Company, Holyoke, MA USA.

Illustrations

I am very grateful to Sean P. McCarthy who conceived and created the cover design for *The Dyeing Room*. Interior illustrations appeared in books, magazines, and postcards of the period. Sources, dates, and artist names are listed if available.

Cover: Sean P. McCarthy, 2014
Facing page 1: *Harper's Young People*, 1879, by T. Robinson
Page 16: *A Handbook of Health*, 1911
Page 28: *Appleton's Cyclopedia of Applied Mechanics*, 1889
Page 40: *The Dyeing of Woollen Fabrics*, 1902
Page 46: *Harper's Weekly*, Vol. 30, 1886
Page 82: *Youth's Companion*, Vol. 78, 1904
Page 87: *Harper's Magazine*, Vol. 115, 1907, by E. S. Green
Page 101: *St. Nicholas Magazine*, Vol. 26, 1898, by C. M. Relyea
Page 110: *St. Nicholas Magazine*, Vol. 39, 1912, by E. C. Caswell
Page 116: *The Girls of St. Cyprian's*, 1914, by Stanley Davis
Page 148: *St. Nicholas Magazine*, Vol. 25, 1898, by C. M. Relyea
Page 151: *Picturesque America*, 1894, by W. H. Gibson
Page 169: Postcard, 1912
Page 257: Photograph, 1908
Page 281: *Oakleigh*, 1898, by A. B. Stephens
Page 288: *St. Nicholas Magazine*, Vol. 30, 1903, by B. Rosenmeyer
Page 301: *Motor Age*, Vol. 41, 1922
Page 305: Photograph by Michael Milsom
Back cover: Mill boy photograph by Lewis Hine, 1909; Suffragettes photo, 1908; engraving of the Haymarket Riot, *Harper's Weekly*, Vol. 30, 1886

Acknowledgments

Although *The Dyeing Room* is a work of fiction, many of the characters, events, and settings have been drawn from the lives of my parents, Ellen S. McMaster and Robert W. McMaster. Memories of my own childhood in Southbridge, Massachusetts, have also been incorporated into the story. One experience in particular, a brief visit to the dyehouse of a still operational woolen mill in Putnam, Connecticut, in the nineteen-sixties, left an indelible impression on me that inspired the writing of this book nearly fifty years later.

More recently I have found both insight and inspiration at the Slater Mill in Pawtucket, Rhode Island, the Museum of Work and Culture in Woonsocket, Rhode Island, the Millyard Museum in Manchester, New Hampshire, and the Heritage Winooski Mill Museum in Winooski, Vermont. I am particularly grateful for the assistance of Laura Krawitt, curator of the Heritage Winooski Mill Museum. I am also indebted to Eileen Crosby, archivist of the Holyoke History Room at the Holyoke Public Library, Holyoke, Massachusetts, for assistance in locating books, maps, and photographs of Holyoke's past including the library's excellent archive of the *Holyoke Daily Transcript*.

During the final weeks of this project, I learned of the death of writer and journalist Mark Ashton, a longtime friend. Mark had urged me to write a sequel to *Trolley Days* and it therefore seems especially fitting to dedicate *The Dyeing Room* to his memory.

Finally, I thank my wife, Susan Milsom, for her advice, support, encouragement, and tireless editing throughout this project.

About the Author

Robert T. McMaster grew up in Southbridge, Massachusetts, a New England mill town. He holds a B.A. from Clark University and graduate degrees from Boston College, Smith College, and the University of Massachusetts. He taught biology at Holyoke Community College in Massachusetts from 1994 to 2014. His parents' reminiscences of growing up in early 20th century America were the inspiration for his two novels, *Trolley Days* (2012) and *The Dyeing Room* (2014).

For more information on the author, his books, and that era, visit **www.TrolleyDays.net**.

TROLLEY DAYS

"A joyful, engaging read from beginning to end..."

-Mark Ashton, *Southbridge Evening News*

"A special gem of historical fiction..."

Winston Lavalee, author of *Dancing in the Dark* and *Tempest in the Wilderness*

Trolley Days is the story of two boys growing up in a great New England industrial city in the nineteen-teens. Jack Bernard, son of a mill worker who emigrated from Canada, is shy and socially a bit awkward; Tom Wellington, son of the mill owner, is self-assured and smooth-talking. For all their differences, the two have much in common. They love fishing, sports, and riding the trolleys that ply city streets and country roads. Each family has been touched by tragedy, wounds of the heart that are slow to heal.

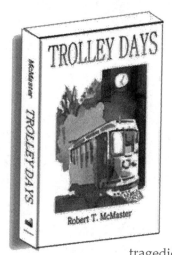

In Chapter 1 Jack is bound for Boston as a blizzard approaches. Tom is in trouble, and while they have barely spoken in nearly six months, in Jack's mind Tom is still his best friend, and no snowstorm will prevent him from going to his aid. Soon they will be plunged into a baffling mystery, even as Tom's life hangs in the balance.

Does friendship have its limits? Can bonds of trust, once broken, be repaired? Can we learn from life's tragedies and move on, or must we carry them like lead weights on our hearts forever? In *Trolley Days*, it seems it is the young who bear the heaviest of life's burdens and must marshal the strength to free themselves and their parents.

Available in paperback and e-book.

Visit **www.TrolleyDays.net** to order

Made in the USA
Middletown, DE
02 September 2015